The Scarab's GAME

JANET OPPEDISANO

The Scarab's Game

ISBN Digital: 978-1-998251-04-9
ISBN Paperback: 978-1-998251-05-6

For everyone who's doubted their power
and found the strength to go on

FREE NOVELLA

To instantly receive the free romantic suspense novella *The Phoenix Heist*, the prequel to the Reynolds Recoveries series, claim your copy at
https://janetoppedisano.com/ThePhoenixHeist

CHAPTER 1

EMMETT

I HAD NOTHING.

Seven high. Offsuit.

If I were playing a proper head-to-head game of poker, I would have offered to make things interesting.

Two of the men at my game—Americans traveling with their wives who were elsewhere—would have been up for additional stakes. The man from Australia would have said no. The woman from Germany was an unknown.

But in the Casino de Monte-Carlo, the game was Texas Hold'em Ultimate. And despite the four others at the table, my only real opponent was the dealer.

It was little more than blackjack—odds and luck over strategy and psychological warfare.

"I see him," came Drew's voice in my hidden earpiece. We'd kept the comms tight for this evening's reconnaissance. Drew and I were working the casino while my sister Scarlett coordinated support from our headquarters. "He's given his keys to the valet. Entering with his assistant, his son, and a woman I don't recognize."

Our intel told us the mark would arrive at the Casino by eight o'clock, but not whether he'd be heading into the restaurant or one of the private rooms. My job was to sit at my table with its full view of the entrance and watch what he did when he arrived.

I probably should have abandoned the table—left my bids, tipped the dealer, and taken my chips. But games of Ultimate were fast. I had at least two hands left in me.

I dropped four hundred onto the Play box.

The pair of Americans raised, while everyone else checked.

I scanned the Salle Europe—the first of three main gaming rooms. It was the same as always, with its ornate paneled walls, soaring ceilings embellished with gold rosettes, and stunning crystal chandeliers. Huge paintings of French pre-Revolution opulence decorated the walls, while the luxurious blue and gold patterned carpeting absorbed the sounds from the crowd of people murmuring all around me.

"What brings you to Monte Carlo?" I asked the man next to me—the only one who'd followed my lead with four times on his raise. "Gambling? Culture? Food?"

He took a sip from his glass, gaze as neutral as someone who watched too many rounds of televised poker and practiced in the mirror. Underneath it, his eyes sparkled the same way they had when he'd held two queens five hands ago. "My wife's here to shop."

The man on his other side chuckled. "You'd better win more, then."

The dealer revealed the flop. Three cards face up, and my seven high became two of a kind.

Drew said over the earpiece, "He's moving through the lobby toward the casino entrance."

I glanced past the dealer as play continued.

If our target steered toward the restaurant, Drew could book us a table while I cashed out. Inside, we'd watch him from a distance before making an approach. That would be a better idea than an early intercept, which provided too much opportunity for his assistant to divert me and suggest I make an appointment.

The dealer flipped over the remaining cards, and my two-of-a-kind became four. Ten-to-one payout as the dealer couldn't beat me. My shit luck from the past four months was finally turning.

"They've split up," said Drew. "The mark and his assistant are heading into the gambling rooms. The son and woman have paused in the lobby. She's taking photos."

Massimo de Rossa came through the main doors and crossed to the restaurant. He wore a loose, camel-colored shirt with long sleeves and more than one gold necklace. White hair hung to his shoulders, combed back with waves curling at his neck. At sixty-five, he maintained his model good looks, which had no doubt helped him build his tremendous fortune in business and the art-collecting world.

His assistant wasn't much younger but dressed in all black, which kept the focus off him.

"Have any of you tried the Rose Salon restaurant?" My question would seem like an innocent inquiry to the players at my table, but it was actually a tip-off for my team.

The dealer dealt their two cards and revealed them, qualifying with a pair. Not enough to beat me, so I won, as did Sparkly Eyes.

"Scarlett, can you arrange for a reservation?" Drew may

have been new to the team, but he recognized my subtle hint. The CIA had created the perfect crew member.

"We can't hack into their system fast enough," said Scarlett. "If the maître d' doesn't have anything available now, slip him a hundred."

The German woman at my table said something about the restaurant as the dealer collected cards and chips, doling out winnings.

"I'll try it out after this hand. Which means it's time to up my wager." I tossed five hundred on the Ante and Blind, adding two for Trips.

"Has anyone ever told you," said Drew over the earpiece, "your team spends money too quickly?"

Scarlett hummed aloud. "Whatever works. And I think you mean—*our* team?"

"Every hundred spent is a hundred less *we* can use to get the scarab." Whether Drew aimed that at me for gambling or Scarlett for the bribe, I couldn't quite tell. He was right, in part, but first, we had to find the scarab.

The ancient Egyptian jewel had been stolen from a museum in Cairo. Our job was to recover it, and our intel said Massimo De Rosa had it.

The dealer spread out the river, face down, and handed out the hole cards. That gave me a nine and a jack, both clubs. If my luck was back, this was a good start. If it wasn't, I'd thrown my money away. I raised four times the ante, as did the American I'd been speaking to, while everyone else checked.

Drew made his way through the room, stopping at the stand outside the restaurant. He spoke to the maître d', who accepted his offer of two hundred euros to jump the reservation line.

The flop gave me two more clubs. Eight and queen. A tiny adrenaline spike hit me. I was heading for either a flush or queen high.

"Table will be ready in thirty," said Drew. "The mark is being seated now."

Scarlett said, "Drew, send me a photo of the unknown woman who came in with Massimo. We'll run her through our databases and see if we can ID her."

His gaze cut to me as he turned toward the entrance. "The son had eyes for her. I'm assuming date, with the hope of more."

"In case she's a factor in the job, send me the photo."

"Will do," said Drew as he disappeared.

Everyone at the table checked, based on the flop.

As the dealer flipped the final two cards, Scarlett gasped, "What the fuck is she doing there? She was supposed to be flying home from Nice today!"

My adrenaline lifted higher. My sister was always in control. She never lost her cool on a job. What was going on?

The cards were the five of diamonds and ten of clubs. I'd won on the Blind and Trips. It was a huge win, but it barely registered.

Don't stand, Em. Don't ask what's wrong. Scarlett will tell you.

Everyone who was still in revealed their cards, and the Americans gave me a slow clap for my straight flush.

Scarlett must have been reacting to the photo Drew had sent. Who was the mystery woman? *Talk to me, Scar.*

"You know her?" asked Drew.

The man next to me slapped my arm, offering congratulations I didn't quite catch.

"Thanks." Distracted, waiting for Scarlett's words, I began racking my winnings, a nervous energy building in my chest. What was causing it? Scarlett's reaction? Or was I rattled closing out my first poker game in four months that didn't end with a gun in my face?

I slid a tip to the dealer and stood, my left hand digging into my pocket before I could stop it. My fingers slid over the textured surface of the hidden poker chip I kept in that pocket every day. The hole pierced through its center. The blue surface. The white edge spots.

Calm down, Em. This is your happy place.

I nodded to the other players, then strolled to the cage, focused on appearing calm to anyone watching. The voices over my earpiece were hurried, keys clacking in the background. The team was furiously researching something. When I was far enough away from the table, I asked, "Scar, who's the woman?"

My sister took in a slow breath, her normal self-control returning. "Jenn."

My step stuttered, and I nearly lost my winnings. There was no way it was *that* Jenn. "Not..."

"Yeah." She cleared her throat. "Jenn Thatcher, my best friend."

"Shit." That was going to complicate things. Unless... "This is perfect. She's our in with the mark."

"No," said Scarlett. "We go with tonight's Plan C. Observe and forgo the initial meeting. You make an approach tomorrow instead. Don't let her see you."

I placed my chips in front of the cashier, who began counting out my money. "I can't approach as Reginald Stone." That was my standard alias for sensitive inquiries.

"And you can't use Emmett Reynolds," said Scarlett, "if they know the company name. This isn't a wise plan."

"Hear me out." I accepted my winnings and slid everything into my long wallet. "How about a compromise?"

"I'm listening."

I weaved my way around tables to take up residence by the bar opposite the Rose Salon. From there, I had a clear view of the restaurant. We had fifteen minutes left until our reservation. If Jenn wasn't inside by then, I'd wait, and we'd re-evaluate. "Emmett Stone. My business cards only have Stone Antiquities written on them, so that covers the De Rosas. And if Jenn balks, I'll wink at her."

"Wink at her?" Drew may have been a talented recovery agent who understood my hints, but he didn't completely understand *me* yet. "What is she? Twelve?"

Scarlett made a noise of assent. "That should work—she knows I've checked into hotels as Ms. Stone for privacy in the past. As long as she remembers that, you're good. Either way, I'll be on comms with you, so if things go off the rails, I can call her. Innocently ask about her trip. It'll be enough to distract her, and if you need more time, I'll pull her entirely out of the conversation."

"Exactly." I caught the bartender's eye and gestured to a bottle of scotch behind him. "It'll kick-start the relationship with De Rosa."

"All right. You're a go," said Scarlett.

I was the lead on this job. I didn't need her authorization, but it settled the queasy feeling in the pit of my stomach. The one reminding me I was going to use Scarlett's best friend as a source.

CHAPTER 2
JENN

The Monte Carlo Casino was one of the most beautiful buildings I'd ever seen. The people milling outside taking photos of the cars screamed tourist trap—although arriving in one of those vehicles, cameras flashing *at* me, was surreal—but the inside made my artist's soul cry.

"Don't fall over," Dante chuckled. His voice was deep, thick with an Italian accent.

I shook my head at myself. Yes, I was busy staring at the huge paintings and the gilded ceilings, which must have been forty or fifty feet high. But what else was I supposed to do? Play it cool and miss everything? "It's breathtaking."

"Designed by the architect of the Paris Opéra."

"I love that building. One of my favorites in Paris." If only I had time to stop there before I flew home.

He guided me toward a dark-wood doorway at the side of the first gambling room. Royal blue walls covered in twelve-foot-tall paintings flanked it, with a decorative wood and glass-work topper. "How long has it been since you visited?"

"Five years, I think?" On an unfortunate holiday with an

even more unfortunate ex of mine. "I'd originally planned on Florence being my next European trip, but Nice came up at the perfect time."

He spoke with the maître d', who ushered us inside the restaurant. "Many would disagree, but I recommend Naples over Florence."

"Is that where you're from?"

"It's where I was born, but we live where the business needs us." He shrugged one shoulder. "Today, it's Monaco. My father's returning home soon while I'll deal with our interests in Paris."

The restaurant was as grand as the rest of the Casino but somehow felt more intimate. I studied the female figures decorating the ceiling, floating on clouds, draped in flowing dark fabrics.

"It was designed as a smoking room." Dante slowed and craned his head heavenward to match mine. "They painted the ceiling in browns to hide the smoke."

Despite the sprawling size, the room reminded me of a Parisian boudoir—warm and cozy. "I appreciate the tour."

Dante stopped and pulled out my chair. "Care to sit, or would you rather see the view from the balcony?"

I dropped my gaze to the room—to the table where Massimo De Rosa and his distracted assistant sat. "I'm good here. Although I might have to come back during the daytime."

"I suspect your days will be long." Massimo leaned back in his chair. "There's quite a lot to complete before the auction."

"I'll have some time after I finish." I'd already canceled my flight home and hadn't rebooked yet, so I had some flexibility. Maybe I *could* swing a trip to Paris?

"We are rather fortunate Dante found you, are we not?" said Massimo. "An art restorer materializes precisely when we're in need of one."

"Very fortunate." Dante smiled as he sat beside me. He and his father dressed in similar casual, yet luxurious, clothes. Their wealth was subtle but somehow obvious. "Nice has been good to us this year."

I spread my napkin across my lap. "And you have tools available at your gallery?"

Massimo nodded. "New artwork arrives often, so our regular man established a small workshop."

"And why isn't he doing the work?" I was only an apprentice restorer, working for my favorite aunt after years in an unfulfilling project management job. I'd worked for her during summers as a student—and sometimes just to get out of the house—so I'd known how to clean and retouch paintings, repair damaged canvases, and craft one-of-a-kind frames long before she hired me. She'd always said I was a natural.

"He's sick and currently in Geneva." Dante leaned closer and lowered his voice to a stage whisper. "Although I suspect he's hiding from his wife."

Massimo's assistant, a man whose name I kept forgetting, typed away on his phone. He sat across from Dante and had hardly looked up. "Signore?"

The two men began a hushed conversation in Italian.

Dante gave a subtle wave to a server with brilliant red hair and bright pink cheeks. He ordered red wine for the table, and she was off. Then he turned his focus to me. "The tools at the gallery are rudimentary."

"That should be fine. It's a simple sprucing up, right? The photos you provided didn't show any damage."

"We've only had it cleaned once, after Papa bought it seven years ago. We'd like it looking its best for the auction on Friday."

If I were listing something in an auction, I would have prepped it much further in advance than a week. But their poor planning was my giant win. Three weeks ago, I'd discovered what a lying, cheating pig my most recent ex was. So I'd begged my Aunt Penny to send me to Nice, in her place, to hand-deliver a painting she'd conserved.

She was the only one I'd told about the pig. I'd almost called my bestie brigade over a dozen times to tell them, but I wasn't ready for the pity looks. Let alone the ones that said I was the last one to figure out what a sleazebag he was. *Again.* "How long has your conservator been out of town?"

"He's not a conservator, per se." Dante placed his hand on the back of my chair, an oddly intimate move for a man I'd only met two days ago. "But he has training, plus a unique passion for art."

"Unique passion?"

"Indeed, he—"

"Jenn?" came a male voice behind me. One that had the hairs on the back of my neck standing at attention. "Jenn Thatcher?"

I turned as he came up beside me.

Emmett.

Freaking.

Reynolds.

Dressed in a black suit with a black shirt, the buttons undone at his neck. My heart forgot how to beat for half a second. When it started again, my brain also reminded my lungs to breathe.

"I thought that was you!" He held his arms wide, as though expecting me to jump up and hug him.

I *wanted* to jump up and hug him. Smell the fresh cologne he'd been wearing for years, with its notes of cardamom and bergamot, plus a hint of vanilla. All I could manage was, "Funny running into you here."

"No kidding." He lowered his arms. "I heard you were in France but didn't expect to run into you in Monaco."

Me, either.

After delivering the painting for Aunt Penny, I'd had a few days to enjoy Nice. Dante and I crossed paths at the Marc Chagall National Museum. He'd commented on one of the paintings—said it looked drab, which was uncharacteristic of Chagall's usual brilliant color palette. I suggested it needed a cleaning, and the conversation somehow stumbled into my job as an art restorer.

Massimo's gallery negotiated a short-term contract job with my aunt, and I'd gotten into Dante's Velatti convertible for the quick drive to Monte Carlo. I'd had a few doubts, but Aunt Penny confirmed he was who he said he was, and he even set me up in a room at the Hôtel de Paris.

Now here I was.

"I'm in town for a contract." I gestured to Massimo. "Massimo De Rosa, this is my friend Emmett—"

"Stone." Emmett winked at me before shaking hands with Massimo.

Stone? What was he talking about?

Emmett produced a simple white business card with black letters and handed it to Massimo—but his assistant intercepted it. "Antiquities broker."

I introduced him to Dante, the courtesy more instinct than anything else.

Why Stone?

Emmett shook hands with Dante. "Pleasure to meet you."

Before I could embarrass myself by not remembering Massimo's assistant's name, the man stepped away to take a phone call.

"And how do you know Jenn?" asked Dante.

"She's my sister's best friend." A lazy smile pulled Emmett's mouth up, tugging at memories best left out of my business dinner. "Known each other since we were kids."

We'd been friends forever.

But he was also the first boy I'd kissed.

The first boy who'd broken my heart.

Now he was the guy using a fake name. Why was he—

Wait. The Reynolds Recoveries company specialized in locating lost things, making special deliveries, and negotiating for the return of stolen items. Scarlett had once told me she sometimes used an alias for privacy. Was that why he'd winked?

"De Rosa, was it?" asked Emmett. "Any relation to the De Rosa Gallery?"

Dante nodded. "It is. And Emmett Stone? Is this a name I should know?"

"I work for a discreet brokerage, dealing in high-value items." Emmett looked from Dante to Massimo, then turned his smile on me. "I'm always on the lookout for potential acquisitions."

That smile settled low in my stomach, bringing back memories I didn't want to relive.

"I'm in Monte Carlo looking for rare Egyptian antiquities for one of my clients."

"We open tomorrow at ten." Massimo lifted his menu, a not-so-subtle hint he was done with the conversation. "I prefer not to speak business after hours."

"Of course." Emmett bowed his head in courtesy. "But I'm sure you can agree a thing of beauty can be discussed at any time?"

Dante shifted in his seat, squaring up toward Emmett without letting go of the back of my chair. "However, we only discuss purchases during business hours."

Emmett gave a faux tip of his hat to the men. "I'll be stopping into Galatea and Brise Galleries in the morning. Perhaps I'll see you all tomorrow afternoon?"

Massimo nodded curtly and focused on the server, who'd arrived with our bottle of wine.

Emmett extended his hand as though to shake mine, something he hadn't—ever?—done with me. "And I'll definitely be seeing you around. Where are you staying?"

CHAPTER 3
EMMETT

Dante released his death grip on the back of Jenn's chair and intervened. He extended his hand, swooping in to shake mine before I could touch Jenn. Drew had called it—she was his date, and he was hoping for more. That wasn't going to happen. The De Rosas had their fingers in too many less-than-legal operations for me to accept him in her life.

Her father's words echoed in my memory. *'She deserves better than the son of a criminal.'*

My smile faltered.

"Enjoy your meal, Emmett Stone." Dante was going to be a problem. If he saw me as a threat, he might interfere in my investigation.

Jenn smiled at me, a slight furrow in her brow. She was trying to figure out what was going on. "See you later."

I turned and left them, sliding one hand into my pocket as I strolled to the other end of the restaurant.

"The son looked like he was about to deck you," said Drew over my earpiece. "She may be more of a liability than an asset."

The problem was that Scarlett's best friends were on the outside. Scar insisted they never know the whole truth of our work, so she'd always have friends who didn't look at her as a heist crew's mastermind.

So here I was, telling barefaced lies in front of Jenn and expecting her to cover for me. I groaned internally. Every year, I grew more like my father—the criminal. The spy. The traitor.

I kept my voice down so no one would think me too strange conversing with myself. "We should finish our drinks and leave, Drew."

"Despite the tip to get in?"

When I reached our table by the window, I scanned the horizon before pulling out my chair. "They're suspicious."

"Go figure," said Scarlett over the earpiece. "You may as well have challenged him to a duel."

That wasn't her second-guessing voice. It was the one she used when she disapproved. Drew wouldn't have noticed—it was subtle enough only our core team would recognize it. She hid her emotions well, except I had years of experience gauging the slightest shift in her cadence, tone, or the breaths she took between words.

I lowered myself into the seat and looked at Drew, as though we were having a polite chat, and I wasn't arguing with my sister. "I didn't like the way he was looking at her."

"It doesn't matter. Jenn has a boyfriend, so nothing will happen between her and Dante."

"This is why it's easier to work alone." Drew motioned to a server for the bill, and the woman nodded. "The more people you let into your circle, the more you risk the work getting too personal."

"The same way it was personal between you and Craig?" My lips tightened to emphasize the taunt.

Drew's frown deepened.

That had been too low.

Honestly, our work had become increasingly personal over the last several months. An enemy that continued popping up during our jobs, the emotional scars my sister had suffered at their hands, not to mention the physical ones I had. I tucked a hand into my left pocket and ran my thumb over the textured surface of my poker chip.

The reminder of what my life had been like five months ago. Before the kidnapping. Before the beatings. Before—

Snap out of it.

On top of everything, the revelation about our mother's past with MI6 lingered like a shadow—a secret Scarlett and I shared only with Drew, hoping his contacts could uncover the truth. And now Jenn was here in Monte Carlo, involved with the very men we suspected held the stolen scarab.

I pulled the crystal tumbler at my setting closer, rolling it between my palms. "I should have said you and Jayce."

Drew's frown softened at the mention of his girlfriend, our team's thief. He'd definitely let things get too personal with her, and he'd be the first to admit it. "We all have our lapses in judgment."

I lifted my glass in salute, forcing myself to remain facing Drew.

Jenn's father was right. She needed a good man. Apparently, she had one at home—although Scarlett complained often that Jenn rarely dated anyone who deserved her. If Mr. Thatcher hadn't scared *him* off, maybe she'd finally found the one she deserved.

She didn't need me protecting her from Dante De Rosa.

So why was every muscle in my body demanding I march back to their table and haul her out of there?

CHAPTER 4
JENN

Tuesday afternoon, I stood in a room off the main office of the De Rosa Gallery. All around me, paintings were stacked against the walls, sculptures lined the shelves, and various antiques hid in their jars and boxes. The gallery itself was minimalist, showcasing some of the finest items Massimo owned or was consigning, while the back office was jam-packed.

A ten-by-twenty area had been earmarked for studying and cleaning pieces, including a tall worktable with an open space underneath it. Tools and chemicals crammed two shelves under the table, while more hid in cabinets lining the walls.

The space was a fraction of what my Aunt Penny had at home, but Dante had explained they contracted out more complex jobs to shops across Europe, depending on the specialists required.

I had the painting out of its frame and off the stretcher and was writing out a plan in my notebook. The painting was an early nineteenth-century pastoral scene by John Constable —two feet by two and a half, typical of his outdoor work. The brushwork was loose, giving an almost hazy appearance to the painting from a distance, but close up, I could see every stroke laid with skill and precision.

Maybe too much precision?

Aunt Penny would have handled something like this at home. However, Massimo's regular conservator had made comprehensive notes the last time he cleaned it, so I had a solid starting point. I simply had to collect solvents, brushes, cotton, and other tools to clean a faint layer of dirt off the top, then apply a fresh layer of varnish.

I ran a hand over the bend at the edge of the painting, where it had wrapped around the stretcher. The small workshop didn't have a heat or vacuum table, so I'd have to use simpler hand-held tools to remove the indentation before cleaning it.

There was a knock at the door, and Dante appeared. "I'm going across the street for coffee."

As I looked up, he paused and smiled, his gaze resting on my outstretched hand. I snapped my hand back. "Sorry. I was getting a feel for the artwork."

He came closer, stopping across the table from me, and ran a finger along the indented edge. "My father always told me not to touch things that don't belong to me."

I swallowed hard. Was I getting in trouble, or was he flirting? "Difficult to clean it without touching it."

"Perhaps you should teach me how, so I also have an excuse." Dante was exactly the kind of man I needed. A smoldering Italian who loved art—clear from the way he caressed the canvas—whose father owned not just one of the yachts in the harbor, but an art gallery in Monaco, and who knew how much else. He was a rich, charming distraction from my reality.

What was he like in bed? *Did you seriously think that?* Maybe he could get me over my cheating ex?

He wouldn't, though. And that wasn't what my trip was about. It was about freeing myself—not getting tangled up again. And the last thing I needed was to get involved with someone, even for a night.

Men are a hassle, Jenn. Remember that.

He rested his hands on the worktable. "Would you like a drink? It would only take us fifteen or thirty minutes."

"Thanks for the offer, but I..." I tapped the stack of notes. "I need to get ahead of the project first."

"I'll bring you something, then?" He was persistent, if nothing else.

"That'd be nice."

He gave a slight bow and left.

Yeah, Dante was the kind of man my father would approve of. Who my friends would high-five me over. No one would give me the side-eye if I brought *him* home.

Why couldn't I have met him when my life was under control?

I sighed and paced the length of the conservation area, considering my next steps. Smooth out the creases, do a quick test along the edge to confirm the required solvents, and away I could go. Or maybe run the tests first to ensure I had suffi-cient materials for the cleaning?

If we had to order anything from Nice, Paris, or elsewhere, it would be best to have the order in as soon as possible. I pulled bottles of acetone and distilled water from a shelf at the back of the room, then donned a pair of nitrile gloves, a mask, and safety goggles. Step one: dilute the acetone.

After double-checking the notes, I rolled a few swabs, creating tools out of sticks and cotton batting. I dipped a swab into the solvent, pressed the edge of the canvas flat, and froze. Aunt Penny normally verified everything for me. This was a Constable. They expected it would fetch over two hundred thousand at the auction on Friday night.

What if I'd misinterpreted something?

What if I had the acetone concentration wrong?

What if I was supposed to warm the solution and had the wrong temperature?

Working without my safety net had my stomach twisting in as many knots as seeing Emmett last night. He said he'd drop by the gallery. I'd put on a little extra eye makeup this morning. My pulse had even jumped every time the front door's bell had chimed.

Maybe that was the real reason I turned down Dante's offer of going for coffee.

What if I missed Emmett's visit?

Scarlett had called me last night, apologized for putting me in a tight spot with Emmett's alias, and explained her team was in town searching for leads on a stolen Egyptian scarab. I'd told her a little about the surprise trip to Monaco but skipped the why. If I told her about Simon cheating on me...

I squeezed my eyes shut and stretched out my neck. He'd brought me flowers afterward. Apologized. Swore it was one time only. Part of me wanted the asshole back.

And that's your problem, isn't it? I opened my eyes and shook my head at myself. *Yeah, that's exactly your problem, Jenn.*

I was almost thirty years old, and my biological clock was ticking. Kelley had just given birth. Heather got close but wound up divorced. And Scarlett? She'd been engaged, but lost her fiancé in a tragic accident two years ago. Her new boyfriend would propose by Christmas—we were all sure of it.

And me?

Instead of settling down with a man who wanted to help me with my clock, I continued dating the most self-centered, egotistical, inconsiderate jerks I could find.

Screw all of them.

"Or focus on work," I muttered to myself. *Quiet.* The last thing I needed was for Massimo or one of his employees to walk in on my self-doubts or hear them as they passed by.

There was no need to fear or worry. I was a strong, capable, intelligent woman.

I flattened the edge and rolled the solvent onto a tiny square, less than an inch. Left it to settle for ten seconds, then wiped it clean with another piece of—

Oh, shit!

The paint smeared as I wiped.

My heart leaped into my throat.

What did I do wrong?

I triple and quadruple-checked the conservator's notes. Re-read the bottles. Examined the cotton in case it had been contaminated.

But everything was right. I was sure of it.

Were the instructions wrong? Were they for a different painting? No. It was a stack of papers, which Dante had delivered in a plain folder. The folder and each sheet were labeled

'Constable, John, "Wheatfield from the Lock," Oil on canvas, 1810.'

"Come va?"

I let out a squeak and spun to face the doorway, where the Italian voice had come from.

A man with a scar across his cheek stood there, dressed in black slacks and a tailored blue shirt. He took a step into the room and smiled. The way his scar puckered, the friendly gesture was unnerving.

"Sorry." I shook my head and tossed the swab and cotton into the disposal jar, doing my best to regain my calm. "You startled me."

"Your work goes well?"

"It does. Thank you." I nodded too rapidly, stopping myself before I apologized again. *He doesn't know your test failed. Stop sounding nervous.* "Although I'm just starting."

"You can finish before the auction?"

Dante had introduced me to the guard on duty that morning, to the man at the front desk, and reintroduced me to Massimo's assistant. He'd advised me the guard would stop in from time to time—which he had—but that everyone else would likely leave me to work in peace for the day.

No warnings about a scary-looking man with a scar.

I picked up the conservator's notes and positioned them over the smudge. "It'll only take a few days."

He came closer, cocking his head. "You're not as experienced as his regular conservator?"

What did that mean? Was a few days too long? Dante had said the regular conservator wasn't full-time, but he had training. *I* had training. "Massimo negotiated a contract with my boss. They discussed my qualifications."

"But Dante hired you, yes?"

What did that have to do with—

Wait. *Does he think you're sleeping with Dante for this job?* I straightened my spine. "I'm sorry, sir, but I have work to finish for the De Rosas."

"He's a handsome man. Wealthy." He leaned on the worktable, ignoring my subtle attempt at asking him to leave. "As is his father."

A few streaks of gray laced the hair at his temples. Paired with the faint lines around his eyes, he was likely in his forties. At his age, he should have known better than to accuse a woman of sleeping her way into a job. They were paying well, but certainly not *that* well.

"They're my clients. I hadn't noticed." Total lie, but it had nothing to do with the job.

He nodded slowly, scanning the painting. "I meant no offense."

"Of course not." I kept my hand on the sheet of paper, just in case. "Now, if you'll excuse me, I have to get back to work."

"Be sure you do your best." He headed for the door. "Massimo has promised we'll see a healthy profit from the sale."

Jackass.

Once I was alone again, I grabbed a loupe from under the worktable and examined the damaged area. If I'd done everything right, the dirt should have lifted, leaving the paint alone. But a tiny section had lifted all the way to the canvas. This wasn't right.

I removed my protective gear before grabbing my phone from my purse. I dialed Aunt Penny's number as I crossed to the farthest corner of the small room. She'd know what to do.

"Jenny Girl," she said in her breezy tone. "How's Monte Carlo?"

"Good." Weird. "But I need some advice."

"You're a talented—"

"Not like that." I didn't need my ego stroked or my confidence bolstered. I spoke quickly—too quickly?—summarizing the steps I'd taken with the painting and my results. "I know I'm overreacting, but..." I stared at the open doorway, cupping my hand over my mouth to ensure no one else heard me. "How could I have gotten it so wrong?"

She clucked her tongue in the way she did when she was thinking. "Have you spoken with the De Rosas about this?"

"No, should I?"

"You have a mismatch between an expert's notes and your experience. The first thing you need to do is figure out which one is wrong."

Wrong? "His notes wouldn't be."

"In that case, the painting may be." Was she saying what I thought she was saying? Did she think it could be a fake? "You don't have much time available, so I'll put you in touch with a conservator I met at a conference earlier this year. He has a lot of experience with fakes and forgeries, and his wife is also an art crime investigator. They'll be able to advise you on the quickest way to figure it out."

I stared at the sliver of canvas I'd revealed with the acetone. *Should I leave? Tell them I'll be back tomorrow? What if Penny's contact calls me back right away? Should I wait and see what he says?* "What do I do in the meantime?"

"Do what I've been teaching you. Do your own experiments. Inspect the paint—is it genuinely oil? Does it feel like it's been on the canvas for two hundred years? Are the polymers cross-linked yet? Does the craquelure look right? Take notes on everything."

Another deep breath. I didn't know what two-hundred-year-old craquelure looked like on a John Constable painting. And it wasn't like Monaco was large enough that I could find a museum with other pieces to compare. Maybe in Nice? Or the Internet.

"You can do this, Jenn. I wouldn't have agreed to the project if I didn't think you could."

So much for a simple cleaning.

CHAPTER 5
EMMETT

THE DE ROSA GALLERY sat at the base of a seven-story terrace house, a five-minute walk from the Hôtel de Paris. My research indicated the gallery took up three stories, while apartments filled the space above. Directly across the street, a shorter building housed a coffee shop and a stamp collectors' store on the bottom floor.

I was alone today with a straightforward goal: Enter the gallery and inquire if Massimo was there. If yes, ask to speak with him and determine whether he'd sell me the scarab. If not, find out if I could purchase it legally.

Our client, a wealthy patron of the museum from which the scarab had been stolen was offering a five-million euro reward for its return. Minus expenses and profit margin, we had four million to negotiate with.

On the open market, a two-inch-long gold and carnelian gem of its quality would be worth no more than a hundred thousand. But this one had been a gift from Pharaoh Khufu to his chief surveyor, which increased its value. I wouldn't have expected that many millions more, but the black market was fickle.

Or the broker who'd put us in touch with the client was setting us up.

I pulled up my suit cuff to check my watch. Black leather and white gold Patek Philippe on the outside. Underneath? Custom Reynolds tech. It was a sin to have taken it apart, but Will—our team's gadget guru—maintained the exterior so perfectly that someone would only know the truth if they popped it open.

Three o'clock. Late enough to have visited the other two galleries as cover, early enough I might be able to spend time with the De Rosas.

And Jenn would be there.

Scarlett had called her last night to gather intel, but Jenn had been tight-lipped, saying only that Dante had brought her to Monte Carlo and she'd be working at the gallery. Something was off with her. But what?

I couldn't read her like I could most people. Something about her had always thrown me, from the first time Scar introduced her as *'my new best friend'* after we moved to Halifax. She'd brought cookies her mother had made for the new kids in the neighborhood. Things went downhill after people started talking about whose kids we were.

'If I ever catch you near my daughter again, you'll regret it.' Her father's words spun around my brain. *'Your sister's bad enough, but you are where I draw the line.'*

I'd quashed his insults fifteen years ago, so why were they haunting me now? None of the other taunts about my father being a spy were bubbling up. Just Mr. Thatcher's. He didn't matter. He didn't know my family; he didn't know the good we did.

My father's incarceration wasn't relevant in my life, so why would it matter to anyone else?

I straightened my cuff and slowed in front of the gallery.

Tall windows flanked the glass door, showcasing two paintings, a jewelry display, and a Greek sculpture roughly my height. Inside, a security guard sat on a chair by a narrow elevator, while a thin man in glasses sat behind a desk straight ahead. Two leather sofas sat off to the right side. Not much on display—the wide, curved staircase by the sofas would take guests to the real treasures.

I pulled open the door and smiled when the man behind the desk looked up. "Good afternoon."

He nodded in return and stood.

As I drew closer, I rechecked my watch—not to find out the time, but to show the indicator of wealth. My greeting made it clear I wasn't there to browse, and the watch made it clear I had the money to purchase. "Is Signore De Rosa in today?"

"He's out." Strike one. "However, my name is Jean-Philippe, and I am intimately familiar with the inventory. Can I help you?" His accent was French with a hint of Spanish—likely from the southwest.

"I have a client in the market for Egyptian antiquities. Do you have anything available?"

"Of course." The man picked up a tablet from his desk and gestured to the staircase. "We have a few pieces on display on the third floor. If nothing suits your interest, we have additional pieces awaiting cleaning or restoration, and I can review them with you."

I followed him toward the stairs, glancing into the back of the gallery, where a few paintings were displayed. "We're looking for jewelry or funerary items. Accessories around five centimeters."

"Very small. Is your client starting a collection or building upon one?"

A short hallway on the main floor led to a door, with one or more doors likely unseen opposite it. Where was Jenn? "They're building upon an existing one. They sold a few coins recently and want to fill the space with something the same size."

"Most of our Egyptian items are pottery, but we have a beautiful scarab that arrived in February."

It wouldn't be this easy, would it? "That sounds like it might work."

"It's an exquisite mold-made scarab in Egyptian blue from the Scarab Factory in Naukratis."

Strike two. "We're looking for something more... gold."

As we reached the second floor, the front door's bell chimed. My guide raised a hand and returned to the top of the stairs. "Ah, Monsieur De Rosa! You're back."

"I won't be staying long," replied a deep male voice with an Italian accent. Massimo or his son?

The father hadn't spoken enough last night for me to get a read on their tonal differences.

"Dante?" That voice, though, I knew. Jenn was downstairs. "I'm just packing up for the day."

"I thought you wanted to get further ahead?" asked Dante.

"Yeah, I did. I mean, I do."

I followed Jean-Philippe, keeping close to the wall so I could watch the conversation unseen.

Jenn approached Dante. "I ran a couple of tests to verify which solvents to use. They need to develop overnight, so I can be sure."

"Any progress is excellent." Dante held up a white bag and a to-go cup. "I bought you some coffee and couldn't resist a few macarons."

She paused. Her back was to me, but I saw enough of her profile to read the hesitation. Brows and lips down. Confused?

Considering how often Scarlett complained about the jerks Jenn dated—I'd only met two and could confirm they were both assholes—she probably wasn't sure how to accept the kindness. Or she was trying to figure out how to turn down his overt flirtation because she was in a relationship.

She accepted the bag, peered inside, and let out a tiny laugh. "Thanks."

Shit. She was buying it.

"Monsieur?" said Jean-Philippe, jarring me back to my job. He was halfway to the next flight of stairs.

How long had I been staring at Jenn and Mr. Coffee?

And *why* was I staring at them? Why did it matter when I had a job to do?

Because the scarab upstairs isn't the one you're looking for. We'd seen our target on display at a gala two months ago in Washington, DC. It wasn't hidden somewhere, waiting for a cleaning.

Which meant it was at Massimo's home, one of his other locations, or stored away from prying eyes. Our source told us it was in Monaco, though. If it wasn't at the gallery, Dante was a better bet than Jean-Philippe to gain me access to their home or offices. I had to take my opportunity before he left.

I dodged Jean-Philippe and returned down the stairs. "Dante, what luck!" I looked at Jenn, feigning surprise, as though I hadn't been spying on them. "And Jenn! I didn't realize you'd be here. Twice in as many days. What are the odds!"

Her cheeks reddened as our gazes met, the bag hanging open in front of her.

"Emmett Stone." I shook Dante's hand, squeezing more than I should have, which he did right back. "Jenn introduced us last night?"

"Sì, I remember." His pretty little smile for Jenn had vanished. No surprise there. "Is Jean-Philippe helping you?"

"I am, sir," said the gallery staffer.

"We were on our way to the third floor. I'm eager to see what you have." I winked at him, letting go of his hand and the testosterone game while playing up our level of familiarity. "My client is looking for a piece of Egyptian jewelry or something small in gold. Jean-Philippe mentioned a blue scarab, which isn't the right material. I don't suppose you have anything in the back like that?"

"This is my father's gallery. I know more about his profit margins than his inventory." Dante gestured to Jean-Philippe. "Our staff are the best people to answer questions for our clients."

Jenn hadn't closed the bag yet. She'd barely moved other than her gaze flicking back and forth to follow my conversation with Dante. "I'm going to pack up."

Dante touched her upper arm. The gesture was too intimate for a work relationship. "Are we still on for dinner?"

Jenn's gaze darted to me, then back to Dante. "I have some research to do. I think I'll grab my laptop and sit somewhere by myself. Maybe tomorrow?"

Dante nodded at her, then addressed me. "If you don't find anything your client is interested in, Jean-Philippe can show you the digital inventory."

Two more people entered the gallery, a middle-aged man and woman, walking close enough they were obviously a couple. They detoured directly to the Greek statue in the front window.

"That sounds perfect." I'd have to call my younger sister before seeing the digital inventory. Brie was our team's hacker, and if I could get my phone next to that tablet while Jean-Philippe was calling up the inventory, she might be able to gather additional intel. I turned to Jean-Philippe. "It appears you have some new customers, so why don't I stop in tomorrow?"

Jean-Philippe nodded.

I stepped closer to Jenn, placing a hand on her back. "Scar said you're staying at the Hôtel de Paris?"

"I am."

"I'm going back there now, so why don't I walk with you?"

"Sounds good. I'll grab my stuff." She left, leaving me with Mr. Coffee.

Jean-Philippe gravitated toward the couple, who eventually waved him over.

"She's your sister's best friend, you said?" Dante folded one arm across his chest, still holding the cup Jenn hadn't taken. He was an attractive man, wealthy, and clearly interested in Jenn. But if Massimo was hiding the stolen scarab, that made Dante the son of a criminal. He was no better for her—or any woman—than I was.

"She's..." I turned in the direction where she'd gone, pretending to consider my words while instead studying the hallway from a better angle than on the stairs. "She's like a sister."

"And you're an overprotective brother?"

I faced Dante again. "It's a quick walk to the hotel, but who knows what could happen to a beautiful young woman out on her own? She might get into a car with a stranger who whisks her off to another country?"

He didn't react to the dig. No appearance of insult or irritation at my suggestion that accepting his drive from Nice might have been an unwise decision. "I'm sure she can handle herself."

"I know she can."

Jenn appeared with a purse over her shoulder and the bag of macarons. "I'm ready."

Dante leaned in to kiss the air at each of her cheeks. "I'll see you at nine tomorrow morning?"

She smiled at him, tucking back a strand of her blond hair that had escaped her bun. Was she flirting with him? "See you then."

I escorted her out the door and into the warm mid-August day. We hung a left, passing a row of parked scooters. I was now officially hours behind schedule. My team wouldn't be impressed.

Hell, *I* wasn't impressed with myself—so many stupid decisions since I saw Jenn last night.

But she was safe from Dante for another day. And that was what mattered most.

It shouldn't have mattered.

But goddammit, it did.

CHAPTER 6
JENN

STILL NO CALL from Aunt Penny's contact. It was four o'clock in Monte Carlo but only ten a.m. in the Eastern time zone. Maybe his office was just opening?

"Were they good?" asked Emmett.

"What?"

He nudged the empty bag in my hand. "The macarons. Did you taste them at all?"

I peered into the empty bag. I hadn't even realized I'd eaten them, let alone tasted them. "Of course. They were delicious."

The smeared paint on the Constable played on a loop in my brain. The hotel lobby's marble floors, statuary, and decorated ceiling had barely registered. Same as the sights and sounds of the city.

Plus, my macarons.

Emmett had walked by my side the entire time in silence. Rare for him.

To be honest, he tried talking to me a few times, but I was poor company.

I may have been relatively new as an art restorer, but I knew how to follow instructions. God, my entire job was about following instructions. I hadn't missed anything or pulled the wrong materials. It was acetone and distilled water, which I mixed to exactly sixty percent dilution, per the conservator's notes. My work had been perfect. I was sure of it.

Something else was going on.

We walked through the white-paneled hallway inside the hotel, along the lush cream and light brown carpet. I had a fourth-floor room with a small balcony overlooking a beautiful courtyard at the center of the hotel.

"You don't need to escort me to my doorstep." I'd told Dante I was going to take my laptop somewhere to sit and think. The truth was, I'd likely take it as far as my balcony, then stare at my phone until it rang.

We passed three doors before Emmett spoke again. "Are you upset about something?"

Something? Try everything. "I'm fine."

His right eyebrow cocked, the same way Scar's did when I wasn't telling the whole story.

But I wasn't ready to confess the niggling doubt in the back of my brain that I'd screwed up—or my suspicion the painting might not be genuine. I slowed as we approached my door, pulling my room key out of my shoulder bag. "Strange."

"What's that?" He stopped just behind me as though he were going to see me all the way into my room.

I shook my head, trying to clear it, then pointed at the Do Not Disturb door hanger. "I was sure I'd put it on for housekeeping this—"

Emmett was in front of me with my room key in his hand before I finished. "Are you sure?"

"I..." My hand hung in the air, as confused about what to do as my brain. "Maybe?"

He held up a finger and pressed his ear to the door. Emmett was normally smooth lines—smiles, crinkled eyes, casual movements. But now? He was sharp angles. He reminded me more of our friend Rav than his usual self.

I glanced around, trying to be subtle in case someone was watching his bizarre behavior. A lump formed slowly in my throat. "You're being weird."

His finger remained up, and he closed his eyes.

The lump in my throat grew. What was going on?

After another minute, he opened his eyes. "I don't hear anything."

"Why would you—"

"Security's tight here, but—" He straightened, the angles shifting back to smooth lines and a lopsided smile. "I was at a hotel in Berlin once, and they accidentally gave a duplicate of my room key to someone else."

"Seriously?"

Or was he changing the subject?

"That's why I always use the safety lock." He chuckled, but it didn't calm the hairs at my nape, all standing at attention. "Let me go in ahead of you. You know, in case someone's sleeping in your bed, and they get a little freaked out."

"Goldilocks?"

He tucked a lock of hair—one that kept falling out of my bun—behind my ear. "You're the only Goldilocks here. I want to be sure there are no bears inside."

"I could just be mistaken about the door hanger." If I didn't know Emmett half as well as I did, I might have suspected he wanted into my room with me. But that ship had sailed a long, long time ago, and it would never sail again. "I don't need a white knight."

"Need? Of course not. But doesn't every woman want one?"

I scoffed inwardly. If only I could convince myself to be attracted to one of those.

Dante acted like he might be one. I curled the top of the white bakery bag. I *hadn't* tasted the damn macarons.

Emmett's eyes crinkled. It was slight and brief, but I was sure of it. He turned to the door, waved the card across the lock, and whispered over his shoulder, "Keep your voice down."

I was so creeped out. What was going on? This wasn't about duplicate keys. And if he thought someone was inside, wouldn't he have insisted we call security? Or at least Rav? Scarlett had told me he was in town with Emmett. "What are we—"

The finger went up again, but he didn't turn around to look at me. He walked slowly—no, he prowled—along the short hallway to my bedroom. At the bathroom and closet doors, he peered around corners like a detective in a movie. More intense, though. If he'd had a gun, I would have called him James Bond.

I wanted to ask what was going on and why he was acting like this, but the words lodged in my throat with that lump.

As he entered the bedroom, he held up a fist. Like soldiers did in movies. I froze.

He was spending too much time with Rav.

Or were there things I didn't know about Emmett?

More secrets from the man my father muttered about every time he saw him?

I poked my head into the bathroom. It was still a mess. My toiletries bag lay open on the counter, two towels hung over the tub's edge, and I'd left the mirror light on.

No, I'd turned that off. I was sure of it.

And my lipstick. It wasn't sitting in the right spot in my bag.

Goosebumps skittered up and down my arms.

Were Emmett's concerns valid? If housekeeping had been through the room, a few things out of place would make sense. But the towels were still lying there. Fresh ones should have been rolled up on the racks over the tub.

A figure appeared behind me, and I gasped, spinning to face Emmett, who was suddenly standing in the bathroom with me. I hadn't heard him move. "Holy crap!"

Emmett put a finger to his lips as he hurried to me. He gripped my upper arms and leaned down so we were eye-to-eye. So close. He whispered, "Keep your volume down."

I pressed a hand against my chest, trying to slow my lungs before I passed out. Instead of speaking, all I could do was nod. What the hell was going on? I was imagining things—that was the only answer.

Emmett drew closer. His lips brushed my ear, and he barely breathed, "Is there anything out of place?"

I nodded again.

"There's no one in your room or on your balcony. There are no signs of forced entry. You're safe here with me. Do you understand?"

I did the only thing I seemed capable of—I nodded.

"I want you to go through the rest of your hotel room. Pretend you're coming back for your laptop exactly like you said you would. Pretend I'm not here. Talk to yourself a little."

My breaths grew steadier as his cologne washed over me. The familiar scent inspired calm. All on their own, and against my better judgment, my arms slid around his back.

He wrapped one strong arm around my waist. "Rav, Jayce, and Drew are here in town with me. They're coming down to look at your room."

The calm vanished as quickly as it had appeared, and I leaned back so I could see him. Was he serious? Why would his team come here? What would they do?

He shook his head, and his free hand found the back of my neck, pulling me close enough to continue whispering in my ear. "I'm not trying to scare you. But I have a feeling someone was in your room. Someone who shouldn't have been here. I need to know if anything is missing, and if it is, what is it?"

I would have been excited to be in Emmett's arms if my heart weren't trying to leap up my throat and out of my body.

Unfortunately, nothing about this trip to Monte Carlo was going the way I had hoped it would. My great restoration coup had transformed into a gigantic failure—either I had no idea what I was doing, or I was working on a forgery. No matter how close I got to Em, he'd never want me the way I wanted him. And now, if his instincts were right, someone had been in my room.

Why?

I slipped away from Emmett, out of the bathroom, down the hallway. I wouldn't say anything if I were really coming for my laptop. But he wanted me to talk to myself.

"Let's see..." I walked to the narrow wooden desk where my laptop and mouse sat. Nothing looked out of place. "Where did I put the..."

Emmett stood soundlessly at the entrance to the room, a

soft smile on his lips that almost made me feel like any of this was normal.

I scanned every surface—the bed, the nightstands, the dresser, the tiny balcony overlooking the patio. My laptop bag sat on the desk chair. I'd left it there, but something wasn't right. Every zipper was open. Sleep had been elusive last night. I'd finally drifted off around two o'clock and slept half an hour later than planned, so I'd rushed through my morning routine.

That rush had included a last-minute panic about where my notebook was. Fortunately, it had been in my laptop bag, exactly where I'd left it, and I'd thrown it into my purse.

My small sketchbook, though? It was still in the laptop bag, spine up.

A shiver ran up my spine.

I never put the sketchbook in with the spine up. If the pages faced the bottom, there were too many chances they'd get ripped, torn, or folded. I always put it spine down to protect it.

Someone *had* been in my room. And they'd gone through my things.

CHAPTER 7

EMMETT

JENN BLANCHED when she checked her laptop bag. She'd seen something that said my suspicions were right—her room had been broken into.

But who?

She was working for Massimo De Rosa, even if only for a week, which meant my top suspects were his staff, an enemy, or hell, it could have been law enforcement. Someone was looking for information from her.

Wrapping my hand around hers, I tugged her gently away from the desk. My team was on the way, and they'd take care of things.

"My sketch—"

I placed a finger against her lips, and her eyes widened. A cursory check around the room hadn't revealed any listening devices, but that didn't mean there weren't any. If I broke into someone's room for intel, it would be to take something, photograph something, or plant a bug. Leaving everything so tidy meant they didn't want her to know they'd been there.

And *that* meant they either had the photographs they wanted or had hidden a bug.

She drew closer as we walked toward the door, wrapping her free hand around my arm. She was afraid, probably confused, and all she had was me.

'Your father betrayed his country. I bet you'd do the same to Jenn.' Mr. Thatcher's words crowded my brain, but I pushed them aside, like I'd been doing since I was fifteen. My father had raised me properly for the first decade, despite being a traitor, and Mr. Thatcher had simply joined a chorus of critics who judged me for my father's actions.

But today, I had higher priorities than my ghosts.

When I opened the door, Rav, Drew, and Jayce filed in. They'd been waiting, knowing better than to make any noise like knocking. The former soldier, spy, and thief nodded as they passed us, while I took Jenn into the hallway to wait.

They'd sweep the room for any hidden microphones or cameras. Depending on what they found, they'd remove the devices, deactivate them, or leave them in place. Cameras would be removed, since they would have spotted me.

But microphones? If there were any in the bathroom where Jenn and I had talked, they'd all need to go—whoever planted them would know we'd found them. But anything else might allow us to trace them back to a monitoring station.

Jenn sagged against the wall and pressed her palms over her eyes.

There'd be questions soon. I'd reacted the way Mum had taught me to—identify all plausible scenarios, determine the most likely ones, and mitigate the risks. In this case, the biggest risk was a person in the room. Finding none, I assumed a trap.

Third, maybe it was an intel-gathering job. A simple break-in was the last item on my list.

Jenn didn't know what Reynolds Recoveries really did. Sure, she knew we recovered missing items and delivered valuables from place to place. But we were more than that. An expert heist crew that recovered stolen items for their rightful owners. Advanced tech, infiltration specialists, spies, and investigators. Our vault specialist was a safecracker. Our art appraiser was a forger. Our cybersecurity team was a group of hackers.

And I'd let her catch a glimpse of that.

I pulled her hands down and kept my voice to a whisper. "Was there something wrong with your laptop bag?"

"It's just for sketches," she muttered. "Flowers, buildings, faces, hands. It's nothing important."

What did that mean?

"The book in my bag." Her chin quivered as she spoke. "It was in the wrong position."

That settled it. Someone had targeted her.

I gave her an easy smile, an attempt to calm her nerves. "Let's go upstairs to my room while the team works. I don't want to bother the other guests with our chatter."

She shuddered more than nodded, and we walked in silence to the elevators, then rode up to the fifth floor. Hand-in-hand, we made our way to the two-bedroom suite I shared with Rav. Our room was safe, clear of bugs. We always swept our rooms for listening devices before settling in and used entry detectors to keep out anyone who didn't belong.

Inside our suite, the two bedrooms were to the right, down a small hallway with a closet and a bathroom. I guided her to the left, to the sitting room, so we could talk. The room was casually luxurious. A delicate chandelier with over a hundred tiny lights, like spun gold, hung over the round table that would be perfect for cards or dining. A low, multi-tiered table sat between the two full sofas in soft brown velvet, with another chandelier above it.

The outside wall was all floor-to-ceiling windows. A wide door led to the terrace, with its thick stone balustrade and seating for two. Jenn lowered herself onto the edge of the sofa, staring out at the terrace and the view of the Mediterranean beyond.

I sat next to her. "Rav and the team will be up in a few minutes."

She continued staring out the window. "What are they doing?"

"Sweeping the room."

"Sweeping?"

"Have you noticed anyone suspicious while you've been in town? Or while you were in Nice?"

She let out a small laugh. "Eccentric, maybe. The man I delivered the painting to in Nice was an odd duck." Her hands rose to her eyes again. "I don't understand any of this."

Talking wouldn't fix anything for her. She'd fallen into a world she didn't understand—my world.

She needed a distraction. I'd deal with the team's results when—

The front door opened, and Rav appeared around the corner. He inclined his head toward the bedrooms.

"Jayce?" I called.

The diminutive thief stuck her head around Rav. "Yeah?"

I flicked my gaze intentionally from her to Jenn and back again.

Jayce scrunched her nose. She knew I wanted her to comfort Jenn and keep her company while I talked business with Rav, but Jayce wasn't the touchy-feely type. At least, not with those outside of her tiny circle of friends. "Drew?"

"Yes?" came her boyfriend's voice from further away.

"Emmett needs us." Jayce strolled into the room and hopped onto the sofa opposite us.

Drew followed her in, a mask of empathy on his face. The former spy wasn't particularly touchy-feely, either, but he had a talent for dealing with people. When I stood, he took my spot and introduced himself. His voice was soft, and he started with simple questions—how did she know me? What brought her to Monte Carlo?

He already knew the answers to these questions. But they were what Jenn needed.

I joined Rav outside his bedroom.

The big man pushed his dark hair from his forehead. A muscle ticked in his jaw—which usually only happened when Scarlett was doing something dangerous. "Two bugs. One was obvious—attached to her bedside table, and it squawked when we got close with the sweep. The other was inside a drawer and didn't make a noise."

Shit. That was worse than I'd been expecting. "One designed to be found."

"And to lull you into a false sense of security so you don't catch the second."

Jenn may have been one of Scarlett's best friends, but Rav had also been one. Scar had her boys, and she had her girls— two separate sets of friends, but all close enough that Rav knew Jenn better than I did.

He didn't have the same fierce protectiveness with Jenn as

with Scarlett, but from how his biceps flexed when he folded his arms, it was obvious he was furious over this. "She needs to go home."

I slid a hand into my pocket, running my thumbnail over the edge of my poker chip. "We need to figure things out before we make any decisions."

"Two, Emmett." He unwound one arm long enough to flash two fingers at me, then re-crossed the arm. "Two bugs."

That fact wasn't lost on me. But there were also too many questions. "Could be mistaken identity. Someone could have been spying on whoever was staying in the room before."

"Or she's the target?"

"You're right." I sighed and glanced over my shoulder, listening. Drew and Jayce were still talking to Jenn. Regardless, I kept my voice low. "We have to assume she's the target."

"Ideas on who?"

I had two obvious choices. "De Rosa's the first and easiest guess. They knew she'd be at the gallery, so the timing's perfect."

"That makes sense."

I didn't want to state my other guess. Didn't want to give voice to my concerns that this job was a setup. Or that I worried Jenn would suffer like I had—as a pawn.

"You suspect Fenix is involved?"

Gripping the chip in my pocket, I nodded. We were one week away from the four-month anniversary of my kidnapping by the Fenix Group. They'd taken me to force Scarlett's hand in a theft. She and the Reynolds team had flown to England on a moment's notice to rescue me despite the danger they put themselves in.

"Then she definitely needs to go home."

"And what if it *is* Fenix?" Sickness twisted in my gut. "What if they want to use her for leverage this time? They followed me to New York to grab me. Why wouldn't they follow her home and take her from there?"

"You're overreacting." Rav's gaze softened as he glanced toward my left pants pocket. Did he know the truth? "You haven't continued with therapy, have you?"

I let go of the chip and folded my arms, mirroring him.

Therapy was a waste. I needed time, and I needed to do my job. Those were the things that mattered. Talking around the truth solved nothing. "They've only messed with our team in the past, but they've seen Scarlett mobilize to save someone she cares about."

Rav's nostrils flared, and danger flashed behind his eyes. "He wouldn't dare."

Scarlett's ex-fiancé—a Fenix captain—was behind my kidnapping. His team almost killed half of ours in Rome. Then tried to kill Jayce and Drew in Washington.

And he'd also been the one to tip us off about the scarab.

"You're probably right—I'm overreacting. Even if Noah was setting us up for the scarab job, there's no way he'd know Jenn would be here."

"If Noah lays one hand on her—"

"You'll have to get in line, Rav."

Rav's gaze slipped past me.

Drew said, "There's something you need to hear."

I turned to see Jenn and Jayce standing with him at the end of the hall.

Jenn clutched her arms across her chest, as though protecting herself. "The painting I'm working on for Massimo De Rosa? I followed his conservator's notes, which didn't match the actual painting. Aunt Penny thinks... *I* think the one I'm cleaning is a fake."

That could explain things. If De Rosa was attempting to pass off a fake, he might want to spy on her progress and any communications she had in her room to ensure she wasn't on to them. Not a quarter as dangerous as Fenix being behind it.

"Drew suggested I back out of the project, but I..." She raked her teeth over her bottom lip.

Jayce rolled up on her toes, all the sitting and standing still likely driving her mad. "She had a video chat with this hottie art conservator—"

Drew's eyes rolled heavenward.

"Not as hot as Drew, of course." She winked at him, and he shook his head in faux irritation. "He thinks Jenn's on to something and suggested some quick tests to confirm whether it's the real deal or not, and then some next steps if it's a fake."

"Drew mentioned Reynolds Recoveries and..." Jenn let out a small laugh, giving her head a tiny shake, as though she could hardly believe what she was saying. "The conservator's wife knows Scarlett. She offered to fly out and help."

How would this play out? Send Jenn home and risk someone going after her when she didn't have anyone to protect her? Let her go back to the De Rosa Gallery and risk... What? Where was the risk? That someone might take her from there? That Massimo and Dante were involved in the stolen art trade? We already suspected that, since they had the stolen scarab.

"I think it's an excellent idea," said Jenn. "The tests are simple, and if they prove it's a fake, I'm sure Massimo would want to know. He and Dante have been so nice to me."

Dante, I growled inwardly.

"I'd like to confirm this for them. And if I'm wrong, I can just finish the job they hired me for."

"You should go home." Rav stepped around me, finally unfolding his arms. "Cancel the contract. They can find someone else."

Relief washed over me. The forceful approach would only make Jenn more determined to stay, which aligned perfectly with my instincts.

Jenn's lips thinned. "I'm not going anywhere."

"Good," I said. "And you're staying here."

"That's what I said." Confidence—whether true or manufactured—radiated from her. If nothing else, her stubbornness was winning over her nerves.

"I mean here. In this room." I scratched my short beard. This was my stupidest idea, but it would keep her safe and keep me up-to-date on everything. "With me."

Everyone's confused stares turned to me.

"I don't want you staying by yourself, in case whoever it was comes back."

She spluttered. "If I need to stay with someone, I can stay with Jayce."

Jayce snorted a laugh. "Drew and I have a one-bedroom suite, and we're not sharing."

"But I could—" A ring came from the sitting room, and Jenn took off, calling over her shoulder as she ran. "That's my phone. Dr. Ferraro's calling back with more details."

Rav must have silently ordered Jayce and Drew to go with her because they followed in sync. I started after them but collided with Rav's outstretched hand. "Scarlett will kill you."

"Why?" I looked up at him, the few inches he was taller than me.

He raised his eyebrows, and I finally caught what everyone else had been eyeing me about.

"Oh shit, Rav!" I swatted his hand away. "I didn't mean in my bed. I meant we shuffle you into another room, and she takes yours. My room's closer to the entrance, so I can ensure she stays safe."

"You're still having nightmares."

How did he know? I hadn't told him about the nightmares since the one time I went to see his shrink.

"I heard you last night."

Fuck. "I have sleeping pills—"

"Which you can't take. If you do, you'll be useless should anyone come for her." Rav was always so fucking reasonable. "Why don't we shuffle *you* to another room so she can stay with me?"

"No." Why did that word come out of my mouth so fast?

"No?" He raised his eyebrows again, suspicion dripping from his single word.

It made more sense for Rav to protect her. Security was his job. I had so much else I was supposed to do in Monte Carlo—figure out where the scarab was, determine if Massimo would sell it, and prove I was over my kidnapping in April.

Shacking up with a woman might have been a fun distraction after we had the scarab, but this was Jenn. And it was during our op.

Rav was right. Scarlett *would* kill me if she thought anything was going on.

I'd kissed Jenn once, when we were teens. She'd been my first crush, the first girl I'd told was pretty.

One stolen, secret kiss. A clumsy thing, but one of the best

I'd ever had. Because it was her. Her cheeks had flushed, but she'd smiled at me like nothing else in the world mattered.

'Who do you think you are, putting your hands on my daughter?'

It was the only kiss we ever shared. I avoided her for months afterward, and Scarlett didn't hide how I'd hurt Jenn. Maybe I should have told the truth about what happened with Jenn's father. Scarlett might have forgiven me. More likely, she —or worse yet, Mum—would have unleashed herself on Mr. Thatcher, and none of us would have seen Jenn again.

One kiss. She got over it.

She wouldn't have gotten over losing her best friend, too.

Just like Scarlett wouldn't get over losing Jenn in Monte Carlo, so I was not about to trust her safety to anyone else.

"I need to do this, Rav."

"That's the problem." He put a big hand on my shoulder and dipped his chin, the hair falling onto his forehead. "But I understand."

At least one person did. Because I was fairly sure I didn't.

CHAPTER 8

JENN

I TOWED my suitcase into the suite, walking ahead of Emmett, who carried my laptop bag. Apparently, the team had swept my bags, as well, in case whoever had broken into my room had done something to them. As the door closed, leaving us alone in a two-bedroom suite in Monte Carlo—how was this my life?—I asked, "Why does your team have equipment to check for bugs and… and stuff?"

He ushered me toward the room Rav had hastily vacated. Housekeeping had already been through to clean up. "We did a job once, where we recovered some jewelry a woman's ex took. It turned out he'd hidden a GPS tracker inside the box we recovered everything in, because she'd been hiding from him."

"Did he go after her?"

"Yes, but we'd found the tracker and suspected the ex was coming. Rav was there when he showed up."

"And Rav took care of him?" I entered the bright bedroom, which had a huge bed and a view of the water. My room downstairs had been a standard single—queen-sized bed with a desk and chair. Here, I had all that, plus my own private terrace overlooking the harbor, including a lounge chair and small table. Space to walk around the bed and stretch out.

"He did." Emmett stopped behind me, giving me privacy in my new room. "She never heard from him again."

I abandoned my suitcase and pulled open the terrace door, inhaling the scent of sea air. The sun would go down in an hour, but the evening was still warm.

"Do you like the room?"

"I was fine downstairs." All the same, I stepped out onto the terrace, leaning on the thick stone railing. The terrace faced southeast, and I could even see part of the Casino to my left. Five stories below, diners ate under large beige patio umbrellas. Beyond that, the avenue that made up part of the Monte Carlo Grand Prix course, parks, the yacht club, and then the water. People milled about, touring the city's grandeur, oblivious to the chaos erupting around me.

"This is for me, not you." He was closer now, his voice a low rumble that settled deep in my stomach.

This was a silly idea. I should have taken Jayce and Drew's sofa or even Em and Rav's. There was no need for Rav to leave.

"What does that mean?" I turned, resting on the railing.

Emmett leaned against the wide terrace door frame, hands tucked casually in his pockets, one leg crossed over the other. He was effortlessly cool, like always. "The way you reacted downstairs when I took you into your room. I think that scared me more than anything else."

"The painting has me stressed out, that's all." *No, that's not all, Jenn.*

Memories of his strong arms around me. His cologne. His warm breath on my ear.

The way he made me feel protected. Safe.

"Drew's going to handle the part of our investigation I was scheduled for tomorrow, so I can go with you."

I shot up from the railing. "You what?"

"Jean-Philippe was going to show me some Egyptian pieces, and if he doesn't have what I'm looking for, we're going to look through the inventory." Right. He'd made his plan while we were at the gallery earlier. It felt like a lifetime ago. "I know you don't need a chaperone, but I'd like to walk with you. We can grab some coffee on the way?"

Damn right, I didn't need someone following me around all day. "That would be nice."

"Speaking of food, do you want anything now? You haven't eaten since we left the gallery, and it's almost eight—dinnertime around here." He smiled, but it wasn't a full Emmett smile. The skin around his eyes crinkled, and the lines deepened around his mouth. But it was missing... What? The sparkle in his eyes? Something in his posture?

Was he stressed?

"How were you so calm earlier? The way you acted, sneaking around my room to find out if someone was there—the call to your team, who was there instantly?"

"Keeping calm is part of my job." He pushed off the door frame, the smile transforming from stressed to forced. "I'm lucky when someone willingly hands over what I'm here to collect, but it rarely works out that way."

"You're expecting a problem with Jean-Philippe?"

"Not a *problem*." He returned to the room, so I followed him. "My goal is to find the stolen scarab and negotiate the best possible price to return it. Getting worked up doesn't help anything."

That made sense.

"Food?" He pointed to where he'd placed my laptop bag on a chair by the door. "Or are you going to work?"

"Food's probably a good idea." I dropped onto the edge of the bed. *So tired.* More tired than I'd realized. "But I think sleep's what I need more."

"Understandable." He let out a sigh. "But listen—if, when you wake up, you decide you'd rather go home than stay here, we'll arrange for your flight home. This can be a one-night deal."

My stomach clenched at the idea of a one-night anything with Emmett. "Thanks. I'll think about it."

He stared at me for a beat, as though he was about to say something. Instead of words, he tipped his invisible hat and headed for the door. He paused and said over his shoulder, "I'll keep my door open. If you need anything, you come get me."

"I will."

"I'll keep you safe."

I know.

Before he left, I stopped him. "Did you tell Scarlett?"

"About your room? Or about"—he turned to me, waving a finger between us—"you staying with me?"

If he'd told her about any of it, she would have called. "Either one?"

He pursed his lips, and I almost combusted. They were full and so kissable, framed by his short beard. The way he inhaled, his broad chest swelled. Those clever eyes never left me.

Calm down, girl.

"I thought about it. But you're a grown woman, and it's not my information to share."

"Thanks for that, too."

He gave me one last smile before vanishing.

I collapsed onto the bed and forced out an extra-long breath. God. I was going to be sleeping one room away from Emmett.

You should call Scar.

And say what? *'Hey Scar, I'm staying in Em's room for the week. Nah, nothing's going on, honest!'*

If I told her about the break-in, she'd flip out. I'd break down—like I'd been working very hard not to do—and then it would be one thing after another until I confessed about Simon. It wasn't the right time. Not yet. When I got home, I could sit with her and have the cry I needed. For now, I had to be strong.

Focus on the job at hand—identify if the Constable was a fake, and if not, clean it.

A white chandelier with dozens of crystals hung from an ornate boss on the ceiling. My original room had a similar one, which I'd stared at last night after dinner in the Rose Salon with the De Rosas. If I only stared at the ceiling, I might have believed everything was the same as before I went to the Casino last night.

My dream trip was turning into a nightmare.

What if I was wrong? Had I been in such a hurry I simply put the sketchbook into my bag upside down? When I'd suggested that to Jayce, she looked at Drew, who shook his head.

I didn't know Jayce well, other than that she was a former

gymnast, full of energy, and she talked fast. Scarlett had told me about Drew, their new hire, who brought *unique skills* to the team. No idea what she'd meant other than he excelled at containing Jayce.

Why are you staring at the ceiling when you should be admiring the view?

I rolled my head to look outside.

You're tired. You should take a nap.

I could do a half-hour of work. Dr. Ferraro—Antonio, he'd insisted—suggested I start with an examination under ultraviolet light to check for evidence of past retouching. Maybe someone had worked on the painting between when their conservator made his notes and now. Maybe they'd used paints that melted under the solvent I used.

That *should* have been my first test today. Taking the notes at face value and assuming they were accurate was a mistake I'd never make again.

The De Rosa Gallery's back room had an area I could close off for the test. I hadn't seen any UV lights, but I hadn't been looking. Surely, they'd have a flashlight, if nothing else. Or a camera with special filters?

That would be step one. It was a logical step and wouldn't raise any concerns.

Antonio also offered to review any photos I took, so he and his wife could act as sounding boards. They'd been cagey when I asked for details about how they knew Scarlett, but they clearly held her in high regard. As though the offers to help were repaying a favor.

I stood and collected my laptop, popping it open on the small desk in my room. Some light research, and hopefully, my stomach would calm enough for dinner.

A gentle knock at my door sent my heart into my throat. I should have closed the door.

"You can work in the sitting room, if you'd prefer. The table's bigger out there."

I swiveled in the chair to see Emmett standing in the doorway again.

He'd switched out of his pale gray suit and now wore a heather blue T-shirt with dark jeans, bare feet instead of dress shoes, and hair just wet enough to drip onto his shirt collar.

My stomach did a few flips, and I imagined running my fingers through his hair.

Mmm, in the shower. Lathering it up for him.

Washing the suds down his...

Okay. *That* was not helping anything.

Emmett held up a clear bottle. "But if you choose to hole up in here, I brought you some water."

"Thanks." I walked to him and accepted the bottle of sparkling water. It had a French label I didn't recognize.

"I can have some wine sent up?" His scent floated around me—not the dark cologne he usually wore, but something lighter. Citrusy. Hotel shampoo from his shower—a blend by a French luxury house I'd enjoyed this morning. "Or a meal?"

"Do you really think I'm in so much danger I have to stay here?"

His eyes softened, and he raised his arm as though to rub mine, but he dropped it again. "Rav says I'm paranoid. Hotel security claims they didn't find anything amiss in your room, either."

That wasn't an answer.

"Besides, your room had no view." He waved his hand vaguely toward the wall of windows. "You can't come to

Monte Carlo for the first time and suffer a view of someone else's window."

That wasn't an answer, either.

One corner of his lips lifted, and he winked at me, causing a flush of heat to run through my body. If he wasn't Emmett Reynolds, I'd think he was flirting. But he *was* Emmett, so I knew it was just him being him. Unfortunately.

"Where's Rav staying?" Surely not in my old room?

"He was aiming for the Princess Grace Suite, but it was already booked." He laughed, a warm sound that melted the edge of my worries. "We arranged another two-bedroom suite. He insisted he needed the space."

"For what?"

"In case you tire of me and need another overprotective big-brother type?"

Big-brother type? What a punch in the gut. *That's what he is, Jenn. Nothing more. And remember you decided men aren't worth the hassle?* "Admitting you're overprotective is the first step, I guess?"

"That it is." He extended his arms to hold either side of the doorframe, stretching his shoulders and grimacing. Was he injured? "Last offer for food, though. I'm putting in a room service order and promise to stop harassing you after I do."

"Some fruit and cheese, I think?"

He snapped his fingers and pointed at me. "Which needs a bottle of red to go with it."

I held up the bottle he'd given me. "Or water?"

"Red wine, my dear." He shook his head in mock sympathy and left again.

My dear? I rolled my eyes and huffed out an exaggerated

breath, loud enough he'd hear it. Sarcasm was my last line of defense with him.

"Made you laugh," he called from the hallway.

That man was going to be the death of me. I should have called Rav and moved in with him. Heat wouldn't be flashing up and down my body every time he stopped by. My breaths would have been regular, as would my heart rate.

Focus on your work. I returned to my laptop and began studying for tomorrow. What equipment did the gallery have available? Which tests could I run? And how fast could I get everything done, so I could prove it was authentic and finish the cleaning?

The painting would go up for auction on Friday.

A memory came back to me, of the man with the scar across his cheek telling me I had to do good work, so Massimo would see a significant profit.

Should I have told Emmett about him? Probably. But if I did—if he thought suspicious people were lurking around the gallery—he would have dragged me back to Nice and thrown me on a plane himself. He wouldn't have put me up in this suite, in a room next to his, and brought me food and wine.

I wanted to help the De Rosas. I wanted to make my aunt proud.

More than anything, I wanted to prove I had control over *something* in my life. I didn't need men telling me what to do and what to think. My father had done that most of my life, and then too many of the men I dated thought they knew better than me about everything.

Including about fidelity.

Stop thinking about Simon the Asshole.

But that was precisely what happened here, wasn't it? Emmett told me to stay with him. And I went along with it.

I cracked open the water bottle, and it hissed.

He told me to drink water. Told me I'd be getting red wine.

Shit.

I *didn't* have control over anything. Not even my feelings for the man in the next room, who'd only ever pretended to want me once, fifteen years ago.

Tomorrow, things would change. I'd do my tests on the painting, prove I was capable...

And I'd damn well flirt back with Dante. That would show Emmett how much control I had.

Wait. Men are a hassle. You're done with them.

But maybe Dante would be the distraction I needed. Better him than the ghost of a fifteen-year-old crush that refused to die.

CHAPTER 9
EMMETT

AT QUARTER to nine Wednesday morning, Jenn and I arrived at the De Rosa Gallery. The security guard let her in and initially resisted my accompanying her. Once I reminded him of my discussion with Jean-Philippe and Dante yesterday afternoon, he acquiesced—particularly since I was such good friends with the owner's son.

Jenn had barely eaten last night, preferring to nibble on snacks while keeping her nose in her laptop. She'd always been smart. Her switch from project management to art restoration two years ago had shocked everyone, but it was clear she loved the change in her career.

This morning, her appetite had returned. We enjoyed room service on the balcony, avoiding all discussion of the break-in, the questionable painting, and any danger.

The denial phase was treating her well.

Maybe I shouldn't have hidden the truth about the bugs planted in her room, but she would have freaked right the fuck out. That wouldn't solve anything, either.

One more thing I was hiding from her. Typical Emmett.

"What's first?" I looked around, cataloging everything I saw. Inconspicuous as possible, I conveyed a fascination with the objects, hiding my ulterior motives. Priority one was finding the scarab—I was fairly certain it wouldn't show up in any inventory, otherwise Jean-Philippe would have suggested it already. He didn't strike me as someone who only knew the public pieces in the gallery.

"Ultraviolet photos." Jenn hung her purse on a hook by the door and donned a gray apron. The apron transformed her from business professional to artisan. Tying it around her waist, she scanned the room. "That is, if I can find an ultraviolet light."

I wandered along the shelves, peering around sculptures and jars, tipping a few small boxes open. Searching for equipment was the perfect opportunity to scout the interior. The room we were in only had one door leading into the office and then the hallway. Across the hall, two doors.

One which required keycard access and was labeled for employees only. Likely restrooms and potentially a break room. I'd need an excuse to explore and verify that nothing was hidden in there. Spending enough money might gain me access.

But the other door?

It was metal, unlabeled, and had a keypad next to it. That was the high-value secure storage. Not off-site. Right across the hall. If the scarab wasn't upstairs or in the digital inventory, it might be behind that door.

I didn't have a safecracking case for my phone, but I'd snapped a photo of the door and sent it back to HQ for when everyone woke up. Unsurprisingly, Brie—my younger sister—

had already responded that she and Will were searching for a match.

Blocks away, Jayce and Drew were preparing to enter Massimo's condo, disguised as cleaners. Like me, they were on the hunt for evidence of the scarab's location. If we confirmed Massimo had it in his possession, that would give us more leverage to force a sale.

If Jayce and Drew came up empty, I'd likely send her into the gallery for reconnaissance tonight. Hopefully, the team would find a match for the security system in their database. If not, I had a small signal jammer in my pocket to leave behind and cover their digital tracks. If we'd had more time, we could have helped Brie take over their security systems remotely.

"Ah ha!" Jenn exclaimed, pulling a three-foot-long light bar out of a cupboard. "There's a camera in there, too. I bet it's for taking UV photos. I can send those to Antonio."

"Dr. Ferraro, you said?"

"Yeah." She placed the light on the large table at the center of the room. "Ring any bells?"

"A few, but it's a fairly common name." In truth, we'd worked for a smuggler named Ferraro a few times, including one job to recover a piece for his nephew. Based on what I'd heard, the odds were good Jenn's source was that very nephew. If she didn't have such a solid contact, I would have suggested we fly Keira—our team's forger—in for a consult.

Jenn gathered various tools while I continued peeking into every space I could.

"You must love working behind the scenes like this."

"Looks like you do, too." She lay the painting on the table, rustling some papers as she did.

I nodded slowly, resuming my exploration. "Museums are

my favorite. Every time I go into a collections department, the vast quantity of items held behind closed doors—out of the public's eye—overwhelms me."

That was one of the few truths I was sharing today.

"Let's give this a shot." With no more warning than that, she shut the door to the office and turned off the overhead light.

I halted my search. Dim light filtered in from under the closed door to the office, while the purple glow of the UV light barely illuminated the room. Not nearly enough to continue poking around.

Jenn passed the bar over the painting, mere inches above it. She leaned over, following closely with her eyes. She hummed aloud as she inspected the bottom edge.

"See anything?" I drew closer, remembering some of my mother's lessons from when I was younger. Lessons that made so much more sense after discovering her tie to MI6. The varnish fluoresced in greens of subtle shades. Variations in the varnish layers would indicate different rounds of conservation. A two-hundred-year-old painting could have been cleaned many times, if not retouched a few.

She hummed again, saying nothing.

"You said it was by John Constable?" I only knew a few Constable works off the top of my head, including *The Hay Wain* and *Salisbury Cathedral*. He was best known for his English landscapes, like the one in front of us.

"Mm-hmm." She was zeroed in on the painting, barely acknowledging me. It was fascinating to watch. "It's called *Wheatfield from the Lock.*"

The golden wheat spread through the middle of the painting, with women working the field and a small boy walking his dog nearby. A stone structure closer to the viewer must have been part of the lock. "Have you ever—"

The door opened, spilling light into the room, and she snapped upright.

"What are you doing here?" Dante De Rosa stormed in, flipping the light on. Unlike the past two days, he didn't even glance at Jenn. This was all about me. "What do you think you're doing back here in the dark?"

Too many responses flitted through my brain. *'Killing time'* and a smirk would probably be met with a fist. *'Getting close to my woman'* would warrant the same. "Jean-Philippe was going to show me your Egyptian collection. We talked about it yesterday?"

An innocent response. *Excellent restraint, Em.* Didn't hurt that it was also true.

"He's out front," Dante snarled. "Why are you back here?"

Jenn set the light bar down and rounded the table, standing between me and the angry Italian. "He walked me over this morning. Jean-Philippe wasn't here when we arrived, so I asked him to give me a hand setting up."

Fire blazed in Dante's dark eyes. We were roughly the same height and weight, and in roughly the same physical shape. He didn't intimidate me—not when I worked with Rav every day. His eyes lowered to Jenn, and all the anger vanished. His smile broke.

And I wanted to tell him she was staying with me.

Petty?

Fuck, yeah.

"You're making progress already this morning?"

"I am." Her back was to me, but I didn't need to see her face. Her smile sounded in her words.

He looked at me again and jerked his head to the side. "Let me see you to the front desk."

"Absolutely." I wrapped an arm around Jenn as I passed her, giving her a full squeeze. Also petty. To her, I said, "I'll be back once I'm done with JP. Holler if you need me."

"Thanks, Em." She closed the door behind us as we left, likely returning to her ultraviolet investigation.

Dante walked me through the small office, past a desk with a computer and a huge monitor. Books and collections lined the walls, stamped with years and auction-house names. In the hallway, he flung his arm toward the front of the gallery. "Your meeting is that way."

Yes, my meeting. With the man who wouldn't likely have the information I needed. I groaned deep inside—it was time to use Jenn a little more. "Jenn had a scare last night."

His arm dropped, and a look of what might have been concern creased his brow. "What happened?"

If I didn't know who he was, I could have believed the worry in his voice. *Come on, Em, he was probably behind it. Him or his father.* "Someone was in her room."

"Someone other than housekeeping?"

I raised a doubtful eyebrow, making it clear I knew he wasn't so thick. "You think that would scare her?"

His eyes left me and searched the hallway, as though he might find answers there. That reaction was more genuine than I'd expected. "Who, then?"

"I don't know." I mirrored him, letting my gaze travel away from our conversation, taking in a few details I'd missed about the hallway, including the security camera I hadn't seen last time. I'd have to warn Jayce about that. "But it scared her."

Dante placed a hand over his mouth and exhaled slowly. "Did the police find anything?"

Was he toying with me? If he had access to the bugs, he'd know the police hadn't been by, so that was an easy question to throw me off. But he'd also know Jenn hadn't returned to her hotel room.

"No." Time for another salvo. "They cordoned off the room and are taking fingerprints this morning."

"Bene, bene," he muttered, his hand slipping to his heart. "I'll arrange for a different room for her. She can't stay there."

I didn't like this. Either he was the smoothest liar I'd ever met, or he was being honest. No tells, no ticks, nothing that said he was searching for the right words. Every twitch of his muscles screamed honesty.

But when you grow up with a father like Massimo, you learn to mask the truth young, don't you?

Speaking from experience, Emmett? Which one of your parents taught you how to twist people until they did what you wanted?

"I've already taken care of it," I said.

His irritation with me flared back to life. "*You* have taken care of it?"

I was supposed to win him over, not taunt him about my relationship with Jenn. "We switched her into a new room with better security, just in case."

"What does better security mean to you?"

To tell him she was staying with me or not? Ensure he ejected me from the gallery or convince him I was an antiquities broker? "Higher floor, with a private balcony, rather than one accessible from other rooms."

"She's here on a contract for us and we're paying for her room. It's not your business to move her around without notifying me."

Jenn hadn't mentioned that part. He was paying for her room?

Of course he was, Em, it's a business contract. "Not to worry—we're covering the cost."

"You think this is about money?"

"When my sister heard, she insisted we pay."

His wandering gaze rested inside the office, no doubt on the door that blocked our conversation from Jenn. "Monaco has one of the largest per capita police forces. How can she be unsafe in her own hotel room?"

"She's a tough cookie. She'll be fine."

Dante turned a glower on me. "This is how you treat your sister's best friend? Someone breaks into her hotel room, and you brush it off as though it were a stubbed toe?"

Well, shit. He really *was* worried about her, wasn't he?

That doesn't make him a good man.

"I only meant to say—"

"You should go to your meeting." He jutted his chin toward the front. "*I'll* check on her and then confirm if I believe she's safe or not."

Great.

Not only had I not won him over, I'd probably driven him closer to her.

CHAPTER 10
JENN

I STARED AT THE PAINTING, darkness all around me, other than inside the sphere of light cast by the light bar. I held it so close it didn't even illuminate the entire painting. And yet I saw nothing.

Nothing other than Emmett and Dante leaving to...

Deep breath out.

Their muffled voices carried through the door, but not clearly enough to make anything out. Except that they were still in the hallway. Instead of Emmett heading to his meeting with Jean-Philippe. No raised voices and no sounds of a scuffle, so they weren't fighting.

What was with the two of them?

Emmett worked with several alpha males, so it wasn't as though he thought he had to be the leader of the pack. Or maybe Emmett could work with the men he'd known most of his life, and the new ones were a problem?

That wasn't it. He was best friends with Scarlett's boyfriend and seemed to get along well with Drew—both of them had been on the Reynolds team for fewer than six months.

Maybe Dante was the problem?

Maybe he was the one causing the stress?

Or maybe it was me? I laughed and shook my head. There was no way Emmett was fighting with anyone over me.

I had to get my head out of the clouds and focus on the painting.

The layer of varnish was even. Ultraviolet fluorescence showed an almost perfect application. The notes from Massimo's conservator indicated his work was isolated to the top left corner. He hadn't mentioned revarnishing the entire painting, so I'd expected the top left corner to appear different under UV.

I extended the light bar's feet so it stood freely on the table and illuminated the room. I retrieved the camera from under the cabinet where I'd found the light. My next step was to take photographs of the painting and send them to Dr. Ferraro in Michigan.

His team would review them and provide their expert opinion. Hopefully they'd tell me I was wrong.

Or did I want to be right?

As I stood with the camera, inspecting settings, there was a light knock at the door. "Come in."

Dante walked in, turning on the lights as he entered. His smile was tight, but different from his reaction to Emmett and me in the dark. "Your friend tells me someone was in your room yesterday?"

Why did he tell Dante?

Instead of a confident art restorer, I was now the damsel in distress. I didn't like that role. "I'm fine. They weren't there when I got back."

"Did they take anything?"

"No." I rounded the worktable and flipped the camera on. "I'm not sure what they could've been looking for. It's not like I travel with expensive jewelry or wads of cash—although I'm sure plenty of people at the Hôtel de Paris do. I think it was a simple mistake the front desk made. They probably double-booked the room and gave a copy of my key to someone else. Airlines do it all the time, right?"

Dante stood across the table from me, resting his hands on the surface. He had such long fingers. Big hands. Strong, corded forearms, visible beneath his pushed-up sleeves. "And your new room? Do you feel safer?"

Safer? I'd have to define that word before providing a proper answer. Or better yet? Change the subject. "I need to take a few photographs of the painting under UV light to study the prior work. I don't suppose there are any cameras with UV filters and Wi-Fi support? So I can airdrop to my phone?"

Dante's head tilted, and his lips pursed in question. "Why photographs?"

"I never rely on someone else's notes. I have to run my own experiments before I apply any chemicals." Not that I'd confess my aunt reminded me of that yesterday, after I forgot her critical lessons.

"No Wi-Fi, but..." He held out a hand, and I passed the camera to him. He turned it to the side, opening the port covers. "I can plug it into the computer in the office and email you what you need."

"Oh no, I can figure something else out. I wouldn't want you to have to hang out here until I was ready."

He returned the camera to me and waved a dismissive hand. "I have some work to do anyway and will be in the office next door for two or three hours. I was worried I might be a distraction with all the racket."

"Racket?" I stifled a laugh. "What sort of office work do you do that causes a racket?"

He shrugged a shoulder, while one corner of his lips and both his eyebrows rose. "I believe I mentioned my father is heading to Napoli soon? He's asked me to double-check the gallery's books before he leaves—three years of reconciliations. I expect there will be a great deal of muttering and swearing. Although I promise all foul words will be in Italian, so it shouldn't be too offensive."

"I'm hard to offend." I nearly snorted. The men I usually dated? Offending me was rarely something they worried about.

"This is good to know." He winked at me and left.

I watched him go, taking in the way his muscles moved under his clothes. His perfectly formed ass and the way his linen pants draped over defined quads. I closed the door before he could catch me eyeing him.

But I wasn't ogling. As gorgeous as he was—and that was an objective fact, like saying the *David* or the *Mona Lisa* were beautiful—I didn't feel the same spark as when Emmett winked at me last night. It didn't shoot through my entire body, land in my toes, and then careen all the way back up to settle between my thighs.

My father's judgmental voice swirled around my brain.

"You don't know anything about them, Jenn."

"Kelley and Heather's parents don't have a problem with Scarlett."

He frowned. "I'll talk with them. Make them see reason."

I stomped my foot like I hadn't done since I was ten. "That's not fair. You can't control who my friends are."

"I'm your father. I have every right to make those choices while you're still a child."

A child? "I'm fifteen. I'm old enough to make my own decisions."

My mother stood behind him, saying nothing. Not coming to my defense.

Hot tears stung my eyes. "I don't care what her dad did. That's not her."

"Sweetheart," he said in that condescending tone he always used, "I know you can't see it now, but one day, when you're older, you'll thank me for this."

"I won't thank you," I sobbed as I marched from the room, "because I'm never speaking to you again."

My threat had lasted all of a week. Until I needed a ride to Kelley's house, and my mother wasn't available.

"Boys learn how to be men from their fathers," he said after ten minutes of silence. "But girls? I looked into Scarlett's mother—"

"You what?"

"The investigation cleared her. It looks as though she was as much a victim as the rest of the country. I'm still not happy about it, but you've made your point. I'm prepared to negotiate a cease-fire. We'll have a long discussion about red flags, and then you can spend time with Scarlett."

He backed down for the first time ever.

My silent treatment had worked! "Thank you!"

His knuckles tightened on the steering wheel. "But not her brother. He's trouble, and I want you to stay away from him."

Dad's warning had come a week too late.

Emmett stopped talking to me the morning my father forbade me from talking to any of the Reynolds kids. No idea why, he just shut down all communication.

One kiss. One knee-weakening, heart-wrenching kiss. He'd intertwined his fingers with mine, and his free hand had slid over my hip. It had been amazing.

But that was it. The end. No texts, no emails, no DMs. Just nothing.

At fifteen, I'd blamed myself. Thought I was such a bad kisser that it scared him away. Or he was disappointed I hadn't tried to go further with him. It took a while to get past that.

I hadn't actually avoided Scarlett that week, like my father thought. After Emmett ghosted me for days, she'd known something was wrong. I cracked under her interrogation and told her about the kiss.

She offered to kick his ass.

I said thanks, but told her to leave it alone.

Emmett and I barely spoke for a year after that. Every time I saw him, I remembered the kiss. Felt the sting of rejection all over again. He'd used me and discarded me.

Like Simon, who'd used me, then slept with someone else.

The guy before Simon? He got angry when I wouldn't loan him ten thousand dollars for something he claimed he couldn't explain to me.

Before that? A co-worker who dumped me after stealing my ideas and getting the promotion I should have. He was the real reason I left my old job.

And before that?

God, who could keep track of all the bad news I'd invited into my life?

But Emmett wasn't like all of them. We were fifteen. No one knew how to express their feelings when they were fifteen. Break-ups were ugly, even if the break-up happened after a single kiss.

He'd taken care of me last night. Wrapped me up in those arms, brought in a team to help, and insisted I sleep close to him so he could keep me safe.

Emmett isn't a bad guy, Dad. And he's nothing like his father.

CHAPTER II

EMMETT

JEAN-PHILIPPE GUIDED me through the third floor, which included their old-world antiquities. Patrons strolled through the space, admiring display pieces, and a few discussed potential purchases.

He was a lean, impeccably dressed man in his early fifties. Keenly aware of the history of each piece in the De Rosa Gallery, he highlighted several Egyptian items while also mentioning a few Greek and Etruscan pieces—in case they caught my eye. He carried his tablet against his chest, glancing at it now and again, but only when he referred to buyers interested in purchasing something he recommended to me.

Considering how easily he rattled off the provenance of several pieces, it was clear he didn't need to check the tablet for anything. He wasn't simply a sales associate—he was a showman.

"Here we have the Egyptian blue scarab I told you about."

It was less than an inch long, a small dome of pale blue dust compressed into a solid mass and then carved. It could almost have passed for turquoise.

"As I'm sure you know, the Egyptians considered scarabs a symbol of rebirth and transformation. They were believed to embody the god Khepri, who renewed the sun each day. Just as the beetles roll their dung balls across the land, so too did Khepri roll the sun across the sky."

I nodded politely.

"This one dates to the twenty-sixth dynasty, and you'll see..." Using his one gloved hand, he unlocked and opened the display case to withdraw the tiny item. He held it reverently in his palm, clear it was for me to inspect and not touch. "The top is carved to resemble the dung beetle, but the bottom is carved with—what our appraiser identified as—an epithet of the wind god, Amun."

"Beautiful." I watched as he turned it over to show me the underbelly and hummed in appreciation. "My client is looking for something in gold, though. A golden scarab would be better."

"Egyptian gold?" He returned the blue scarab to its display case, between a set of five canopic jars and a beaded wesekh collar necklace in deep blue.

"That *is* what I'm hunting for." The blue scarab was a beautiful work of art. However, it wasn't the artifact I was looking for. Either way, making a purchase could provide access to more items and might give me an excuse to enter the employee restroom. If neither Jean-Philippe nor the digital inventory produced the results I hoped for, Jayce would need me to plant the jammer for tonight. "Although, now that I think of it, I may have another client who'd find this one interesting."

Jean-Philippe paused before locking the case, clearly encouraging me to continue.

"Before we discuss that..." I smiled, angling my gaze to his tablet. "You mentioned you have other pieces not on display?"

"Certainly." He finished with the case and held the tablet away from his chest, tapping and swiping at it. "We have a few gold items from Egypt. You said your client was looking for one or more small pieces, though?"

"Smaller than my palm." I held out my palm, measuring the length with the fingers of my opposite hand.

He continued scanning the tablet without turning it for me to see. "Budget?"

I chuckled. "Much larger than my palm."

"We have a buyer's room on the second floor." He inclined his head toward the stairs and then led the way. "It's more private."

"Of course." Hopefully, a private room would allow me to get my phone close enough to his tablet. It needed prolonged proximity for my sister to attempt hacking into the De Rosa inventory.

Behind a door at the top of the curved staircase up from the main floor, two antique damask sofas welcomed us. They faced each other across a long carved wooden table, where Jean-Philippe placed his tablet. "I believe this is closer to the right size and material?"

I sat opposite him and peered at the item the tablet displayed—a gold finger ring with a large flat top depicting two seated characters. "It is. Can I take a photo to send to my client?"

"Certainly."

I nodded and pulled out my phone, tapping out a quick text to Brie: *Putting my phone by the tablet. Do your best.*

She replied with a thumbs up, and the text vanished. My

younger sister controlled the software inside all our tech. The text and email apps were full of cover-appropriate messages, in case I was caught. While I was at the gallery, my phone was on an open communication protocol, so I could send her any details she needed, and she could wipe all traces immediately.

Jean-Philippe slid the tablet closer to me.

I snapped the image and placed the phone on the table, within the distance Brie needed. Rather than allowing Jean-Philippe to lift the tablet and interrupt whatever the team at home was doing, I studied the ring, pinching to zoom in on the photo. Swiping to view it from other angles. Reading the provenance.

My phone buzzed with an email notification. Absently, I glanced at it. My stockbroker was advising me of an opportunity he wanted to discuss.

Perfect.

That was the sign from Brie she was in.

"How much?" I continued scanning details, flipping between the images and text.

"Twenty-three thousand euros."

I nodded slowly. "It *is* stunning."

He extended a hand at my hesitation, as though to retrieve the tablet and show me additional options.

Once Brie had established a connection, did she need me to keep the phone next to the tablet? Or would a few feet make a difference?

I tapped the image of the ring. "Do you have it on-site so I can see the real thing?"

"It's with a local goldsmith currently, having the band cleaned."

My phone buzzed again, this time with a call notification

from Eloise—Scarlett's cover name. That wasn't the signal I expected from Brie to indicate she'd finished. But Scarlett was at home with her, so they must have been coordinating something.

I dismissed the call and leaned closer. "As I mentioned, a scarab would be perfect—*if* it was gold. My client saw one at a charity event in Washington, DC, a couple of months ago."

Jean-Philippe sat forward again and picked up the tablet, swiping through items as I spoke.

"The organizers told them it came from a gallery in Monaco."

He nodded, continuing to swipe, not looking up at me. "We *did* have one, but it's been sold."

Sold? Fuck.

"We have a stunning nineteenth-century Fabergé presentation box arriving next month. Do you think they might be interested?"

"Who was it sold to?" The question was too blatant, but the tip that Massimo had it was the cornerstone of our entire trip. However, that tip was two months old.

He flipped the tablet around so I could see the presentation box. "It's truly exquisite and would be a stunning centerpiece for a new Russian collection."

My phone buzzed again—another call from Scarlett.

What did this one mean?

We had plans for the stockbroker email. A text from my assistant asking about my flight home would signal she was having problems accessing the digital inventory. And when she finished? That was supposed to be an email from an auction house about a Jackson Pollock sale.

But two phone calls from Scarlett? Not good.

"I apologize." I dismissed the call again and clasped my hands, portraying my regret. "Can we continue in a few minutes? I need to call her back and, honestly, I need to use your facilities."

"Of course." Jean-Philippe stood and gestured to the door. "It's the door next to the elevator."

Not where I needed to go.

Collecting my phone, I stood and looked at the door. Looked back at him. And at the door. I wasn't aiming for full-on disdain, but certainly for a level of minor disgust at using the same restroom everyone else did. "The public one?"

"Why, yes. Our employee facilities are not—"

"If I'm spending twenty thousand euros on—" The phone buzzed, and I immediately dismissed the call without looking down. What was wrong with Scarlett? This was recon, not an op. She didn't need to be in constant contact with me.

"But of course, Monsieur Stone." Jean-Philippe bowed his head, curling the tablet against his chest again. "If you'll follow me to my desk, I can provide you with a guest keycard."

"I'll be down once I finish with my phone call. Can I take it here?"

He nodded again and left.

As the door swung shut, my phone rang yet again.

I swiped to answer, wishing there were a button to smash. "What?"

"Rav and I just had a little chat." Her words came out quickly, showing her frustration. This wasn't going to be fun.

"You interrupted my meeting for that?"

"I was looking over some operational details this morning and noticed the change in the hotel rooms. Not just a change"—she took a deep, intentional breath, designed to convey how angry she was—"but the addition of a whole new suite."

Were there cameras in this room? Recording devices? It would make sense from a security standpoint to ensure no one walked off with anything. But it wouldn't make sense from a customer service standpoint. Which one was more important?

Jean-Philippe allowed me to stay in the room by myself, so I expected there was some sort of monitoring device.

I had to keep my cool and not reveal anything. "He insisted."

"I don't like this, Em." Of course, she didn't. Rav had warned me Scarlett would be pissed. At least she hadn't flown to Monaco to deliver that message.

I strolled across the room, toward a four-foot-tall Impressionist painting. Boats on the water at sunset. The painting was so serene—I had to absorb some of that quality. "We had to do something."

"*Something* would have been putting her up with Jayce."

"She tried, and it was a no-go."

Scarlett was quiet for a moment, no doubt scrunching her toes in her shoes to discharge her pent-up emotions. She'd likely said all the same things to Rav. To keep the peace—the big man was always trying to do that—he probably also explained why, tactically, it was a better choice for Jenn to stay with me.

"You may not have cared, but you really screwed her over when we were kids. Don't you dare pull that shit again."

I threw my head back as if I could find more serenity written on the ceiling than in the painting. I'd never told anyone what really happened with Jenn's dad.

Scarlett had thrown her anger at me back then, and I'd

taken it. What other choice was there? Repeat Mr. Thatcher's words? Tell my sister I wasn't good enough? Tell her that *she* wasn't good enough to be Jenn's friend? Blame our father for everything? He'd been in prison for five years already when Jenn and I...

Deep breath.

My sister had always treated me like an irresponsible child, even after I grew out of it—or most of it. The rest of the team appreciated that I stood up to her behind closed doors when she was being unreasonable, but none of them realized how much I kept bottled up.

What was the last thing she said to me before I flew to New York and was kidnapped?

Right.

She'd said, *'Don't get arrested.'*

"Eloise," I drawled, using her cover name, which she'd used for the call display. "You're overreacting. I have an excellent team backing me up, and we have everything well in hand."

"Two. Separate. Rooms."

I meandered along the wall to the next painting. Similar to the first, but with grass and people standing about. "I wouldn't take advantage. You don't need to worry."

We didn't have conversations like normal siblings. She knew where I was and what I was doing. Knew I had to keep my words measured in case someone was nearby. She knew I'd be smiling while seething underneath. While I knew she was in her office because she wouldn't let anyone hear the hint of anger and disappointment in her voice.

"Emmett."

"Eloise?"

She let out another slow breath. "Brie can't find any record of the scarab in the inventory."

If they'd sold it, there'd be a paper trail. "None? Not even a sales history?"

"No. And Jayce and Drew came up empty at Massimo's."

"Our buyer could be mistaken?" I suggested.

Scarlett and I had argued about this trip to Monte Carlo almost daily since she confessed her conniving ex was the one who gave her the tip. Rav and Malcolm—Scarlett's boyfriend —both suspected it was a trap. They thought Noah was luring her to town so he could grab her.

Otherwise, she and Mal would have joined us.

"He wasn't wrong." How she still had so much faith in Noah was beyond me. "You're sending Jayce in tonight?"

And just like that—when the topic switched to her potential mistakes instead of mine—we returned to the professional discussion.

"That's the plan." Sensing the conversation was nearly over, I drifted toward the door. "What about the painting?"

"*Wheatfield from the Lock* is in their inventory. It's marked as going to auction on the weekend, but it doesn't have an indicator about being cleaned. A few other paintings have notes about that."

Maybe the difference was because it was being cleaned in-house. But suggesting that might sound suspicious to any cameras in the room. "Solid provenance?"

"Massimo De Rosa bought it legally at an estate sale, but a section of the sale history from about fifty years ago isn't sitting right with me. I'll touch base with the Ferraros and see if we can coordinate on that angle—maybe run a few other pieces through some stolen art databases."

"Excellent idea." I put a hand on the door. "Anything else before I go?"

"She has a boyfriend, Em. He's an ass, but she's taken. Don't forget that." Scarlett clicked off, and I stared at the phone momentarily before shoving it into my pocket.

Then made my way downstairs to Jean-Philippe and the guest pass.

CHAPTER 12
EMMETT

Behind the keycard-protected door, a short hallway provided access to two restrooms, plus a break room at the end. The latter included a kitchenette with shelves and racks for hanging personal items. Off that room was a small storage area with cleaning supplies.

The public restroom was likely far nicer, but it wasn't close enough to the secure storage for my signal jammer.

I ducked into the first room and locked the door behind me.

Jean-Philippe might have told me the truth, and they'd sold the scarab. But his refusal to provide details—even when I asked again after my phone call with Scarlett—and the fact it was missing from the inventory didn't add up.

So, where could I hide the jammer in preparation for Jayce's recon tonight? It was the size of my palm, disguised as a container of mints with a fake lid that wouldn't open. A magnet on its back would hold it in place if there were any appropriate metal surfaces. But the sink was marble, attached to the wall with a single shelf underneath. Over it, a slim-profile mirror with a gilt frame. A low-profile toilet completed the room. Next to the standing toilet paper holder, a wall panel controlled the bidet functions.

Without any lower cupboards or a skirt around the sink, the only hiding spot was behind the small waste bin in the corner. But a cleaner would easily find it, then either throw it out with the trash or alert someone to our work.

The ceiling was plaster, as I'd have expected in such an old building, so the ceiling was out, too.

Okay, Plan A didn't work.

Plan B? I'd peeked into the other restroom, which was exactly like the one I was in. No options there, either. Could I place it in the break room? It didn't have a locked door, so I'd have to be fast in case someone came in. But was it too far from the storage room door or the cameras?

I pulled out my phone and texted Brie: *Range on the device? I don't have a lot of options close to the security panel.*

She immediately replied: *50 ft. Steel walls will reduce that a bit.*

I sent her a thumbs-up emoji. Hiding it in the break room would be risky, but it was the best option.

As my hand landed on the door handle to leave, I heard another door open and close nearby—the keycard-protected door. Someone—more than one someone—walked toward the restroom.

If they went to the break room, my opportunity to set the jammer was gone unless they were in and out.

"The truck will be here at midnight." The first voice was soft but masculine, speaking English with a light Scottish accent. Definitely not one of the gallery staff I'd met. "We've prepped the pieces for the yacht and still have to finish with the auction items."

"Bene."

Ice shot up and down my veins, and my head grew light. My knees wobbled, and I rolled away from the door, hand against the wall to keep myself upright.

I knew that voice.

I'd know it anywhere.

He spoke again. "I wish we were flying to Napoli instead of sailing. It takes so fucking long."

A bag flew over my head, shutting out the world.

"Massimo has so much junk to transport."

A fist to my face. Stars in my eyes.

Deep breath, Em. You're not in Venice.

The kick to my ribs would come next.

You're safe. The door's locked. He doesn't know you're here.

It was Enzo.

The man who'd beaten me. Not the brains behind my kidnapping, but the sadistic muscle.

I sank slowly to the floor, fumbling for the poker chip in my pocket. Breathing. Trying to suck in slow breaths, so he wouldn't realize I was still conscious.

No. *You're not in Venice, Em. The slow breaths are so he doesn't find you in the restroom.*

The Scottish man spoke, quieter this time, as they moved past my door. "And we'll be picking more up at the auction."

I gripped the poker chip, holding it against my lips. Breathing. Still breathing.

"Once we have the disc," said Enzo, "we're almost done. The boss will be happy."

Listen to them. This is important. Stop freaking out.

"Any chance we won't win it from the auction?"

"None," said Enzo. "No one will outbid Massimo for a simple golden disc, no matter what the auctioneer says about it."

"And we leave as soon as we have it onboard?"

A bead of sweat rolled down my back, and I flattened my palm against the cold marble floor.

Their voices grew muted, they must have gone into the break room. If it had been someone else—the guard or Jean-Philippe, maybe even Dante—I could have strolled in and found some way to divert their attention long enough to shove the jammer under the sink.

But not...

Deep breath.

Not Enzo.

How long would they be there? Someone would get suspicious if I stayed in this locked room too long. If Enzo was one of those people, I was done for.

I pressed my cooled hand to my forehead, wiped the sweat away, and focused on calming my heart.

Swallowed.

Breathed.

I was in the room closest to the exit. If I slipped out quietly enough, they wouldn't peek their heads around the corner, and I'd be out of the gallery in under three minutes. There'd be no stopping to finalize the blue scarab's sale with Jean-Philippe. Someone else would have to come back for the scarab.

I'd need an excuse to leave.

Or not. I could slip out the back door and no one would ever know.

But Jenn.

I'd be leaving Jenn here with Enzo in the building. A wave of nausea flowed through me. I couldn't leave her alone here with the wolves. But I also couldn't let her see me like this.

Call in backup? No, I couldn't let the *team* see me like this. Scarlett or Mum would force me home and into therapy. They'd ban me from doing any ops until a stranger decided I was ready.

Fuck that.

I was better than that.

After one final clench, I stuffed the poker chip back into my pocket and braced myself against the wall. Stood up. Knees weak but functional. My pulse thrummed in my neck, but I had more important things to worry about.

Step one: Slip out of the restroom, out of the employee hallway, and across to Jenn.

Step two: Tell her we need to go. Concoct some excuse about her safety and escort her out the back door.

Step three: Run for it? Fuck, no. If I let her see my panic, she'd lose her rock. That's what I was for her last night in her hotel room. She'd been losing it, and I was her rock. If I couldn't keep my shit together, I'd be useless.

Still not good enough.

Never good enough.

The real step three: Channel all my mental energy into willing Enzo to stay in the gallery long enough for Jenn and—

"And the scarab?" Enzo's voice snapped me back into the moment. They were passing my restroom again. "I heard it was back from the goldsmith?"

I stood my ground, pressing my ear to the door. *Sold, was it, JP?*

"We'll take it to the auction coordinator tonight. I'd planned to take it with the painting, but the art restorer's not finished yet."

"Bene. I'll be in Nice this afternoon," said Enzo, "but will be back when the truck's ready. Check on the restorer before you leave. I don't like what happened at her—"

The door exiting the short hallway opened and closed, shutting me out from the rest of their conversation. I leaned my forehead against the door and went inward. *Find your control. Focus on what's important.*

Enzo was in Monte Carlo. He was one of the Fenix Group's captains. They were here.

Massimo and Dante were working with them.

The scarab was going to the same auction as the painting Jenn was working on. Jean-Philippe's lie about it being sold and Brie not finding it in their inventory were of little import now. Cozying up to Massimo didn't matter, either. He was working with fucking Fenix.

I fumbled for my phone and texted Scarlett with shaking hands: *Can't talk. Tell the team Enzo's in town.*

Her shocked *What?!* reply came quickly, but I didn't have time for a discussion.

Protecting Jenn was now my priority. It wasn't about my conscience anymore. Or about mistrusting a man who wasn't right for her. Or the look in her eyes when she started panicking in her room last night. It was about keeping her safe. Enzo didn't sound like he knew her link to Reynolds Recoveries—we had to keep it that way.

Now all I had to do was put my professional face back on, hide the jammer in the kitchenette, pay for my little blue scarab, and get Jenn the hell out of here.

CHAPTER 13

JENN

I DROPPED a cotton ball into the waste jar and straightened from my stooped position. I stretched my back, twisted at the waist, and rolled my wrists. I was a quarter of the way through the cleaning process, the bright colors of *Wheatfield* springing back to life.

No matter what the conservator had written in his notes, he'd used Merrivar varnish. After doing my own tests, I'd been able to grab a bottle of Merrisol mineral spirits to remove it, and the layer of grime came up quickly.

My body had been growing accustomed to this sort of work since I started with Aunt Penny, but between the poor sleep last night and my worries about the painting's authenticity, my muscles were crying for a break.

I checked my watch. Emmett had left me three hours ago. Two hours ago, I'd taken the camera to Dante, who gave me digital copies of the UV photos, which I forwarded to Dr. Ferraro. He didn't expect results until tomorrow, but he and his wife were on the case.

And so, I cleaned the painting. Fake or not, a thin layer of dirt coated it, as though someone had hung it over an open fireplace.

"Che cazzo," muttered Dante from the next room. He'd left the door open once I no longer needed the dark.

"What now?" I called while wrapping cotton batting around another stick. "More of your father's handwriting?"

True to his word, Dante made a ruckus while he worked. He talked to the payroll ledger, complained to himself about sloppy work, and recounted more than a few stories for me about clients from their gallery here and another in London. "It's a good thing he didn't teach me."

"Don't you have employees who can do that for you?"

"We do." The wheels of his chair squeaked, and he approached, stopping in the door frame. "As someone once said, sometimes you have to do your own experiments, rather than rely on someone else's work."

"Wise words." I dipped the swab into the thin, clear solvent and applied it to the next two-by-two section of the painting. The old varnish and dirt on top of it swelled as I agitated it with small circular movements. "Sounds like my experiments were more fruitful."

"Sì, it does." He squeezed his eyes shut and pinched the bridge of his nose. "Do you want lunch yet?"

My back screamed *Yes!*, but I said, "Thanks, but no. I'm in the zone and only have forty-eight hours."

He came closer, leaning on the table to see what I was doing. "You think it will take that long?"

"Not the cleaning itself." I slid the cotton off the end of the stick and into the waste jar, then grabbed another small wad to clean off the residue. "The varnish I'll use dries in twenty-four hours, so if you want it ready for the auction, I need to finish by tomorrow midday."

"We'd hoped to have it ready by end of day tomorrow."

Then they should have worked harder to find another restorer or conservator before Dante hired me.

"Just be happy it didn't need retouching." I disposed of the dirt-laden cotton ball and shook my head. "That would have meant letting the paint dry before I could varnish it."

"I appreciate your honesty." He stood up and leaned a hip against the table. "I imagine many others would have claimed the additional work was required."

"Perhaps you should choose your contractors more carefully." I began winding another swab.

"Contractors..." He hummed, a low sound like frustration. "And so many others."

I rolled the Merrisol against the painting, glancing up at him as subtly as possible. His eyes were closed as he massaged his temples. Was I supposed to ask for more details? Ask if he was all right?

"Time to blow this—" Emmett came to an abrupt halt, one step into the room. A small white bag with the De Rosa Gallery logo hung from his hand. "Dante. I didn't realize you were still here."

"Mr. Stone." Dante gestured to Emmett's bag. "Did you find what you were looking for?"

"Not exactly, although I did find something interesting."

Dante angled his head, prompting for more.

Emmett lifted the bag and smiled. "Jean-Philippe was quite convincing. That man deserves a raise."

Dante returned the smile. He looked friendly enough—

they both did—but I could feel the testosterone flooding the air. "I'll advise my father."

"Good." Emmett turned his focus to me. "I'm ready to go. How much longer do you need?"

"I've only finished part of the cleaning." I circled my hand vaguely over the area I'd completed, before wiping the last of the mineral spirits I'd applied away. "There's a lot of work still left to do. You go ahead."

Emmett came closer, dipping his forehead and raising his eyebrows. The look may as well have been a pat on the head. "Do you remember what happened yesterday? I'm not comfortable leaving you here alone."

Of course, I remembered what happened yesterday. I'd barely stopped thinking about the way he'd held me in my hotel room. How he'd made me feel better. Kept popping into my room while I was preparing for today. How I'd glimpsed him heading to the shower this morning, wearing only his pajama pants, the strong muscles of his back inspiring one too many fantasies about running my hands up and down his body.

Down, girl.

"I'm not alone." I gestured at Dante, the proof I'd have company.

Emmett frowned. "Can I have a moment alone with Jenn, please?"

Dante checked with me, and when I nodded, he left for the office.

I dropped my swab into the jar and folded my arms.

Emmett placed his small bag on the worktable and gripped my upper arms. He kept his voice so quiet Dante wouldn't hear him. "I know you think this is ridiculous, but I'm worried about your safety. I've barely been able to think straight the entire time I've been here. Someone targeted you—"

"Targeted?"

He let go of me, shaking his head. "That's not what I—"

"You said Rav called you paranoid?"

"He did."

"And this is why? You said you'd walk me over this morning, but now you assume I'll leave with you, even though I have a professional responsibility?"

Something flashed behind his eyes—something I'd never seen before. Worry? Fear? Panic?

No, Emmett Reynolds never panicked. He was always the picture of control.

His features softened, and he picked up the bag. "Why don't we discuss this over lunch? We can walk to the Café de Paris, across from the hotel."

I unfolded my arms and stepped closer to him, looking up into his deep brown eyes, full of faux concern. "Why?"

"Because I enjoy your company."

Emmett had said I wasn't allowed to stay in my own room.

Wasn't allowed to stay with Jayce.

Wasn't allowed to come to the gallery on my own or stay unless my quote-unquote bodyguard was there.

Going to lunch wasn't about enjoying my company. It was about controlling me. Emmett was doing the same thing every other man in my life did.

I grabbed a fresh stick and a wad of cotton. "I'm in Monaco for work. I only have so much time to get this done. Going out for lunch is not a luxury I can afford right now."

Was I overreacting?

Honestly, I hadn't wanted to stay in my old room or even in a new one last night. Not alone. Having him in the next room was the only reason I'd been able to get any sleep at all.

I *was* overreacting.

But so was he.

Emmett stared at the painting, fumbling with something in his left pocket.

Dante entered the room. "Is everything all right?"

As I nodded, Emmett said, "When do you expect you'll finish?"

"When they kick me out." I finished rolling the solvent on, disposed of the cotton, and pulled off another chunk, wiping away the dirt from the painting.

Dante said, "We close at eight."

I tried not to look, but I could almost hear Emmett's jaw tighten.

He really *was* worried about something. What was he not saying? "I'll swing by and—"

"No need," said Dante. "I also have a great deal of work to do, so I'll still be here. I'll be certain she makes it back to the hotel safely."

Emmett didn't look at Dante. Throughout the whole exchange, he just stared at me. It was unnerving. "I told Dante about the break-in at your hotel. And while I appreciate his offer, I promised my sister I'd watch out for you."

Dante added, "Security will be here, as will two of our men reviewing the inventory. Plus, Jean-Philippe."

Emmett gave me a smile that was somehow less genuine than the one he'd given Dante earlier. He came closer and kissed my cheek, causing my heart to bounce. "Call me ten minutes before you leave."

The same thing my father used to say. I always had to check in. Always had to let him know where I'd be. Still, for some reason, I said, "I will."

Emmett left, pausing at the door to look at me over his shoulder. That strange tension didn't leave his face. What did it mean?

His shoes clacked on the polished floor and gradually faded away until the chime over the door announced his departure.

Air filled my lungs again. What was it about that man? How did he irritate me so much, yet every time he got close, my body reacted like he was a special drug designed just for me?

Dante leaned his elbows on the worktable across from me. "You cannot keep working for seven more hours without food. I'm starving. I'm going to order something, and I'll order some for you. Eat or don't eat, that's your choice. But there will be food here for you within thirty minutes."

I discarded the cotton ball, covered in its brown gunk. "That, I can do. Let me know how much."

"Business expense." The corner of his lips lifted. "You're of no use to me if you can't complete this painting."

"At least you won't be withholding food until I'm done?"

"I won't. Plus, you and I are having dinner once you finish for the day. After reconciling accounts for so long, I'll need a good meal and good company."

"No, thank—"

He held up a finger to stop me. "You will also be of no use to me tomorrow unless your belly is full tonight and you get a restful sleep."

Were the bags under my eyes—which I'd tried to cover with makeup—that obvious?

"It's a business expense." He winked as he pushed off the table. "You *are* here for business, are you not?"

I was.

But somehow, it felt like he was asking for more.

CHAPTER 14
JENN

DANTE HELD his wineglass up as the sommelier retreated from our table. "What shall we toast to this evening?"

Like a good girl, I'd called Emmett ten minutes before eight o'clock, as Dante and I were preparing to leave. I still hadn't heard from Dr. Ferraro, so I'd simply cleaned the Constable until the gallery closed. Emmett had tried five different ways to convince me not to go to dinner and come directly back to the hotel. He'd even offered to take me out himself, if that was what I wanted.

Instead, I told him Dante had already made reservations at Le Ciel, a rooftop restaurant on the far side of the Monte Carlo Casino, and that I'd be back when I was done. Emmett had told me to enjoy myself, as though it were his choice, not mine. Honestly, I'd been surprised he hadn't insisted I call to let him know when I was walking back.

"To this amazing view." I raised my glass toward the railing next to us, inhaling the hint of the sea wafting in from the Mediterranean. It was the only glass I'd have all night. It was late, and I was exhausted—more than one would put me to sleep where I sat. Before taking a sip, I shifted the glass in his direction. "And to new friends."

Dante's smile widened as our glasses clinked, his dark eyes never leaving mine. "And to beautiful women with a passion for art."

Heat flared up my cheeks, and I covered the blush with one hand as I returned the glass to the table.

Dante reached over and moved my hand. "You're embarrassed by this?"

"No, it's..." I glanced away from him. "I'm just not used to..."

"To what?" His thumb traced over the back of my hand in a gesture so delicate, the hairs on my neck stood up. This didn't feel like a business dinner.

"Being complimented." The words slipped out before I could stop them. It wasn't entirely true—men said nice things to me all the time, but they never seemed so... "Or at least, complimented honestly?"

"This is truly a sin." He let go of me and pressed a hand against his heart. "On behalf of all men, I apologize."

I laughed quietly and finally looked at him again. "I suppose I can find it in me to accept your apology."

There was such sincerity in his eyes. Behind it, a smoldering intensity. It was like a touch, an energy pulsing off him. So why was I still thinking about Emmett?

"This is excellent news. Because I must confess..." He leaned closer, lowering his voice. "My intention for this evening was to invite you to my apartment when we were done."

His apartment?

"I can think of little more I would enjoy tonight than an evening of pleasure with you."

Holy shit—that was unexpected. "Pleasure?" Or was it completely expected?

"Whether that pleasure turned out to be thoughtful conversation, a glass of wine, or hours of passionate love-making would have been up to you."

"Would have been?"

"I am a man who takes what he wants." He paused for a moment, scanning my face as if searching for permission to go on. He must have found it, because he did. "But the one thing I will not take is another man's woman."

"I'm not..."

He leaned an elbow on the table and ran his thumb over his lips. "We would have had a lot of fun, you and I."

"I... I didn't say no." Why did I say that? Because I shouldn't have been saying no. I should have been throwing down my napkin and saying, *Yes, please!*

"Perhaps not with your words, but with every other part of your body." His gaze skimmed down my face and neck, slowly crawling along what the table didn't hide from him. "When we first met in Nice, I felt an immediate attraction to you. It was obvious in your eyes and your smile you felt the same, but still, there was hesitation."

"I just came off a nasty breakup." Why did I tell him? I hadn't even told my friends yet.

The intensity in his eyes softened, then they narrowed. "I saw the same spark when we first came to Monte Carlo. But it changed when we went for dinner with my father."

Changed?

He nodded slowly and picked up his glass, watching the deep liquid, rather than drinking. "Emmett."

A nervous flutter spread through my stomach at his name. *Damn it!*

"There's nothing going on between us."

"I've seen that. However, my father is a shrewd businessman who's taught me a great deal. One of those lessons is to know which battles are worth fighting and which aren't." Dante looked out at the water and took a sip of his wine. His eyes fluttered closed as he held the wine on his tongue for a moment before swallowing. "Winning you over would have been an entertaining battle for both of us, but you belong to someone else."

How was I not saying no, and yet somehow saying no? "I told you, I just broke up with my boyfriend."

Dante placed his wineglass on the table. "I'm not referring to titles like boyfriend or legal entanglements like marriage. I'm talking about your heart."

My heart? It had no idea what was going on. "Emmett and I aren't a thing."

He whispered, "Then why is he at a table with three other people, but he can't take his eyes off you?"

My spine snapped straight. "What?"

No way. He wasn't here. He wasn't spying on me because I'd told him where we were going for dinner.

I turned to the side, but my back still faced most of the restaurant. Even if Emmett was watching, it didn't matter, because I didn't care. Honestly, I didn't care. That overprotective, self-absorbed jerk did not drag his whole team to Le Ciel because he didn't trust me.

"Jenn, my father also taught me how to read people. You

and Emmett have more history than either of you will admit to, I think."

Our history included all of one kiss. A hand that drifted, but didn't touch anything off-limits. It included years of my father's judgment. Half my life, being close to Emmett, but never close enough.

"Sometimes, I find brilliant women miss things that are right in front of them."

What was I missing, other than living my own life? Tasting the flavors of the world?

"But if you tell me your heart does not belong to him, you and I will have our night together. As many nights as you want, until you leave."

I don't belong to Emmett. The denial sat awkwardly in the pit of my stomach. Part of me always wanted him, despite everything. Or maybe because of everything. Because he'd rejected me, and I never got over it? Childish imprinting? Craving the bad boy?

"I thought so." He sighed. "Before my ego insists I attempt to seduce you anyway—which will lead to neither of us having what we want—can we make a promise to each other?"

Dante genuinely wanted me. Only for a few nights, but he did. And he was honest about it. When was the last time that happened? Actually, it happened three boyfriends ago. The co-worker who stole my plans at work.

He hadn't really wanted the sex anyway. He wanted my ideas.

But Dante? He'd wanted the night, and rather than pushing it, he was pushing... what *was* he pushing? He was turning me down, wasn't he?

I was so tired, and nothing made any sense.

"We shall be friends, you and I." Dante brought my fingers to his lips. "You will allow me to continue flirting with you. No expectations of anything to come later, simply one single man enjoying the company of a stunning, almost-single woman. Is this fair?"

"I don't understand, Dante."

He continued holding my hand, resting my fingers against his chin. "How long has he been in love with you?"

Air spluttered out of my lungs, and I almost laughed. "Since never."

"As I said..." He pulled my fingers to his lips and kissed them again. "Brilliant women..."

CHAPTER 15

EMMETT

ACROSS THE RESTAURANT, Dante paused in kissing Jenn's hand long enough to tuck a lock of hair behind her ear. He smiled at her, and my fist sent a message to my brain that punching him would relieve a lot of my tension.

She was still wearing the navy blouse she'd worn to the gallery. The setting sun painted her with a soft glow, as warm as the blush that normally decorated her cheeks. If I were sitting across the table from her, I'd be able to see the candles flickering in her dark blue eyes. She'd be smiling at *me*, not *him*.

Her hair was tied back in a low ponytail, letting too many strands escape its hold. A knot tightened in my gut. Every one of them was a target for Dante.

"She deserves better." My words came out closer to a growl than I'd intended. Hell, they came from my outside voice. Also not what I'd intended.

Rav nudged me with his foot under the table. "Jealous?"

Hardly jealous. Jenn deserved someone better than me,

too. But Dante was a criminal, and she refused to listen to my warnings.

"He's working with Fenix, for fuck's sake." I had the poker chip out of its home in my pocket, unable to stop clenching the tiny thing. "Why are we letting this go on? She should be on a goddamn plane home."

"We already talked about that." Rav shifted in his seat so I couldn't see Dante anymore. "If Fenix wants her, she's safer close to us, where we can watch out for her. And if I recall, keeping her here was *your* idea."

How much had I missed while she was working through the afternoon and evening? What had Dante said? Had Enzo come back early? Jenn looked happy, which meant she was oblivious to what was really going on, other than the potentially fake painting. That was my fault, in part. We'd kept her in the dark about what we genuinely did for years.

I was the one putting her in danger.

"Have you figured anything out from the bug in her room?" I asked Rav.

He shook his head. "It was deactivated this morning."

"After she checked out. It had to be for her. Fenix must be targeting her."

"It could still be a coincidence." Drew broke open a roll from the table and placed it on his bread plate. "It's possible you were mistaken about who you heard at the gallery."

"Not a chance." I would have recognized Enzo's voice anywhere. It was the same voice I heard in my nightmares every night, and the only one that would have caused me to cower like an abused dog. If Jenn weren't in the mix, I would have launched myself out of the restroom at Enzo and... and what? I could barely stand while he was on the other side of a solid wall.

First, the taunt, then the fist. *'You'd better hope your sister finishes the job quickly.'*

It was four months ago. Let it go, Em.

Pathetic.

"Put a tracker on her," Jayce said around a mouthful of food. She was on her third roll and had eaten half of Drew's calamari, in addition to her own appetizer. "Worked for us."

Drew grinned at her across the table, and she winked at him. "Not a bad idea. You packed a few, didn't you?"

Jayce nodded. "Toss one in her purse, another in her pocket, just in case."

Dante and Jenn's food and a fresh bottle of wine arrived. What was his end goal? Obviously, he wanted to sleep with her, and she looked like she was about to go along with his stupid plan. She wasn't the cheating type, though. She was pure and honest. She was loyal.

'What do you know about loyalty?' Mr. Thatcher's words swirled around my brain again. How would he feel if he knew an antiquities thief was wooing his daughter? A man hip-deep in an organization that kidnapped and extorted to get what they wanted?

My own words began swirling. *'Why did he do it, Mum?'*

My mother had never answered the question. Never made excuses. And she'd never turned her back on my father.

What did *I* know about loyalty?

A lot more than most people.

"Em?" Rav nudged me again.

"What?" I snapped. Clearly, the conversation had carried on without me.

"Do we need to switch seats?"

Probably. "No."

"Can we discuss this auction?" Drew patted his lips with his napkin. The former spy was good at keeping us on point. Nothing too personal—except for his constant subtle flirtation with Jayce—and he always focused on the matter at hand.

With Scarlett at home, keeping the team on task was supposed to be my job. Rav could usually be relied on to remind me, but he was more concerned about me than the job. He'd suggested we cancel the entire thing the moment I confirmed Fenix was in town.

Their presence wasn't a surprise. But it had hit me a lot harder than I'd expected.

Drew continued, "The conversation you overheard indicated the scarab will be up for sale?"

I picked up my fork and moved my salad around. Anything to stop myself from looking at Jenn and her Fenix boy toy. "They're moving it tonight. Since you didn't find any evidence of it at Massimo's, we'll assume it's at the gallery. If Jayce can find it before their truck arrives, we can be in Cairo by the morning."

"Which leaves Jenn alone," said Rav.

"Good point. Staying in town would be a risk, but our best course of action would be to fly Jenn out with us." Our private jet was in Nice, a forty-minute drive away—alternatively, a seven-minute helicopter ride. Everything would be easier if I told her the truth, but her reaction would introduce too many variables into our plan. "Plan A, we get it tonight and lie low afterward. As soon as she's done with the painting, we leave."

"Plan B, the auction?" asked Drew.

I nodded.

Rav said, "Brie's team didn't find any indication of a legal auction this weekend."

"Which means..." I speared a radish, not planning on eating it, then placed the fork on the side of the plate. "It's probably going to be at the Casino Rocher."

Jayce fidgeted in her seat, eyeing the food being delivered to other tables. "Why at a casino?"

"It's not *quite* a casino. At least, it's not *only* a casino." I slid my chip back into my pocket and pulled out my phone. I opened the satellite map, zeroing in on the old town. "Monaco-Ville is the historic district, built on the rock they call Le Rocher, where the original stronghold was built in the thirteenth century."

"We visited there yesterday." Drew and Jayce had gone sightseeing while they were off the clock. "Toured the Oceanographic Museum and watched the changing of the guards at the Prince's Palace."

"The best strongholds have emergency tunnels, both for soldiers to escape if they're overwhelmed or for the populace to get into the stronghold if the city is attacked." I pointed to a spot directly west of Monaco-Ville. "The caverns under the Exotic Gardens are a big tourist destination. It's all roped with rough steps and paths for people to follow, but if you go deep enough, there's a connection between those caverns and a large one inside Le Rocher."

Rav frowned. "And you know all this because..."

I raised an eyebrow at him, knowing he knew the answer. "Because in the end, it houses one of the world's most interesting casinos."

"And black market auctions?" added Drew. It sounded like a question but obviously wasn't one.

"The native Monégasque people aren't legally allowed to gamble in Monaco. The Casino de Monte-Carlo was originally built in the mid-nineteenth century to help get the country out of debt, and they didn't want their own people to go further *into* debt by gambling their money away."

"Where there's a will, there's a way?" asked Drew.

"Exactly." My gaze inadvertently wandered over Rav's shoulder, to where Jenn was enjoying her meal. She hadn't turned in our direction once, and Dante hadn't seemed to notice us either. *Focus, Em.* "They hold special events—poker pots so high they'd make your eyes water, betting on the behaviors of people they watch through closed-circuit feeds, and adrenaline raffles—for the insanely wealthy. There's plenty of gray market activity. Far more than black most of the time. The police visit occasionally, ensuring there's no violence, weapons, or whatnot, but they otherwise turn a blind eye to what's going on."

Jayce sat up, leaning forward to whisper. "And if I don't find the scarab tonight, we break in and take it?"

"Plan B is winning it at the auction. But yes, Plan C is breaking into the auction site." I zoomed in closer to the Oceanographic Museum. "There's one entrance in the public elevator here. And another one..." I swiped and pinched until I had an image of the back of the Museum. The Rock's face jutted out of the water, with the back of the building continuing straight up from the cliff. I pointed at a door at the base, close to sea level. "Here."

"With guards?" asked Jayce.

"Yes." I zoomed out again and pointed at the Exotic

Garden. "Which means we need to find one of the tunnels from the public caverns."

"It won't be a service tunnel built out of concrete, will it?" Drew's jaw clenched as he eyed Jayce. He hid his worry for her well, but I could still see it.

"There's some element of spelunking required."

"Sweet!" said Jayce, bouncing back into her seat.

"They take their security very seriously." I picked my phone up, and the next step in the plan formed in my brain as I spoke. "The regular entrances include metal detectors to ensure no one brings weapons in, and you need to check your digital equipment into Faraday cases so no one's snagging blackmail material inside."

Rav sat back, folding his arms. "Which means no comms."

Our digital communications all ran through our phones. If my phone was inaccessible and no one had another Reynolds phone nearby, my earpiece wouldn't work. "We never break rule number one."

The first rule on any op for Reynolds Recoveries: Never turn off your earpiece.

We instituted the rule after one of our jobs went horribly wrong, and we lost Noah.

And now he was back, screwing with us.

Such irony.

"Will mentioned a prototype recently." I tapped his profile on my phone and held it to my ear. "Hopefully, it's far enough along we can use it."

He answered on the first ring. "One sec." His voice grew muffled. "It's work. I know it's late. I need to take this. Yes, it's —Katie—no, just give me—yeah—five minutes."

A door closed on his end, and a long, slow breath came over the line. "Thank you."

"For what?"

"Katie flew in this afternoon." His younger sister lived in Seattle, the last I'd heard. "She had some sort of blowup with her husband and is using me and Mum as an excuse for some time away from him."

Will's temporary situation in London had started with his father's funeral and comforting his mother for a couple of weeks. During that ordeal, he'd discovered they'd hidden her early-onset Alzheimer's from the rest of the family. Over the past year, he'd become her near-full-time caretaker.

He'd only let it interfere with a few ops, and the team had rallied to cover for him. But tough decisions were in his near future.

"I would have thought the extra help would be welcome?" I said.

He groaned in frustration. "She's a nurse, so she can manage everything, but she's insisting I take a vacation."

"You need one of those." Even though the timing was shit for us.

"Not while you're in the middle of a— Sorry, you didn't call to hear me complain. What do you need?"

A little quid pro quo. I needed something from him, and he needed a distraction. "We're going somewhere we won't have access to a phone, so I was wondering—"

"Can you wear a watch?" His voice brightened. "I have a prototype we can hook up to one of our earpieces and amplify its secure signal."

"That's what I was hoping you'd say."

"It still needs a little work, though. Who's going to wear it?"

"Me."

Will chuckled. "I warn you, the prototype is *only* an Omega, so you may hate it."

"I'll be wearing a tux. Promise me it won't stand out."

"Black leather strap and face with gold accents. You'll look great."

"I'll suffer. Can you ship it tonight?"

"One sec." Will grew quiet. Maybe checking something on his computer. Maybe checking the prototype.

I glanced over Rav's shoulder. Dante had moved his chair closer to Jenn's. Another course was being delivered, along with a new wine.

Son of a bitch.

"Will, do you have any jewelry for a woman with an embedded GPS tracker? Or something you could easily add one to?"

"I do. For Jayce?"

"It's for Jenn." I closed my eyes, forcing myself to stop looking at her enjoying her time with *him*. "With Fenix involved in the gallery and her working there, I'd feel more comfortable if I knew where to find her at all times."

"I have a few options."

"My watch will also need to work underground. May not get a strong cellular or satellite signal."

"It's not ready for that, but I should be able to..." Will trailed off, muttering to himself. He was likely already pulling tools to start the job.

"How much time do you need? I want it for the initial recon tomorrow afternoon."

"It'll be tight. I was working on the scarab decoy, but I can put that aside—"

"We might need the decoy."

"Hmm... I can work through the night, but..."

"If I send the jet, can you hand everything to them at the airport in the morning?"

"Doubt it. But here's what I can do: Katie wants me to get out of town for a few days and relax. How about I pack up the tools I need and hop on the jet myself? I can work on the flight and make any tweaks required tomorrow afternoon."

That was the best idea I'd heard all week.

Once Will and I finished sorting out the details, I texted everything to HQ so they could coordinate with our flight crew. My luck was definitely turning around. Will had the equipment we needed, and his sister's visit had come at the perfect time. He even had something to help with the Jenn situation.

"Will should be here sometime tomorrow morning. If Jayce finds the scarab tonight, we'll fly to Cairo and then home as soon as Jenn's done. Otherwise, we'll scout the Casino Rocher in the afternoon and discuss our next steps."

"This was supposed to be an intel-gathering trip"—Rav leaned closer—"not a heist."

Exactly why the scarab decoy wasn't ready yet. We'd thought he had a month or more before needing it. This op was evolving quickly.

"Then they decided to auction it off." I shrugged. "Friday night, it'll change hands and vanish. We'd have to start this entire job over again from scratch."

"Contact the police about the auction," said Rav. "They can recover it."

"I told you." I leaned forward, matching him. "As long as the Casino follows certain rules—no violence, no human trafficking, no prostitution, no drugs—they operate with impunity. If we tip the police off, someone tips off the Casino. The auction doesn't happen, and the scarab's gone."

Rav was right to share his concerns. We were moving fast, juggling more risks than even *I* liked.

Fenix's appearance had been our top concern, and they were in Monaco. We'd discounted the possibility of Massimo working with them, since Noah—who also worked for Fenix—gave us the tip. He'd told Scarlett in June that the group was fracturing. I just hadn't expected it was fracturing *so much* that Noah would sic us on his opposing faction.

But what I wouldn't announce to the table?

If we had a chance to shove a wedge into their organization—the one who'd destroyed my life—I was prepared to face all those risks.

Jenn laughed at something. From all the way across the restaurant, I recognized the sound. I didn't look. I didn't want Rav to know she was a factor in my decision. Fenix was screwing with *her* now. It wasn't only about me and my team. It was about people we cared about.

I didn't give two shits about our client anymore.

All I wanted was to ruin the men who'd ruined me.

CHAPTER 16

JENN

THE SOUNDS of roaring engines and chatter filled the air as Dante and I walked past the front of the Casino. He spoke endlessly, telling me about the history of the buildings, the country, and a few tangents about Paris. He was an excellent tour guide, and my nerves had calmed after he'd laid everything bare at the restaurant.

I wasn't berating myself for not being more attracted to him. I was simply enjoying his company.

The Place du Casino—the area directly in front of the beautiful Monte Carlo Casino—was lit up with old-fashioned street lamps, bulbs entwined around the palm trees, and lights covering the surrounding building facades.

We walked through the crowd who were filming the arrival of Ferraris, Lamborghinis, and Bugattis. As many people wore shorts and T-shirts, as wore tuxes and evening wear. Women strolled through the area in impossibly high heels and even more impossibly minuscule skirts. Valet drivers took keys, parking the ridiculously expensive vehicles, while the onlookers pointed and stared.

"Have you ever taken part in this spectacle?" I asked.

He'd driven me from Nice in his Velatti convertible, which would have been a rare jewel in any crowd. "When I was younger."

"When you had more to prove?"

"When I was less certain about myself." He slipped an arm around my waist as more than one woman eyed him up and down. Who could blame them? Dante De Rosa was a definite catch. "I suppose I also had something to prove, but I'm not sure to whom."

"Friends?" I paused as the traffic crawled along the Avenue de Monte-Carlo, which separated the Casino from the Hôtel de Paris.

Dante raised a hand, and the cars halted for us to cross. "I've never been here with my friends."

"So, your dad?"

"This sounds likely."

He and I were worlds away—the rich Italian with homes around the world and the plain girl from Eastern Canada. Yet we both grew up thinking we had something to prove to our fathers.

"What about your mother?"

Dante's jaw tightened. Did he have a story he wasn't prepared to tell? He let go of my waist and took my hand as though helping me up the stairs to the hotel. "Care to make a wager?"

"About?"

He slowed as people filed into the revolving door. "Emmett will be waiting for you in the lobby."

"He won't."

"So you'll take my bet?"

"How much?"

"One kiss."

This was him *not* attempting to seduce me? What would he have done if he were going to try? Or was this a tactic?

"If I'm right about him, he wants you, so he'll be waiting for you. And perhaps if he sees me kiss you, it will remind him to do something about his feelings."

"And if you're wrong?"

"Then I've kissed a beautiful woman." The corner of his lips lifted into a smirk. "And still, I win."

"And if he's not there?"

"Name your price." He brought my hand to his lips. "Because I know he will."

Emmett had apparently left Le Ciel before our dessert arrived. He could have been anywhere—in the room, at the Casino, at a club, or with his co-workers. What would he do in Monte Carlo when he wasn't searching for an ancient Egyptian scarab? It was after ten, so he might have been asleep already.

"Take me to the auction on Friday as your guest."

"This is your bargain? A date?"

"Not a date." I pushed through the revolving door ahead of him. Once we were through, I tilted my head and said, "A business expense."

He took my arm, and he laughed. "You use my words against me."

We continued into the cavernous lobby, with its soaring ceiling, supported by columns topped with intricate carvings. The marble floors were polished, reflecting the chandeliers and wall-mounted lights. The grand staircase beyond a huge floral display added to the sense of elegance. Along either side of the lobby, people sat in plush chairs and sofas, while staff delivered food and drinks.

I paused beside the statue of Louis XIV near the entrance.

No Emmett anywhere to be seen.

My heart sank. Somehow, Dante had built the moment up as though it were a certainty, and I was... I was disappointed. Let down, almost.

"Do you know about the statue?" Dante gestured to Louis's form on the back of a horse. He pointed at one of the front knees, which was far shinier than the rest of the statue. "Rubbing the horse's right knee brings good luck."

A few days ago, I'd thought I was the luckiest woman in the world—if I blocked Simon out of my brain. A trip to France, a whirlwind in Monaco, and an amazing job opportunity. It was someone else's life.

But all I could see was how none of the people in the lobby were Emmett. He didn't actually care. The faux concern at the gallery was nothing more than macho posturing. A desire to control me that ended the second I was out of sight.

Dante took my hand and placed it on the shiny knee. "You have to rub it, not stare at it."

Under his firm touch, the palm of my hand slid over the spot where the patina couldn't take hold. What luck could I hope for? Emmett already wasn't there, so—

"Jenn!" came a man's voice that shot goosebumps up and down my arms.

I turned, my hand still in Dante's, and blinked.

Emmett walked out of the lobby bar in his dark jeans and a collared shirt. "I thought you were out for the evening."

"That counts," said Dante. "I win."

Was he right? Had Emmett been waiting for me, and his greeting was a cover? Or was this a coincidence?

If he'd been waiting, it was about the break-in, not his feelings for me.

Surely.

Surely?

Dante stepped around me, put his hands on my shoulders, and leaned in slowly. Instead of my lips, he pressed the softest, most chaste kiss on my cheek.

That was his bet-winning kiss?

As though reading my thoughts, he whispered, "You belong to another man."

"I don't *belong* to anyone."

"Your heart does." He winked at me.

"Dante, good to see you." Emmett stopped next to us and held out his hand.

"And you, Mr. Stone." Dante released me and shook hands with Emmett.

"Call me Emmett, please." He smiled, but the way their fingers turned slightly red told a different story. It was the same battle of wills as at the gallery yesterday.

"Emmett. Of course." They finally released their grips. Who'd won? "Did you find anything else to purchase for your clients after you left the gallery this afternoon?"

"No." Emmett scratched at his short beard. He'd complained this morning it was at the worst length, and either he'd have to deal with the itchiness or shave it off. "I've been looking for a gold scarab for some time now, but no one is selling quite what I'm looking for. Jean-Philippe wouldn't have held out on me, would he?"

"I doubt it, unless he already had a buyer for such a piece."

Emmett's eyebrow raised. "You're sure *you* haven't heard anything?"

"If I had, I would provide what help—"

I forced a yawn, big and quite unladylike—anything to break up the tension between them.

Dante had said he'd show me that Emmett was in love with me. Was that what this was? Was Emmett jealous? And Dante was taunting him, so I'd see it?

Was he playing matchmaker?

Another yawn. "I need to get upstairs. If you two will excuse me?"

"I'll walk up with you," said Emmett.

"Thank you for this evening." Dante pulled me close and kissed my other cheek. "Until tomorrow."

As Dante retreated, Emmett said, "How much work do you have left on the painting?"

"Two or three hours." I shrugged and started deeper into the lobby, toward the elevators. "Dr. Ferraro hasn't called me back with any new information, so I don't even know if I'm cleaning the real thing."

He made a noise of assent but said nothing. All the way to the elevator bank and while we waited for a car to arrive—just silence. His jaw flexed, and he avoided looking at me. But once the elevator doors sealed, he started. "You two a thing now?"

The judgment in his voice stung, and I practically snapped back, "No."

Emmett kept his gaze on the climbing numbers above us. "He kissed you."

"It was a cheek kiss." I shook my head. "He's Italian."

"You were out late."

Me? "You were still at the bar when I got in."

"I don't have anything scheduled in the morning. I can sleep late."

"It was a working dinner." Sort of. I *thought* a lot about work, at least.

"Where'd you go?"

"Le Ciel. He said he saw you at one of the tables."

The door opened on our floor, and he waved me out ahead of him. "Awfully posh for a working dinner."

"You don't like him, do you?"

He fell into step beside me, pulling out his phone when it buzzed, then shoving it back into his pocket. "I didn't think he was your type."

My type? Bad boys. Liars and cheaters. Awful men. *Why do you keep choosing men like that?* I rolled my eyes, more at myself than at him.

No, Dante didn't seem like my type at all.

Emmett was that type.

At least, that's what my father always said. Emmett used to get into fights when he was younger and was suspended too many times to count. He always did well in school, but had a temper. Then something happened around the time of our one and only kiss, and all that changed. Scarlett never knew what it was, but she thought Emmett and their mother had a talk that helped him.

After he stopped getting into trouble, my father still insisted he was bad news. No matter what Emmett did as he grew up, my father would talk about him like he was still a kid, getting into scuffles.

And my dad never let go of what Joseph Reynolds did, either. Some of the boys we knew thought Emmett was cool because his dad was a spy. Emmett never thought that. He never wanted to talk about his father. Scar said it was even like that at home.

We walked down the curving white hallway, past the gold paintings and the embossed doors, to our suite. Why did he care if Dante was my type?

"What exactly do you think my type is?"

He frowned, deep lines creasing around his mouth. "That's none of my business, is it?"

Was Dante right? Did Emmett want me and *that* was why he'd been acting weird?

If it was, why not say something? He always knew what to say and could talk anyone into anything. Why not come closer to me last night?

Wait.

Emmett kept coming back to my room last night, getting me settled with the water and then with the food and wine. I'd assumed he was worried about my mental state after the break-in. Had he been imagining the two of us together in the same bed, instead of rooms apart?

Heat pooled in my core, and I drifted closer to him as we walked. "Were you waiting for me downstairs?"

"I needed a drink." That was bullshit, wasn't it?

"You had wine in the room last night. Why not order room service again?"

He slowed and produced his keycard as we approached our door. He didn't answer me. Just opened the door and held it while I went in.

I stopped in the small vestibule, rather than heading for the living room or down the short hallway to my room. I was tired. My back hurt. My eyes were sore.

Dante's words kept circling around my brain. *'How long has he been in love with you?'*

"Emmett..." I barely got one word out before my throat closed. What was I going to say? I couldn't ask him if Dante was right. I couldn't tell him how I honestly felt—all I could manage was his name. I couldn't stand to turn around and look at him.

"What do you need?" The earlier irritation had vanished from his tone, and his body drew closer to mine. It was that same soft tone he'd used in my hotel room yesterday. The tender one I'd dreamed about.

I need everything.

No, not everything. You.

I took a small step backward and made contact with him, my pulse kicking up.

Show me some luck, King Louis.

He gripped my upper arms, not separating from me. He just stood there, all tall and solid muscle, crowding my air with his. "Are you all right? Did Dante—"

"I don't want to talk about him." I wanted to talk about what Dante *said*. But how? Pull out my seduction game, as pathetic as it was? The men in my life had always been the instigators. I'd never had to do much to win them over.

His phone buzzed again, but he didn't move. "Is something else going on?"

God, what would I do if I tried something and Emmett rejected me again?

"Jenn? What's the matter?" His phone buzzed again— three short bursts—and he let go of me. Frustration coated his words. "It's work. I have to take this."

My heart crashed. Now what? Do what I should have been doing? "I'm going to take a shower. My back's killing me."

"I have painkillers in my bag." He strolled into his room, gaze locked on the phone. "Let me know if you need anything."

Anything? I needed him to join me in that shower. Or maybe I'd clean up and put Dante's theory to the test.

CHAPTER 17

EMMETT

THE SHOWER DOOR closed inside the bathroom. Jenn would be in the shower for at least a half hour, if her morning routine was any indication. Considering how she'd sagged against me when we came in, she'd likely head straight to sleep afterward.

Plenty of time for the op. I retrieved my earpiece and headed for the living area. The team was already in progress.

Jayce and Drew had skipped out early from dinner to follow Jenn and Dante from the restaurant. I'd refused to believe she'd go to his place after—she had a boyfriend at home, and Scarlett insisted that meant something to Jenn.

Then again, Dante had escorted her to the hotel. He'd held her hand and kissed her cheek, when it had only been air kisses yesterday. He'd planned on coming upstairs with her. Fucking slimy Fenix asshole.

And she was eating it up. Maybe she wasn't as loyal or as good as I'd thought she was.

Even still, she wouldn't have brought him upstairs, because I might have been here. If not, she would have had to explain the two-bedroom suite. No, she wasn't planning on bedding him tonight, but just in case, my team had followed them.

I'd been waiting for her arrival to save her from herself.

Jayce and Drew had headed to the gallery after confirming I had Jenn. They were a fantastic team, who almost didn't become a thing because they'd been too stubborn to realize they were perfect together.

A smile tugged at my mouth. It had taken a lot of work to convince them they were getting in the way of their happiness, but I was a damn fine matchmaker.

I popped the earpiece in, and video feeds fired up on my screens.

"You finally ready, Emmett?" came Scarlett's voice from HQ. That was unexpected. Monaco was *my* job, not hers. We needed Brie's tech skills tonight, but the plan was for Scarlett to sit out. Not surprisingly, my older sister had never been happy on the sidelines.

"I am." I sat at the table in the living area, where I had more space for my laptop and external screen than in my room. "Everyone in place?"

"Yes," said Rav, who was broadcasting a video feed from the park catercorner to the gallery.

"No," came Jayce's voice in my ear. "You said the truck wasn't supposed to arrive until midnight, but it's here now."

"What?" I was sure Enzo's guy said midnight.

"That's why I've been trying to reach you." Scarlett's voice was calm, but she was using her commanding tone that may as well have been a lecture. Although it explained why my phone had buzzed three times—that was the emergency signal.

"Could be a different truck, if they're an hour and a half

early." I watched Jayce's feed, which showed three men loading items from the gallery into the truck. The feed wasn't clear enough to recognize the men's faces. "Anyone we know working the truck?"

"No one," said Jayce.

That eliminated Enzo and Noah, at least. They were the only ones I was worried would come after us. It also meant neither Massimo nor Dante was there. Those two were the money, so they wouldn't likely dirty their hands with something as tedious as loading boxes.

Dante could certainly manipulate Jenn, though. Maybe I'd have to play the big brother and scare him off instead of scaring her off. I didn't need to schmooze him anymore since he wouldn't confess to his father having the scarab.

"—after they're gone." Scarlett's voice snapped me out of my head.

I'd missed something. How much?

Fuck. This is why she's on the comms. I was ten minutes late, and my sister was covering my ass.

The guys on the video lifted a long crate into the back of the truck—the right size and shape to house a three-by-four-foot painting. Minutes ticked by as they left the truck, returned to the building, and came out with more.

Had they already packed the scarab? It was small enough to have been in a pocket.

My team was patient. They'd go in after the truck left. Or would they? Is that what Scarlett had been talking about? Dante could have removed the scarab when he finished work, planning to drop it off with the auction coordinator. The team had monitored them from the moment they left the gallery, and they'd walked straight to the restaurant, so he hadn't detoured to Le Rocher.

Unless someone met him at the gallery?

Or he went to the Casino after he dropped Jenn off.

After he'd kissed her. Twice.

C'mon, Em, it was only the cheek. That's normal.

It wasn't fucking normal. The way he'd taken her hand and rubbed the statue's knee. How he'd held her. Touched her face at the restaurant.

"We missed it, didn't we?" I muttered.

"Missed what?" Jenn's voice had me practically jumping out of my seat.

Rav grunted over the earpiece, meaning he agreed with me, while Jayce sounded optimistic about breaking in to explore, anyway.

Jenn was barefoot, dressed in a long, plush hotel bathrobe, with her hair in a towel. She'd only been in the shower for twenty minutes, tops. Rogue water droplets clung to the side of her neck, one daring to roll down her collarbone, vanishing underneath the robe's fabric.

Lucky fucking water.

Unbidden, an image flashed through my brain of following the path of that water droplet, and the one following it. With my thumb, then my mouth. Undoing the thick tie at her waist and peeling the robe back slowly. So slowly.

My cock twitched.

"Is that Enzo?" whispered Jayce over the comms.

My gut clenched, and the budding fantasy vanished.

I angled my laptop, so Jenn couldn't see the video feed. "It's just work stuff."

Scarlett asked over the earpiece, "What's she doing in your room?"

When Rav stayed with me, we both set up in the living area of our hotel suite. If I were trying to hide what I was doing from Jenn—which I should have been—I would have been in my bedroom, behind a locked door.

Now I was facing a bigger question: How did I answer Scarlett without making Jenn suspicious?

"How was the shower?" *Shit.* I shouldn't have said that.

In one ear, my sister asked, her voice thick with accusation, "Shower?"

All of my senses absorbed Jenn's movement toward the balcony door. The scent of her perfume, airy and citrusy, with a hint of jasmine underneath. The light padding of her feet on the hardwood floor, silenced when she stepped onto the thick rug under the sofas. The sway of her hips as she dodged between the coffee table and a sofa.

What would her freshly washed skin feel like? What would every inch of her taste like?

Fuck, man. What's going on? Why was I suddenly so aware of her?

She bent her head back, letting the towel fall into her hands, then dropped it onto the nearest sofa. "I *love* that shower."

"Emmett, tell me she is not in your bedroom after having a fucking shower." Scarlett's voice was distant. Not really, but I was doing my best to tune her out. Everyone on the team learned quickly how to distinguish between the conversations in your ear that were meant for you and all the noise in everyone else's background.

That's where I was putting Scarlett—in the background.

And that was a mistake. I had a job to do that didn't include eyeing up the woman I'd sworn to protect.

"The view from the sitting room is beautiful, isn't it?" There. I answered Jenn, while providing the information Scarlett needed. And responding to Jayce, I added, "When Jayce was here after we arrived, she thought she saw someone from the balcony that she knew, but she was mistaken."

Jenn ran her fingers through her wet hair and turned to face me. "What a strange coincidence."

I shrugged.

Over the line, Jayce said, "You're right. This guy isn't ugly enough."

Drew asked, "Enzo's supposed to be here for the truck, right? Was anyone else coming? Did Dante say anything to Jenn?"

I grimaced deep inside. Back to using Jenn for intel. "What was Dante up to this evening?"

Jenn blinked at me a few times, framed by the faint light from the hotel's exterior. She looked like an angel, albeit a confused one.

"Did he mention any plans? I was surprised he brought you back so early."

Her shoulders fell, and she returned to the sofa. Sitting down lightly, she said, "Sleep. His father's working him hard while they're here."

Oh, the sacrifices they must be making for their dear Fenix. "He's doing the same to you. Working until eight, then keeping you out all night at a *working* dinner? You should get some sleep."

"I'm kinda wired." She eased back on the sofa, propping one foot on the coffee table. The robe rose with her leg and slipped, revealing far too much skin. Toned muscle all the way to her upper thigh.

Avert your eyes, Em. She's taken. Although she didn't seem to mind Dante's interest.

"I'm still not adjusted to the time zone." She yawned, stretching her arms behind herself and bowing her back as though she were working out her muscles. "And my back's killing me. Too many hours at the worktable."

Was that true, or was it an excuse? Had the break-in rattled her more than she'd let on, and was she afraid to go to sleep? The way she worried her bottom lip and lowered her eyes— she was uneasy. How could I fix her mood while the team prepared their own break-in?

If she were any other woman, I would have offered to massage her back. Encouraged her out of that robe. Found something in my toiletry bag to pass for massage oil.

Or skip the oil and the pretense.

"I have sleeping pills. Would that help?" Not that I'd use them while she was staying with me.

"No thanks. Can we talk instead?" She settled back, grabbing a cream-colored throw pillow from the end of the sofa, which she hugged to her chest. "Dante said some things this evening that got me thinking..."

"Truck's packing up," said Jayce.

My gaze flicked to the video feed on my monitor, then back to Jenn. Sure enough, the men closed and locked the gallery's back door. The next stop would be Massimo's yacht or the auction site.

Jenn looked up at the intricate chandelier over the table. "If *Wheatfield* turns out to be a fake, what do I do?"

"Call the authorities?" Which wouldn't do anything unless the police acted before the painting went to the auction.

"That was my original plan." She looked out the window into the darkness.

"Truck's leaving," said Jayce. "What's your call, Em?"

If I'd been paying attention earlier, I might have been able to answer her. Scarlett had likely given some options. The original plan was to use the jammer to take down their cameras. After that, Jayce and Drew would bypass their security system. With the truck potentially whisking the scarab away, following it would have been options two and three.

"Look for the money, then follow it," I said.

"Good call," said Scarlett over my earpiece. "Jayce, plant a tracker on the truck, then head into the gallery."

"Exactly." Jenn sighed. "If they *knew* the painting was a fake, why pay a stranger to clean it? They couldn't have vetted me that closely. If I discovered the truth, I could be shady and extort money from them or immediately call the police. Why take that risk? I doubt they know."

"Or that's why Dante's attempting to distract you."

"What?" snapped Scarlett, no doubt at me. After she'd warned me not to touch Jenn, Jenn had gone off and found someone else to test her loyalty.

"Distracting me?" Her brow furrowed. "You think that's all he's doing?"

"I don't trust him. I know people, Jenn, and he's got an agenda."

"He's a good man. Surprisingly honest."

"Tracker's in place," said Jayce.

Thanks for the reminder. I had to sneak one into Jenn's purse before she left in the morning, until Will brought me something more reliable to always be on her. "People don't become as wealthy as the De Rosas without more than a few skeletons in their closets, not to mention a string of broken hearts behind them."

She let out a quiet laugh, as though my words had hurt. "Something you know a lot about, right?"

I had more skeletons than she could understand.

"Watch yourself, Em," said Scarlett. Yet again, my sister didn't trust me to make wise choices. At work, she trusted me implicitly. But in the real world?

"I'm sorry." Jenn stood abruptly, dropping the pillow and letting the robe's hem fall so it covered her again. "I'm interrupting your work. I should leave."

Drew and Jayce bickered in my earpiece about her lingering too close to the truck. She'd seen the lock on the back and wanted to sneak inside while it was moving. Drew called her reckless and the rest of the team got involved.

Jenn hadn't made a move to her room yet.

I tapped a button on my keyboard, breaking rule number one: Never turn off your earpiece. Although that mostly applied to people in the field who were in danger. I was supposed to lead the crew, so I had more latitude, but Scarlett could coordinate them. Brie was on the line with her, so they'd be fine without me for a few minutes.

"Yes, I have work to do." I rose from my chair, pinning her in place with my eyes. "But if I couldn't handle the interruption, I would have locked myself in my room."

"You promised to leave your door open."

"I did." I started walking toward her. "More importantly, I need you to understand what's going on here."

Her lips tightened. What was going through her head?

She'd come out in a playful, teasing mood, and now she seemed on the brink of tears. Or of yelling at me.

"We suspect they asked you to clean a forgery." I stopped so close to her that she had to tilt her head back. "We also suspect they have the scarab we're looking for."

"Suspect? You didn't ask Jean-Philippe?"

"I did. He told me they'd already sold it, but it was a lie." At least I could thank Enzo for that tidbit. "They're sending it to the auction, too."

"I don't understand." She scrunched her nose. "If they have it and you want to buy it, why lie? Why not just sell it to you? Or what if he was telling the truth and the new owner—"

"It's worth millions. They believe I'm an antiquities broker who'll do his due diligence before buying such an expensive piece." Mental note: The scarab wasn't in the inventory because it was a stolen piece. Instead of comparing their inventory against stolen art databases, I'd need Jayce to take photos of the storage area and compare *those* to the databases. "If they can list it at an underground auction, with some level of anonymity, they wouldn't be attached to its original theft."

"Underground?" Her eyes widened slightly, and she shook her head. "Dante wouldn't..."

She was so naïve.

I dealt with people like Dante and Massimo all the time. Thieves and criminals who thought the world owed them something. Thought their money and their polished exteriors put them above everyone else.

That's why my team existed. We reminded them that all their money didn't keep them safe from the truth.

Money and the truth. My stomach twisted in a knot.

How much did the Russians pay you, Dad?

That information hadn't been in any report from his brief trial. My mother must have known—she was too smart to have missed the signs. Still, an investigation into a CSIS officer selling secrets must have included his wife, let alone everyone he knew. They must have gone after Mum, although she shielded us at the time. We were too young.

She never told us the details.

Discovering she was with MI6 once upon a time, though? Of course, she knew how to keep secrets. Had she been in on Dad's crimes? Did he know she was an intelligence officer, too?

Whatever the truth was behind my parents, Mum made her own version of lemonade from those lemons. She rebuilt her entire life after they locked him up. Now she ran a company that helped the victims of charlatans and thieves like her husband.

I took Jenn by the shoulders. Her perfume filled my senses, and it was all I could do not to breathe her in. Imprint the moment on my brain.

Fuck, she was beautiful. Her hair was drying, and she didn't wear a stitch of makeup. It was just her, plus her intoxicating scent.

"Promise me you'll be careful. Don't let him sweet-talk you into anything. Men like him are dangerous."

She moistened her lips, and I almost lost it. But she nodded and whispered, "I need to get into bed."

I pulled her closer, wrapping her up in my arms. The tension in her shoulders evaporated, and she sank against me the same way she had when we first came in. If the team hadn't been waiting for me, I could have stayed in that moment forever.

But my team *was* waiting. Prepping for another crime.

I'd last visited my father in September. Next month, Mum would force us all there for our annual visit. Every year, he asked if I'd met anyone special. And every year, I avoided the question.

A one-night stand didn't care who my father was. They didn't have time to learn my secrets. And they definitely weren't around long enough for me to start crafting lies about my career.

You're no different from your father.

I squeezed Jenn closer, then released her. This cozy sweetness was better than I deserved. "Get some sleep. I'm sure your back needs the rest."

She gave me a weak smile. "Don't stay up too late."

My hand found its way to her cheek, against my brain's orders. "Will you have time for breakfast on the balcony tomorrow morning?"

"You said you were sleeping in."

I barely shrugged, unable to let her go. "I don't sleep very much."

She touched my hand, holding it against her face, and her eyes fluttered closed. "Breakfast would be nice."

So beautiful. My thumb swept across her cheek, which grew redder the longer we stood there. My cock twitched again, reminding me it hadn't gotten its way in four months.

That was my cue.

I pulled my hand back and headed for the table. "I'll let you know before I call room service, so you can put in your order."

"Thanks." She padded out of the room as I sat.

I waited for her door to click closed before turning my earpiece back on. "Sorry, folks."

In full command mode, Scarlett said, "We're going to have a chat when you get home."

"More than one, no doubt." *Don't piss her off too much.* "Rav, I'm going to toss a tracker into Jenn's bag in the morning. I won't be able to stick around the gallery again, so I'd like you to stay close to her. Keep an eye out."

Rav was tireless. The military trained him to function on little sleep, so asking him to forgo a night wasn't unusual. "Text me when she leaves."

"What's going on?" asked Scarlett.

"I'm not sure yet." I wasn't overreacting. It wasn't jealousy, despite what Rav said at dinner. It wasn't even *just* Dante. Something wasn't adding up.

Jenn was right about them hiring her. They'd given her their own conservator's notes about the painting, which had turned out to be wrong. If they'd known it was a fake, why give her the notes? Why not have her figure out the right steps for the cleaning on her own? That would have avoided questions.

There was something else going on, but what?

"Jammer's engaged," said Drew.

A graph on my screen dipped, showing we'd disrupted the Wi-Fi signal at the De Rosa Gallery, taking their security feed down with it.

Time for me to sit back, monitor the team, and hope Jayce found what we were looking for.

The sooner we finished, the sooner we could get everyone out of Monaco.

Including Jenn.

CHAPTER 18
JENN

EMMETT'S LIPS found my collarbone, and I sighed. His tongue danced along the length of my neck, and I shivered, reveling in the press of his body against mine. He moved with a fluid, predatory grace that threw my pulse into a frenzy. His fingers traced fiery paths down my sides, each touch sending electric shocks through me.

"Jenn," he whispered, his breath hot against my skin. His voice was gravel and velvet, rough and smooth in all the right ways. "You taste so good."

Heat erupted in my belly, spreading like wildfire. It felt real. It felt right. His words echoed in the dark, and his body moved next to mine the way I'd always imagined—the way it was meant to be.

His lips trailed down my chest, and I arched into him. His hands cupped my breasts as he kissed his way down my body, each touch leaving a burning imprint on my skin.

"Emmett..." I moaned his name and squeezed my eyes shut.

His tongue circled my navel and continued further south.

The sensation was mind-numbingly intense. As he pushed one of my legs to the side, my fingers clutched at his hair as if he were an anchor in a storm.

I had to watch him. I couldn't keep my eyes closed.

But when I opened them, we weren't in my room anymore. We were in the Casino. I was naked in the middle of the Monte Carlo Casino, propped up on a bed of pillows on a platform. The clatter of roulette balls and slot machines filled the cavernous space as the gamblers went about their business with an eerie indifference.

"Emmett," I hissed. No response. "Emmett!"

He looked up at me, confusion on his features. "I told you to be careful."

"I—" My eyes snapped open, and I shot up from the bed.

Faint light spilled in through the crack between my curtains.

I was in my bed. Pulse pounding. In my hotel room.

Shit.

It was a dream. Just a dream and nothing more.

I flopped back onto the pillow, pressing my hand to my chest, urging my heart and lungs to slow down. How else was I going to get back to sleep and enjoy the rest of that dream?

Other than the part about being at the Casino.

Minutes passed, and my brain remained on high alert. The dream began to fade.

That was the closest I'd ever get to him. I blew out a slow breath. Dante had been so wrong.

After I'd showered last night, I *had* been wired. Every drop of water had me thinking about the possibility Emmett wanted me. That he'd insisted I stay with him, he'd followed me to the gallery and restaurant, and he'd been waiting for me to arrive after dinner—not because I was Scarlett's best friend, but because I was me.

So I'd put on some perfume, made a ridiculous display with my hips, and nothing! I put my foot on the table so the robe would expose my leg—and almost a lot more—but he didn't react.

No, he *did* react. He kept checking his laptop.

I scrubbed my hands over my face.

Emmett couldn't get back to work fast enough.

I was officially the worst femme fatale in the history of the world.

A soft noise from Emmett's room broke my thoughts. I sat up again and cocked my head, listening. Was it my imagination or was he still awake? The clock by my bed proclaimed it was three in the morning. Did he have that much work to finish?

The sound came again, louder.

An icy burst crawled up my spine. It *was* him, right? Someone hadn't broken in?

I slid out from the bed and crept toward my door. Pressed an ear to it. The sound came again, but it was definitely from the wall between our rooms, not the hallway.

Curiosity and adrenaline urged me forward.

Quietly, I eased my door open and stepped into the hallway, my feet barely whispering against the hardwood floor. His door was open—exactly like he'd promised.

The noise came again, obviously from his room—a low groan, guttural and filled with pain, followed by heavy breaths. My stomach clenched as I drew closer.

"No," he murmured.

It was a nightmare. I paused before I reached his room,

wanting to check on him, but not wanting to. This was crossing a line—stepping into his personal space uninvited. Not just uninvited, but while he was sleeping.

He rustled the sheets, followed by another soft cry. Before I could second or third-guess myself, my feet carried me the final distance to his room. His curtains were wide open, with the moonlight dancing across his sweat-slicked skin. The covers were a mess, half off the bed, and three pillows were on the floor. His face twisted in discomfort as he fought some unseen enemy in his dreams.

"Emmett," I called softly, stepping further into the room. His head jerked to the side, a grimace overwhelming his features. It was getting worse.

He tossed the sheets again, revealing how little he wore— boxer briefs only.

You shouldn't be here. He wouldn't want you to see him like this.

Then he shouldn't have convinced me to stay with him.

"Em, wake up."

His body jerked, and another groan tumbled from his lips.

I reached out, pausing before I touched his shoulder. Waking someone from a nightmare was dangerous. Why was I doing this?

Or was that an old wives' tale?

"Emmett," I said more firmly this time, giving his shoulder a gentle shake. His skin was hot to the touch, feverish even.

His eyes flew open with a start, wild and unfocused. He shot upright, his hand darting beneath his pillow.

Re-emerging with a handgun.

Pointed directly at my chest.

"Get out!" he bellowed.

I stumbled backward, fear twisting my insides. Heart leaping into my throat. Hands raised. "It's me!"

"What—"

"Jenn!" I tripped over something, falling hard onto the floor. No escape. Nowhere to go. He had to hear me. "It's Jenn!"

"Jenn—" He leaped out of the bed, eyes still wild but recognition dawning. The gun clattered to the floor as he lunged forward, dropping to his knees beside me.

Why did he have a gun under his pillow?

"Jenn, I'm so sorry," he whispered, voice hoarse. He reached out, hesitating before his hands found my arms. "Are you okay? Did I hurt you?"

I shook my head, hiccupping in breaths. "I'm fine. Just startled."

"I'm sorry," he repeated, softer this time. His eyes roamed over my face, searching. He brushed back a strand of hair, fingertips lingering for a moment longer than necessary. "I didn't mean to scare you."

"It's okay." It wasn't. My vision blurred as tears collected on my lids. I should have stayed in my room.

It was a gun.

Emmett took my face in his hands and brushed away the tears rolling down my cheeks. "I'm so sorry. I would never hurt you, I swear."

I nodded rapidly, almost as rapidly as the shudders wracked my body. What else could I say? What could I do? My sweet, kind, amazing Emmett slept with a gun. And he had horrible nightmares.

He leaned forward and pressed a kiss against my forehead. "What are you doing here?"

"You were having a nightmare." I sniffled, wishing I didn't sound as pathetic as I must have. "I heard you from my room. You sounded... like you were in pain."

"I'm fine." Emmett's voice held the barest tremble, a vulnerability so unlike him that my heart would have ached if it weren't so busy trying to escape my body. He glanced at the discarded gun on the floor. "It was only a dream."

I put my hands over his, trying to steady my breathing.

He picked me up and settled me on his lap. Strong arms wrapped around me, pulling me close. "Don't cry. You're safe."

Too late.

I buried my face against his neck and fell apart.

A gun.

Pointed straight at me.

All I could see was Emmett yelling at me, with the gun pointed at my chest.

Despite the tremor in Emmett's voice, his embrace was solid and confident. He traced soothing circles on my back, the warmth of his body a comfort. The thin layer of sweat he had from the nightmare cooled my skin, and I was suddenly aware I was sitting on his lap, both of us practically naked. My tank top and boy shorts only hid a smidge more than his boxer briefs.

Heat—stupid, poorly timed heat—crawled its way up my chest.

"I'm sorry." I tried pulling away, but he held fast.

"Don't apologize," he whispered near my ear. "You didn't do anything wrong."

I could feel every contour of his muscles pressed against me, and it sent a confusing blend of comfort and embarrassment rushing through me. My thoughts jumbled into an incoherent mess, a swarm of butterflies filling my stomach. Such awful timing.

"Emmett," I started, my voice catching.

His grip loosened, and he separated from me, but only enough we could see each other. His eyes were bloodshot, exhaustion etched into every line of his face. But the way his gaze caressed me, I could almost believe he didn't want to let me go. As though maybe, just maybe, holding me was the one thing keeping him together.

The silence stretched between us as we sat in the dark, slowly transforming from a shared fear and regret into something darker. Something dangerous.

Something I'd wanted almost as long as I'd known him.

I pulled my hand from around his back and traced his jawline, raking my fingers through his short beard.

His lids flickered shut for a moment. Was he enjoying it or trying to come up with a way to tell me no? When his eyes reopened, they burned with an intensity the dim light couldn't hide. A rumble formed in his chest, reverberating through me.

My core tightened in response, a desperate ache building. Flashes from my dream hit me. His lips on my breasts. His hands digging into my hips. His whispers as I threaded my fingers through his hair. I ground down on his cock, searching for friction, making my need clear.

"Fuck," he groaned, eyes sliding shut again.

There was so little fabric between us. Did he feel how wet I was?

"Jenn," he ground out. One of his hands moved into my hair, wrapping his fist around the strands, holding me in place.

When he reopened his eyes, a war raged inside them. Desire battled with restraint, and for a moment, I was terrified he'd push me away.

I grazed my fingers up his jaw, through his hair, and settled them at the nape of his neck. I urged him closer, our breaths mingling in the scant distance that remained. His eyes locked onto mine. I could almost taste the desire radiating off him.

What had he been dreaming about? What scared the unflappable Emmett Reynolds?

"You are so fucking beautiful." He dipped his head slightly, lips hovering just above mine, his breath dancing against my skin. And he paused. No more than an inch between us. "But we can't do this."

Underneath me, he hardened, and I rubbed myself against him, the heat growing unbearable. "Why not?"

"You have a boyfriend." His forehead dropped to mine, a tinge of regret in his words.

"I broke up with him before I left for Nice. He was cheating on me." It should have been a lot sooner than that. *Focus on the moment, Jenn.* "For once, I want someone who cares about me."

"I care about you." He let out an ironic laugh. "I care so much, I can't... can't touch you. I promised Scarlett I'd keep you safe."

"Safe from you?"

He nodded, but didn't separate from me. "You deserve someone..."

We sat in silence for seconds that felt like minutes, until I realized he wouldn't say more. I applied pressure to the back of his neck, hoping to encourage him forward, but he resisted.

So I drifted my fingers down his jaw again, tracing my thumb against his lips. "Someone what?"

His lips parted, and he pulled in a ragged breath. His tongue followed, dragging across the pad of my thumb. Slowly. Excruciatingly slowly. He leaned back, shaking his head. "Someone who takes you back to your room when you need sleep. That's what someone who actually cares about you would do."

Cutting off any protest I could offer, Emmett slid his hands under my knees and around my back, lifting me effortlessly. Too confused and overwhelmed to argue, I let my head rest against his neck. I imagined he was lifting me to his own bed, to do everything Dream-Emmett was doing in my fantasy.

Did Awake-Emmett want me the same way? Was he making excuses to avoid me again, or did he believe what he was saying? Was running my hand over his hard pecs going to turn him on or embarrass me come morning?

"I'm sorry I scared you, Jenn." He swallowed hard. "It's the last thing I ever wanted.

Why did he have a gun in Monaco, let alone sleep with it under his pillow?

The gentle rocking from his steps as he carried me down the dim hallway calmed me. His warmth seeped into my skin, his pulse a steady rhythm against my ear, relaxing me.

We reached my room, and he nudged the door open with his foot, stepping inside without breaking stride. He moved through the bedroom with the ease of someone who'd carried a hundred women to bed this way.

I pushed that thought aside.

"You're safe." He laid me on the messy bed, pulled the

cover over me, and pressed another kiss to my forehead. "I'm not going anywhere."

"I know, I..." I curled up on my side. *So tired.* Break-ins and forgeries and staring down the barrel of a gun. This trip was supposed to free me, not bring everything crashing down.

"You need rest." He rounded the bed, slid in behind me, pushed a thick arm under my head for a pillow, and draped his other arm over my waist. "I'll stay until you're asleep."

I nestled against him, breathing in the scent of his cologne. Cardamom, bergamot, and a hint of vanilla. Dark. Mysterious. So sexy.

So not the right time to think about that. I snuggled against his muscled body, hoping to rub my ass against his erection, but it was gone. No matter how hard he'd been, he didn't genuinely want me. Not that way.

"Don't think about anything. Just sleep."

He was one to talk. He'd been the one having the nightmare.

But the gun? Holy shit. Scarlett never said their jobs were so dangerous they slept with weapons next to them. Rav, I could understand.

Not Emmett.

Not voice-like-silk Emmett.

I yawned and placed my hand over his.

Not always-knew-what-to-say Emmett.

Not the Emmett who Dante swore was in love with me.

"Nothing bad's going to happen." He stroked my abdomen with his thumb. "I've got you."

I know.

CHAPTER 19

EMMETT

JENN'S ALARM PINGED, prompting a small groan as she rolled over to shut it off. Despite our legs remaining tangled, the lack of contact felt wrong. She nestled back against my chest with a soft sigh, pulling my arm over her. She mumbled something that sounded like, "One snooze."

I didn't respond to her groggy words. Instead, I pretended I was still asleep. Pretended I was an ordinary man, holding my woman in the morning.

Last night, I'd planned to wait until she fell asleep, then leave. At worst, I would have gone back to my room for the gun, hidden it in the bedside table drawer, and snuck back in next to her. But sleep had taken me too quickly. For the first time in four months, it had been peaceful. No pills, no alcohol, no anything.

Just the woman I couldn't have, snuggled safely in my arms.

It had taken all my self-control to bring her to this bed and tell her to go to sleep. Every fiber of my being wanted to press my lips against the slope of her shoulder, let my hands travel the landscape of her skin, and feel her pulse quicken under my touch.

Fuck, she'd been so wet in my lap last night. But her heat was nothing against the visions in my dream. I couldn't shake them, even with her grinding against me.

I'd seen Rav's doctor once after the ordeal in April.

He'd wanted me to talk about the dreams.

I wanted nothing to do with that.

I'd figured I had all the time in the world to deal with my demons. I hadn't considered being with a woman since then—barely wanted to spend time with anyone outside of the company.

But then Jenn... urging me to kiss her, to throw her into the bed, to feast on her soaking pussy for hours?

Her breathing became steady again as she drifted back to sleep. I slowly tightened my grip around her waist, feeling the curve of her body tucked against me. If my hand wandered, I could claim I was sleeping. Sink between her legs and stroke her into wakefulness. After last night, I knew she'd say yes.

My cock reacted.

But I had to resist.

She was still Scarlett's best friend, and Scarlett had been right to warn me off. I was trouble. I was a liar, a manipulator, and was incapable of long-term relationships. No matter what she said, Jenn wouldn't want a one-night stand. She deserved forever with a reliable man.

And that wasn't me.

While it also wasn't Dante, considering he was working with Fenix, at least her revelation about her boyfriend confirmed she was as loyal as I'd thought. She hadn't been out cavorting, thinking about cheating on her significant other.

Her alarm pinged again, and she sighed. "I need to get ready."

I didn't let go; instead, I held fast, making her pause in her stretch for the phone. "Are you all right?"

She relaxed against me and put her hand on top of mine.

"I know I scared you, and I'm more sorry than you can imagine."

Her alarm continued, but we both ignored it. "Why do you sleep with a gun?"

It had been by my side every night for four months. But that wasn't a detail she needed to hear. I only had to confess something that would convince her not to delve deeper. "Someone broke into your hotel room."

She threaded her fingers between mine, a gesture too intimate and so welcoming. "That's why you kept your door open? In case someone sneaks in?"

"No." I should have told her about the monitor attached to the door, which would emit a high-pitched wail if anyone attempted to breach it. The noise would disorient an intruder and give me enough time to react. All the Reynolds team members used those in our hotel rooms. We knew how easy standard security was to break. "That was in case you needed me."

"I see." Her voice was hushed, a hint of regret lacing the words as she said, "I need to get ready."

Reluctantly, I loosened my grip on her waist. "I know."

She sat up slowly, the sheet sliding down to reveal more of her back—the little tank top barely hid anything. The curtains were slightly open, letting the sun streak across her body, dancing along her elegant spine.

My fingers itched to trace each vertebra, but I clenched them into a fist instead.

She stood, turned off her phone, and left.

The absence of her warmth was immediate and jarring. I rolled onto my back, staring at the ornate chandelier, wrestling with memories that wouldn't let go. The sound of water running in the bathroom almost had me racing to join her. We'd been close last night—the raw connection we'd nearly made.

With an exasperated sigh, I reached down and smoothed a hand over my hard dick. *Stupid shit.* I usually had excellent control—critical in my line of work—but instead, it was ready and willing, excitedly awaiting Jenn's return.

Keep it under control, Em. There's work to do.

I imagined green felt. Leather bumper. In my mind's eye, I cupped my hole cards for a preview. Two jacks—I had a six percent chance of a pocket pair on a fifty-two-card deck. But jacks were dangerous. The chance of a higher card showing on the flop was fifty-two percent. I moved through the game, faceless dealer and players calling, raising, folding.

Percentages crammed my brain, multiplying and dividing with each card the dealer revealed.

Five minutes of stats and my hard-on finally calmed down.

I hurried to my room for a tracker and my phone. Making sure not to disrupt any of the contents of her purse, I buried the tracker inside a small zippered compartment, then slid back under the covers.

Maybe I should have settled in my own room or gone to the sitting room and ordered breakfast—or grabbed more clothes—but this bed was warm and smelled like her.

As though summoned by a need to interrupt my thoughts,

my phone buzzed, showing Rav's name. I answered on the first ring, keeping my voice low, though Jenn was still in the shower. "Did I miss anything last night?"

Everyone else on the team had slept in yesterday, knowing it might be a late night; the team at home was five hours earlier than us, so they'd been fresh from the start. I'd been the outlier, up early to escort Jenn to De Rosa's before spending hours with Jean-Philippe. Try as I might, I hadn't been able to focus long enough for Jayce to finish searching the storage room at the gallery.

"No scarab, but Jayce took a video, as you requested. Brie's parsing it to scan stolen artwork databases in case there's anything else of worth there."

In this case, items of worth would be anything we could return to its rightful owner or tip the police off about. Not our top priority, but taking anyone with Fenix down a notch was a worthwhile endeavor in my mind.

"What about the truck?" I watched the open door, listening for the water to shut off.

"As we expected, it offloaded everything onto a yacht at Port Hercule," he continued. "Brie ran a check and confirmed it belongs to Massimo De Rosa."

"Makes sense. Any idea whether the scarab was in that shipment?"

"Brie found the yacht's schematic, and Jayce wanted to board it, but there was too much activity. One of the men from the truck stayed onboard, one left on a tender, and the other drove to a parking garage in Nice."

That meant the scarab could have been on the yacht, in Nice—or wherever the final driver went afterward—or somewhere on the water. "Did you see where the tender went?"

Rav grunted, expressing his disappointment. "He left the port and headed west, but I lost him after he rounded the tip of Le Rocher."

"That doesn't help at all." I paused, listening. The shower turned off. I had to wrap up in case she came out instead of staying in the bathroom to do her makeup. "Although the lesser-known entrance to the Casino Rocher is at the base of the rock, by the tip. If that *is* where the auction's taking place, it's possible he dropped off the scarab."

"Brie's team is looking for the auction catalog so we can confirm details."

"Dark web?"

"She expects so."

"I'll have to talk to—" The bathroom door opened, and I shifted the conversation sharply. "Benedict with ham, coffee, and some—"

Jenn walked in, wearing the robe like last night. Eyes down but darting up. "Yogurt and fruit?"

I put up a finger and nodded, pretending to finish my conversation. "Tea, yogurt, and fruit. How long?"

"Mais oui, but of course, monsieur." Rav let out a chuckle. "I'll call the order in for you. Mine was twenty minutes, so you can give her that estimate. And don't forget to text me before she leaves."

"Twenty minutes, perfect. Thank you." I hung up and dropped the phone onto the bedside table.

Jenn glanced at the table, then back at me. "Why'd you call on your cell phone? The hotel phone's easier."

"I was too comfy to move." I shrugged. "And it was all the way over on your side of the bed."

She crossed the room, heading for her suitcase. "But you

went to the other bedroom to grab your phone? You didn't bring it with you last night."

Why did I come back to this bed when staying in my room would have been wiser?

"And if you'd left to get it in the middle of the night, I would have woken up." She opened the suitcase with her back turned slightly to me. She pulled out something black and tiny, stuffing it into an oversized pocket of her robe. Panties. Had she worn any under her sleep shorts? Had she soaked through those, too?

My dick twitched again, like the stubborn appendage it was.

"I'm stealthy like that." I folded my arm behind my head and propped against the headboard, letting the sheet slip to my waist. Why was I still in her room? Old habits?

Ego?

Honestly? I wanted to see the hunger in her eyes by the light of day.

Fuck, who was I tempting more?

"Are you walking me over this morning?"

"I am."

"And hovering all day while I work?" She turned so I could see her profile, but she didn't look at me. Was she embarrassed about last night? Or this morning?

"Can't imagine Dante would appreciate that."

"Yeah." She took in a slow breath. "About last night..."

I let my arm drop and sat up straighter. The gun. My dreams were so bad I could have killed her. I shouldn't have been replaying how much I'd wanted her last night. I should have focused on how much of a danger I was. "Again, I'm sorry. I never wanted to scare you."

"Not that." She turned a little more, fidgeting with a black lace bra. "I think you've got Dante wrong. He's a good man. Generous, kind—"

"Handsome and rich?"

Blue eyes snapped to mine, and her mouth gaped in shock.

I was *not* jealous, especially after having her in my lap last night.

"After what I... I said... did..." Her cheeks flamed red, even more obvious because she hadn't put on any makeup yet. She turned back to the suitcase, wet hair falling to hide her cheeks.

Why was I being such an ass? "Fear makes people say and do things they wouldn't normally do. I understand."

"Yeah, I guess you're right." Jenn flung one hand in the air as though dismissing her words. "Fear makes us act... differently."

Guilt twisted in my gut. I was lying to her, pretending I didn't want her when she was *all* I wanted. But she deserved better than what I had to offer, which was nothing more than a lifetime of lies, danger, and a man incapable of a real relationship.

"Why don't I leave so you can get dressed?" I shifted to the side of the bed, keeping the sheets over me.

She hesitated, finally glancing over her shoulder at me. Those blue eyes held a flicker of uncertainty, almost like she wanted to protest.

I forced a reassuring smile. "I should put more clothes on, anyway."

After a moment, she gave a slight nod.

I slid out of the bed, very aware I was only in my underwear. Grabbing my phone, I headed for the door, pausing to look back at her. Committing her tousled hair and makeup-free face to memory. Filing the image next to that of her robe falling away last night, revealing her long leg while I was trying to focus on the job. Her hot sex pressed against me in the wee hours this morning. My hand on her curves when we woke.

She dropped the bra into her open suitcase, turned to face me, and her gaze raked down my torso.

If Jenn didn't have a boyfriend anymore, Scarlett lost her reason to tell me to keep my hands to myself. Jenn was a grown woman. I was a grown man. We could make our own decisions.

She moistened her lips.

Breakfast, the gallery, and the scarab mission be damned. My whole body screamed at me to lunge across the room and grab her. My boxer briefs didn't hide how my dick reacted to her, and I didn't care. *Let her see it.*

"Em..." Her fingers curled around the edge of her robe, her knuckles grazing her chest. "It wasn't fear."

I jolted as my phone buzzed in my hand, yanking my attention to another phone call from Rav. Fucking bad timing. No, it wasn't bad timing. I wasn't thinking straight. Maybe the call was the best timing. "It's work. I need to take this."

Jenn let go of her robe and spun back to her suitcase, the moment vanishing as quickly as it had started.

"I'll let you know when breakfast arrives." Without waiting for a response, I slipped out of her room and closed the door, giving her privacy. Or giving it to myself? I leaned against her door, staring up at the decorative ceiling, poker scenarios running through my brain so I wasn't talking to Rav with a raging hard-on.

What the fuck was wrong with me?

What isn't wrong with you? If you flop a three-of-a-kind,

the odds of making a full house or better by the river go up thirty-four percent.

Letting out a rush of air in frustration, I headed for my room while answering the phone. "What?"

"Will's on the plane. He'll be here in three hours."

That could have been a text. An email. Could have waited until Jenn and I were done. I clenched my back teeth rather than curse at him. "That it?"

"Mm-hmm."

I clicked off without another word. Why was I being an ass to him? Was I angry he'd interrupted us?

Or grateful he'd saved me from myself?

CHAPTER 20

JENN

"Damn," I muttered to myself. A section above the trees in the background glowed green under the ultraviolet light. "How'd I not see that?"

Probably because you were so tired when you worked on that section yesterday.

Not like I'd had any better sleep last night. Four blissful hours in Emmett's arms couldn't fix staying up too late and nearly being shot at three in the morning.

It was only nine, and the De Rosa Gallery was eerily quiet. Emmett had walked me over after breakfast, and the security guard opened the door for me early, before any other staff had arrived. Emmett had lingered, telling me to be careful, like I was a child.

Did I really try to invite him to touch me again this morning?

'It's not fear,' I'd said.

And what did he do? Left to take a call again. He'd never seemed like a workaholic, but the last two days painted a different image of him. Serious, focused, and more interested in his work than me.

Drop it, Jenn.

Two hours, tops, and I could finish the cleaning. Next, check for structural issues with the stretcher and remount the canvas. Then varnishing, drying overnight... I did some quick mental math.

Cutting it close, but doable.

I adjusted my goggles and reached for a thin wooden stick and cotton wad, rolling another fresh swab. *Dip in the solvent. Roll over the section under the UV. Wait while the varnish swelled. Clean it off with another swab.*

This was my favorite part about the job—the repetitive, almost meditative work, watching the painting return to life. I moved through instinct, my mind a jumble of thoughts. More than anything, I kept revisiting my memory of waking up next to Emmett, his arm draped over me, his bare chest rising and falling against my back.

Such a good memory.

I dropped a dirty swab into the disposal jar and examined the painting, finding another tiny spot in the clouds. "Freaking clouds."

"Buongiorno." Dante's voice carried through the closed door, making me jump. He knocked and opened the door. "You're in early this morning. And in the dark again."

"Occupational hazard." I clicked off the light bar as he turned on the overhead. "I wanted to ensure I finished everything on time for the auction."

"Need any help?" He walked around the table, coming close enough to kiss my cheek, as though we were old friends.

I hesitated, torn between my desire to prove myself and accepting his company. "No, thanks. I've got this."

"Bene." He bowed his head slightly. "How did our wager turn out last night?"

I was *not* having a discussion with Dante about Emmett. "I have a lot of work to do."

He tilted his head, as though hoping I'd open up. When I didn't respond, he nodded instead of prying. "Don't hesitate to ask if you need help or wish to chat. I'll be working on the ledgers again today, so I'll be nearby."

"Thanks."

After I had the ultraviolet light back on, he left me in the near dark. The clouds called to me, and I took care of three more spots I'd missed yesterday.

The longer I worked, the more Emmett invaded my thoughts. The memory of our single, stolen kiss fifteen years ago flashed through my mind. I'd waited for a repeat that never came. His taste, a mix of mint and the popcorn we'd had at his house, lingered in my imagination.

Time had undoubtedly distorted those memories, but I held onto them.

How many men had I dated since then? How many sexual experiences had I had? Why did my brain keep circling back to *him*? Not only during my trip to Monaco, but ever since he dumped me. Not that he actually even dumped me. He just stopped talking to me.

And last night?

Again.

Again!

He turned me down, but I couldn't stop thinking about him.

"He cares about me," I grumbled to myself, immediately checking the door to be sure Dante had shut it all the way. *Cares enough to take me to bed for a good night's rest.*

My phone pinged, the cheerful sound mercifully pulling me from my spiraling thoughts. A call from Dr. Ferraro at this hour? I peeled off my gloves, pulled down my mask, and retreated further into the room to avoid disturbing Dante.

"Jenn Thatcher speaking."

"Ahh, Jenn," said Dr. Ferraro, his Italian accent thicker than Dante's. "I hope it's not too early?"

"Not at all." Time had passed quickly. It was already eleven o'clock in Monaco—five a.m. in Michigan, where he lived. "You?"

He chuckled. "Samantha—my wife—thought to visit the Courtauld and speak with an associate about your case."

They flew to London for this? Who did that? "In person?"

"Sì, she did. And I think you'll be glad for it."

"You found something?"

"We did. My wife is sending you an email with the details now." No sooner did he say that than a notification popped up on my phone.

My first thought was to put him on speaker and look at the email. I glanced at the closed door. Would Dante hear me? "I'm not somewhere I can open it right now. What is it?"

"Samantha's contact maintains auction catalogs dating back decades," Dr. Ferraro said. "We found one which included your Constable painting, recording its sale in 1956. We compared the catalog photograph to the one you sent and found a discrepancy with the signature."

My heart skipped a beat. "A discrepancy? What kind of discrepancy?"

"The letters B and L are not the same."

An excited female voice chatted in his background—which must have been his wife. "Tell her how."

"In the original painting, the letters touch, but in the photos you sent, they do not."

"They don't?" I echoed, my mind racing to keep up. I looked at the painting, lying on the worktable, so innocent. "No professional would change a signature."

"Precisely," he said.

A trained conservator or restorer would work around a signature. If it was damaged, they'd often leave the damage in place to maintain the painting's integrity. A signature wasn't like a leaf, a flower, or a hand, which would be corrected.

His wife's voice came across from his end. "Tell her she's dealing with a fake."

His voice grew fainter as he said, "Bella, per favore?"

"Yeah, yeah," she said.

What if the one in the catalog was the fake, and I was working on the original?

"As I was saying," Dr. Ferraro continued, "there were two catalogs which included the painting. The one from 1956 included a photo and a complete provenance. Another, from 1932, had a line drawing of the painting. We can't use that one to confirm, but it was part of the intact chain of provenance."

"Shit," I hissed. "What now?"

"Have you told the owner?"

"Not yet."

"You should find out what they wish to do."

I nodded slowly, unable to rip my eyes away from the painting. "I will. Thanks."

"And my wife would like for you to email her if you have any further questions."

I thanked him again and clicked off.

Emmett had been right. How did he know? And what did this mean for Dante and the gallery?

I pulled up the documents Dr. Ferraro had sent and reviewed the 1956 catalog photo, placing it next to the *Wheatfield* I'd been working on. The signatures definitely didn't match. It was slight, and they were close, but the connection between the B and L was different.

Dante had hired me to work on a fake. But why? It made no sense. He couldn't have known the truth. Unless it was *all* about getting me in bed? Would he go that far? And then simply give up because he claimed Emmett was in love with me?

A strangled laugh burst out of me.

Ridiculous.

Me and Emmett. *So* not in love with me.

I leaned against the worktable.

Dr. Ferraro said to tell the De Rosas about it being a fake. But could I trust Dante? Did he know it was a fake? Had I been wrong about him this whole time?

Face it, Jenn, your judgment when it comes to men is seriously screwed up.

I added a few notes about the conversation to my notebook, stuffed it into my purse, and threw myself back into the cleaning. My thoughts were an even more chaotic mess than before. Muscle memory took over.

What was I going to tell Dante? If this painting was a fake, it couldn't go to auction. But if Dante was involved in something shady and found out I knew the truth, what would he do to me?

Now you're being ridiculous. You've seen too many movies.

Or you've listened to Emmett too much.

Of course, someone *had* broken into my hotel room. Someone *had* gone through my things.

But Emmett was the only one who'd pulled a gun on me.

Once I finished the cleaning, I turned on the lights, remounted the painting on its stretcher, and made some repairs to the frame. Too soon, the varnish was drying, its glossy surface catching the light.

And I was out of excuses to avoid confronting Dante.

I stripped off my protective gear, took a deep breath, and went to his office. My knock was met with a distracted, "Yes?"

Dante looked up as I entered, his tense face giving way to a smile, then back to tense. "Is everything all right?"

"We need to talk," I blurted out before I lost my nerve.

He shifted his posture away from the computer and leaned his elbows on the desk, giving me his full attention. "About?"

"The painting."

He clasped his hands in front of himself, his brows drawing down. "Will it not be ready?"

I hesitated, studying his face. Was it genuine confusion, or was he a talented liar who knew I was about to tell him I'd figured it out?

"You need to see something," I said finally, gesturing for him to follow me into the workshop.

I stopped in front of the painting, where it sat near the edge of the table. "When I started cleaning, I noticed a few things that weren't quite right, so I called an associate and sent him the UV photos you helped me with."

Dante watched me instead of the painting.

I was alone in a back room of a gallery with a man I'd just met—a wealthy one who Emmett warned me was dangerous. Was I risking my safety? *Deep breath.* I opened the email on my phone and placed it beside the drying canvas. "This photo was taken in the '50s, when the painting was sold at auction. If you look closely, you'll see the signature from the auction catalog and the painting I've been working on don't match."

Dante leaned in, hovering over the phone and the painting. "They're close, though?"

Close? Close didn't count in authenticity. Accuracy did.

"This can't be right," he murmured, moving slowly back and forth between my phone and the painting. "Your associate? Who is this? Someone we can trust?"

"His name is Dr. Antonio Ferraro, and he—"

Dante straightened immediately. "Ferraro?"

"Yes, his family—"

"I know his family." He cupped the back of his neck, gaze drifting to the open door to the office. "I need to check something."

He left without another word, and I followed. Through the office, turned into the short hallway, and to the secure storage room. He punched a code into the panel by the door and pushed the door open.

Emmett's voice was as clear as if he'd been standing there, saying, *'Don't go in there with him.'*

But one glance inside captured me. The room was a trove of art and antiquities I had to explore. Glorious marble sculptures lined the walls. Empty frames, paintings in dozens of slots, jewelry boxes, and drawers that hid many treasures.

Emmett had explored the workshop yesterday morning. He would have loved this room even more.

"My father keeps a copy on his yacht." Dante pulled painting after painting out of the storage slots. "When we arrived, he had everything brought here, because it was more secure while the boat was docked."

His fingers danced over some larger pieces, and he resumed pulling out everything of roughly the same size as *Wheatfield*.

"It's not here." He opened a large chest at the back, pulling out masses of fabric and dropping them unceremoniously on the ground. "He wouldn't..."

I scanned the room, searching for anywhere a painting of the right size could be hiding.

Dante finally stopped, hands landing on his hips. He turned to me, his expression grim. "He cleared out a lot of his favorite pieces recently. His yacht is being prepared for his trip to Napoli."

"Maybe the real one is on his yacht?"

"He's not a criminal." Dante's eyes hardened, betraying— what? Doubt? Why would he leap to defend his father against an accusation I hadn't made? "And I'm going to prove it to you."

CHAPTER 21

EMMETT

I leaned against the stone half-wall at the garden's edge, overlooking the Port Hercule yacht club. Normally, I'd admire the display of wealth below me—million-dollar yachts crammed in between multi-million-dollar yachts—but I couldn't rip my focus from the tracker app on my phone. Watching. The little dot representing Jenn had left the gallery, heading for the marina.

"What's she doing?" I muttered, inadvertently using my outside voice again.

"Visiting Massimo's yacht?" Drew's tone was maddeningly reasonable. He barely knew Jenn, so maybe I could excuse it, but he was in work mode. Observe. Orient. Decide. Act.

"Where else would they be going?" I glowered at him, which he ignored.

Drew shrugged, his posture relaxed in a way that only pissed me off more. "Monaco's not very big, but there are a lot of yachts."

"Where is it?" I held my phone so he could see the map. "You were there last night."

Drew barely glanced at the phone. "I can't see her, but the GPS looks like they're heading in the right direction."

I splayed my fingers on the stone in front of me, the rough surface almost enough to anchor me in the present. Was this payback for last night? For this morning? The memory of Jenn in my arms, her lips so close to mine, flashed through my mind. I'd wanted to kiss her so fucking badly. But I couldn't. Wouldn't. No matter how much I—

"What's the story between you two?"

"What?" I snapped. *Get control.* I forced my voice to soften. "Nothing. There's no story."

"I doubt that." Drew's eyebrows rose, his expression skeptical. "For someone who claims to be just friends, you're awfully worked up about who she spends time with."

"It's not about that. Dante's father is a criminal. They're mixed up with Fenix. What if... what if Enzo's on the yacht?"

The name alone sent a chill down my spine, memories of my captivity threatening to surface. I pushed them down, focusing on the present danger.

"I understand your concern, but I don't believe it's the only reason you're glaring at your phone."

I opened my mouth to argue, then thought better of it. I wasn't going to fool Drew. Instead, I changed the subject—to one only slightly less awkward. "Tell me more about the intel on my mother. You said an old colleague remembered her from MI6?"

Drew leaned his hands on the half-wall, not taking his eyes off the marina. "You don't need details about my source, but suffice to say he worked with Evelyn in the late eighties, before she left the service. She went by Evelyn Stone back then."

"Stone?" My mother had been the one to give us our aliases, so it must have been linked. "Her maiden name is McCall. Are you sure it's the right person?"

"He recognized her photo. You didn't ask me to dig deeper, but I can."

"No." We'd eventually talk to her about it. Or get Brie to do the research. "You trust this guy?"

"He's solid. No reason to lie about it."

"I don't understand." The blip on my phone slowed on the other side of the marina. Were they at Massimo's yacht now? "Why would she hide it? Why not tell us the truth?"

"Occupational hazard." Drew shrugged. "When I was in the Agency, I told everyone I was a general government worker. My fiancée at the time figured it out before I told her. Any signs you might have missed with your mother?"

I thought back, memories flooding in. Mum teaching me to pick locks when I was twelve, calling it a *valuable life skill*. Showing me how to read micro-expressions and body language. All those lessons on controlling my emotions, masking my tells. "Somehow, I think we all knew."

"Denial?"

I let out a long sigh, my gaze climbing from my phone. "Scarlett always said Mum was overprotective after everything with Dad."

Drew nodded. "Maybe she gave you the normalcy you needed?"

"Normalcy?" She'd shown my sisters and me how to track people, earn their trust, and get their information. How to hot-wire cars, navigate unfamiliar terrain, and that you always needed an exit strategy. "But with all the secrets we've proven we can keep, why wouldn't she say anything? Why stick to the accountant cover story all these years?"

"Probably started with her thinking you were too young to know. At some point, it would have felt too late to tell the truth."

"The truth…" Not a Reynolds specialty. "What's it like? Being CIA, unable to tell anyone in your life what you really do?"

"Honestly? I didn't have family, and almost all my friends were in the business. My fiancée was the exception, but—" Drew's jaw tightened, and he leaned more onto the half-wall. "—you know what a shitshow that was."

His former fiancée had gotten tangled up in our job in Washington, which led us to Monaco. And shitshow was a good word for all of it.

"That's why we keep Jenn in the dark about Reynolds. And the rest of Scarlett's close friends." We wanted to keep them safe.

But as for my friends? Outside of my co-workers, I didn't have the sort of close circle Scarlett did. When I was a teen, I got into too many fights over other kids taunting me about my father. Rav and Declan had sometimes helped when people targeted Scarlett or Brie, but mostly, I'd been on my own.

"How did I miss it for so long?" My mother had taught me how to avoid the fights and how to defend myself. When I'd asked how she was so good at those things, she'd said it was from movies. "Looking back now, it seems so obvious."

"I've been thinking…" Drew hesitated, finally looking at me. "Your dad worked for CSIS before the Russia incident, right? I suspect there's more to their story than you know."

I stared at him. "How did you know about Dad's CSIS connection?"

Drew frowned, dipping his head, as though surprised—not by the question, but that I'd bothered to ask it. "You think I'd work with your team without doing my homework? We uncovered that tidbit prior to my first contract with Reynolds."

Footsteps approached from behind us. As we turned, Will smiled and extended a hand toward Drew. As they shook hands, Will said, "Nice to meet you."

Drew gave Will a quick once-over. He'd only been with us officially for two weeks, although he'd been a constant fixture with the team since the June contract in Washington, so the two men were familiar with each other. "I'm interested to see what you've brought."

"He'll hate it." Will grinned at me while pulling a sleek watch box from his backpack. His accent had grown steadily thicker since he'd moved to London, and the smile deepened lines around his eyes that made him look like he'd aged ten years. His mother had declined quickly after his father's death, and Will had taken the brunt of it.

I accepted the box and opened it, revealing a stunning timepiece inside. The polished metal gleamed in the sunlight. I shook my head ruefully, thickening the tone of faux disappointment. "The modified Patek you made me is already so perfect. I can't believe you're making me switch."

Will held up his hands. "Not forcing anything. It's just the prototype I had ready. Give me a few weeks, and I can fit the new tech into your usual watch if you prefer."

Drew tsked at us. "More money down the drain."

In truth, I had a sizable watch collection and wouldn't

complain about anything Will provided. But I took a swipe at Drew, all the same. "Don't spies all wear Rolexes for easy bribes?"

He frowned. "Cash is more portable."

"True. I also have a prototype tracker we can attach to a piece of paper money. However, I haven't figured out how to incorporate full comms into something so thin." Will pulled out another small box. "I thought about using something like that for Jenn, but the risk of her misplacing whatever we attached it to was too high. Scarlett and I discussed it—I was originally planning something based on Brie's preferences, but Scarlett overruled everything I suggested."

"Smart move," I said. "Brie's not your typical jewelry wearer."

A tiny smile tugged at the corner of Will's mouth, his voice growing almost wistful. "Yeah, I didn't think Jenn would appreciate a habit-tracker ring or a necklace pendant she could fiddle with incessantly."

The note of fondness in his voice almost had me pushing for more. I'd half expected something romantic to develop between him and my younger sister over the years, but it never had—both regularly dated other people.

I filed the thought away for later and opened the box Will had handed me, revealing a delicate gold bracelet. Nothing too flashy or attention-grabbing, but a motif resembling screws dotted its surface. And it came with a gold screwdriver to ensure it stayed on. "You're kidding me."

"What?" Will asked, sliding his backpack on again.

"This is a Cartier Love bracelet." The iconic design was unmistakable. How could I give this to Jenn?

"Scarlett came up with the idea a few months ago, so I'd

had this prototype almost ready." Will tapped the screwdriver in the box. "It's discreet, and the screw closure means no one takes it off."

It made sense. Neither Jenn nor a security guard—nor a kidnapper—would bother with it because it was too difficult to discard. But still. I was going to give Jenn a Love bracelet?

"Sorry, but it's what I had." Will shrugged.

Fuck me. After everything that happened last night—how clear she'd been about wanting more from me—telling her the truth might have been less risky than giving her something like this.

"I finished both of those on the flight." Will lowered his voice. "The scarab decoy should be done tonight, so long as I can get several uninterrupted hours of work."

Closing the box, I sighed. The bracelet would help keep Jenn safe, so I couldn't argue against it. "Have you checked into the hotel yet?"

"I left my bags with the concierge on my way over. Checking in is my next stop."

Mine should have been to the training facility Jayce was at—a large office space with high ceilings that we'd rented for preparations. But could I leave my vantage point? I was close enough to Jenn I could do something if she was in trouble. Going to the office would leave her exposed.

And I'd sworn to keep her safe.

CHAPTER 22
JENN

I stepped onto the deck of Massimo's yacht, *Lustra II*, trying to understand everything happening around me. The sea breeze whipped my hair across my face as Dante spoke to one of the crew members. Several people busied themselves with cleaning, no doubt preparing for the yacht's departure.

"Grazie," said Dante to the man, who headed off with his cleaning materials. He turned to me. "My father's not here."

"Now what?"

"They're setting sail tomorrow after the auction." Dante ran a hand through his dark hair, frustration evident in his tone. "Perhaps he's at the apartment overseeing the packers."

I chewed my lower lip. Dr. Ferraro was certain the painting I'd been working on was fake, but Dante insisted it was genuine. Was he covering for his father? Or truly in the dark?

Was Emmett right about the De Rosas being dangerous?

"It used to hang in the upper deck lounge." Dante waved me toward a wall of glass, which slid open with a whisper as we approached. "Maybe someone rehung it."

As we walked through the yacht's luxurious interior, I

couldn't shake the prickles skittering up and down my arms. The staff moved about as though everything was normal, but something was off. Unless it was just me, and Emmett's warnings were simply tainting everything I saw.

Or Dante's irritation had me on edge.

At the top of a narrow circular staircase, we entered the lounge. The room was decorated with sleek white leather furniture, a small table for four at the center, and a bar off to the side. The subtle scent of leather and lemon polish permeated the air.

My eyes were immediately drawn to a painting hanging by the bar. I stepped closer to examine it. "Is this—"

"The copy," Dante finished. "At least, that's what I thought it was, but now you tell me."

I pulled out my phone to compare this version of *Wheatfield* to the old auction catalogs. I zoomed in on the signature. It was so obvious, it practically screamed at me. "These are identical, Dante. Even the craquelure is the same."

"It can't be." Dante pinched the bridge of his nose, his lids falling shut. "This has to be the copy."

"Willing it to be true doesn't make it so." *That should have been my motto.* "The one I've been cleaning is the duplicate."

He shook his head and let out a long breath, finally opening his eyes to look at my phone. "There must have been a mix-up."

This explained why the painting had smeared when I tried to clean it using the conservator's notes. He'd written those instructions for the painting staring at me from the wall, not the one I'd finished varnishing this afternoon.

"Perhaps"—Dante's eyes flicked back and forth as he spoke, as though searching for an explanation—"the movers were told they'd be bringing *Wheatfield* onto the yacht, and they were confused. Perhaps they simply brought the wrong one?"

"When did they do that?"

"Last night." He frowned at the painting. "While the one you're cleaning sat in the workshop, out of its frame."

"And you honestly think they accidentally delivered a fully intact painting?" I left my greater fear unsaid—that he'd swapped them intentionally. But if that was the case, why bring me on board and show me the truth?

Fear crawled up my spine.

If Emmett was right, and this was all an act, this yacht was the last place I should be. And accusing Dante was the last thing I should have been doing.

Dante's gaze slid toward the wall of windows beside the bar. "It has to be a mistake. But..."

I wanted to believe him—hoped this might all be a simple misunderstanding. But a nagging doubt persisted.

"The ledgers," he muttered.

Ledgers?

Before I could respond and ask what he meant, movement outside caught my eye. I turned, my heart nearly stopping as a familiar figure passed by the window.

Blond hair. Chiseled features. Strong nose.

Noah.

Scarlett's former fiancé.

Noah—my heart beat too fast in my chest—who died two years ago.

At least, that's what I'd thought. I'd gone to his funeral, after all.

Noah.

Did he have a twin I didn't know about?

Dante saw him, too, the faintest relief washing over his face. "We should speak with Noah."

My throat tightened. Not a twin.

"He's one of my father's associates, helping coordinate items for the auction and my father's departure. He may have some idea of what's going on."

My mind reeled. Noah. Alive. Working with Massimo. The funeral... Scarlett's grief... What was going on?

"I... I'm feeling a bit seasick," I murmured, my voice tight as I tried to steady my breathing. Heat prickled at the back of my neck, and I put a hand against the wall, forcing myself to stay upright.

"We're not moving." Dante's expression shifted to concern as he steadied me. "And the waves are barely—"

"Weak stomach." My pulse thundered in my ears, and I avoided glancing toward the windows again, where Noah might still be visible.

"But of course. I'll speak with him later."

I started to shake my head, but my stomach churned like I was genuinely going to be sick. "No, no. I'll be fine. You talk to Noah and see if he has more information. I'll..."

What? What was I going to do? Go back to the gallery and stare at the fake *Wheatfield*? I had nothing to do until the varnish dried.

Talk to Noah? What would I say?

No, I needed to... to what? Think. I needed to think. "I need some fresh air, that's all. On dry land."

He nodded, his forehead creased in worry. "All right. Sit and have some water at the yacht club. I'll meet you there."

I forced a smile and darted for the stairs, carefully keeping my face away from Noah's direction. I disembarked and hurried along the dock, my head light and legs shaky.

What was going on? The painting, Noah... I needed to talk to someone and make sense of all this.

Scarlett? God, no. What would I say to her?

Maybe Emmett or Rav?

As I reached the yacht club, I spotted Rav, sitting at a small table and reading a newspaper. Suddenly, it clicked. This was why Emmett hadn't insisted on staying with me at the gallery, despite all his talk of danger. Rav wasn't actually reading a paper. He'd been watching me the whole time.

I marched over to his table, fire burning in my gut, replacing the nausea. I hauled out the chair facing him. "We need to talk."

Rav lowered his newspaper. "About?"

"Noah."

No reaction.

"I saw him. Not five minutes ago, on Massimo's yacht."

He didn't express shock or confusion. Just a flicker of irritation in his eyes.

"You knew," I breathed, my legs almost giving out under me. "You knew he was alive?"

Rav grunted, folding his paper and laying it on the table. "We can't talk here."

"But—"

"I warned him." He stood. "Let's go."

"Where?" I asked, my mind whirling with questions. "Warned who?"

Rav pulled out his phone and typed a quick message. "You need to talk to Emmett."

CHAPTER 23

EMMETT

My phone buzzed. I pulled it out to find a message from Rav: *Heading your way with Jenn. She spotted Noah.*

"Shit." I flashed the message to Drew and Will. "So much for keeping her in the dark."

Will grimaced. "That complicates things."

Another text from Rav came through: *Call Scarlett re: how to handle this.*

I frowned at the phone. This was my op, but he was deferring to Scarlett? *He's not deferring, Emmett. He's looking for her best friend's input on explaining the news and cushioning the blow.*

Jenn wasn't a mark or a target. She was a friend. One who might be in danger.

How close had she gotten to Noah? Had they spoken? How many Fenix members were in Monaco in addition to Enzo and Noah?

And how many of them were as interested in Reynolds Recoveries as those two were?

"Drop this off in my room." I handed the bracelet box to

Will as I dialed Scarlett, who answered on the first ring. "Scar? We've got a situation."

After a brief discussion, we decided there was no choice but to tell Jenn a partial truth—that we'd only learned Noah was alive four months ago. It was technically accurate. As I'd learned long ago, the best lies were always rooted in truth.

Once I hung up, I said, "Scarlett's sending over the full auction catalog they found on the dark web. The Constable painting is listed, along with our scarab."

Right on cue, my phone buzzed with the incoming file. I opened it, and Drew and Will did the same on their own devices.

As I scrolled through the list, an item caught my eye—a golden disc from China.

Drew hummed aloud. "You were right about the location. Casino Rocher, Friday night."

"This disc..." I tilted the phone to show them. "Enzo mentioned Massimo bidding any amount to win a golden disc at the auction. What if it's another item on Fenix's shopping list?"

Will said, "Everything they've gone after so far has been bird-related. How does a flat disc tie in?"

Drew's brow furrowed. "If it was spherical, you could make an egg connection. Maybe the disc represents a nest? Or a bird flying toward the sun?"

If Massimo was buying the disc for Fenix, maybe we could go after it instead of the scarab. Sure, our client was paying us to retrieve the Egyptian artifact, but the chance to get one over on Fenix? After everything they'd done to us?

To me?

So tempting...

Movement on the path caught my eye. Jenn marched in our direction, her face a storm cloud. Rav trailed a few paces behind, looking wary.

I cleared my throat, casually tucking my phone away. Will mirrored me, while Drew kept his out, so we didn't look as guilty as we were.

"What the hell is going on?" Jenn demanded when she was fifteen feet away, her blue eyes flashing with anger.

I gestured to Will, keeping my voice calm and even. "Will's joined us for—"

"I know Rav texted you!" She came to an abrupt halt in front of me. "I saw Noah. He's alive!"

Rav was better than that. He should have hidden that he was texting me. As if reading my thoughts, he said, "My priority was getting her away from the marina safely."

"You didn't see him arrive?" I asked Rav.

He shook his head. "I would have let you know if I had."

Jenn huffed out a breath. "Will someone please tell me what's going on? It's obvious this isn't a surprise to any of you."

I held up a hand, trying to project a calm I wasn't sure I felt. Smoothing things over was my superpower—but with Jenn thrown into the mix? "I need you to walk me through everything first. Where exactly was he? What was happening?"

Jenn's lips tightened, and she spoke in a rush, obviously wanting to get to the part where I told her the details. "The *Wheatfield* painting in the gallery is a fake. I told Dante. He took me to Massimo's yacht to see the real one. Noah was on the yacht, and I left the second I saw him."

"He didn't spot you?"

Her mouth opened and closed, and she glanced at the

other men. The flush in her cheeks dimmed. "I don't think so."

"Good." I pulled out my phone and showed her the auction catalog. "Look at this."

She zoomed in on the image of the Constable, her brow furrowed. Diverting her attention was the key to diffusing her anger at this moment.

"The scarab we're after is in there, too," I said. "The De Rosas have been hiding it this whole time."

Jenn's brow furrowed deeper, conflict playing out on her face. She'd been so adamant about defending Dante, but now?

Gently, I said, "The scarab was stolen, Jenn, and now they're selling it."

"This says the painting..." She looked up from my phone, her face hardening again. "Back up and tell me what's going on with Noah."

So much for the diversion.

CHAPTER 24

JENN

EMMETT SIGHED, running his nails over his short beard. His eyes, usually warm and inviting like melted chocolate, held a wariness that made me want to shake him. "We found out in April. He showed up out of the blue while we were overseas."

"And why did no one tell me?" I demanded, anger burning in my gut. "I'm supposed to be Scarlett's best friend."

Rav put a hand on my back and dipped his head. "Nothing that happens here changes how much she cares about you."

He was always so freaking calm and reasonable. I wanted to be mad! But no one else was rising to the occasion.

"Scarlett was in shock," Emmett explained, his voice irritatingly soft. "She was devastated and lost. And you know how she gets when she's upset."

I scoffed, crossing my arms. "I'd say she normally clams up because I think that's what you're going for, but she hasn't acted like anything was wrong. In April, she..." The anger in my stomach settled into a slow roll. "April is when Malcolm showed up. He knows, too, doesn't he? A man she only just met knows that her formerly dead fiancé is actually alive, months before I do?"

Emmett nodded slowly.

"And..." I flung a hand toward Drew. "The newbie? He knew?"

Everyone looked at Emmett, who said nothing more than "Yes."

I shrugged away from Rav's attempt at comfort and took a few steps to the garden's edge, where the wall overlooked the yacht club. The sun glinting across the Mediterranean seemed garish and fake, like my relationship with my apparent best friend. Everything felt wrong, like I'd entered some bizarre alternate reality.

Scarlett went through that without me. I leaned against the short wall, watching small boats motor in and out of the port. *Am I such a terrible friend she couldn't confide in me?*

Emmett came up next to me. He touched my arm, and I sidestepped away from him.

"I was there when Scarlett buried Noah's ashes." The memory of that day, the grief and finality of it all, flashed through my mind. Scarlett *did* get quiet when things went wrong, but I'd thought it was because she'd lost him. "Whose ashes were they?"

"It was just ash. Not a person." Emmett folded his arms and turned to face me, one hip resting against the wall. His words were barely audible over the distant sounds of the marina—the creaking of boats, the clink of rigging, the muffled voices.

"I was by her side every day after he died." Or didn't die? "I don't understand."

"We haven't been able to piece everything together." He

took a deep breath, glancing at his team, who'd given us space, then back at me. "But the truth is, Noah was in a car alone while we were working overseas. He was driving too fast and went off the road into a river. It was a long way down from a high bridge. So when we couldn't find the car, and there was no trace of him, through police or hospitals, we all assumed he was dead."

I shook my head. None of this made sense. "So why concoct the whole story? Why didn't Scarlett tell me what happened? Why bring ashes home and bury them?"

"We'll have to talk to Scarlett about why she made the decisions she did," Emmett said. "Maybe she wanted to pretend there was no chance, rather than spending a lifetime hoping she might see him again someday. And if everyone around her believed the same thing, I think that made it easier for her."

"Easier? She kept all his clothes." How many times had I told her to pack them up, instead of wearing his shirts when she was alone? "Why's he on Massimo's yacht? And why didn't he come home with Scarlett in April?"

She'd brought Malcolm home instead.

Emmett's jaw tightened. "He's working with an organization called the Fenix Group. Thieves who steal antiquities from around the world."

"And Noah..." I looked down at my hands, flexing them against the rough stone. How was any of this true? "You think Dante's involved. That's why you didn't want me going near him."

They should have been questions. But everything was clicking into place now.

At the same time, nothing made any sense in my world.

Emmett pulled out his phone and showed me another auction listing. A small red jewel. "This is the scarab we're here for. We came based on a tip that it was in Massimo's possession. Jean-Philippe wouldn't confess to having it, likely because it's stolen and they're dumping it on the black market."

My stomach churned even more. I'd been spending all this time with Dante and in the gallery. I'd gone out to dinner with him, laughed with him, started to trust him. He'd acted like a friend. "You knew Dante was working with Fenix, didn't you?"

"I suspected." He placed a hand on my back, and I didn't shy away this time. "All I knew was that Massimo had the scarab somewhere. At first, I'd wanted to give him the benefit of the doubt because it's common enough for people to be duped when buying antiquities and art."

"What changed your mind?" I stood still, craving his touch and fearing I'd collapse if I moved.

If Dante was such a horrible person—a liar and a thief— why would he have encouraged me to find out Emmett's true feelings? Could I trust any of it?

Of course, I couldn't.

Emmett had turned me down last night, hadn't he? He rubbed my back, small circles that should have soothed me. "I didn't want you to find out any of this."

I pulled back to look at him, searching his eyes for the truth. "You wanted my best friend to continue lying to me for the rest of my life?"

He didn't shake his head, disagree, or tell me the question was silly. No, he just said, "You should probably talk to her."

I nodded slowly, tears pricking at my eyes. *No crying in*

front of him. Not again. I pulled my phone from my purse, ready to hit Scarlett's number, but Emmett put his hand over mine.

"Use my phone," he said. "It's a secure line."

Secure line? What did that matter? And why was his phone secure?

Emmett hit the speed dial and put the phone to his ear. After a moment, he said, "I've got Jenn here. I told her about Noah's body vanishing in the river, that you were too distraught to talk about searching for the body, and that he's working with the Fenix Group now. She wants to talk to you."

My hands shook as I accepted the phone. I couldn't find my breath, and all I could do was stare at the phone. She'd been lying about this for two years.

Emmett and the team backed away to give me privacy.

Bringing the phone to my ear, I whispered, "Hi."

"I'm so sorry," Scarlett whispered back.

"What am I supposed to say?" My voice trembled, and I swallowed hard. I had to push through this. "Am I supposed to say I'm sorry you didn't think you could tell me the truth? Or I'm sorry I couldn't tell something was going on? Or sorry I—"

"You don't need to apologize for anything," Scarlett said in a rush. "It was all me. It was grief. A whole lot of denial."

"They honestly never found his body? You would have had police scouring every inch of the water for miles."

"Oh, Jenn." She let out a slow breath. "I should have told you."

The sick churning in my stomach and the tears in my eyes faded, replaced by a fire in my belly. "You're right, you should have. And then, when you found out he was alive, you should have told me that, too."

"He's not who we thought he was."

I scoffed, bitter laughter bubbling up. "Heather always had him pegged. She always thought he was a passive-aggressive jerk."

Scarlett gave a quiet chuckle. "Well, she was right."

"So what now?" I dropped my head, exhaustion overwhelming me. "I'm in Monaco, supposed to be working on the job of a lifetime, hired by some rich Italian to clean a painting, and now it turns out it's a fake. And Noah's alive. And they're working together."

And your brother turned me down last night, Scar, but he slept in my bed.

"Well, it's an adventure, isn't it?" Scarlett said, a lightness in her tone.

The absurdity of it all hit me suddenly, and I couldn't help but smile. "I wish you'd trusted me."

"It was never about trust, Jenn." She was quiet for a beat, and I straightened, looking out toward Massimo's yacht.

He was out there. Noah.

And Scarlett was five thousand miles away, not answering my questions.

"Why did you lie about it?" What I really didn't understand, though, was how she could have left him behind. Scarlett was a strong, intelligent woman. Her company found things—that's what they did. Why couldn't she find him?

"Listen..." Her voice turned serious. "I need you to trust me until you come home. When we're in the same room, I'll tell you everything."

What other choice did I have?

I turned toward Emmett. He'd kept the secret, too. All of them had.

"For now," said Scarlett, "do whatever you feel is right. Except, don't go anywhere near Noah. You can't trust him."

My stomach roiled. Did I still trust Scarlett and Emmett? They'd both lied to me about something so big for two years. I'd been defending Scarlett to my father since we first became friends.

And now?

My father was right. Both Scarlett and Emmett were more like their father than either of them thought.

Don't think that way. She'll explain when you get home.

Their father had sold secrets to the Russians. Hiding something—even something like this whole cover-up with Noah's death—wasn't the same thing. But still, Dad had been right about them, at least a bit.

"I'll keep this secret from Heather and Kelley," I said, barely believing my own words. "But when I'm home again—"

"We'll talk, I promise," Scarlett said. "Can you pass the phone to Emmett?"

"Yeah." I held out the phone, and Emmett approached, accepting it.

"I'm sorry," he said softly. "It's a lot to absorb."

I held up a hand, cutting him off. The last thing I wanted was another Reynolds apologizing to me. "She wants to talk to *you* now."

He nodded, stepping away to take the call.

Everything had changed in a few short hours. My best friend's dead fiancé was alive and working with criminals. The painting I'd been working on was a fake. And the man I'd wanted for half my life—

What was I supposed to think about Emmett now?

The sun felt too hot. The breeze too strong. "I'm going back to the hotel. I have more work to do on the painting. It only needs to be reframed tomorrow, but—"

Rav held out a hand to stop me. "Wait until Emmett's done with Scarlett. We'll need to make some decisions."

CHAPTER 25
EMMETT

I PACED AWAY from Jenn and my team toward a bend in the park's walkway. I pressed the phone to my ear. "What's up, Scar?"

"You should have given me some warning," Scarlett said, her voice tighter than usual. "I knew you were going to tell her things, but I wasn't ready to talk to her myself."

I sighed, pinching the bridge of my nose. "You're ready for everything."

"What are we supposed to do now?"

I frowned. This was unlike my sister. She rarely asked for anyone else's opinion. A lot had changed since she met Malcolm. She got along better with our mother, occasionally let people catch a hint of her emotions, and apparently was asking for my advice.

"When I heard Enzo..." I trailed off, swallowing hard against the bile rising in my throat.

A bag flew over my head.

A punch to my face, the taste of metal flooding my mouth.

The boot to my stomach would come next.

I shook off the memory, my fingers instinctively reaching for the poker chip in my pocket. The smooth, worn face grounded me, its texture bringing me back to the park. To Monte Carlo. "I was suspicious enough of Dante inviting Jenn here after their brief meeting in Nice. After I discovered Enzo was in town, I assumed Dante's approach was part of a bigger plan. But I figured Jenn was safe because Enzo wouldn't know her. Unless Fenix were surveilling you at home or Noah was feeding them an awful lot of extra intel."

"But now that Noah's there?"

"They took me to get to you." I withdrew my hand from my pocket, sank onto a bench, and leaned back—acting casual for Jenn's sake—while my mind was a jumble. "Would they take Jenn for the same reason?"

"I understand Malcolm and Rav are worried Noah will come after me, but it doesn't make sense. He didn't try anything in Washington and hasn't reached out since then. Maybe he's found someone else for the job he wanted me for."

Noah had tried to recruit Scarlett to join the Fenix group. She'd obviously said no—kidnapping me hadn't exactly endeared the organization to her. But for some reason, she trusted Noah enough to send us all to Monaco after the scarab.

The scarab.

I frowned, pieces clicking into place like tumblers in a lock. "If Noah's working with Massimo, why would he send us the tip about the scarab?"

Scarlett hummed thoughtfully. "Good question. Noah said there was a division in their ranks. Massimo must not be on Noah's side."

Unease churned in my gut, a familiar sensation that had

become my constant companion since Venice four months ago. I wanted to look back at Jenn but stopped myself. "Is this a power play? Are we pawns in the middle of Noah's game?"

"I wish I knew."

Another massive cruise ship was making its way toward the port, its horn bellowing a deep, resonant note that echoed off the tall buildings crammed into this tiny country.

I'd been to Monte Carlo over a dozen times, but I could still remember the thrill of my first visit. The way my heart raced as I stepped into the famed Monte Carlo Casino, the clink of chips, and the hushed murmur of high-stakes games filling the air.

Today, the glitz and glamor faded to a dull sheen.

Instead of being my favorite city, it was the backdrop for another battle with Fenix.

"I'm not sure if you heard," I said, "but the Ferraros sent Jenn some information about the *Wheatfield* painting. The one Dante brought her to clean is a copy. Dante just showed her the original hanging in Massimo's yacht."

"I don't like this, Em. We should abort the scarab mission."

I ran a hand over the outside of my left pocket, feeling the poker chip. Memories of Venice danced in my head. Sequestered in a small room. Patched up from one of the many beatings. The musty smell of damp stone. "If we have a chance to divide this organization further, we're taking it."

"This isn't about us or revenge," Scarlett argued. "This is about Jenn's safety. I'll call the museum in Cairo and our client so they can deal with the auction. You come home instead."

"You know that doesn't work, Scar. By the time the

authorities act, it's too late. You think any police force will work on this by tomorrow, based on an anonymous tip? Go in and break up an auction at the Casino Rocher? Plus, nobody touches the Casino—not for a tiny stolen jewel."

"So we fly Jenn out of Monaco. If you need to continue this mission, we get her out first."

"We already talked about this," I snapped. Laughter from a passing group of tourists grated on my nerves. "If they're genuinely targeting her, what's the difference between grabbing her here or at home? What are we going to do? Hire private security to tail her for a year? Do the same with Heather and Kelley? Their families? Are we going to add security to every one of our employees?"

"It's better than any plan you're proposing!" Her voice had raised—something she rarely did. This was a sensitive topic for her.

"Then she stays with me. Every second, every day."

"They took *you* in New York," Scarlett said softly.

The words hit me like a physical blow, knocking the air from my lungs. The phantom pain of bruises long healed throbbed beneath my skin. Memories of the headaches. The blurred vision for two months. "That's because we didn't even know they existed before New York, let alone that they might take one of us. But today? Monaco may as well be my home turf, and we're not going in blind. She'll be safe with me."

"Rav has more experience in that role. Ask him to—"

"I don't have time for this. This is my op, my decision." I hung up on her. *Stupid move, Em.* I stared at the phone, waiting for her to call back.

Second-guessing each other was in our nature, but this was different. Since the kidnapping, there were too many pitying looks, too much checking if I was all right with the smallest thing.

I was fine.

I told them that over and over, but no one believed me.

No matter what my reaction to hearing Enzo was, I was fine.

I could protect Jenn. I could keep her safe.

If you say it often enough, maybe you'll believe it.

I ran my fingers over my short beard. If Fenix was crumbling from the inside out, I could help destroy it. We had plans to make—checking out the Casino and searching for the secret tunnels leading to the Exotic Garden—but how was I supposed to do any of that and keep Jenn as close as I'd sworn I would?

Let Jenn in on the big secret?

Hardly.

Text the team the plan? Possibly.

Double-talk and hand signals?

With a long sigh, I stood and launched the photo app on my phone. Returning to the group, I swiped through the hidden folder containing the photo that would confirm how much danger Jenn might be in.

Jenn started, "Rav wouldn't let—"

I lifted my phone to show her a photo the team had snapped of Enzo when they first encountered him in London. "Have you seen this man?"

The way her eyes widened and how she sucked in a quick breath—I had my answer.

I shoved the phone into my pocket to conceal any possible tremble. "You're with me until you leave Monaco."

She blinked rapidly, as though I were speaking a foreign

language. Her blue eyes, usually so warm, flashed with defiance. "That's ridiculous."

"The man's name is Enzo." I shook my head, trying not to show my frustration. "With him, Noah, and the Fenix Group involved, this city's too dangerous."

"So, what, you're going to be my bodyguard now?" she asked, folding her arms.

"We have work to do and don't have time for arguments." Not from Scarlett and not from Jenn.

Jenn spluttered, "I have to finish the painting."

"The fake?" The words came out harsher than I'd intended, but this wasn't the time for apologies.

I could almost see the gears turning in her head. She spun to face the water—angry and hurt, but hopefully she'd listen after she took a few breaths.

"I'm going to the Casino Rocher to speak with someone. The rest of the team has an appointment at the Exotic Garden." I looked pointedly at Drew, who considered for a moment, then nodded.

"We'll be in touch about what we find," Drew said, inclining his head to the north.

Will turned to Rav. "I need to check into the hotel before we go to the Garden."

Drew added, "Jayce is in our room, waiting for us, so we can all go over."

Rav, Drew, and Will headed toward the hotel.

Once they'd left, I touched Jenn's arm, stepping in so close Rav would have given me a side-eye. "I'm sorry for all of this. But I—"

"You have a meeting." Her shoulders fell, and her gaze dropped to my chest.

I tried to hug her, reassuring her that I was doing all of this because I cared, but she backed away.

"We should go." Before moving, I scanned the yacht club. Had Noah seen Jenn? Was he watching us now? "It's a short walk, but we'll cab it."

We walked out of the garden and into a parking lot, where a car picked us up, and we rode in silence. So much had changed in her life in the past hour—what could I possibly say to make any of it better?

Nothing, Emmett. Except maybe a little truth.

As we climbed the edge of the Rocher, all of Monte Carlo was on display from our elevated vantage point.

Jenn stared out the window, taking in the view. The Monte Carlo Casino and our hotel were practically invisible between the relentless tide of high-rises, towering apartment blocks, and steel facades. "Hard to believe I can see the entire country from here."

"Almost forty thousand people in less than one square mile." The mountains framed the edges of the tiny country, giving them little space to expand. So they built into the water, creating land where there had once been sea, each new land-mass covered in buildings that blocked out the vista from those behind.

The car made a turn into the old town, cutting off the view of anything other than the surrounding buildings.

Jenn turned to me. "What's at this casino?"

I raised my voice, making it clear I was speaking to the driver. "Ici, s'il vous plaît."

He nodded at me in the rearview mirror and pulled off to the side. He would have looped the entire Rocher to get to the

Oceanographic Museum, while Jenn and I could cut between buildings to arrive in under a minute.

I paid the driver, and we were on the move again. "Since talking to Jean-Philippe about the scarab failed, we'll try the auction. I'm hoping we can buy it outright, but failing that, buy it from whoever wins. Either way, I have a contact who can give me more information."

Jenn frowned, watching her feet instead of looking at me. "But you said it was stolen. How can they auction it?"

"Welcome to the world of high-end art theft." The irony wasn't lost on me—how often were we stealing those same pieces right back? "Some bidders will be remote and anonymous, but the auction coordinator will get a commission from the sale and as a broker if it comes to that. They might help for the right price."

I didn't tell her we were actually scouting the location. If our first two plans didn't work, Jayce would need to sneak in and steal the scarab. The secret tunnel out of the Casino would be her best bet to escape unseen.

Jenn was quiet momentarily, then said softly, "I can't believe Noah's involved in all this."

I glanced at her, noting how her back was hunched, telling me more about her feelings than the sad note in her voice. It was a far cry from her initial anger after seeing Noah. "I'm sorry, Jenn. I know you two were close."

She shook her head, her hair dancing as a light breeze caught it. "I thought I knew him. And now Dante... What am I supposed to think anymore?"

"About Dante?"

Jenn sighed. "I want to believe he's innocent and didn't

know about the fake painting. But why bring me here to clean it?"

Dante might have been as innocent as she wanted to believe. More likely, Noah was behind all of it, including the break-in at her hotel room. But why?

"Men like him are used to getting what they want." *Careful. Don't hurt her more.* "They can be very charming and persuasive when it suits them."

"You think he's using me?"

If I said yes, that might have broken her. "I'm just saying keep your eyes open."

She was quiet again as we walked. We switched to single file to avoid being bowled over by a tour group, all wearing their cruise ship stickers. Once we'd passed them, she said, "I feel so stupid, Emmett. Like I've been played this whole time."

I stopped us at a crosswalk. The urge to pull her close, to shield her from the world, was almost overwhelming. "You're not stupid. These guys are professionals at manipulation. You couldn't have known."

Jenn's eyes finally met mine again. The sun glinted in their blue depths, and I was immediately dragged back to last night, when we stood like this in the sitting room. Her in her robe, wet hair and all. She was in pain, and all I was thinking about again was kissing her. "How do I know who to trust now?"

Kissing her would be a bad idea. Right? "Trust your instincts. And remember—I've got your back, no matter what."

She gave me a small smile, a ghost of her usual radiance. "Thanks."

We waited for a pair of scooters to pass and crossed toward the Oceanographic Museum. I needed to focus on the mission. But I couldn't help wondering what it would be like to have her look at me the way she had last night in the sitting room.

Before I pulled the gun on her.

What would it be like to have her trust me completely? She'd seemed ready to forgive me this morning in her hotel room. I pushed the thoughts away, locking them in a box in the back of my mind. There was no room for distractions or complications.

We had a job to do, and it didn't involve Jenn's lips on mine.

CHAPTER 26
JENN

TRUST MY INSTINCTS? Had Emmett seriously said that to me? After last night? After this morning?

God, after believing Dante?

My instincts had only been right about *Wheatfield*—the fake.

My heart was still in my throat since the phone call with Scarlett, but I couldn't help staring at the imposing Baroque facade of Monaco's Oceanographic Museum. It loomed over us, almost blocking out the sun. I should have been sightseeing inside instead of skulking around with Emmett.

He guided me toward an outdoor elevator near the end of the building, his hand hovering near the small of my back. "This goes to the parking garage below, and it's also the entrance to the Casino Rocher."

As we stepped inside, a couple tried to follow us.

Emmett blocked their path.

"Sorry, private tour," he said with a disarming smile, so smooth the couple smiled back instead of protesting. Once the doors closed, he punched in a combination of buttons. "Code for the casino level."

"Why so secretive?"

Emmett's lips quirked into a half-smile. "It's an underground facility, and not just physically. They operate outside the law, but close to it."

My stomach twisted. Were we criminals for going inside?

"Security's tight. We'll surrender our phones—they'll be stored in Faraday bags. Empty pockets, purse search for you, metal detectors for both of us."

"Seems excessive."

Emmett shrugged. "It's partially required for some of the clientele but mainly a marketing ploy. Like the Monte Carlo Casino, they play up the exclusivity. Dress code in the evenings, top-shelf alcohol, the works. It's not actually a secret, though."

The elevator stopped, doors opening into...

The only casinos I'd visited were the big one here and a few in Vegas. This room reminded me more of a private screening room at an airport than a casino lobby. I whispered, "This isn't what I expected. There are no flashing lights."

"Security first." Emmett approached a burly man in a black suit, standing behind a long metal table. "No photos allowed inside. That's why we go through the checkpoint before seeing anything."

The guard placed two small trays on the table and said in a thick French accent, "Place all items in here, then proceed through the metal detector."

Emmett emptied his pockets: watch, phone, wallet, and a white poker chip with a hole drilled through it. No gun. Did he leave it behind because of where we were going? Or did he only keep it on him at night? The security guard placed Emmett's phone in a pouch, handing him a small chip in return. That must have been to track where Emmett's phone was stored, since the security guy placed it into a slot behind himself.

As Emmett went through the detector, I surrendered my phone and let them search my purse. Another guard waved a wand over Emmett, pausing at his belt before waving him through.

Once we'd collected our belongings, I couldn't help but ask, "What's with the poker chip?"

Emmett's hand closed around it possessively before tucking it into his left pocket. "Good luck charm."

"Why the hole?"

"It's from a game earlier this year. The hole prevents me from using it again."

Did I see it right? Five thousand written on its face? "You didn't cash it in?"

A muscle ticked in Emmett's jaw. "Let's head inside," he said, steering me down a short hallway.

The passage opened into a breathtaking cavern. Natural stalactites and stalagmites rimmed the edges, while the main area gleamed with polished floors and sparkling chandeliers. Gaming tables, elegant bars, and patrons in designer clothes filled the space. Modern classical music drifted through the air, mingling with the soft clink of chips and the murmur of voices.

It was magical.

So magical, I could almost forget the insanity my life had become.

Almost.

Emmett nodded to a few dealers as we passed, but kept us moving. The ceilings rivaled the Monte Carlo Casino in height, but the atmosphere seemed more intimate, more exclusive. It didn't smell like wet earth or stone, as I would have expected, but something richer. Like some combination of Emmett's cologne and power. Wealth.

"Who are we meeting?" I asked, trying to keep my voice steady despite the growing knot in my stomach.

Emmett slowed near a blackjack table. "You know how to play?"

I glanced at the layout. "Face cards are ten, aces one or eleven, numbered cards their value. Beat the dealer to twenty-one without going over."

Emmett withdrew his wallet, counting out a thousand euros in hundred-euro notes. "Table minimum is ten, maximum a thousand."

The dealer exchanged his money for chips. The soft clatter as they hit the felt was oddly comforting. But I wouldn't spend his money. "I have my own cash."

"Business expense," Emmett said without skipping a beat. "I need you here, but I also need to have a private conversation with someone."

The words echoed Dante's earlier excuse for taking me to dinner, setting off alarm bells in my head. Business expense. As though no one could simply enjoy my company.

Emmett reviewed a few more rules. "Bet before the cards are dealt. Dealer gets one up, one down. Use hand signals—flat hand to stay, tap for another card—"

"Why hand signals?"

Emmett's eyes flicked to a light fixture. "Cameras everywhere. They don't record sound, but they track every move. If you like your cards and want to increase your bet, you can double down by matching your original wager."

I watched the other players while Emmett detailed strategy, payouts, splits, and surrenders.

Surrender.

That should've been my word of the day. No more forged paintings, no more dead men rising from the grave, no more cloak and dagger.

"How long will you be?" I asked, trying to sound as neutral as he did.

"An hour or two." Emmett flagged down a passing drink server. "Don't bet too high, or you'll burn through the chips. Just have fun and stay put."

I frowned. "I thought you said I had to stay with you for the rest of my trip?"

Emmett's expression tightened. "You're safer here than almost anywhere in Monaco."

"And you're genuinely that worried about my safety?"

Scarlett's warnings about Noah swirled around my mind. What had really happened when they found out he was alive? What did she mean when she said he wasn't who we thought?

Emmett's hand ghosted over my arm. "In general, yes. Scarlett's got me paranoid. Our primary concern is that Noah and his team are also after the scarab. We need to get it first."

"What if they win the auction?"

Emmett's smirk was pure ego. "No one gets the better of me."

There was the Emmett I knew. Where had he been hiding?

He leaned close, his lips brushing my cheek as he whispered, "One more thing. Your name is Krista Stone, and you're my wife. Got it?"

I pulled back. "Wife?"

He moved in again. "And I'm Reginald Stone."

Stone. The alias he used with the De Rosas. "Reginald?"

"And Krista. With a K."

His cologne enveloped me, dark and dangerous. He'd warned me about Dante, but here he was, asking me to play pretend. Why all the deception? Why the games?

"I like to stay anonymous in places like this, so that's how anyone would know me here." He gave me a peck on the cheek, sending heat blooming through my chest.

My mind flashed to the early hours of this morning, when he'd held me through my terror. When I'd almost believed he wanted me the way I wanted him. Before I learned the truth about *Wheatfield*. Before Noah. Before realizing my best friend and her family had lied to me for years.

"Have fun, honey." Emmett winked at me, sending a fresh wave of heat through my body. He paid the drink server with another hundred, told her to take care of me, and then he was gone, sauntering away with his infuriating confidence.

He disappeared into the crowd, and I tried summoning anger over his betrayal. Instead, all I saw was the swagger that had always drawn me to him.

With a sigh, I sat and placed my first bet. The hands flew by in a blur as I lost myself in the opulent surroundings, barely paying attention to the cards. Emmett's strategy lecture went out the window, and I lost hand after hand.

I made small talk with a German couple next to me, who were celebrating their thirtieth anniversary. They'd been married as long as I'd been alive. Five kids. Twelve grandkids.

And what did I have?

A string of broken hearts. A cheating ex.

I placed another bet, thinking of the gorgeous Italian who should've been a fun distraction—until I learned he was likely a criminal and working with a man I'd thought was dead.

The worst part? I'd liked Noah. I'd thought he was good for Scarlett.

How had my judgment in men gotten this bad? How had it gotten even worse since leaving Simon, the cheating asshole?

I skipped a hand, lost in thought.

A new player joined our table. Middle-aged and soft around the middle, but impeccably dressed in what had to be a bespoke suit. His eyes raked over me like I was on the menu. "Just decorating the table, beautiful?"

Seriously? I was still in the work clothes I'd worn to the gallery—nothing spectacular, and certainly not an invitation.

"Waiting for my husband," I said coolly.

He leaned on the table. "How long's he going to be?"

I was supposed to wait here, but suddenly, I wanted to be anywhere else. I stared at my chip stack. If I lost it all, I'd have an excuse to find Emmett. He'd probably lecture me about staying put, but at least I'd be away from Mr. Bespoke's leering.

I glanced around. No sign of Emmett.

"This is my last hand," I announced, shoving all my chips forward. *Business expense this, Emmett.*

The dealer slid me a jack. Ten to her nine. As she delivered cards to the other players, I considered my face card. Emmett had once told me the jack was originally called the knave. The trickster. Dishonest. Untrustworthy.

Was that Emmett?

My next card was a seven. I was supposed to stand on seventeen.

Standing was the safe play.

But hadn't I come to Monaco for an adventure? To break free?

Screw it. I could make one decision for myself.

Even if it was colossally stupid.

If I won... I looked out at the glittering casino. At the chandeliers, the flashing lights, the sounds of triumph and despair. Emmett, handsome in his pale gray suit, acting like he was born for this world, was nowhere to be seen.

If I won, I was taking control.

I'd order room service and make my move tonight, long before bedtime. Eliminate all his excuses.

And if I lost? Well, I'd just be continuing my current streak, wouldn't I?

The dealer's attention turned to me. I tapped the table.

She hesitated. "You have seventeen, madame. Normally, you want to stay on seventeen."

I muttered, "I'm tired of staying when I'm told to."

"Anything above four will bust." She held my gaze a beat longer.

I tapped again.

And wouldn't you know it?

She dealt me a fucking five.

CHAPTER 27

EMMETT

THE CASINO ROCHER felt different this afternoon. Typically, it was a place I visited for fun, but it was all business today. I rarely had a problem mixing work and pleasure, but it usually meant having a beautiful woman on my arm. If only Jenn were that woman, and not someone I was looking out for.

Could Noah have been behind the break-in?

Maybe he'd spotted Jenn in town, assumed she was working with Reynolds Recoveries, and planned on gathering intel. But he wouldn't make a rookie mistake like moving any of her items, let alone replacing the housekeeping door hanger in the wrong direction. Noah was damn good at his job and wouldn't slip up like that.

I scanned the room, taking in the layout. As fate would have it, the natural cavern formation mimicked the Monte Carlo Casino—some said the Casino had been designed based on the cavern, which predated the Casino by millennia. Three huge central rooms with several offshoots. One large room off the second for a small restaurant, another for special events, and yet another offshoot from the third main room that led into the storage areas. Any item already delivered for the auction would be in secure storage.

I ducked into the men's room for privacy. The restroom was like the rest of the casino, built into the stone, with marble and porcelain fixtures gleaming under soft lighting. Two men stood at urinals, and another washed his hands. I slipped into a stall, the cool metal door closing behind me with a soft snap. I retrieved the hidden earpiece from my wallet and popped it in.

After following Will's instructions to connect it to my new watch, I heard his voice crackle through.

"I have—from Emmett. To—me?"

The watch connection worked, but the signal was shit. I flushed the toilet to avoid suspicion and left to wash my hands.

Will's voice came through again. "I don't—signal?"

I lathered up and extended my hands under the water. "Water's a bit warm, isn't it?" I said, loud enough for the man next to me to hear, but more importantly, to find out if Will could hear me.

The man grunted in agreement, but said nothing.

When no response came from the team, I strolled out of the men's room and whispered, "Can you hear me?"

Will replied, "—but the—not good."

No kidding, the signal wasn't good. "I'm turning off my mic," I said slowly, letting each word hang in the air. "Will can do some work on the signal."

Hopefully, enough of the message got through, and they could piece it together. I wouldn't focus on communicating with the team. Having the earpiece in was all about Will fine-tuning the equipment from his place in the cavern. I'd listen in on the team's conversation, but they didn't need me narrating my progress.

The rest of the team was exploring the caverns beneath the Exotic Garden, searching for the magic path that would deliver Jayce to the Casino Rocher. She was a talented thief and sneak, but there was no way she'd bypass security at the main door or the water door. The latter was lower security, but still had metal detectors. And they didn't allow just anyone to use that door.

But if they found the secret path from the Garden to the Casino?

That she could navigate, then sneak through the Casino during its busiest hours.

My goal inside the Casino was twofold. One, I'd see if the manager would sell the scarab before the auction. A long shot, but possible. The starting bid listed in the catalog was two million euros, which gave me plenty of wiggle room to get up to four million, the purchase limit my team had set.

And two, I was there so the team could ping the GPS in my watch and use me as a target in their exploration. Hopefully, the GPS signal was better than the comms.

The game room at the back housed the higher limit tables, and another small offshoot from the back led to the private gaming salon for the true high rollers. It wasn't likely full at this hour, but sometimes people went in early.

I slowed to observe a poker hand starting at a table near the back. Not Ultimate. Traditional.

My breath caught in my throat, memories of the last game I played flooding back. My knees were weak, and I shoved my hand into my pocket to grip the old poker chip. The smooth surface grounded me, a lifeline to reality.

Deep breaths, Emmett.

The kidnapping. It was in the past.

Deep breath. There's no bag over your head.

Someday, I'd sit at a table again. Instead, I stood still for several more minutes, studying the players as they went through hand after hand.

A woman in a V-neck sweaterdress dominated the table. At the end of the third hand, she strung along the last man standing, who was talking himself into a frenzy. He flattered her, she smiled politely, he insisted she was bluffing, and she returned to a neutral expression.

A husky female voice with a lyrical French accent filled my ear. "Does she have him beat or no?"

I didn't turn around. The woman speaking to me was the one I'd been looking for. "I've only watched a few hands so far, but if I were him, I'd be all in. I don't think she's got anything."

The woman came to my side and threaded her arm around mine. "She's a former model from Greece who started coming here three years ago. She usually sticks to the high-value tables. Her practiced disinterest fools a lot of men."

I nodded, keeping my eye on the model's opponent, who continued to waffle on whether to fold. "I imagine her cleavage has a lot to do with it, too."

The woman next to me hummed in agreement. "Swimsuit model."

The man at the table finally folded, and his opponent collected her winnings without revealing her cards. Still agitated, he said, "You've got to show me what you had."

The winner simply shook her head. "What I have is your money."

I leaned in to kiss the woman on my arm on the cheek. "A pleasure to see you again, Martine."

"It's been too long, Emmett."

I raised an eyebrow at her.

Martine patted my arm. "Fine, fine. It's been too long, Reginald."

She was a stunning woman in her mid-60s who'd been working at the Casino Rocher for as long as I'd been coming. My mother had originally put the two of us in touch.

I'd thought they were simply old friends. But now? Was Martine one of Evelyn's sources from her MI6 days? Did Martine know her as Evelyn Stone? Was she secretly smiling every time she heard me called Reginald Stone?

This knowledge about my mother changed things. So many things, it was hard to list them all without stepping through my entire life.

I said, "I understand you're hosting an auction tomorrow."

Martine used my arm to turn me away from the poker table, where the Greek model and her opponent switched seats, so they sat beside each other. Perhaps she was planning on using the proximity to win more at the table or to win something in the bedroom this evening.

Martine said, "Have you seen the catalog?"

A server approached us with two glasses of champagne on a tray. Martine's standard. Both of us accepted the glasses but remained arm in arm.

"I have. But at least one piece in the auction is stolen, and we were in Monaco looking for it. If someone had told us you had it—"

Martine said, "You know I don't deal in stolen goods."

We both knew she would. She'd been the Casino's manager for years, walking the narrow line between black and gray market on the regular. It was the perfect position to gather secrets from the ultra-wealthy, wasn't it? Would she also have been MI6? French intelligence? Just a source?

"Sometimes provenance research is challenging," I said. "No one would accuse you of doing anything like that intentionally. However, if I can provide evidence, perhaps you'd consider releasing this particular piece early? Immediate purchase instead of sending it to the auction block?"

Martine took a sip from her glass. She surveyed the crowd as she always did. Watching? Waiting? "If I did that and word got out, what would my clientele say? Why, I'd be little more than a consignment shop and not an auction house."

I chuckled and took a drink of my own. "You're the manager of one of the best casinos in the world. You're not Sotheby's or Christie's."

Martine stopped us at a roulette table. The dealer spun the ball as the wheel turned, its rhythmic click pairing with the players chanting under their breath.

I suppressed a head shake. *The house always wins.* That's why I preferred poker. It wasn't about the house. It was about the players.

"The Egyptian authorities have been searching for it for some time."

Martine gave me a long glance and fluttered her eyelashes. "Oh, Reginald, darling," she drawled. "Don't even pretend you think the police will do anything about my auction."

I kissed her cheek again. "I wouldn't dream of it. But I would suggest some particularly enterprising young Egyptians might take it upon themselves to retrieve it."

"Or some particularly enterprising Canadians?"

"How about a trade? Is there anything I can do for you that might change your mind?"

The roulette ball landed on red twenty-three, and two men jumped up from beside the table, arms in the air—a five-hundred-euro win on a straight-up bet.

Had I given too much money to Jenn? How much of it had she spent? How much of it had she lost? Jenn and Scarlett often played cards with their other two best friends—their game was poker or Euchre, only for dimes, and Scarlett always lost.

Such a strange relationship she had with those women. Which was the real Scarlett? Heist crew mastermind who strategized high-stakes thefts around the world or the woman who couldn't bluff her way past her best friends?

Or was she somewhere in between?

Martine urged me along, each of us sipping our champagne. The dealers didn't acknowledge us, but everyone saw her.

More than that, it was clear they all saw me with her.

She said, "This is an appealing offer—a trade of favors. But I cannot. The auctions are a gateway to more and bigger business."

This would make things difficult. I hadn't expected Martine to agree to any of it, so talking to her had been a calculated risk. She now knew the Reynolds team might attempt to take something, and when the scarab turned up missing, she'd know it was us. She'd be more cautious and put more security on the inventory. If we stole it during the auction, that would be a problem for her. And as one of

Evelyn's contacts, what was bad for Martine was bad for Reynolds.

"And what if this item went missing, but no one realized it?"

"Someone always figures it out." Martine frowned playfully. "No matter how good your replica is."

How did she know we had a replica? *Because she's your mother's friend.* After imaging the scarab in Washington this past June, Will had constructed a perfect copy, right down to the gold base and the worn hieroglyphs. Short of running chemical analysis, no one would figure it out.

Although whoever created the fake Constable painting no doubt thought the same, and our contacts still identified it.

"What if..." I lifted my champagne flute to disguise my lips moving. "What if we do a job for you?"

A sly smile slid up Martine's face. She leaned toward my ear, using her hair to conceal her words. "Why don't I call your mother, and we can sort out the details?"

CHAPTER 28

JENN

THE GERMAN WOMAN'S sympathetic gaze was like salt in the wound of my epic loss. I forced what smile I could, trying to mask the sting of defeat and the growing unease in my stomach. So much for putting my love life in the hands of fate.

Fate had just given me a great big middle finger.

Mr. Bespoke pulled out the chair between us and patted it. "Why don't you come over here and sit with me? Maybe I can help you turn your luck around." His voice oozed slimy charm, and his predatory glare made my skin crawl.

I stood. Grabbing the drink I'd been nursing since Emmett abandoned me, I tried to keep my movements casual, my smile polite but dismissive. "I have to find my husband."

How convincing was a fake marriage without a ring? Not very, but it was enough to shake off Mr. Bespoke's unwanted attention.

I wandered between gaming tables, staying close to the blackjack area in case Emmett appeared. The glamor and excitement that had initially dazzled me now felt oppressive, each laugh and clink of a glass reminding me how out of place

I was. After watching several more hands of blackjack at another table, then drifting over to observe a few rounds of baccarat, I drained my glass. The alcohol did little to settle my nerves.

Emmett had said he'd be an hour or two, and it had already been one. My fingers itched to check my phone, to lose myself in the numbing scroll of social media, but it was still locked up with security. Going back through the checkpoint wasn't an option—knowing my luck, Emmett would come looking for me the moment I left.

"Excuse me." I caught the attention of a passing server, a young woman with a pretty smile and a tray laden with colorful cocktails. "Can you tell me where the ladies' room is?"

She nodded, gesturing toward the second large room. "Past the door to the restaurant, second turn on the right."

I thanked her and headed in that direction, dodging between casino patrons.

How many were tourists like me, and how many were locals? Surely the people of Monaco didn't spend all their time here, despite the surprising number of occupied tables. It wasn't as packed as the Monte Carlo Casino had been the night Dante and Massimo took me to dinner at the Rose Salon, but it was close. Maybe it was more popular in the evening?

I slowed as I passed the restaurant, peeking inside. The ceiling was lower, with fewer natural variations in the stone than in the main rooms. Had they intentionally done that for food safety?

And where was the kitchen? How did they vent heat and exhaust? How much effort went into bringing supplies down here?

Did everything come through the elevator Emmett had brought me through earlier, or were there other access points I hadn't seen?

After passing the restaurant, I turned down the hallway toward the ladies' room. Just past the door, an enormous fresco adorned the wall. Reminiscent of Botticelli's *The Birth of Venus,* it featured a naked woman, her breasts and pelvis covered by her hands and hair, with laurel leaves and cherubs in the background. Odd place for such a stunning piece of art.

Drawn closer, I inspected the fresco. Chips and cracks littered the surface, but the colors remained vibrant, as though someone had recently cleaned it. Strangely, an ornate frame surrounded it, designed with leaves that mimicked the laurels in the fresco.

Except...

Laurel leaves were lanceolate—like the head of a lance, with a rounded bottom tapering to the top. One foot above my eye level, a series of four leaves stood out as linear, thin, and straight. I reached out to trace the intricate design. I never could keep my hands off a beautiful frame.

The leaves—olive?—were rough and cool to the touch, as though crafted from the stone of the Casino's cavern. The laurel leaves were warm, like wood. I pressed harder against the wooden frame, slipping my fingers into the grooves, and closed my eyes as I traced the patterns with my fingertips. I breathed deeply. My nerves began calming with the soothing movement.

But as my fingertips slid over the olive leaves, the stone gave way under my touch. A section sank into the wall. My eyes shot open. The wall in front of me shifted, grinding stone against stone as it slowly opened.

Another enormous cavern loomed behind it. What the—

"Qu'est-ce que tu fais ici?" A suited man seated behind a desk leaped to his feet.

Before I could respond, another man materialized, a gun pointed directly at me.

Shit, shit!

I threw my hands up.

"I'm sorry! I was looking at the fresco." I stumbled backward, my mind reeling. Twice in less than twenty-four hours, I'd stared down the barrel of a gun.

This was the last time I ever came to Monaco.

The armed man lunged forward, his grip crushing my upper arm. He spun me, shoving me back the way I'd come, pressing the gun against my spine. A stream of French curses filled the air, the words harsh and guttural.

"It was an accident!" I pleaded, my voice high-pitched and frantic.

We were heading back into the Casino. *You'll be safe in there. Someone will fix this.*

His only response was to squeeze my arm and dig the gun deeper into my back. "Move."

My shoe caught, and I went down hard, pain shooting through my knees. The impact knocked the breath from my lungs, and for a moment, all I could hear was the pounding of my own heart. Before I caught my breath, he yanked me back to my feet, forcing me forward once more.

"I can follow the hallway on my own," I gasped, desperate to put some distance between us. "I promise I won't—"

"Save it for the boss," he snarled.

Tears blurred my vision, the glittering lights becoming a kaleidoscope of color. Could this trip possibly get any worse?

Not only did no one come to my rescue, but no one seemed to care that a man was holding a gun to my back in the middle of a crowded casino.

I swiped at my eyes, trying to regain my composure. *You were trespassing, and he's a security guard, that's all. You'll be fine.* But didn't security guards normally just tell you to turn around?

"Stairs. To your right."

I hadn't even noticed them, carved so seamlessly into the cavern wall they were nearly invisible. With each step, dread settled deeper in my stomach. Who was the boss? What was waiting for me?

And what would Emmett say when he couldn't find me?

This was all a colossal misunderstanding. I'd simply taken a wrong turn. Surely someone—hopefully his boss—would listen to reason.

But wait. How strict were the police in Monaco? Would I go to jail for trespassing?

No. Emmett said this place operated outside the law, so they wouldn't call the police.

Oh shit.

At the top of the stairs, my captor nudged me through a door. The room was elegantly furnished with plush velvet chairs and gleaming mahogany tables that wouldn't have looked out of place in the Prince's Palace. Crystal sconces cast a warm glow across smooth stone walls. The whole space radiated old-world luxury, a stark contrast to the rough tunnels below. A man and a woman stood at a bank of tall windows overlooking the casino floor below, their backs to me.

"Martine," the man behind me announced, "this one came through the back entrance."

The pair turned, and my heart stopped.

The man at the window was Emmett.

His face was a mask, giving nothing away. He leaned toward the woman—short graying hair, with sharp eyes that cut right through me—and whispered something in her ear.

The woman waved a dismissive hand at the man still holding the gun to my back. "Go back to your post. I'll handle this."

As the armed man retreated, Emmett's eyes met mine, and for a moment, I saw a flicker of something—relief? Concern? Irritation? Then, a soft smile. "Martine, I don't think you've met my wife, Krista."

CHAPTER 29

EMMETT

Martine gave me a knowing smile. "Wife? Now that sounds like a story I would love to hear."

What was I supposed to do now? Martine not only knew who I genuinely was but also knew my mother. The wife story wouldn't fly. But if I dropped it, Jenn would get suspicious. She was the one I truly had to hide things from, and having her in Martine's office was not part of my plan.

Why did I bring out the Krista cover in the first place?

Because you're so accustomed to lying to people that you can't control yourself?

I crossed the distance to Jenn. Fortunately, she slipped in next to me so I could wrap an arm around her waist. Whether it was because she was smart or scared didn't matter. She went along with it.

"The poor thing hates it when I sneak off to do business."

Martine idly fiddled with one of her gold bracelets. "And yet she was the one sneaking around my casino?"

"Sorry." Jenn looked up at me, as though begging for help.

No matter how many times I tried to convince myself

there could be something between us, my job would always prevent it. Not just my past. Not just my father. "Did you get lost, honey bear?"

Jenn nodded vigorously. "I was looking for the ladies' room. Someone told me it was right beside the restaurant, but the cave walls... there was this painting. There were all these little nooks and crannies everywhere, and the lights, and..." She took in a shuddering breath.

Martine came closer, chin and brows drawn down as though attempting to put her prey at ease. "The architecture can be quite bewildering your first time here."

Jenn tensed. She was even more scared than after the break-in or after finding out about Noah. Too many things were piling on top of each other, pressing her soul down.

Will's voice came over my earpiece. "Little longer. Almost —location."

I kissed Jenn's temple and let go of her, holding my hand out to Martine. "A pleasure, as always."

She held her hand out, expecting me to kiss it, which I did. "I'll be in touch, Reginald."

With my mother, she meant.

Martine withdrew her hand and held both of hers out for Jenn to take them. Martine blinked slowly as she wrapped her hands around Jenn's, the faux smile not leaving her face, "You should track down a wedding ring, my dear."

Jenn snapped her hands back, staring at the left one. "I know. I lost it—"

I finished for her, "I suspect it went down the shower drain last night. We'll do one more pass of the hotel suite, and if we don't find it, I'm afraid I'll be paying for a new one."

Martine strolled back to her wall of windows and waved a

hand over her shoulder to dismiss us. "Make sure he buys you a bigger one, darling."

She *knew* we weren't married. She *knew* Jenn wasn't a particularly convincing liar. So she *must* have known Jenn wasn't part of the game. But Martine had kept up the ruse, for my benefit.

Which told me Martine was going to help us.

I took Jenn by the hand and escorted her out of the office. Her steps were tentative, so I held her as we walked down the stairs—partially to keep her moving, partially in case she tripped and I had to catch her. "You were supposed to stay at the blackjack table."

"You didn't say you were meeting with the manager."

"She's the auction coordinator."

"I've met auction coordinators before." As we reached the bottom step, she was still shaking. "They're not usually scary women who watch out of an underground bank of windows like they're a cartoon supervillain with armed guards and secret passageways inside a—"

I stopped, spinning her to face me. "Secret passageways?"

Jenn raised her hand, pointing toward the ladies' room. "It's over—"

I seized her wrist, yanking it behind me, attempting to make it appear like I was pulling her into a quick embrace. "Don't."

"Don't what?" She tried to pull away, but I held her tight.

Hopefully, I'd moved fast enough to disguise her pointing at the hidden tunnel. I leaned closer, both to whisper and so she wouldn't see me turn my earpiece microphone back on. "Do you forget what just happened? A man was guarding a secret door you stumbled through. You don't point it out to everyone else."

"Two men."

Will, I hope you heard that part. "Two armed men?"

"Yeah." She stopped resisting, and her body went soft against me. This wasn't fair to either of us. The cover was all wrong, no matter how right it felt. "There was a section of a fresco on the wall—it stood out. I pressed it, and the wall swung open. One guard was sitting behind a desk, and the other one jumped me."

If Jayce was going to sneak in that way, we'd have to do something about those guards.

Will said over the comms, "—her by the—"

What was that supposed to mean? Her by the what?

Think, man.

Will and the team were searching for a way through the tunnels between the Garden and the Rock. What were the tunnels like besides the beautiful caverns under the Garden? Narrow? Wide enough for supplies? It had been used as an escape tunnel more than once to keep the inhabitants safe so there'd be room for a lot of people to pass.

And if Martine had two armed guards on the other side, it wasn't a complete secret.

I had to position myself in roughly the right area so my GPS would be helpful. I pulled back from Jenn and cupped her cheek in my palm. "I'm sorry."

She blinked rapidly, but didn't flinch from my grasp. "For what?"

"I should have asked if you were okay. Were you scared?"

"Terrified." She spluttered a laugh. "And I fell, so my knees hurt, but then I saw you..."

"Do you need to sit?" I glanced down at her pants, which were no worse for wear.

"I'm okay." Her eyes glistened, and she nodded quickly. "But I lost all your money."

I couldn't help but laugh. It was so preposterous. The money wasn't important. She'd found the secret entrance for us, and that was what mattered. "Have you tried roulette yet?"

The roulette tables were near the ladies' room. *Using her again, aren't you?*

"I honestly think I have the worst luck in the world."

I slid my hand down from her face, along her arm, and took her hand. "Mine's pretty good. Maybe it'll rub off on you."

Her fingers flexed in my grip, and I glanced at her long enough to witness her cheeks reddening. "How do you know the manager?"

I towed her through the crowd, which had thickened since we arrived. "I've been here a few times."

She stayed close to me, wrapping her free hand around my arm. "This whole situation feels like something out of a spy movie."

I chuckled, trying to keep my tone light. "Oh yeah? Which one?"

"I don't know—James Bond?" She glanced around nervously. "That Martine woman could pass for a Bond villain or something."

Hopefully, Martine's far from a villain. We arrived at a roulette table, and I pulled out a chair for her.

"Although..." Jenn sat, looking up at me with amusement in her eyes. "What if everyone thinks she's the Bond girl, but it turns out to be a case of mistaken identity?"

I grinned at her. "What does that make you?"

Her cheeks reddened more. "The real Bond girl?"

When the dealer was ready, I pulled out a few hundred euros and placed them on the table. "The temptress? Here to uncover my secrets?"

Jenn's fingers trembled slightly. She was flirting to distract herself, wasn't she? To get over what happened?

My turn to play along. It wasn't a hardship, despite knowing the danger she was in and how much I was keeping from her. If it kept her calm and distracted from the very real threats around us, I'd suffer.

"So, Miss Temptress"—I gestured to the roulette wheel— "where should we place our bet?"

Jenn bit her lip, considering. "If you've got the luck, you should pick."

I winked at her. "It's not luck, it's skill."

Her playful smile faded, and her gaze dropped to my lips.

The wink might have been taking it too far. She'd been open about her feelings for me, and I was using those feelings to manipulate her.

To make her feel better.

That was a supportive thing, right? Not selfish?

"We're close," said Jayce over the earpiece.

I reached past Jenn and picked up my chips. Straightened. Held them in front of her. *Blow on them,* I mouthed.

Definitely too far. But damn, it felt good.

Jenn moistened her lips, dark blue eyes locked with mine. I felt that all the way in the pit of my stomach. And when she blew on the chips, the sensation dropped lower.

Then her father's voice wove its way through my brain. *'You're not good enough for my little girl.'*

What was I doing?

"Can you hear me?" Jayce snorted. "Just flirt some more if you can't talk."

I hadn't heard Rav's voice yet. Hopefully, he was far enough away, and my signal was still scrambled so he couldn't make out my words. "You choose the bet, Krista."

"Who's Krista?" asked Jayce. Her voice came through so clearly, she must have been close. "Where's Jenn?"

I carefully placed the chips in her hand, my fingers lingering for a moment longer than necessary. With deliberate movements, I shifted behind her chair, my heart racing as I gently ran my hands over her shoulders.

Jenn hesitated, then placed a small bet on red. She took my hand from her right shoulder, pulling me closer as the ball spun. She twisted her head to look at me from the corner of her eye. "So, if I'm the temptress in this scenario, what's my evil plan? To seduce you away from your mission?"

"Maybe you're working with me, but you're a double agent? Trying to throw me off my game?" I should have been able to talk Massimo out of the scarab at the restaurant, or convince Jean-Philippe or Dante to hand it over at the gallery. But every time Dante looked at her, the right words flew from my brain. She *was* throwing me off my game.

"Am I succeeding?" Her eyes met mine with an intensity that almost pushed her father's voice—and the idea of my team listening to our conversation—out of my head. As the word '*Yes*' formed on my tongue, the ball landed on black. Jenn groaned, letting go of me and slumping back in her chair. "See? Even your luck isn't enough to rub off on me."

"I have eyes on them," whispered Jayce. "Security desk with two armed men."

Drew said, "—areful." Proximity must have played a large part with the watch-connected earpiece. No doubt, he'd told her to be careful, but was farther away from me than Jayce was.

"It's a little early for dinner"—I tossed a chip onto the table, and it rolled, eventually settling on red fifteen—"but did you want to visit the restaurant and grab something to eat?"

Jenn stood and faced me. She might have been disappointed with another loss, but her nerves had calmed from earlier. "You sure? I'd like to avoid the real world a bit longer."

"I'm free for the evening." I'd finished my conversation with Martine but had to wait for her proposal to Mum. Jayce was close enough that she'd mapped a route to the Casino. They didn't need anything else from me. "I'm all yours."

The ball clattered into a slot on the roulette wheel behind Jenn. A few cheers rose from the players and observers.

"Quinze, rouge," droned the croupier. "Fifteen, red."

Jenn's lids fluttered shut, and she grumbled, "Seriously?"

I shrugged, holding down the self-satisfied grin I wanted to flash. Thirty-five-to-one odds. "Guess I got lucky."

CHAPTER 30

JENN

"ARE YOU ALL RIGHT?" Emmett's voice was full of concern, as though I were a fragile piece of pottery that might break if he looked at me wrong.

The elevator dinged, and we got off on our floor.

I hadn't thought my life could get any more crazy after seeing Noah this afternoon. But an afternoon in an underground casino with secret passages, armed gunmen, and my best friend's brother? My life had turned into a movie.

But who was the Bond Girl? Me? Or Martine?

Was that the problem? Did Emmett have a thing for older women? Or for women who were in control?

Control. Was that *my* problem? I was showing him I wanted him—giving him opportunities to tell me he wanted me, too. But I hadn't *told* him. Hadn't demanded anything.

Maybe the direct route was what I needed. "You're not working tonight?"

"I finished everything I needed at the Casino." How did none of this faze him? Was this what their work was normally like? "I'll meet with the team tomorrow afternoon to review our auction strategy. The support staff back home is searching for information on people who might be in town to buy the scarab, in case I can talk them out of it."

"I didn't realize what a complicated operation it was."

He pulled out his keycard and unlocked the door, holding it open for me. "The higher the value, the more of the team involved."

As the door closed, I considered asking how much the scarab was worth. It didn't matter. What mattered was that we were alone in our hotel suite. We were safe. And he had nowhere to go.

Deep breath. You can do it, Jenn.

I turned to face him. Dropped my purse. Held my breath and grabbed him by the neck, pulling him closer. His eyes widened in surprise, but I didn't give him a chance to protest. I kissed him, pouring all my pent-up desire into the moment.

His mouth didn't open for me. He stood frozen, lips firm against mine.

It's shock. That's all. It's not another rejection.

"Kiss me," I whispered against his lips.

His rich brown eyes flicked back and forth between mine.

Don't say no.

His arm snaked around my waist, yanking me against him. I gasped, and his mouth claimed mine in a bruising kiss, stealing my breath. His tongue swept into my mouth, rich with champagne and need. Raw hunger blazed between us as he devoured me, stealing my air, my control.

My heart thundered against his grip. Heat scorched through my veins, igniting places I'd dreamed of him touching.

He was greedy.

So greedy.

My pulse pounded, a fire growing deep inside me. Every inch of my skin tingled. He was the man I'd wanted for so long, and now I had him.

The feel of his strong body against mine, the taste of his lips, the low moan from deep in his chest... All my worry and tension melted away, replaced by a primal need that consumed me. My panties were already soaked, and the tightness building between my thighs needed to be released.

Not by myself this time.

His fingers blazed a path down my side, gripping my ass and pulling me closer. His other hand tangled in my hair, twisting until my neck arched back.

Time to tell him what you want, Jenn. Don't worry. He wants the same.

"I'm so wet, Emmett." I raked my teeth over his bottom lip. "Take me to bed."

He squeezed my ass, but pulled his mouth away from mine. "The things you said last night..."

Which things? I'd said a lot, smart and not so much.

"I can't do this." His forehead pressed against mine as his hands dropped away. The muscles in his arms flexed, his fingers curling tight as though he were fighting himself. "You're Scarlett's best friend."

What did that have to do with last night? "We're adults. That sister's best friend stuff got old ten years ago."

"She made me promise—"

"To keep me safe."

He lifted his forehead, not taking his hungry eyes off me. Not moving away. Not closing the tiny gap between us either, though. "I promised I wouldn't touch you."

"Just one time." I flicked open a button on his shirt. "No one has to tell her."

Emmett Reynolds was trouble. People had been saying that from the day they found out who his father was.

None of it had mattered to me. I'd wanted Emmett for half my lifetime. And maybe my horrible track record with men was because of him. I'd fallen in love with every bad boy I crossed paths with, trying to find the same thrill Emmett had given me. Trying to fill the void he'd left when he dumped me at fifteen.

None of them had quenched my thirst.

One night with him would close the open loop in my heart, and I could finally move on. No more cheaters, no more liars, no more men who put themselves ahead of me. I'd find myself a good man, settle down, and have the picture-perfect life I'd always wanted.

I undid another of his buttons and slid my fingers under the loose fabric of his shirt, doing my best to hide the nervous tremble.

"Just one night."

That would solve all my problems.

He dragged his teeth across his bottom lip and finally moved his damn hand. It landed on my hip, and he clenched hard. "She'll kill me."

Summoning every ounce of courage and sex appeal I could find, I purred, "It'll be worth it."

His nostrils flared, and his gaze dropped to my lips. Heat pulsed through my body as his mouth eased open, his breaths growing ragged.

He was going to say yes this time.

He had to.

His other hand locked onto my waist, and he forced me back two steps until I touched the wall.

"This is wrong," he growled, grabbing my arms to take my hands off him.

"I don't care."

He lifted my hands over my head and pinned my wrists against the wall. Leaned in close, so his hot breath skated over my cheek. Teeth grazed my earlobe, and I moaned, bowing my back to find his body with mine. There was too much space between us.

CHAPTER 31

EMMETT

Fuck me.

Fucking fuck me.

What was I doing? Why did I grab her?

How had I already undone three of the buttons on her blouse?

Because you want her. You want to kiss those lips, rip those clothes off her, and taste every inch of her. Fuck her against the wall until she screams your name.

Because you've always wanted what you can't have.

I held her hands steady over her head, ghosting my free hand along her arm, down the side of her breast, and stopping at her waist. I pulled back only far enough to see her face.

Jenn's wet, swollen lips parted. She knew what she wanted, but hadn't planned on asking, had she? Or she didn't think I'd take her up on it.

Raw need slammed through me as my fingers traced her hip, keeping a razor-thin space between our bodies. Blood pounded through my veins. My body screamed to consume her. My cock demanded I claim her. But my brain?

It was the only part of me that realized I had to stop.

Scarlett had been right to warn me away from her. I wasn't what a good, smart woman like Jenn needed. I was little more than a con artist.

I was a man whose father betrayed his country.

You're no better than him. You used Jenn to get close to the De Rosas.

I was a man who froze at the sound of Enzo's voice.

He kidnapped you. What did you expect to do when you heard him?

"It can just be physical, Emmett." She swallowed, the sex kitten growing apprehensive. "I don't need any promises of what comes tomorrow or next week or when we get home."

"You deserve more." Like a man who could tell her the truth, who wasn't hiding an entire career she didn't understand. Who wasn't hiding his sister's lies. I'd told Jenn a few truths to win her trust, but the rest of it? How would she react?

Her voice dropped, and she flexed her wrists under my grip. "I deserve to be happy."

I couldn't make her happy.

"What you're asking for…" The words were bitter on my tongue, but I forced them out, anyway. "It's not something I can give you. Not now, not ever."

She flinched, hurt flashing across her face before she masked it with determination. "You can. We've always been friends, and I know you."

"You don't know the real me." I took a step back, creating distance between us. It was for her own good, even if it felt like tearing out a piece of my soul.

She stared at me, easing her arms down and blinking as though trying to understand what I was saying.

"You *do* deserve to be happy, but I'm not the kind of man who's capable of giving you that."

"That's a shitty excuse." Her chin lifted defiantly. "One night, Emmett. Not forever."

Fuck. One night? It would be too easy to give in, to lose myself in her for a few hours. But one night would never be enough, and I'd only end up hurting her more in the long run.

"Jenn, listen to me. You don't understand. There are things about me, things I've done... You wouldn't want me if you knew the truth."

"It's not me, it's you? Seriously?" Her gaze dropped, cheeks flaming as red as ever. Tears welled against her lids. "What's wrong with me? Why do I always—"

"Stop that, right now." My gut twisted. Every dream I'd had of her over the years came rushing back. She was the pure fantasy, always out of reach. If I told her how long I'd wanted her, she'd never buy it.

"My god, I can't believe I..." She pulled her gaping shirt closed, curling her shoulders in. "Just go to bed and pretend this never happened."

She was crying.

Because of me.

Because I was letting every little voice into my head. Her father's. My sister's. Rav's.

Goddamn Noah and Enzo for showing up and making this fucking trip worse.

"It's not..." *Fuck. Fucking fuck.* I stood there, pathetic, as her tears fell. Every instinct screamed at me to pull her close, to wipe away those tears. But I couldn't.

'You're not good enough for Jenn. You never will be,' her father had said.

My hand slipped into my pocket, fingers closing around the poker chip. The weight of it, the memories it carried, anchored me. I'd been running for so long, hiding behind lies and half-truths. I couldn't keep doing it, not with her. She deserved… something—some kind of explanation.

Tell her the truth. For once, tell someone the truth.

I took the chip out of my pocket. Holding it lightly between two fingers, I let someone else see it for the first time. "I'm damaged goods, Jenn."

Her shoulders heaved with her quiet tears. She tried walking away from me, but I put a gentle hand out to stop her.

"At the end of April, I was at a poker game in New York City with Malcolm." I rolled the chip over my knuckles. Its blue face and white edge spots flashed with each turn. I could have done it blindfolded. Described every millimeter of the chip without hesitating. "Three masked men broke in and took us."

My story must have confused her, because she stopped crying.

"They beat me—" I stopped when the words stuck in my throat, and I swallowed hard. *You can do this.* "They forced Scarlett and the team to do a job to pay the ransom." I held the chip face out to show her the hole punched through the middle. "I was beaten regularly and shipped to Venice, where the team came for me."

Jenn's brows drew down. The pity look.

Great. What was sexier than that?

"After it was all over, I went back to New York for one of

the chips from the game." I wrapped it in my fist, pressing the textured face into my palm. "It's been in my pocket for almost four months now."

"What does that have to do with..." She let her hands drop from her shirt, fanning them as if to say, *'All of this?'*

"I saw a doctor who said I'm dealing with post-traumatic stress, and"—I glanced down at the chip—"I'm having a tough time dealing with what happened."

With trusting people. With my confidence. With sleep.

At least I wasn't having daily headaches or jumping at every loud noise anymore.

Her brows shifted from pity to confusion.

There was too much else going on I couldn't confess to. What the ransom had been, what Noah's plan was, and that I'd only seen the doctor once. I'd thought I had plenty of time to get over the issues.

But then I arrived in my favorite city in the world, the men behind my kidnapping showed up, and the woman I'd wanted for as long as I could remember told me she wanted me, too.

"Noah was their ringleader."

Jenn gasped, apparently forgetting how upset she was, because her hands landed on my chest. "Seriously?"

"That's why I wanted you to stay here with me. They've —" I didn't want to talk about Fenix. I wanted my life back.

Fuck. I wanted to be the man she thought I was. I dragged my hands through my hair, the weight of her gaze making my chest ache. There wasn't a single part of me that could give her what she *deserved*.

But I could give her part of what she *wanted*.

I stuffed the chip back into my pocket and drove my fingers through her hair. "You're right."

She sucked in a quick breath. "What do you mean?"

"I do want you," I whispered as I wrapped one fist in her hair, taking in her smooth skin, her dark blue eyes, and the little freckle by her right eye.

She'd grown more beautiful every year since we were kids. And she wanted to be mine for one blissful night. She didn't understand who I was. What I'd been through. What I couldn't do for her. Still, my lips brushed hers, and she sighed softly. She tasted sweet, like the chocolate souffle she'd enjoyed at the Casino's restaurant.

The kiss deepened, our tongues tangling with a deliberate patience that made my body come alive. The desperate urgency from earlier melted into something more dangerous. Each gentle stroke threatened to unravel the careful walls I'd built, but I couldn't bring myself to stop.

She moaned deep in her chest and pulled my shirt from my pants. Her hand circled around me, running up my back, under my shirt.

My fingers caressed her arms, guiding them upward until her wrists crossed above her disheveled hair again. My cock strained against my zipper. Patience was my forte, and this woman would come for me before any of my clothes came off.

Jenn's soft whimper filled the air as she arched her back, breasts straining against the black lace bra she'd chosen with care this morning. For a fleeting moment, she'd held control, but now she was at my mercy, her body pleading for my touch.

I traced my tongue across her skin, marking her with wet heat. Her breath caught when I reached the swell of her breast, and I paused. "May I?"

"Oh god, please."

I pulled the cup down, teasing my way to her nipple. Her

heart raced beneath my lips, her quickened breath urging me onward. As my mouth explored her smooth skin, my hands wandered lower, deftly undoing her button and sliding her zipper down. I nipped at her flesh, eliciting a tiny gasp that went straight to my cock.

"Please, Emmett." Jenn moaned and writhed, but kept her hands away, even though the restraint was obviously a challenge. "I need you inside me. Now."

"Not yet, honey." I kissed my way down her stomach as I peeled away her pants and underwear. I guided her to step out of them, then knelt and hoisted one of her legs over my shoulder. "I need to show you how much I want you first."

Her pussy glistened in front of me, clit swollen and begging for my attention. I licked her seam slowly, savoring her flavor, committing every gasp and cry to memory. My tongue circled her clit before returning to dip inside her. She clenched my hair, holding me steady as I worked her closer and closer to the edge.

I slipped two fingers into her warmth, her slick heat enveloping me. Her hips bucked, seeking more, and I obliged. Curling my fingers, I found the sweet spot inside her that made her shudder, while my mouth continued its assault on her sensitive nub.

Her breath caught, her grip on my hair tightening. She was close, but I took my time, wanting her to revel in every moment.

"Fuck, Emmett," she panted, her hips grinding against my face. "Don't stop."

Fuck stopping.

I kept up my steady rhythm, fingers pumping in and out of her, my tongue swirling and flicking. Her inner walls began to pulse around my fingers, her body tensing as she climbed higher and higher.

Suddenly, she cried out, her climax crashing over her like a tidal wave. Her body shook as she rode out the crest of her orgasm, and she held my head right where it wanted to stay. I didn't slow until she went limp, her fingers slipping from my hair, her breath coming in shallow gasps.

I slowly withdrew, giving her one last, gentle lick that made her quiver.

Jenn's eyes fluttered open, meeting mine. There was a satisfaction in her gaze, a contentment that made my chest...

What was my chest doing? It was more than my pulse pounding or the knowledge I'd brought her to ecstasy. There was something else.

Something warm? And happy?

No, no, no.

Jenn was the first woman I'd been with since—

Stop thinking about the kidnapping. That was all it was. Not a feeling. My long dry spell was screwing with my brain. There were *no* feelings involved.

"Wow," she breathed.

I stood, skimming my hands up her sides, over her breasts, until I cupped her face again. "You only asked for a kiss, but I hope the rest was all right?"

She lifted onto her toes, encouraging me to kiss her again. Her soft hum when our mouths met increased that strange feeling inside my chest.

Sneaking a hand around her as we kissed, I undid her bra, preparing for round two. "Stay here."

Jenn nodded, her hair a mess, her lips thick from my assault. I strode into the bedroom, my dick hard enough to pound nails. I grabbed a few condoms from my toiletry bag. If this was going to be one night only, it was going to be an unforgettable one.

I returned to find her teasing her own nipples, the rosy peaks taut with need. I gave one sharp tug of her hair to expose her throat. My teeth grazed the length of her neck, drawing a desperate sound from her. Her spine arched, surrendering herself to my mouth. When I bit down lightly near her collarbone, her cry sent a jolt through my body.

I'd wanted to do that for so long.

My fingers slid down her stomach, over her silky skin, to the thatch of curls between her legs. She moaned as I played with her, then gasped when I pushed two fingers inside her again.

Her sex clamped around me, and she slapped one needy hand over mine. She rocked her hips, guiding my hand as I pumped my fingers in and out. Her pants and moans filled the room, and she let go of me to tug at my belt, fumbling with the buckle. "Get these off."

I withdrew my fingers to help, unfastening my pants and shoving them down far enough to free my cock. I tore the condom wrapper, sheathed myself, and lifted her against the wall. "This doesn't hurt your knees, does it?"

"They're fine."

"You ready for this, honey?"

"Yes."

I held under her ass, letting my tip play at her entrance. She was so wet and ready. So easy to drive inside her. Her pussy gripped me like a vise. I wanted to take my time, to savor her luscious body, but my cock had other plans. I drove into her, again and again, taking my fill. "Fuck, yes, Jenn."

Her head dropped back, and she latched one leg higher up my back to give me better access.

"Oh, god, Emmett," she panted. "Yes, yes, yes."

My lips found her throat again, and she mewled. Her inner walls spasmed, milking my cock, and I had to grit my teeth to hold on. I wanted to come, but not yet. Not until she came again.

"Emmett," she gasped. "I'm—oh, god."

She began shaking, gripping my shoulders to help slam herself onto me until she finally fell apart. And with a few more thrusts, I followed her over the edge, spilling myself into the condom.

I kissed her softly, then rested my forehead against hers. This was a mistake. A huge mistake. But it felt so damn amazing.

"Definitely better than just a kiss." She wrapped her arms around me, holding tight as our breathing slowed.

"Jenn," I whispered as I pulled out and put her down. "My Jenn."

"I don't suppose you have another one of those in you?" Apparently, the sex kitten had returned.

"Well, now that we've ensured Scarlett and Rav are going to kill me..." I bent, tossed her over my shoulder, and headed for the bedroom. "I'm going to take you to your room, splay you out, and feast on your gorgeous body until you beg me to stop."

Her squeal of delight zipped around inside of me, almost making me think I *could* be the kind of man who'd make her happy.

CHAPTER 32
JENN

I woke slowly, savoring the warmth of Emmett's arms around me. A smile crept all the way out of my chest when I remembered where I was and what had happened last night.

Yesterday morning, we'd woken up like this too, but that had been a semi-innocent co-sleep between friends. This? This was post-three-orgasm bliss.

I nestled closer to Emmett, careful not to wake him. My mind drifted back to our encounter last night, replaying every touch, every kiss. Every lick. Every nip.

Hold on to those memories, Jenn.

Next came the replay of Emmett's confessions. Kidnapped. Beaten. Trauma responses.

He wasn't the kind of guy who normally expressed weakness. As an adult, Emmett was always in control and always easy-going. He'd always been strong—a survivor. But the way he'd opened up, showing me his physical and emotional scars? God, it touched me in ways I hadn't expected.

And how he'd hesitated, struggled with his desire, and his promise to keep me safe. The conflict in his eyes had been clear. My soul hurt just thinking about it. His vulnerability, his honesty—it had melted something inside me.

And the sex? I'd completely forgotten about all the crazy things going on around us. The fake painting, Noah being alive, the De Rosas, the underground casino—all of it was nothing compared to how he'd wrecked me.

I shifted slightly, considering my options. I'd gone into last night swearing it was about getting him out of my system.

That probably meant I should climb out of bed and not get carried away with silly emotions. That would be the wise thing to do, right? Put some distance between us and get my head on straight?

But I didn't want to move. I wanted to stay right here, in Emmett's arms, for as long as possible. Was I pathetic? Was it leftover teenage feelings? Or was there something deeper? Something real?

I closed my eyes, listening to Emmett's steady breathing, and snuggled back a little more, risking waking him up.

And what I felt was morning wood behind me.

Would he still want me this morning?

My bare back to his bare chest, with the light smattering of hair that tickled my skin. He rubbed his short beard against my shoulder, showing me he was awake.

"Emmett..." I whispered, snaking one hand behind me to stroke his hard cock. "Good morning."

"Fuck," he groaned, the guttural noise echoing inside me.

"Do you want to..." I continued stroking him, reveling in his obvious need.

He groaned again, his teeth grazing my shoulder. "Yes, woman."

I reached for the bedside table, grabbing another condom for him.

Once it was on, he pushed into me slowly, filling me in one lazy stroke. Stretching me. Overwhelming me in the best possible way. His hips rocked gently, as if neither of us were fully awake.

"Yeah." This was what I'd wanted. "Right there. Like that."

"Still so wet," he breathed, his hands roaming my body. He cupped my breasts, his fingertips teasing my nipples. "Is this how you wanted to start the day, honey?"

Honey. He was still calling me honey. "Perfect."

He tweaked one of my nipples. "Are you going to beg me to stop, like you did last night?"

"No." Not yet, at least.

"You will." His teeth raked across my shoulder, and he continued with the torturous pace, building a fire inside my core. In. Out. In. Out. How long could he go on like this?

"Oh, god, Emmett, I need more."

His speed remained constant. He *was* trying to kill me. "Beg me."

"Please," I whimpered, arching my back to invite him deeper. "Fuck me harder."

"Close enough." His pace quickened, and he gripped my hips with newfound urgency, holding me in place as he owned every inch of me. Slamming into me, he growled, "Is this what you want?"

"Oh god, yes, yes, yes," I panted, the entire world vanishing as stars lit up my vision. The orgasm ripped through me, shattering me.

He tensed behind me, his breath hot on my neck as he

found his own release. For long moments, he held onto my hips, his fingers digging into my skin as if he needed the anchor to reality. Finally, he relaxed and kissed my shoulder. He rolled out of bed to take care of the condom, giving me an opportunity to watch him move.

Emmett's body was a masterpiece of lean strength. Defined muscle, like a Grecian sculpture, rather than a bodybuilder. He was even more gorgeous naked than in his fancy clothes. And the way the morning light filtered through the curtains, catching the thin sheen of sweat on his skin? Too delicious for words.

Three long scars marred his back, though. Was that from his kidnapping?

When he slid into the bed, he didn't pull me back into his arms. Instead, he lay on his back, an unreadable expression on his face, one arm tucked casually behind his head. "Thank you."

I rolled over, laying my head in the crook of his arm, and pulled a knee up over his hips. "Seriously? I should be the one saying that. I'm still up by two orgasms over you."

He chuckled, kissing my forehead. "That's a good thing, right?"

"So good." I drew circles across his chest. There were so many words I wanted to say, but I kept them inside. I didn't need to tell him how long I'd wanted him, how he'd been the only man to put me first, or how magical it had been—that would all be too awkward. "Think we should try and even that count out later?"

His breathing was slow and easy, his heart beating a simple rhythm under my ear. When he didn't answer, I chanced a look.

His eyes were closed, features relaxed. "You didn't bring an evening gown with you, did you?"

I sat up slightly at the odd subject change, but Emmett eased me back down.

"You'll need something for the auction tonight."

Work. We were back on the work topic. So much for the magic. "I didn't bring anything fancy."

He began idly sweeping his fingers along my back. "We'll go shopping later."

Aunt Penny paid me well, but not well enough for an evening gown in Monaco. "I don't—"

"Business expense. My treat."

How did I feel about that? I'd wasted a thousand euros in the Casino last night, but with one careless toss of a chip onto the roulette table, he'd more than won it back.

Emmett yawned, and the hand on my back slowed. "Are you happy?"

"Yes," I whispered. *So much, yes.*

"Good." He kissed the top of my head and moved the arm he was propped up on. He twisted his fingers around mine and rested our hands on his chest. "Me, too."

That, combined with him calling me *'My Jenn'* last night and *'Honey'* again this morning, sent a bundle of jittery energy spiraling around my insides. Was this more than one night— plus a morning? More than a vacation fling? I shifted so I could kiss him. Soft and tender. Trying to show him nothing mattered but the moment we were in. Hopefully, there'd be more, but this was all I needed for now.

He lifted me so I lay on top of him, and we just kissed. Tongues and lips and roaming hands. Warm bodies pressed together, our heartbeats syncing. He drew patterns on my back, and time slowed. The world narrowed to only us, wrapped in each other's arms. The weight of my naked body on his felt right, like we were designed for this.

Shit.

It was just my luck.

Instead of getting him out of my system, I'd ensured he would never leave it.

CHAPTER 33

EMMETT

LATER FRIDAY MORNING, after ensuring all of Jenn's physical needs were met, I dropped her off in a shop on the Monte Carlo Promenade. She was in the expert hands of a professional shopper, who'd help choose her outfit for this evening.

Across the road, where I could still see the shop, I joined my team at a small outdoor seating area. A thick stone half-wall shielded our table from the port, and a large yellow umbrella concealed us from the view of anyone in the buildings above.

As I approached, Rav, Will, Jayce, and Drew looked up.

"Morning, all," I said, taking my seat.

Will was pulling a small device from his backpack—a compact black metal box, only three inches long. He flicked a switch on its top, pressed a button, and a green light illuminated. "Interference is on."

We'd debated whether to meet in the two-story open office we'd rented for training, one of our hotel rooms, or outside. Will's jammer provided us with a cone of silence and invisibility, and he could have disrupted any video feeds or listening devices indoors or out.

The decision came down to Jenn. She wouldn't question the group of us sitting around a table and chatting across the street from the shop. But if we'd gathered in one of our hotel rooms or at the office, I would have needed an excuse to leave her alone, and that wasn't an option.

Next, Will pulled a watch box from his bag. "I've upgraded the receiver in the watch, which I believe caused the problem yesterday."

I opened the box, inspecting the modified Omega for any sign it wasn't the real thing. Naturally, there was none. "Any changes to the earpiece?"

Will shook his head. "The watch manages the extended signal. The earpiece just needs to connect to it."

Two gelato cups sat in front of Jayce from a small snack shop nearby. "We stuck around for a few hours after locating the right tunnel. The guards rotated every half hour, always in pairs, and if one had to leave, another filled in temporarily."

Rav said, "One of them responded instantly when Jenn walked through the door, yes?"

I nodded.

Will placed a tablet in the middle of the table. The way it dimmed when I moved my head suggested it had a protective layer, ensuring no one beyond our table could read it. A floor plan of the Casino Rocher appeared.

"Where'd you find this?" I asked.

Will grinned at the tablet, almost as if to himself. "Brie's a genius."

For over a decade, Will and my younger sister swore they were nothing more than friends. I'd noticed the sparkle in her eye when she spoke to him years ago, but this was the first time I'd seen the same from him.

You need to address that, Emmett.

"The guards." Rav pointed to the spot where someone had marked an X on the floor plan, indicating the concealed entrance. "When the crowds are thin, their job appears boring. If something went awry, I suspect the second guard is a backup. Some sort of distraction or disturbance might get rid of both at the same time, or one after the other, without allowing them to secure the door quickly enough to stop Jayce from slipping in."

"The hidden doorway is at the end of the corridor leading to the ladies' restroom." I zoomed in on that section of the map. "Any distraction that gets Jayce through the door can have her in the restroom before anyone notices." I looked at our acquisitions specialist. "If you can change quickly enough—"

"Not an issue," Jayce said, covering her mouth as she swallowed a spoonful of her gelato. "I have another dress like the one I wore in Washington, but in all black. It'll work for stealth and changes quickly into formal attire."

Drew added, "The distraction will have to be something that doesn't shut down the auction or cause chaos."

With a smirk, Rav quipped, "So, no explosives?"

Jayce snorted. "No explosives."

Will slid another small box to Jayce. "This is the replica of the scarab. It'll fit in the pouch hidden in your dress, right at your hip bone."

Drew said, "I must say, she tested the hidden pouch last night, and it worked perfectly. Engineering, goldwork, *and* tailoring skills? That's an impressive resume."

Will shrugged. "I can build anything out of anything else."

Jayce held her spoon near her lips as she said, "Will's like our own MacGyver."

"My mom loved him." Will gave a small laugh, staring at the tablet, likely remembering better times with his mother. He was in a lot of pain. This trip was hardly the vacation his sister insisted he take, but it would help him find some normalcy for a few days, at least.

"I could smuggle a phone in, too," said Jayce, around another mouthful.

"Too risky," I said. "If they catch any of us sneaking tech in, we're out of the game. Drew and I need to keep as clean as possible so we can help you without worrying about ourselves."

Jayce shrugged. "Fair."

"The plan for tonight is simple. If I win the scarab at the auction, we're done. If I can't, the next move is to woo the buyer into giving it up. If that doesn't work, we get Jayce into the storage room." I zoomed out on the floor plan, shifting to the third main room. I tapped the hallway near the high-rollers' room, where the secure storage was located. "Jayce swaps the scarabs, takes the genuine one, and leaves through the hidden doorway into the caves. If the buyer realizes they've been duped, the blame will fall on the Casino first. Martine—the manager—had a lengthy chat with Mum last night."

Drew asked, "They know each other?"

"Yes. From way back, according to my mother." I held Drew's gaze for a moment longer, and he nodded. Scarlett and I had kept the MI6 story under wraps, except when we needed Drew's assistance. When would we inform Brie, Rav, and the rest of the crew? We hadn't decided yet. "She's highly regarded in all the right circles, but there's always an element of buyer beware in the black market. She and Massimo have some history, so she'll pin the blame on him, claiming he gave her a fake."

Much like the Constable painting his son hired Jenn to clean. Poetic justice.

The black market was a strange thing indeed. A Picasso could go for a song if used as leverage, or a small golden artifact might fetch many times its actual value if someone desired the rare piece enough.

"Why don't we go right now?" Jayce scraped the bottom of her first cup of gelato. "It's probably quiet, with fewer people in the way."

"Quieter, but not empty." Casino Rocher operated twenty-four hours a day. Mornings and early afternoons saw the fewest people, but the security was still high. "And too empty for you to sneak into the storage room."

Jayce shrugged and switched to her second cup of gelato. "What if we staged a fight? Get a couple of drunk guys to start swinging near the ladies' room?"

Drew shook his head. "They're guarding the other side of the door. They wouldn't handle disturbances inside unless it threatened their position."

"Fair point." Jayce reached out, idly moving the image around on the tablet. "How about a medical emergency? Someone collapses near the hidden door? Surely they'd come running if someone yelled for help?"

"Still won't work," I said. "You'd wind up with more people gathered around that entrance, and possibly paramedics to contend with."

Suddenly, Will snapped his fingers. "What if we don't

create a distraction ourselves? What if we let someone else do it for us?"

"Go on," I said.

"Have you ever heard of urban exploration?" Will leaned in. "People love finding hidden spots in cities. What if we leaked the location of the secret door on some adventure websites?"

That idea had potential. "A bunch of thrill-seekers descend on the guards at once from the cavern side of the door?"

Rav nodded thoughtfully. "It would overwhelm the guards. They'd try to keep people away, possibly call in backup, and the chaos allows Jayce to slip past."

Will folded a small keyboard out from his phone and began typing. "I'll talk to Brie. Her team will set up the website posts and make it look like there's a lot of interest. Arrange for multiple confirmations at the right time."

"Make it two waves of explorers," I said. "One to mask Jayce's ingress and one for egress."

"I like it. Stealth, skill, and I bet it'll be hilarious." Jayce's eyes gleamed as she offered Drew a spoonful of gelato. That was a change—she didn't usually share food. "We've been rehearsing movement through the Casino, and I can make it to the storage room in three minutes and twenty seconds without looking more suspicious than I normally do. I'll have Brie's remote access thingamajig so she can futz with the security feed."

"Good." I was too well-known in the Casino to be sneaking around.

But Jayce? Not only was it her job, but she'd be bringing in the electronics. Everything fell on her shoulders. "You're working on access to the room itself?"

I nodded at her. "Martine's provided the passcode. That'll be the easy part."

Rav, speaking like the head of security he was, said, "Can we trust her?"

I'd asked the same question. Scarlett had said no—she never trusted the team's safety to outsiders. But Mum had overruled her.

"If Mum says we can," I said, "we can."

Rav nodded, obviously not fully satisfied, but willing to accept the answer. "Drew should be inside the Casino, while you work the caverns with Jayce."

I wasn't about to be pulled from my own op. "No, we've already—"

He held up a hand. "Noah and Enzo have only met Drew once, so a light disguise will ensure no one recognizes him."

Part of me wanted to shut Rav down. But Drew and Jayce *did* work well together. Maybe it was a good plan. I said, "Then Jayce can hand off the device to loop the security feed. Drew can plant it in the right spot and keep moving. The less time anyone spends near that room, the better."

"Getting me through the secret door is a far bigger risk than Jayce," said Drew. "I'll have to come in through the main entrance, which means no phone."

Will said, "I don't have another watch, and your comms will be awful inside the cavern."

"Drew takes the watch," said Rav. "And Emmett stays in the caverns."

Not a chance. "I'm not arguing with you, Rav. This is my job, and I'm going in."

Drew waved a hand. "I worked solo for years. Don't worry about me."

That came close to breaking our cardinal rule—never turn off the comms during a heist. But I turned to Will. "If Drew had his earpiece, he could still communicate with me and anyone who gets close enough in the cavern, right?"

Will nodded. "It should work. Plus, we can still use the earpiece to track him if something goes south."

"Done." I pointed at Drew. "You go in near-blind, and I go in with the watch."

Rav frowned. "That's not the right call, and you know it. You don't have anything to prove."

"You're right, I don't." *But you do, Em.* My fingers twitched. They wanted to touch the chip. *Don't let him see it, Emmett.* "Martine's agreed to work with us, but that includes an auction invite for me, not Drew. We're not jeopardizing the mission."

Rav folded his arms as though challenging me. "And Jenn?"

"What about her?" I asked, a little too fast. *He doesn't know what happened last night or this morning, so calm down.* "She's my plus-one tonight. I'll keep her with me, which means she'll be safe."

"She'd be safer in the boat with me." Rav's job was to monitor the water door in case Jayce needed to use it as an emergency exit. There was a security presence at that door, but between the two of them, they'd be able to get her out. "Jenn's a liability tonight."

"He's right." Drew, as sour as Rav at times, nodded. "You're not at your best when she's around."

What?

"Don't give me shit about it getting personal, Drew. What

did you do when she"—I jabbed a finger in Jayce's direction—"was in danger?"

Jayce nudged too-serious Drew with a shoulder. "He jumped in front of a bullet for me."

Drew opened his mouth to rebut.

I turned the finger on him before he could defend his hypocrisy. "Exactly. Sounds like *too personal* worked out pretty well for you."

"We're not stupid, Emmett," growled Rav, his huge arms flexing. "You're going to get her hurt."

"Noah's the one who gave us this tip. He wants us to take the scarab to screw over Massimo. He won't hurt her if that ruins his plan."

"That's not what I'm talking about."

Did he know about me and Jenn? Had Jayce said something about me flirting yesterday? Had Rav's earpiece reception been better than he'd let on?

"Anyway." Jayce's singsong voice was a blatant attempt to break the tension. When that didn't work, she stood, plucking at Drew's shirt. "We should head back to the office and run through the virtual maps again. I'd like to do it with the actual scarab and consider Drew on the inside."

Rav didn't take her bait and stayed focused on me. "You're playing house with a woman who's already taken."

"She broke up with Simon before she left home." *Shit*. I *definitely* said that too fast.

Rav stood as he unfolded his arms and leaned on the table. Fists balled. Menace in his eyes. "I swear, if anything—"

"Noah's not after her." I also stood despite how stupid it was to square off with Rav. "If he were, he would have tracked where she was every second. She wouldn't have seen him until it was too late. He's not stupid, either, Rav. Think about it."

He glowered at me, his extra three inches feeling like a foot. He could have thrown me over the short wall without stopping to think. It was what he'd trained for. He excelled at strategy and tactics. A surveillance expert and marksman who possessed a level of grit I'd never encountered before.

And he was so loyal to his friends he'd die for any of us.

That included Jenn.

"You remember the first time you broke her heart?"

It was one kiss. Hardly her whole heart. And who'd told him? *Jenn and Rav have been friends that long, too, remember?*

"I should have kicked your ass back then instead of letting Scarlett stop me." The intensity in Rav's eyes didn't break until he finally pivoted to Jayce. "Let's go."

Drew collected Jayce's garbage, and they headed for the garbage bin.

Rav turned back to me, burning a hole through me with his gaze. "And for the record? You know the Casino best, so you should be joining us at the office. If this job fails..." Rav's finger aimed at my chest. "It's on you."

CHAPTER 34

JENN

I TIED my new pink silk scarf around my neck, donned my new sunglasses, and tucked Emmett's credit card into my purse.

Chloé, the amazing shopping assistant, handed over the last of my bags. "Have an unforgettable evening."

"I will." After last night, this morning, and now the shopping, unforgettable was a given. "And thanks for all your help."

Emmett had come in with me, setting both a minimum and maximum amount for me to spend. Not trusting me to reach the threshold, he'd told Chloé to help me shop until I hit twenty thousand euros. I had the requisite dress, shoes, jewelry, and handbag for this evening, along with new underwear and everyday accessories.

'This is how undercover works,' he'd said. *'If you don't fit the part, no one will buy you as my date.'*

Scarlett dressed like this on a regular basis. I'd always known she spent a lot on clothes, but had no idea how much.

It wasn't all business expenses, was it? Did she and Emmett honestly make so much they could afford all of this?

Maybe I needed a career change.

I stepped out into the warm August day. Across the street, a small snack shop sat amidst several tables and chairs. Emmett and Will sat at a table isolated from the others. A couple, a family, and a few other people scattered around the rest of the seating area. Beyond them, the port was full of yachts and superyachts.

Including Massimo's.

With the fake Constable.

I glanced down the street, watching for a break in traffic. Rav, Jayce, and Drew were further down the sidewalk, out of earshot, unless I yelled. I could practically see the storm cloud gathering around Rav's head.

What was going on?

You're supposed to meet Emmett. Stay on track. I stepped in between a couple of parked cars, watching as a Ferrari and a Bentley motored by. Monaco really was a whole other world.

I darted across the street when there was an opening, focused on Emmett. My stomach did a few flip-flops, and I did my best to hold down the smile that would give us away. Although, Will wasn't the type to figure out something like that. Not like Rav. If I smiled at Emmett the way I wanted to, Rav would know in an instant.

Although, had Emmett already given it away? He'd said we wouldn't tell anyone yet. Emmett was always so smooth. But could he hide...

Wait a second. Did Emmett's feelings exist outside of the bedroom? Well, outside of the hotel suite? They certainly hadn't been confined to a bedroom last night. Or this morning.

Emmett's rich brown eyes met mine, and he gave a curt nod. Yep. He was hiding it plenty fine. No problem at all.

Will craned his neck around to face me. Just as serious.

Had their meeting not gone well? Was that why Rav was marching off, with Jayce practically running to keep up with him?

As I approached, Emmett said, "Looks like you did well."

I sat at the table, put down my bags, and fished Emmett's credit card out of my purse. "I have all the receipts."

"That didn't answer my question."

I peered into the bags and pointed to them in order. "Shoes, clutch, dress, jewelry. The shoe and jewelry selection was limited, but Chloé selected some beautiful pieces. She also had a few dresses that arrived last week, so I've got something brand new from a local designer."

An array of boxes and gadgets littered the table in front of Will—his default, as long as I could remember. Will was Scarlett's little sister's best friend, so he'd been a part of my life almost as long as the rest of the Reynolds family. His father had been a carpenter and taught Will how to carve and fit woodwork. As he grew older, the materials grew more complex. He and Brie used to spend hours assembling electronics of all sorts.

"Will," I said, "I haven't seen you since your father passed. I was sorry to hear about it."

Will gave me a tight-lipped smile.

"Are you still living in London with your mom?"

"I am."

"Any thoughts of moving back home?"

"My sister's staying with her right now." Will looked up at Emmett and then at me. "I expect when I get home, we'll start talking about assisted living."

Emmett said, "Brie mentioned you were already looking into it?"

"She's so young." Will pulled the dark tablet from the center of the table, staring at it. "Whenever she's in the hospital or gets particularly bad, I look into options. The wait-lists are so long... And when she comes out of whatever spot she's in, we switch back into our normal routine, and I don't have time to think about it."

I put my hand on Will's. "It might be better to start the process early and defer if you have to, rather than waiting until it's too late?"

"Some voice in my head says I can fix her like I can fix anything else." Will nodded slowly and started packing his things into his backpack. "But I can't."

Despite my father being a judgmental jerk at times, at least I had him and my mom.

"You're a good son to—" My phone rang, and I pulled it out of my bag. *Shit.* I showed it to Emmett. "It's Dante."

After I'd retrieved my phone from security at Casino Rocher last night, I'd found one call and a few texts from Dante, asking if I was all right. I'd messaged him, claiming my stomach was still upset, but I'd be fine.

"I should go," said Will, standing with his backpack. "I'll see you—"

"After the auction," said Emmett. He gestured to my phone. "Let me listen."

I took a deep breath and answered the call, while Will wandered away. "Hello, Dante."

"Jenn, how are you feeling?" Dante's voice was warm with concern. "You left the yacht so suddenly yesterday."

I glanced at Emmett, who leaned close enough to hear both sides of the conversation. "I'm much better. The seasickness passed this morning."

"I'm glad," Dante said. "I wanted to update you on... Papa confirmed there was indeed a mix-up, and we suspect the conservator was behind it. That's likely why he's not returned to town. We believe he swapped the paintings, planning to eventually sell the real Constable on the black market. We'll ensure the correct one gets to the auction tonight."

Emmett shook his head, a subtle frown expressing his skepticism.

"Will you be returning to the gallery to finish work on the copy?" Dante asked. "We were all fooled, but you still did excellent work and deserve to be paid."

"Oh, well, anyone can put it into the frame now," I said. "Once the varnish is no longer tacky, it should be fine. Since it's not actually a Constable, you don't need me."

Dante paused before he spoke again. "I was hoping to speak with you, Jenn."

My stomach twisted almost as much as I'd claimed it had yesterday. "I'm sorry. I'm quite busy at the moment."

"Of course," Dante said, his tone shifting slightly. Suspicious? "How did everything go with Emmett?"

'He's in love with you,' Dante had said.

That was *not* what was going on with Emmett. Was it?

"Everything went well," I said carefully, not wanting to give him an opportunity to probe deeper. I wasn't prepared for Emmett to hear Dante's theory. "But I need to go."

"Of course. And thank you for your discretion about the painting."

After we hung up, Emmett frowned. "Discretion? That's likely the real reason he called. He wants to ensure you don't tell anyone they hired you to clean a fake."

"I don't know." It didn't make sense. Dante had been so nice to me. He'd been so encouraging. How could he be caught up with kidnappers?

"You believed in him, and it's hard to shake that." Emmett's hand dropped to my lap, and he stroked my thigh. "You're holding up so well despite everything that's happened."

I pushed my sunglasses into my hair. "Your whole team's gone?"

His gaze flicked past me, scanning where they'd vanished. "They are."

"So what now?"

"Is there any lingerie in those bags?"

"I might have had Chloé toss in..." I bit my lip, trying to invoke the woman I'd been last night. "Something special for you."

"For me?"

"For tonight." I rummaged in the accessories bag and pulled out a small black box. "I know it seems silly to buy you something with your own money, but—"

"No, it's thoughtful." He pulled the lid off, revealing a gold silk pocket square. "For tonight?"

"Yeah." I pulled out the V-neck of my shirt and tucked the square into my bra. "I'll hold onto it until we're almost ready to go."

"It'll smell like you." He took hold of my scarf and pulled me close, his lips grazing mine. "I love it already."

I draped my arms over his shoulders. "There's more in the bag for after the auction."

He gave me a quick peck on the lips, let go of my scarf, and sat back. His eyes crinkled as I sat back. "I got you something, too."

He pulled a white bracelet box from his jacket pocket. He handed it to me with a look that was hard to decipher—something between excitement and hesitation.

When had he bought this?

I opened the box, and my breath caught. A thin gold bracelet nestled inside the box beside a small gold screwdriver. It wasn't just any bracelet. It was a Love bracelet. Iconic, ridiculously expensive, and meaningful. My mind raced. Was our relationship advancing this quickly? "Emmett, this is... I don't know what to say."

"You need to dress the part for tonight. I hope it matches the rest of the jewelry you bought." He rubbed the back of his neck, looking almost shy.

Dress the part. Right. This was how undercover worked, and I was reading too much into it. It was another business expense.

Right?

And why didn't I want him to confirm?

"Let me put it on you," he said, his voice softer, almost tender. He took the bracelet from the box and used the delicate screwdriver to secure it around my wrist. "Perfect fit."

I looked up at him, searching his face for any hint of his honest feelings. *Was* this all business? Or was there more?

Unfortunately, Emmett was a master at keeping his emotions in check, revealing only what he wanted me to see.

"It's beautiful."

"*You* are beautiful," he whispered, before leaning in again.

His lips met mine, soft and warm. The kiss was tender, almost achingly so. His hand ran up my neck, his thumb gently caressing my skin. I melted into him, savoring the sweetness of the moment. There was a depth to this kiss that felt different from everything last night or this morning. It was slower, more deliberate, as if he was trying to convey something he couldn't put into words.

Maybe it was the lingering doubt about what this all meant, or the fear it might end as quickly as it began. Whatever the reason, I clung to Emmett a little tighter, trying to memorize every sensation.

When we finally parted, I searched his eyes, hoping to find answers to questions I wasn't even sure how to ask. Did he regret what we'd done? What would come next? Did he feel the way I did?

He took a slow breath, his thumb continuing to stroke my cheek. "I don't want to spoil this moment, but I need to tell you something."

My heart stopped. *What now?*

He just kissed you, so calm down.

"I need you to understand..." He raked his teeth over his bottom lip, brow furrowing. "It was your father."

What was my father? "What?"

He sighed and cupped my cheeks, his touch firm yet uncertain, as if bracing me for bad news. "When we were fifteen. He saw me kiss you that night and confronted me. Said I wasn't..."

My heart started again and sank. My father? Considering the horrible things he'd said to me about Emmett, what would he have said to the boy himself?

"It doesn't matter what he said. I thought you should know I didn't do it on purpose. I was..." He shook his head. "I was young and didn't fight for you."

He'd had to fight so many people when he was younger. But kids. Teens. Not adults. At least, I hadn't realized it was adults, too. Scarlett hid everything so well.

"Why are you telling me this now?"

Emmett peered over my shoulder, his hands dropping to my scarf. "Rav suspects something's going on between us. He said some things about back then and..." He let his head roll forward, so I couldn't see his eyes.

I ran my fingers through his hair and kissed the top of his head. "That was fifteen years ago. It's in the past."

He whispered, "I'm not a bad man."

So many people told him he wasn't good enough, including my own father. And now Rav? I lifted his face so he had to look at me and truly absorb my next words.

CHAPTER 35

EMMETT

"YOU DESERVE TO BE HAPPY," Jenn whispered.

Did I?

I *wasn't* a bad man. But I *was* a selfish one.

I'd wanted Jenn for fifteen years, and now that I had her, I wasn't letting her go. Wasn't about to trust her safety to anyone, not even a pilot, an airline, and five thousand miles of distance. Not that I could tell anyone, but it was the truth, deep in my soul.

Rav was right about so much. The members of our high-profile team all had histories of relationships that failed because they couldn't handle the secrecy. Jenn might have been different, but Scarlett would never let her in on what we really did. So he was right—I was letting myself enjoy the moment, but I'd have to hurt her in the end.

How my own heart dealt with it didn't matter.

She was what mattered.

Fuck, man, let her go.

I wrapped my fists in her scarf, forcing her close enough to kiss her again. Taste her. Just be nothing but the man making her sigh and smile.

Where Rav was entirely wrong was about how much I had to prove. To Jenn, to her father, to my sister, to Fenix...

To myself.

I wasn't my father. No matter how many lies I told Jenn, I was doing everything to protect her.

Except her heart.

But in the end, I *was* selfish. I let her believe I was putting her wants above everything else, when honestly, I was putting my needs first. I needed to feel normal and in control again. She gave me both.

Fuck, last night, I'd had my first real sleep in four months. She gave me the peace I needed for that. I hadn't even brought the gun into the room. The night before, I'd thought about it, but last night? I'd completely forgotten.

I broke from the kiss and wrapped my arms around her. "Let's go back to the hotel. We have a few hours before we need to get ready, and I can think of a few things I want to do with this scarf."

How would I survive going back to the real world without her?

CHAPTER 36

JENN

"Once we hand over our invitations and enter the auction room, I'll be in work mode." Emmett held tight around my waist as we walked through the first grand room of the Casino Rocher, past the blackjack table where I'd sat yesterday. He looked dashing in his tuxedo, the pocket square I'd bought him matching my gold evening gown perfectly. My new shoes pinched a bit—I'd tried to break them in, but my feet weren't used to heels anymore after two years of casual dress at Aunt Penny's studio.

"I'll be more focused on the other attendees than you. Don't take it personally."

"What do you mean?" I asked.

"I'm watching for thieves who might take the scarab and whoever else might bid for it."

That seemed excessive, but maybe that's just how black market auctions worked. "Why isn't the rest of the team with you?"

"Drew will arrive soon to cover the casino, but everyone

else is support staff. We only secured two invitations for the auction—for Reginald and Krista Stone."

"Shouldn't you have gotten invites for Drew or Rav?"

"Neither of them looks as stunning in a dress as you." Emmett's lips quirked.

I couldn't help but smile, his hand on my waist a reminder of our shower this afternoon. I could almost feel the hot water cascading over my skin, Emmett's strong hands lathering me up. If I closed my eyes, I'd be back in the shower, with his lips tracing a path along my collarbone, while his fingers... oh, god, his fingers.

How had so much changed in just a day?

Emmett had always been the one I'd wanted, even when I was fifteen and he was the troubled boy my father warned me about. Our sexual chemistry was so natural; being with him was like wrapping myself in a warm blanket. We'd fallen into this new rhythm quickly. Too quickly? Was there any chance we'd still be together when we got home?

Think about that tomorrow. "I bet they don't look as stunning in a tux as you do, either."

"They don't." Emmett squeezed my waist and kissed my temple without missing a step.

I took in the grand surroundings, the sweeping lines of the cavern's ceiling, and the sea of black-tie attire. "What happens if one of these people walks into the auction and finds out what's actually going on?"

"It isn't *entirely* black market. There will be some less-than-legal transactions, but most of the items are legitimate. Martine told me she's enticing the clientele with exclusivity, lower fees, and the Rocher experience."

"The Rocher experience? Privacy and legal flexibility?"

"Something like that."

The idea of selling stolen art didn't sit well with me, so Emmett's mission to return the scarab to its rightful owner made me proud.

Midway through the second room, Emmett stopped and flicked his gaze up to the windows of Martine's office. "I need to speak with her for a moment." He gestured to a doorway built into the cavern wall opposite the office. "Why don't you go into the auction room and wait for me inside?"

I placed my hands on his chest, sliding them to the nape of his neck. "I'll miss you."

Emmett ran his fingers down my arms and kissed me. It was chaste, a kiss that wouldn't mess up my lipstick, but it lingered, as much breath as lip. When we parted, he scanned my face, his gentle smile warming me from the inside. He'd been so vulnerable and honest with me since I'd moved into the suite. Somehow, I'd grown to want him even more than I had before.

"I'll see you inside," Emmett said, kissing my cheek before leaving.

As I watched him go, the same thoughts that had been trying to creep in all afternoon pushed into my brain. '*It was your father*,' Emmett had said. My father had chased Emmett away. How could he have done that to me? My parents let me believe Emmett had simply lost interest, but my father was behind it the whole time.

Although, it shouldn't have surprised me.

How different might my life have been if my father hadn't interfered? What if Emmett and I had been given a shot?

Honestly? You were fifteen. It likely wouldn't have worked out, anyway. Sure, some people stayed with their high school sweethearts all their lives, but would that have been us? Or would we have dated, broken up, and ruined my friendship with Scarlett?

Maybe it had been for the best, after all, and now we had a chance to try again?

You're getting ahead of yourself, Jenn. It's only been a day.

I headed to the auction room, presented my invitation to the security guard, and went inside. It was more of the natural cavern, with a lower ceiling than the main rooms, but also decorated with elaborate chandeliers. Rows of chairs were set up near the front, while various objects were displayed near the back. Obvious security guards lined the walls, sweeping the room with their eyes.

Soft, stringed music melded with the voices surrounding me, playing from hidden speakers. At the front, the auction block stood higher than the chairs, with large screens above it, looping through items for the auction.

A server greeted me with champagne. "Bonsoir, madame."

"Good evening," I said, both advising him I spoke English and accepting the drink.

He nodded. "The auction items are on display until the auction begins. Then our staff will move everything to the storage area, where they will be prepared for pickup or delivery to the winners after the auction is completed and payment is confirmed." He handed me an auction catalog from his tray. "No digital devices are allowed inside the Casino Rocher, so you may use this to follow along."

I thanked him and began flipping through the pages. Once I found the listing for the scarab, I wandered over to look at the tiny item in person. Two million euros to start. Amazing. And five of Emmett's team members came to Monaco for it.

What were they doing as support while he and Drew were here? Why so many of them, when the entire job had been Emmett talking to people, and tonight bidding on the item? Surely he could have done it alone.

Scarlett had always been vague about her job, which I took to mean she thought it was boring. It certainly *felt* boring. Not nearly as active or involved as *my* job.

Speaking of my job...

I searched for the *Wheatfield* painting, eventually spotting it across the room.

Nervous energy swirled around my stomach as I stared at it.

Had Dante been honest about Massimo mixing up the paintings and ensuring the right one made it to the auction? Should I check it out? What if it was still the fake? What would I do? What *could* I do if I didn't want to get kicked out?

Curiosity won out, and I moved through the crowd.

Some people smiled as I passed, while others looked me up and down. I gripped my black studded clutch tighter. I didn't belong among these people with such blatant wealth—so many diamonds and exotic leathers.

You're wearing five figures' worth of designer clothes, Jenn. You belong.

At least, I looked like I belonged.

Five feet away from *Wheatfield*, my heart sank. The B and L in the signature didn't quite touch, which was the error in the copy. Even from so far away, it was unmistakable. Dante had lied. Probably told me to stay quiet about the painting and assumed I wouldn't attend.

Emmett was right again.

Inwardly, I groaned at myself. My father was right again, too—I had terrible judgment in men.

"You said"—Dante's deep Italian voice startled me—"you were too busy to come to the gallery. I hadn't expected you meant you were too busy attending the auction."

I should have known he'd be here tonight. Should have prepared what I'd say if he and the copy were here. I'd been too focused on Emmett to think through what tonight would bring. "And you said you'd ensure the real Constable painting was at the auction."

He exhaled slowly, a frustrated noise. "Sì, my father said he would."

I pointed at the signature. "Then what's that?"

Dante leaned in to inspect the painting. His jaw clenched, a muscle twitching beneath the skin, and his eyes flashed with anger and something deeper—probably irritation because I'd caught him red-handed. His voice was low and tightly controlled when he spoke, each word measured as if he were afraid of what might slip out if he let his guard down. "Since you're not here as my date, I wonder how you got in? Are you accompanying Emmett Stone?"

"You're the one who told me to pursue him."

"Things certainly changed quickly." The way his lips thinned and he didn't look at me—was Dante jealous? Had he expected Emmett to reject me? Had he thought I'd come crawling back to take him up on everything he'd offered me at dinner?

"Not as magnanimous as you sounded the other night."

"Don't tell anyone about the painting." Dante cleared his throat, his features darkening. "I'll take care of it."

Sure, he'll take care of it. Just like he ensured it wouldn't be here. "Why did you give me your conservator's notes?"

"Because I didn't know." His nostrils flared, and he stared at me for a beat before turning away. He dodged people on his way to the second row of seats and joined his father. He and Massimo leaned their heads together. Neither of them looked upset, and Dante obviously wasn't chastising his father.

Mix-up, my ass. Didn't know? Not likely. They must have planned this all along. How many times had I tried defending him to Emmett? God, I was so gullible.

Dante was nothing more than a criminal who wanted me to keep his secret. Oh, and wanted to get me in bed.

Another man approached me from behind. "So they brought you into the fold after all?"

The air rushed out of my lungs. I remembered that voice. I'd spent so much time with him while he and Scarlett were engaged—dinners and barbecues at their house, evenings out, and card games with friends.

Noah continued, "I never expected Scarlett would read you in."

Little breaths. Stay calm. I was in so far over my head. I didn't know what was going on with Dante. Didn't know what Noah was talking about. But what I *did* know was that both of them were awful people. I turned to face him. "Funny running into you here. Thought you'd be too busy in your evil lair to mix with the masses."

"You've heard about my change in status." Noah's gaze raked over me, as if peeling back my layers. He'd always been sharp, but an unfamiliar danger lurked in his eyes. His head cocked, and a curious smile broke. "But you don't know about *them*, do you?"

"Them?" I asked.

Noah mused, "No earpiece."

What was he talking about?

"There's something bigger going on," Noah said.

"Bigger? I already figured out your little game with the painting." I gestured to the De Rosas. "I told your partner in crime that he didn't fool me."

"You're kidding?" Noah laughed and shook his head. "You're the restorer, aren't you? The one Dante brought in from Nice?"

My gut twisted. Why was that funny? Had Dante said something to him about me? "I am. I'm working for my—" And why did I need to justify myself?

"Scarlett isn't here with you, is she?" Noah glanced around the room, a flicker of something in his eyes. Of what? Hope? Longing? Was he still in love with her, despite whatever made him pretend he was dead?

I was probably imagining it, layering who he used to be on top of whoever he was now. "I'm here with Emmett."

"It's good to see you again, Jenn. But as much as I'd like to catch up"—Noah patted my arm and I yanked it away—"it would probably be smart for you to leave. Both of you."

As he wandered off, the butterflies in my stomach mixed with the bile rising in my throat. Dante, I could handle. Maybe. But Noah? Why should we leave? What was really going on?

CHAPTER 37

EMMETT

I'D TOLD Jenn I needed to speak with Martine, but unfortunately, that was code—a lie—for *I need to go into the men's room to sneak my earpiece in without you knowing*. Everything would have been easier if Scarlett weren't so uptight about her friends uncovering the truth about her job.

On my way out of the men's room, I said, "Everyone in place?"

Rav's gruff response came over my comms first. "In position on the water. No movement at the museum's water door."

Brie chimed in next. "HQ is up and running. Scar and I are ready for the drone feed. We have everyone's GPS signals and Jenn's."

Drew caught my eye from where he stood at a craps table. He must have arrived minutes after Jenn and me. Had he seen us together? "Good roll," he said, clapping at the player beside him, donning his cover perfectly.

"Drew's comms are solid inside," I told the team, since none of them would be able to hear him yet.

Will finished the check-ins. "Jayce and I are in the caverns. Drones are prepped and ready for deployment."

"Copy that." I nodded, despite Drew being the only one who could see me, then started my circuit around the room. "Proceeding to check the tunnel and storage area."

I strolled through the Casino, my steps measured but outwardly casual. The path to the ladies' room had no line and an unimpeded flow of women in and out. Perfect cover for Jayce. "Nothing out of the ordinary at the tunnel to the secret entrance. Checking the storage area next."

The team continued to chatter over the earpieces. I tuned it out, focusing on my surroundings—none of their words were for me. My gaze swept over the crowd, cataloging faces and potential threats. That's when I spotted the Grecian former model, fluttering her chips.

Our eyes met, and she shot me a flirtatious wink. I returned a smile, briefly entertaining the thought of joining her for a hand after the auction. Not because she was beautiful —I had a far more perfect woman waiting for me in the auction room—but because she'd be a challenge at the table.

A jolt of anxiety crashed through me, and my throat constricted.

Calm. Deep breaths.

Jenn may have helped chase some of my demons away, but clearly not all of them. I still wasn't ready for poker. Shaking off the moment, I continued my sweep, confirming there was no additional security guarding the storage room.

Satisfied, I reported my progress and made my way to the room where the auction was being held.

The room was packed—easily over two hundred people in attendance. Unable to spot Jenn in the crowd, I moved to the side of the room, using my height advantage to look over the seated guests.

As I searched, I noted familiar faces. Dante and Massimo, deep in conversation in the second row. A Russian oligarch, who I was sure had one of the missing Fabergé eggs. A Nigerian businessman who'd once tried to hire Reynolds to recover some of the Benin Bronzes from the British Museum.

Finally, my eyes landed on Jenn, and my breath caught in my throat. She was talking to a woman in front of a painting. Absolutely fucking stunning. She'd pinned her blond hair up, highlighting her long neck, the gold dress she'd bought earlier skimming her curves like I intended to do tonight. Underneath, the special lingerie she'd hinted at with a mischievous glint in her eye.

She fit in seamlessly, exuding confidence as they discussed the artwork. A pang of doubt hit me. Should I have sent her home like Rav and Scarlett suggested? Was I risking her safety for my own pride? For my refusal to run from Fenix?

Will's voice over the earpiece pulled me out of my thoughts. "Are you seeing this?"

Brie chuckled. "There's got to be a hundred of those urban explorers!"

Good news for us. More of the explorers meant more chaos in the tunnels. More chance Jayce could slip in unseen if I didn't win the auction.

I was about to head over to Jenn when the auctioneer stepped to the front, greeting the crowd. People began moving to their seats as the large screens behind him finally stopped their scroll. On the left screen, images of the scarab appeared, along with notes on its provenance and bidding information.

The right screen displayed a list of the items to follow: a Velatti Aereus roadster, then the golden Chinese disc.

The disc. *Was* it one of Fenix's targets? What did they want with it? Hell, what did they want with any of their acquisitions?

My gaze drifted back to Jenn, alone now that the staff was removing the auction items. Face pinched, she flicked her eyes from me to the front of the room. What was she—

Noah. He was taking a seat behind Dante and Massimo. He looked up at me. Smiled.

Fucking asshole.

He started in my direction, and my chest constricted. Pain streaked up my throat when I tried to swallow.

He's not Enzo. Calm the fuck down.

I dug a hand into my pocket, gripping my poker chip and tensing to hide any shudder. With my other hand, I gestured for Jenn to stay put. She couldn't get caught in whatever game Noah was playing.

"She looks different than I remember," Noah said as he reached me, inclining his head toward Jenn. "Don't tell me you two finally hooked up?"

The auctioneer started bidding for the scarab at two million, and I raised a hand, partly to bid and partly to keep Noah at arm's length.

"As if you don't know why she's here," I said.

Noah cocked his head, settling in beside me as I split my attention between the auction and him. "Initially, I assumed it was because she was working with you, but obviously not."

Scarlett hissed over the earpiece, her voice full of venom. "Tell that jackass—"

"Scarlett, please," I muttered, cutting her off. The last thing I needed was her distracting me, too.

The Nigerian businessman raised his hand, outbidding me. Probably just to be a pain in my ass.

"Is Scarlett in town with you?" Noah asked, a smirk playing at the corners of his mouth. "Tell her and her new little boy toy I say hello."

At least Scarlett didn't respond to that. And neither did Malcolm, the 'boy toy' in question.

I ran my fingernail around the edge of the chip. "What do you want?"

Noah raised his glass to his mouth, hiding his words. "What I wanted *two months ago* was for your team to grab the scarab. You're so late it doesn't matter anymore."

"Why?"

"My team's getting too cocky." Noah sipped the champagne, his eyes glued to the front of the room—but I knew him well enough. He was watching everything. "They need to be reined in."

Anger flared in my chest. It was clear Noah was manipulating the Reynolds team into doing his dirty work, which was precisely what I'd told Scarlett was going on. I clenched my fist, the poker chip digging into my palm.

"I hadn't expected you to come now, though," Noah continued, his tone casual. "You really should cut your losses and go."

I raised an eyebrow. "Afraid we'll mess with your grand schemes?"

"Afraid?" Noah chuckled—the sound grating on my nerves. "You haven't stopped us from securing anything we've wanted. Sure, you've had some of our team members arrested, but none of them were critical to our end goals." He took another sip as I raised my bid. "You're little more than an irritating fly. We have loftier goals than you can understand."

I kept my face neutral—he was feeding me intel, but what exactly? "So, why are you here talking to me?"

Noah shrugged. "Not everyone in our organization realizes this truth. You should be grateful our lines of communication are so poor. Enzo was certain the pretty restorer Dante brought in from Nice was an undercover operative."

My heart skipped a beat. That explained it. "The break-in at her hotel?"

"He thought she was seducing Dante in order to uncover Massimo's secrets. If he'd found out she was working with you—"

"She's not working with us." My words had come too quickly, betraying how much his presence got under my skin.

"Let me rephrase." Noah frowned slightly. "If he'd found her link to Reynolds, she would have been in a lot of trouble. Fortunately for her, he didn't find any damning information in her bags, and she miraculously switched to another room shortly thereafter. Be happy he got bored pursuing her."

Happy? If Enzo had found out where she was staying, that would have led him straight to me. A knot tightened in my gut, and I fought to relax my muscles. I couldn't let Noah see that reaction. I raised the bid again, trying to focus on the auction. We were up to three and a half million euros. I only had half a million left to grab it legally.

Noah continued, "Although if Enzo or Massimo had bothered to tell me her name or that a Stone was poking his nose around, I would have figured it out before five minutes ago."

"You gave us the tip about the scarab. Don't tell me you would have scared us off the job?"

"I would have scared you out of Monaco altogether."

"Why?"

Noah's eyes finally met mine, cold and calculating. "This is our place right now. We may have more significant concerns than Reynolds Recoveries, but Enzo will kill any of you on sight because he believes his little failures at your hands are important. He wants revenge."

My stomach churned at each mention of Enzo. Of the memory of what he'd done to me when it *hadn't* been revenge.

Jayce said over the earpiece, "The first explorers are nearing the secret door. Are we a go?"

I stared at the auctioneer. The Nigerian had raised his bid to four million euros. That was my upper limit. I glanced at Jenn across the room, apprehension and worry written all over her face.

The auctioneer called for any further bids. Everyone else had dropped out.

I raised my hand, pushing the bid to four-point-one million euros. It was close enough to our target, and I wasn't losing over a hundred thousand. I'd cover that if Mum balked at it.

Noah used his glass to conceal his words again. "Why bid on it if you're just going to steal it? Jayce not so sure of her abilities anymore? I hear her leg's getting worse."

I froze. Of course, he knew our plan. Of course, he knew about Jayce. He knew everything about our team, and we knew next to nothing about his.

Fuck.

Noah was distracting me even more than Jenn. Did he

have some bigger game going on? *He always has a bigger game going on.* But if Fenix considered Reynolds nothing more than irritants, we had to stop thinking Fenix was after us.

Unless Noah said all of that to manipulate me?

Double fuck.

I looked at Jenn again, and calm settled over me. Her presence grounded me, reminding me of what truly mattered. I was getting too worked up during this job, but in the end, I had the most important thing—her.

The auction, Noah's mind games, even the scarab itself seemed to fade into the background. Turning back to Noah, I changed tactics. Go on the offensive. "Why come here to buy the disc when you could have just kidnapped its owner?"

Concern flashed behind Noah's eyes, his composure slipping for just a moment. "If you touch it—"

"Don't worry, we're only here for the scarab." I watched his reaction carefully, searching for any truth leaking out.

The Nigerian businessman increased his bid to four and a half million.

Noah clucked his tongue. "It would appear Osaze's still sore about those Bronzes."

Goddammit. An extra hundred thousand over our limit was one thing, but the next bid would eliminate most of the profit Reynolds would get when we handed the scarab over. The reward was five million. Frustration flooded my body— going that high would be stupid.

Before I could respond to Jayce, Scarlett's voice came through my earpiece. "Osaze won't sell us the scarab for less than a million profit. Jayce, you're up."

Jayce's confident reply came through, "You got it, boss."

Scarlett said, "Be careful."

"What fun would that be?" Jayce was so reckless at times. But she was ready.

Noah stepped in front of me, blocking my view of the auctioneer. His proximity had me clenching the chip again, and I resisted the urge to step back. "Don't forget, my team's here tonight. And I also have a past with Martine."

He winked and walked off, leaving me with a growing sense of unease.

As Noah wove his way through the crowd, my mind raced. Had we been double-crossed? Did Noah plan on us being here? Was Enzo waiting for Jayce? The possibilities made my brain spin.

"Shit," I muttered under my breath. "Be extra careful, Jayce. Keep an eye out for Enzo."

"I will, too," said Drew. No one else could hear him, but everyone knew he'd do anything for Jayce. Rav had been right to insist Drew work on the inside. He thought on his feet well, and if he spotted anything going wrong, he'd choose Jayce's safety. I could trust in that, at least.

Apparently ignoring everyone else, Jayce said, "The guards are distracted. I see my opening."

I blew out a deep breath. Time for the real game to start.

CHAPTER 38
EMMETT

STARING at the auctioneer was nothing more than cover. My peripheral vision—and my brain—was trained on Noah. He took a seat behind Dante and Massimo. When he leaned forward to speak with them, Dante craned his head back, then spun to glower at me. But I kept my gaze on the action everyone else was there for.

Over my earpiece, Jayce made random quips at people as she passed them, demonstrating to us she'd gotten in. Brie and Scarlett kept everyone up-to-date about Jayce and Drew's locations and the video feed from the drones inside the tunnels. The guards had the first wave of urban explorers nearly under control. Everything was going to plan.

"Brie," I whispered, "can you have one of your team members research this golden disc? I want to know what it is."

"We're on it," Brie said.

Jayce said something to Drew over the comms—a sarcastic comment about him colliding with her. In reality, she'd snuck the device that would allow Brie to hack the security feed into his pocket.

Jenn approached, threading her arm around mine. "You okay? You were talking to Noah for an awful long time."

"Fine."

Jenn sighed. "Fine? I'm still in shock."

The auctioneer introduced the golden disc.

Massimo took the first bid.

"I mean… every time I turn around here, something else crazy happens." She held my arm tighter. "Can you believe they brought the fake painting to the auction?"

"The fake's here?" I asked, momentarily distracted from the auction.

Jenn nodded and put her head on my shoulder. "At least one good thing's happened. You and I—"

"Massimo's bidding on a golden disc." I inclined my head toward the front before she could mention anything going on between us. I couldn't let the team hear that. "Considering how much gold he already has in the gallery and no doubt in his home, it's a curious purchase."

Jenn opened her auction catalog. "This one's from China, originally part of a fengguan from the ninth century. His gallery doesn't have much from East Asia."

As Jenn spoke, Brie filled in more details on her end. "It came from the inventory of a Chinese noblewoman. In that period, the dragon represented the emperor. And can you guess what represented the empress?"

"The phoenix?" I guessed.

"Yes, how'd you know that?" Jenn asked, flipping pages in her auction catalog, as though searching for information. "The fengguan is also known as a phoenix crown."

Shit. Drew had called it. I was more distracted than I'd

realized. I shouldn't have responded to Brie while Jenn was talking to me.

"You're right about his interest in antiquities," I said, trying to recover. "Jean-Philippe mentioned something about Massimo's fascination with phoenixes, specifically. I was wondering if this might be related, but a nest or feathers would seem more appropriate."

That was a reasonable cover.

I watched the auction intently, my mind racing with possibilities. Massimo and three others were locked in a bidding war, the price skyrocketing past three million.

The reward money for returning the scarab might be enough to snag this mysterious disc. You should bid on it.

No, Emmett, that's a bad idea.

Jenn closed her auction catalog and tucked it under her arm with her clutch. "I'm not sure about other periods, but the phoenix was often depicted with a halo in medieval European iconography. Maybe in Chinese mythology, the crown—"

"That's it!" I blurted, my eyes darting between her and the auction. "The Fenix Group, as far as we're aware, has collected a talon, a feather, and a beak. All made of solid gold, ancient pieces from various cultures around the world."

"You think they're collecting parts of a larger statue or something?"

"That's got to be it!" I said, with a couple of voices over my earpiece echoing the comment.

Jenn's brow furrowed. "And you think this confirms Massimo and Dante are *part* of the organization? Not just working with them?"

The auctioneer's gavel fell with a resounding crack. "Sold

to Monsieur De Rosa for five million, two hundred thousand euros!"

Massimo and Dante stood, embracing despite an obvious tension between them. Massimo gestured toward the entrance, exchanging words with Noah, who nodded in response.

The senior De Rosa said his goodbyes and left through a side door.

For my team's benefit, I whispered, "I think Massimo's headed for the water door."

Jenn looked up, but didn't question me.

Rav's voice sounded in my ear. "There's a tender heading toward the door. It came from a yacht waiting a kilometer or so away. Will, can you dispatch one of your drones to make a positive ID on the yacht?"

Noah strode purposefully toward the casino door, while Dante settled back into his seat, looking decidedly pissed.

"Noah's leaving the event room. Probably going to retrieve the disc for Massimo?" Normally, I had a lot of leeway when coordinating a heist. So long as the people around me didn't realize what I was actually doing, I could easily use code for my observations or orders.

But with Jenn standing next to me?

I was giving a play-by-play of everything happening in the room, and she was following my every word. I should have been more careful, but I didn't have time for that.

Noah glanced in my direction, frowning at me before he vanished through the exit.

"You're acting weird. What's going on?" Jenn's arm tightened around mine. "Noah warned me we should leave. Should we?"

Leave?

Fuck Noah for dismissing us as minor irritants.

Fuck Enzo for breaking into Jenn's hotel room.

Fuck all of them. Those bastards would *not* win again.

"If the disc is what Fenix wants," I said, an image of shoving the words down Noah's throat too appealing, "I want it more."

Jenn asked another question, but Jayce's voice in my ear drowned her out. "Well, I'm in the storage room already. And it's sitting right in front of me. It doesn't fit as nicely into my dress, but I can grab it."

Scarlett began to protest. "That's not part of our—"

"Do it," I snapped, my mind made up.

"Do what?" Jenn's confused voice practically melded with the background noise. "Leave?"

My focus was on the unfolding situation. On my team. On Jayce.

Noah was en route to the storage room to collect Massimo's prize. He knew Jayce. He'd spot her. What would he do if he caught her with the disc?

Shit. What if Enzo was in the Casino somewhere? Why hadn't I planned that out earlier?

We were so close to our goal. I had to act fast.

CHAPTER 39

JENN

I STARED UP AT EMMETT, who seemed to be somewhere else. His eyes were distant, focused on something other than the auction or me. It was as if he'd suddenly transported to another world, leaving me behind.

Frustration bubbled up inside me. Was this more of the spy stuff I'd teased him about yesterday?

Emmett's jaw tightened, an internal struggle playing out across his face. He was holding something back, something big.

"I said, should we lea—" I began, but Emmett's face snapped toward mine.

He gave me a brief kiss on the cheek. "I need to talk to somebody about the man who won the scarab."

I barely had time to say, "But can't you just talk to him? He's right here," before Emmett strode out of the auction room.

Was I supposed to go with him? Stay here? Sit at the blackjack table like a good little girl?

Everything else in the room was completely normal. The

auction continued, people drank, and the staff milled about the room. So why did I feel so completely lost?

The auctioneer dropped his gavel on a ruby-encrusted necklace and moved on to the next item.

"*Wheatfield on the Lock*, a stunning painting by John Constable," the auctioneer announced, reciting information about the original first in French and then in English. Year painted. Medium. Highlighting the characters and the clouds. "As you can see from our provenance documentation, this lovely piece has been in the possession of royalty and celebrities around the globe. The current starting bid is two hundred thousand euros, certainly a steal for such an illustrious piece."

It's a steal, all right.

Dante should have had it removed from the auction, like he swore he would. But what else could I expect from a man working for an organization that kidnapped and beat people to get what they wanted?

Rage built inside my chest, hot and immediate, demanding action. I marched around the perimeter of the chairs and up the center row, landing in the seat next to Dante. "Are you going to do something about this, or am I?"

Dante's eyes widened in surprise, then narrowed as he processed my words. "Jenn, I—"

"Don't," I cut him off. "Don't give me more excuses. That painting is a fake, and you know it. You promised me you'd take care of this."

The auction staff didn't know me from a hole in the wall. What could I do with my little accusation? Even if they believed me, Emmett said black market items were common here. Would they care? They *should* care, considering the copy wasn't worth a fraction of what the winner would pay.

Dante's surprise gave way to anger, and he growled, "He swore—"

"Yeah, yeah, your dad swore. You keep saying that, but it's nothing more than words. The copy is still up there, about to be sold to some unsuspecting buyer for a small fortune."

Small fortune? I'd been in Monaco too long if hundreds of thousands was small.

Dante's jaw clenched, and for a moment, I expected he'd argue with me. But he stood abruptly, maneuvering around me and stepping up to the front of the room.

He walked right up onto the platform, causing a stir among the other bidders. The auctioneer's microphone cut out, and they had a brief, hushed conversation. What felt like minutes ticked by until Dante waved for me to join him.

You go, girl. Twice in only two days, I'd stood up for what I believed in, told people what I wanted, and they did it. I rose from my chair, smoothed out my dress, and joined the men at the front.

As I approached, the weight of dozens of curious stares hit my back.

The auctioneer turned to me, his expression a careful mask of professionalism. "Monsieur De Rosa tells me the authenticity of this painting is in question?"

I nodded. "I had a firm in the States confirm it was a replica. The most telling feature is the signature—the letters are slightly off compared to an auction catalog we uncovered from 1956."

"And the name of the firm?"

"Caine-Ferraro Fine Art Investigations," I said.

The auctioneer nodded and gestured for one of his assistants to join us. "Show them to the preparatory room and record her details."

The assistant nodded and made her way down the steps, toward the door Massimo had taken. To the water door? That's what Emmett had called it, wasn't it?

"Once we have the information, we'll take it to the coordinator to confirm," said the auctioneer. He turned toward another of his assistants and pointed to the screen behind them. "For now, we'll move on to the next item in the auction."

CHAPTER 40
EMMETT

Thirty minutes had passed since the last auction items were moved to the storage room. Jayce was already inside, and she hadn't reported any problems. She must have swapped the scarabs and had the disc safely stowed in her dress. The op wasn't going perfectly anymore, but it was all within acceptable parameters.

Except for Noah. He was the one variable I'd hoped we wouldn't have to deal with. At least I hadn't spotted Enzo anywhere.

"I said"—Scarlett's command tone was in full effect—"Jayce, put the disc back."

Jayce blew a raspberry. "They tried killing me. Twice. And my man."

"And you don't think taking that disc will lead to a third attempt?"

Over my comms, Rav said, "I think Enzo's piloting the tender. He's picked up Massimo at the water door. The yacht in the distance must be his. No need for the drone, Will."

An icy pain spread through my body at the mention of

Enzo's name. *A bag flew over my head. Then the fist.* I pushed the memory aside, focusing on the present. On the Casino. On the op. He was outside in a boat, not inside. Everything was fine.

Will's response was quick. "It's halfway there already. I only need one to monitor the cavern."

Why were Enzo and Massimo leaving without Noah? Noah was on his way to the storage room, but the auction pieces weren't supposed to be available until after the auction ended. Could Noah be trying to pick up the disc early?

He must have made some sort of arrangement with Martine. That was what he meant when he said he had a past with her.

"Jayce," I said urgently, "I think Noah's on his way to the storage room. Get out and duck into the high-rollers' room. It's right next door."

And take the disc, Jayce. Show them we aren't scared of them.

There was a pause before Brie's voice came through. "Jayce just sent a text. Two staffers are inside the storage room now, so she can't talk."

"Shit," I muttered under my breath, scanning the room for Drew. When I caught his eye, I made a subtle hand signal indicating he needed to join me. I positioned myself by a craps table, surrounded by a large crowd, and waited.

Drew sidled up next to me, his expression neutral. "What's she done?"

I almost laughed at his immediate assumption that Jayce was wreaking havoc. "There are two workers inside. Jayce is hidden but can't leave."

Drew laughed and clapped at a winning roll on the table.

His ability to mask his true feelings and blend in was impressive. "Time for Plan J3?"

Whether or not she was leading the op, Scarlett ensured the team had enough backup plans to cover any eventuality. Since Martine had only promised to provide the passcode and no other help, we had multiple contingencies.

Plan J1 was if Jayce couldn't sneak past the guards and into the Casino—Drew would have crashed the secret door from the inside to add an extra distraction. Plan J2 was getting Jayce into the storage room undetected if Brie's hacking skills weren't up to snuff—which they always were. J3 was if Jayce got stuck in the storage room.

"J3 it is. But we also need to account for Noah."

Drew shook his head with the crowd as the next roll didn't go well. "Can she hear me?"

"She might, if the signal's strong enough inside the cavern." I tilted my head slightly. "Talk to my left ear if you want to be sure."

Drew leaned in close. "You're going to owe me for this one, sweetheart." He then wandered off.

Brie's giggle came through the comms. "Jayce's text says she's looking forward to it."

Will's voice followed, tinged with amusement. "I don't think I want to know."

I tuned out Brie and Will's subsequent conversation, focusing on Noah's movements. "He's at the storage room."

He pressed the buzzer by the door, and the door opened. Noah started to enter but stopped. His irritation was visible even from a distance. The door closed, and Noah exited the short hallway, checking his watch and surveying the area.

"I think the staffer's gone to retrieve the disc," I said, my mind working through the possibilities.

Brie said, "Jayce gave two taps on her comms."

I felt a small surge of relief. Two taps meant everything was okay, and Jayce didn't need a rescue. But Noah was still waiting, and that made me uneasy.

"Did you grab the disc?" I asked, hoping for confirmation.

"Two taps again. I think that means yes," Brie replied.

Will's update came next. "The second wave of urban explorers is almost at the guard desk. Some of them are turning around because the first wave is passing them on their way out."

Brie added, "People are posting about the armed guards on the message board. Although one guy did post about seeing a hidden door, which is attracting attention."

"They'll be at the guards in ten minutes. That's Jayce's window," Will said. "Post instructions about how to open the door. That'll keep more of them going forward."

"On it," Brie confirmed.

How long was Noah going to stand at the entrance to the storage room? And if he was there for the disc, what would happen when he found it missing? If he'd had to wait for the auction to end—which he was supposed to—we would have been long gone before he discovered it was missing.

The door behind Noah opened, and someone came out. Noah turned his back to me, engaging in conversation with the employee. Their body language told me they were arguing. The employee's hands went up in apology, and Noah jerked forward, shaking his head vigorously.

I said, "I think Noah figured out we took the disc."

Scarlett said, "Emmett, we need Jayce out of there. Now."

Noah flung his hand out and spun around, storming out of the hallway. Eyes narrowed, he scanned the room.

I ducked, pretending to tie my shoe and shifting until I could spot him again. "Noah's pissed. He's searching, probably for me or Jayce. I don't see Drew."

Drew wouldn't have abandoned his girlfriend. No doubt he was somewhere close, watching for his opening.

Noah approached a security guard, pointing at the storage room, then somewhere past me.

The guard touched his ear—engaging his comms—and nodded.

I stood, but stooped to ensure I didn't stand out. The guard walked from the third giant room to the second. He met up with another guard, and they stopped in front of the ladies' room entrance.

"Two guards have taken position in front of Jayce's escape route," I said.

Plan J3 transitioned to J5—the one where Drew risked himself to get Jayce out through the secret door.

Two women approached the guards, who pointed toward the third grand room, indicating where they could find another ladies' room.

This was a problem. If Jayce tried to leave through the main door, she'd have to go through the metal detector again, and they might find the scarab or disc on her. Maybe we'd have time to use the water door before Enzo returned for Noah—*if* he was coming back.

Noah started up the stairs to Martine's office.

I said, "Noah's heading to the manager's office, and the guards aren't letting anyone pass into the hallway to the ladies' room."

Will said over comms, "The second wave is arriving at the guard post. It's now or never, Jayce."

Drew—where was he?—said, "Wow, sorry. I was looking for the men's room."

A gruff male voice responded to him, "How did you open the door?"

Drew said, "It just opened."

I took my eyes off Noah for a moment to find Drew. He was at the storage room door, in someone's face. He must have been covering for Jayce.

"Don't touch me!" snapped Drew.

Jayce whispered, "I'm out."

Drew stumbled away from the storage room as though someone had shoved him. After he cleared the area, he straightened his tux. "What's the plan now?"

I said, "Two guards are blocking her path. We can handle them."

Drew said, "You're going to owe me twice."

She made a kissing noise and said, "Okay, Mr. Grumpy Face."

Noah vanished at the top of the stairs.

"Here we go, folks," I said. "Noah's out of the picture for now. Drew and I will get Jayce through. Will, bring the drone close enough so the guards can hear it. Hopefully, it will disorient them even more. Jayce, time to move."

I walked up to the guards, putting on my best concerned-husband act. "Excuse me, gentlemen. Could you check if my wife is still inside? She's been in the ladies' room for twenty minutes, and I'm getting worried."

One of them put out a hand. "I'm sorry, sir, but if you—"

"Wait," said the other. "You were with the boss yesterday, yes?"

"I was."

They looked at each other and straightened. This was precisely why I'd wanted to make a show of parading around with Martine—immediate respect.

Jayce stayed close to the wall, inconspicuous and casual.

The man who'd recognized me turned his head and touched his ear, speaking quietly. He was calling for a female guard to join us. More security would ruin our plan, not improve it.

"That's not necessary." I touched the man's arm, and the second guard swiped it away. I put up my hands in surrender, not interested in bringing more attention to us. "Just tell her it's time to—"

Drew appeared out of nowhere, tripping into both of the guards. They all careened away from Jayce's direction. Then three men came barreling out from the ladies' room, slamming into the guards, taking Drew and me to the ground with them.

The newcomers were all dressed in khakis and hiking boots.

Will's excited voice came through the comms, "They got the door open!"

No kidding.

"Wow!" One of the urban explorers, tangled up with Drew and me, attempted to stand. As he did, he pulled out his phone to take a photo. "They said the tunnel would lead somewhere amazing, but—"

The guards recovered first. The one who'd been calling for backup grabbed the explorer's phone and smashed it. He yelled at the invaders to stay down. Another guard, newly arrived from the secret passage, helped Drew and me stand.

No sign of Jayce, but she said over the earpiece, "I'm out. The guards didn't see me."

I mouthed to Drew, *She's safe*. Then I huffed out a breath, straightening my tux. "Thank you, gentlemen. I'll let Martine know what a splendid job you're doing."

"This was supposed to be an exclusive event." Drew looked down at the men on the ground in disgust. "I'm leaving."

"And if my wife comes out, tell her I've gone back to the auction." I ran a hand through my hair, ramping up my faux irritation, while still providing critical details to the team. "It's so much calmer in there."

I glanced toward Martine's office.

Was Noah still upstairs? Was he watching us?

Was Martine helping him more than she'd promised to help us?

CHAPTER 41

JENN

"Merci, madame." The auction assistant, professional and composed, closed her notebook. "I will take this information to the auction coordinator, who will confirm."

"Thanks. And I'm sorry for the hassle." I offered her a polite smile, pride and worry battling in my stomach. We'd done the right thing, but what consequences might I face for it?

The assistant left Dante and me in the small room off to the side of the auction. Like the rest of the Casino, it was carved directly from the rock. The ceiling hung low, creating an intimate, if somewhat claustrophobic, atmosphere. The soft lighting cast eerie shadows across the rough-hewn surfaces, accentuating the natural contours of the rock.

There were only two doors. One led back to the auction, the other presumably to the water door Emmett had mentioned earlier.

I studied Dante, trying to reconcile Emmett's warnings and the charming man who'd whisked me off to Monte Carlo for the job of a lifetime. If he was truly as evil as Emmett suspected, why would he have helped me expose the painting? But then again, he'd let it get this far. Was this all just an elaborate act to cover for his father?

Dante planted his hands on his hips, staring after the departed assistant. His jaw clenched, betraying his irritation. "They won't be happy to hear about this."

"They?" Did I want to know who?

"You look beautiful tonight." Dante turned to face me, his expression softening slightly. "I neglected to mention it earlier."

Seriously? After everything that had gone on, was that really all he had to say? "I don't know what kind of game you're playing—"

"Me?" Dante jabbed a finger at his chest, his eyes hardening again. "Marone. Of everyone here, I'm the—"

"Jenn," a familiar voice cut through our exchange. We both turned to see Noah standing in the doorway to the auction room.

A jolt of panic ignited in my chest, and I scanned the area behind him, searching the crowd for Emmett. Where was he? He wouldn't have left me here if it wasn't safe, would he?

The door closed behind Noah, and my first reaction was to run back through. But I needed answers.

Noah blew out a deep breath as he approached, his gaze intense. "What lies did Emmett tell you about me?"

Dante looked between Noah and me, his brows knitting together. "You two know each other?"

"Yeah, I've known this lying asshole for six years." I let out a bitter laugh. "Minus the two years we all thought he was dead."

Noah's expression tightened at my words, but he turned to Dante. "Can you give me a couple of minutes with her?"

Dante angled his head toward the door. "We can all return to the auction and speak there."

"I have things to..." Noah's head bowed, as though he were fighting to push out the right words. "I'd like to speak with Jenn privately."

Dante raised his eyebrows to ask for my approval. When I nodded, he said, "I'll be right outside the door."

Once the door shut behind Dante, I was alone with Noah. The little voice in the back of my head that wanted to leave grew louder.

"Scarlett doesn't understand. I've tried explaining everything to her." Noah ran his hands through his hair, frustration etched across his face. His voice was low, almost pleading. "I told you to leave. I said the same thing to Emmett—that it's too dangerous here—but he abandoned you for his job."

"What are you talking about?" I crossed my arms, attempting to project defiance, while I was actually disguising a subtle tremor. "How could you possibly know what Emmett said or did?"

He took a step closer, and I instinctively backed away. "Jenn, please. I didn't remember anything for the first several months after the accident. And after that? I stayed quiet to keep Scarlett safe." He held his hands out, palms up, begging me to understand. "You have to believe me."

I studied his face, searching for any sign of deception, but I'd never been able to tell when a man lied to me. I saw pain, a raw vulnerability that tugged at my heart despite my better judgment. "Then tell me the truth, and I'll give them the details."

Noah nodded, relief washing over his features. "I wasn't behind what happened to Emmett—the kidnapping. I had to go along with it, or they'd find me out."

"So, who *was* behind it?"

"Did they tell you about Enzo?" Noah asked, his eyes darting to the far door as if checking we were still alone. "The man with the scar?"

I held my shaking arms tighter, remembering the overwhelming urge I'd had to bolt from the gallery workshop when Enzo had checked in on me. I nodded slowly.

Noah glanced at his watch, a flicker of urgency crossing his face. "Did Emmett tell you why Reynolds is here?"

"We were talking about Enzo."

"They're stealing the scarab," Noah blurted out.

I blinked. Surely, I'd misheard him. Stealing? "What?"

"They wanted to appear legitimate by buying it outright, but once they failed, Jayce broke into the storage room and stole it."

"Jayce? Jayce Monroe?"

She wasn't even in the Casino.

Noah's expression hardened. "She's a thief, and he's a con man."

My mind spun, unable to keep up with his changes in topic and ridiculous accusations. I shook my head. "You're not making any sense."

"Did Emmett say anything unusual while you were here this evening? Like he was carrying on a conversation with someone other than you, but trying to hide it?"

That was precisely what talking to Emmett during the disc auction was like. My heart leaped into my throat, and I tried to keep my face neutral.

Noah must have seen my reaction, because he pressed on. "That's why I took my opportunity to leave Reynolds. They're nothing but a heist crew. All of their"—he made air quotes—"recoveries? Thefts. They're criminals."

"That's not possible," I whispered. My best friend was *not* a thief. This had to be another lie. "Why are you saying all this bullshit?"

Noah's eyes softened, a hint of sympathy in his voice. "I worked with them for four years. I was Scarlett's second-in-command. She didn't love me. She used me for my strategic skills."

"No." I held my hands out between us, creating a barrier, as though it would shield me from his words and force him to tell the truth. "You're lying."

"Didn't you wonder why there are so many other Reynolds team members in town, but Emmett is the only one at the auction tonight?"

My stomach sank. Of course, I'd wondered that. I'd even asked Emmett why. Grasping for an argument, I said, "Drew's in the Casino. Emmett didn't need him for the auction."

"I have more proof." Noah walked to the far wall and opened a hidden panel, revealing an elevator. "Come with me."

I stood rooted to the spot, my mind a whirlwind of conflicting thoughts. Everything Noah said made a twisted kind of sense. Years of Scarlett's vague answers about her regular trips overseas. How they could spend twenty thousand euros on my clothes as a business expense. How no one told me Noah was alive.

He pressed the call button, and the elevator's ancient dial

began climbing. "There's a security desk on the bottom floor where we can review footage. It'll show you everything."

I bit my lip, torn between curiosity and caution. *You're smarter than that, Jenn. No matter what Noah says, you need to hear the story from Scarlett or Emmett, not from him.*

Noah looked at the ceiling, balling his fists as I hesitated. "For fuck's sake, Jenn."

Taking a deep breath, I steeled myself. I didn't need to figure out if he was trustworthy or not. I just needed to find Emmett. "I'm sorry, Noah, but I can't go with you."

Something dark flashed across his face. "I didn't want to have to do this." Before I could react, he lunged forward, clamping a hand over my mouth and the other around my waist. "Emmett's left me no choice."

Oh god, oh god, please no!

My heart slammed against my ribs as I thrashed and fought, desperate to break free, but Noah's iron grip crushed me against him. Each attempt to scream died against his palm, swallowed by applause from the auction beyond the walls. My legs flailed wildly, finding nothing but air as he hauled me backward toward the waiting elevator.

Emmett! Dante! Somebody help me!

Please! Anybody!

The elevator chimed its arrival like a death knell, doors sliding open with a whisper, and he hoisted me off my feet.

I kicked my feet up to stop the door from closing, but he pivoted his weight, slamming us into the wall.

The fake wall began to close as the elevator doors slid shut.

It was too late.

CHAPTER 42
EMMETT

I HEADED BACK to the auction room. The lightness in my chest at the prospect of seeing Jenn warred with the pressing need to get her out of the Casino. Before handing security my invitation, I cast one last glance at Martine's office. No sign of Noah. The absence of his smug face should have been reassuring, but it only heightened my unease.

My team had done their job well—snagged both the scarab and the disc without triggering any alarms.

Not just minor irritants anymore, are we, Noah?

Once inside, I immediately checked the spot where I'd left Jenn. She wasn't there. A quick scan of the room yielded nothing. No flash of gold dress, no glimpse of her radiant smile.

Where are you?

Dante stalked toward me, his usual frown—at least for me, since he was all smiles for Jenn—morphed into barely concealed anger.

"Who *are* you?" Dante demanded, his accent thickening with emotion.

What game was he playing?

"Emmett Stone," I replied, falling back on my cover. "Antiquities—"

"Che cazzo." Dante's hand sliced through the air, cutting off my practiced introduction. "You and Noah Pierce—how do you know each other?"

Pierce? We'd assumed Noah had been using an alias since we hadn't been able to find any trace of him under Noah Turnbull, since we discovered he was alive and well.

"That's none of your concern," I said, keeping my voice level.

Dante's jaw clenched, his eyes flashing with anger. "Are you two here to check up on me?"

"You two?" I asked, genuinely confused. Was he talking about Noah and me?

A bitter smile twisted Dante's lips. "It's always a pretty woman."

"What are you talking about?" I asked, still searching the room for Jenn. Had she stepped out, and I missed her? Passed right by her? Maybe she'd seen the commotion outside the ladies' room? Not something I wanted to have to explain to her.

"I don't need a babysitter," he spat, ignoring my words.

"And I don't have time for this." I tried to push past him, but Dante's hand landed square on my chest, stopping me in my tracks.

"You can tell my father I'm holding onto his secrets," he growled, leaning in close. "He can stop sending his little spies."

Spies? Massimo's secrets?

Noah's cryptic warning about the break-in at Jenn's hotel room came back to me—Enzo thought Jenn was trying to seduce Dante to get at Massimo. How did this all fit together?

"Listen, Dante," I said, forcing calm into my voice. We needed to leave before Noah could retaliate. "I don't care what you think is going on, but I need to find Jenn right now. Have you seen her?"

"Why should I tell you anything?"

I took a deep breath, trying to keep my voice steady. "Because our mutual friend's going to wander in here any second, and I'd rather not be here for it."

Dante's face contorted. "Friend?"

"Noah."

A flash of disgust crossed Dante's face. "He's not my friend." He paused, his brow furrowing. "I thought you were working with him?"

"You're the one"—as the words left my mouth, I knew they were wrong—"working with him."

Dante's disgust deepened. "I'm not working with any of those—"

"Where's Jenn?" I asked, my gut twisting. I read people for a living, and I'd misjudged Dante from the start—he had no reason to react so strongly to the idea he was working with Fenix. If it were a con, he should have brushed it off, not looked like he'd swallowed a bottle of poison.

Dante's head tilted, and the same realization I'd just had was mirrored in his eyes. "You're not working with Fenix?"

"I said, 'Where's Jenn?'" I practically shouted, drawing a few curious glances from nearby guests.

"She was talking to Noah," he said, pointing toward the side door. "In the—"

I sprinted for the door, my heart pounding in my ears.

Jenn was alone with Noah. How could I have been so stupid? He hadn't gone to see Martine—that was a distraction, so I'd finish the job with Jayce. Leaving Jenn unprotected.

How could I have left her vulnerable like that?

A bag flew over my head. Then the fist. The boot would come next.

I was safe.

But was Jenn?

I tore open the side door, sick fear climbing up and down my arms. The room was empty, with no sign of Jenn or Noah. Panic clawed at my throat.

"Brie, where is she?" I demanded, my voice echoing in the vacant space.

Over my earpiece, Brie said the words I didn't want to hear. "Her GPS signal says she's right next to you."

I spun around, searching every corner of the room. Nothing. My mind raced, trying to puzzle out what happened. Had Noah found the tracker? Had he—

No. I couldn't let my mind go there.

And then—

Ice spread up my spine, and I froze in place.

Her clutch.

On the floor.

Under a chair at the side of the room.

"Altitude reading," I barked as I snatched her tiny bag from the floor. I fumbled with the buckle and tore it open. No bracelet.

Thank fuck! She still has it on.

Scarlett's voice came through my earpiece, unusually quick for her. "She's a hundred feet below you!"

My stomach dropped. The water exit. Of course.

I raced to the false wall concealing the elevator—thank god I knew this place so well—swinging it open with such force it slammed against the rock next to it. I jabbed the down button repeatedly, willing the elevator to arrive faster.

"C'mon, c'mon," I muttered, staring at the ancient elevator dial.

It's not moving, Emmett.

Even if someone was in the car, the dial should have been moving by now. Fuck. Was Noah in the elevator with her on the bottom floor? Or did he disable it somehow?

"Em, she's moving southeast," Scarlett's voice came through again, the worry in her tone heightening my dread.

Southeast. Toward the water. Noah must have jimmied the door to stop it from coming back up.

Shit, shit, shit!

Rav's calm voice cut through my spiraling thoughts. "The tender's on its way back."

I looked at the other door, which led to the rough-hewn and dangerous stairs down. The elevator still wasn't moving. I couldn't wait any longer.

"Rav, start up the boat," I ordered, already moving toward the stairwell. "I'm taking the stairs. We can't let them get away with her."

CHAPTER 43
JENN

I STUMBLED as Noah half-carried me from the ancient elevator, his arm tight around my waist. We emerged into a security room similar to the one at the entrance, though much smaller.

He wasn't covering my mouth anymore. Now was my chance.

"Let me go!" I screamed, twisting and pushing against him with all my strength.

But Noah was still stronger. He anticipated my every move, deflecting each desperate attempt at escape with infuriating ease.

"I told you—both of you—that you should have left," Noah grunted, his voice a mix of frustration and something almost like regret. Before I could process his words, he hoisted me over his shoulder.

I gasped, the sudden change in position disorienting. "Put me down!" I demanded, fists pounding against his back. I kicked my legs, hoping to connect with something that would make him release me.

His grip remained firm.

As we passed the guard's desk, my eyes fell on the metal detector wands scattered on the ground. There were no guards in sight.

Blood splattered across the wall behind the desk.

Ice splintered down my spine, and for a moment, I stopped fighting. "Are they..."

I couldn't finish the question.

I already knew.

Noah's voice was surprisingly gentle when he said, "Close your eyes."

Those words sent a wave of nausea through me. What had Noah done?

Oh shit, what had I done by staying to talk to him?

Acid burned up my throat, tinged with the flavor of champagne. Why had I let Dante leave?

We exited through a heavy door, and the cool evening air hit me like a slap. A light spray from the water misted my legs, dangling awkwardly in front of Noah. I pushed up a few inches, desperate to get my bearings.

It was so dark.

When Noah turned, the lights on a small boat nearby shone directly onto us, and I had to avert my eyes. Spots crowded my vision, and I craned my neck to see the museum looming high above us.

We were on a stone dock with a few stairs leading down into the Mediterranean.

"Please, Noah, don't!" I pleaded, my voice cracking. "Don't take me!"

The gentle purr of the boat's engine slowed next to us. From my position over Noah's shoulder, all I could see was the tip of the port to our right. It was at least a quarter of a mile away. If I screamed again, would anyone hear me? Would it bounce off the water and the cliff above us, stopping anyone from figuring out where I was?

Noah walked down the stone steps toward the small boat and passed me to someone else. The exchange was quick and rough.

The scar. The snarl. The angry—

Oh shit, it was Enzo! The one Emmett said was behind his beatings.

"Don't hurt her," Noah said, his tone carrying a warning.

Do. Not. Freeze.

I sucked in a deep breath and screamed with all the power in my lungs.

But Enzo's hand clamped over my mouth, his grip painful. He growled, "No noise, bellissima, or I'll have to ignore Noah's suggestion."

I whimpered against his palm, my eyes darting wildly between Enzo and Noah. How was this happening?

Enzo dropped me onto a padded U-shaped bench at the back of the boat.

I scrambled to sit up, my hands gripping the edge of the seat as if it could somehow anchor me to safety.

"Do they know we have her?" Enzo asked Noah, who was climbing into the boat.

Who were *they*? Emmett? The police?

"They'll figure it out soon enough." Noah scanned the horizon before pointing at a set of lights moving in our direction from the port. "I stand corrected. I suspect that's theirs."

My pulse quickened. Was it Emmett coming to rescue me? No, he wouldn't have been able to get out of the Casino so fast. Was it a coincidence? Had he called the police? Surely they'd have flashing lights or something, wouldn't they?

Noah extended his hand toward Enzo. "Give me one of your guns."

My internal panic reached a fever pitch. This was real. This was happening. I was being kidnapped by armed men. Why? Where were they taking me?

I huddled on the bench, trying to make myself as small as possible. My mind raced. The fake painting. Dante's evasiveness. Emmett's warnings. Noah's cryptic messages. How had I ended up here?

Noah closed in on me, shoving my head from one side to the other, looking at my ears. Patted me down. Breasts, thighs, everything.

"Don't touch me!" I swatted at his hand, but he snatched mine.

"She's clear—no surveillance." Noah's voice was devoid of the warmth I once knew. He released my arm. "Let's go. If the boat closes any distance, I'll need you to threaten her. They won't believe me."

I pulled my legs up to my chest and stared at Noah. What had happened to him? Upstairs, he'd been like his old self— right until he grabbed me. And now? Had he killed the guards? No, he hadn't had a gun when we left. But Enzo... my eyes darted to the scarred man. It must have been him.

Enzo sat at the helm, turned up the engines, and slowly maneuvered us backward from the dock. When we were only ten feet away, Enzo began to turn the boat, until a loud noise caught everyone's attention.

The door flew open and slammed against the wall as Emmett charged through. "Jenn!"

Enzo cut the engine.

Hope surged inside me. Emmett had come for me! He cared. He was here to save me.

But he stopped suddenly, extending a hand as if he'd lost his balance.

"Emmett!" I cried.

He didn't look at me. His gaze was fixed on Enzo.

And Enzo did exactly what Noah had asked him to—he pulled out his gun and walked toward me, his movements slow and deliberate. As he approached, I shrank back against the bench.

Why wasn't Emmett doing anything?

Was he really just a con man? Had his feelings for me been nothing but pretend? Another part of some elaborate game?

I searched Emmett's face for answers but found only fear and indecision. He wasn't coming to rescue me.

He'd just... stopped.

Noah took Enzo's place at the helm. "Tell your boat—I'm assuming that's Rav—to stop."

Emmett stood there, doing nothing but sucking slow breaths. He'd said it was post-traumatic stress—that he'd been having a hard time dealing with it. But this? What had Enzo done to him?

He wasn't doing a fucking thing other than breathing.

In the distance, the approaching boat slowed to a stop.

"I see Will's improved the earpieces," Noah said, sounding genuinely impressed. "It picked me up from all the way over there?"

Emmett's lips moved, his voice barely audible at first. But as he spoke, his words gained volume and strength. "Let her go. She has no part in this."

"You brought her into it." Noah shrugged his shoulders dramatically. "If you'd left her and the bug in her hotel room and avoided her—as I recall, something you've done often throughout your shared history—she would have finished with the painting and left Monaco without ever learning the truth."

A bug in my hotel room? The Reynolds team had swept it, but hadn't told me about any bugs. Was that why they'd moved me?

You should be asking why they didn't tell you.

"Truth?" Emmett's voice was thick, guarded.

Noah's face took on a mock-sympathetic expression that made my stomach churn. "I'm afraid I had to tell her about Reynolds Recoveries being a group of thieves."

Emmett's eyes finally met mine, wide with shock. Or apology? Shame? No signs of denial. No hints Noah was lying.

"I also told her you stole the scarab," Noah continued, twisting the knife deeper into my chest.

No, Emmett wasn't debating anything Noah said. Noah was the only one who'd told me the truth. My world tilted on its axis, and I had to brace myself against the back of the bench.

Noah's voice took on a darker tone. "I didn't tell her that when I went to pick up the Chinese disc for Massimo, it was already gone. I must confess, I'm surprised you got the jump on us this time." He paused, gesturing at Jenn. "But if you want her back, you'll have to hand over the disc."

Emmett nodded, his face a mask of calm I now recognized as practiced deception. "Jayce, did you catch that?"

My heart shattered into a million pieces. He was in communication with Jayce this whole time. Noah was telling the truth—Emmett was a liar and con man. And if he was working this job with Scarlett, that meant Scarlett was a thief, too.

My best friend.

The person I trusted most in the world.

"Emmett?" I choked out, my voice barely above a whisper. "Is it true?"

He just stared at me, his silence more damning than any words could have been. The truth was written all over his face. My father's warnings echoed in my mind, a cruel reminder of how blind I'd been. Emmett *was* dangerous. He *was* no good for me. And I'd fallen for him all over again.

"We'll be on Massimo's yacht." Noah started the engine. The low rumble increased the churning in my stomach. He raised his voice as the engine grew louder. "You have thirty minutes. Enzo won't wait any longer."

I couldn't look up at Enzo, who still had the gun trained on me.

What would he do in thirty minutes?

CHAPTER 44

EMMETT

THE BOAT SPED AWAY, while I stood stock-still on the dock.

You fucking coward. You let them take her.

The calm sea and the wake behind their boat mocked me, reminding me of my failure to act, jump in, or do something —anything—to save her.

"Where's the disc?" I demanded.

Scarlett's voice sliced through my earpiece. "I told you it wasn't the job you were—"

"Shut it, Scar!" I snapped, fear twisting into anger. "Where's the fucking disc?"

Jayce's reply came swiftly. "I'm almost back to the Exotic Garden."

Could we deliver the disc to Noah in time? What would Enzo do to Jenn if we didn't? The image of the dead guards flashed through my mind—Enzo's handiwork, no doubt. More memories flooded over me—the cocky taunts I'd shot at him before the beatings started in New York, the first time I saw myself in the mirror at the hospital in Venice—

Oh god, what he might do to *her* that he hadn't done to me.

I swallowed hard. "How fast can you run it down here, Jayce?"

Rav's boat pulled up next to me.

Drew chimed in. "I'm faster and almost at the Garden, anyway."

"Not faster in your dress shoes," Jayce retorted.

I tuned out their bickering, my gaze fixed on Noah's boat. The sooner I had the disc, the sooner Jenn would be safe in my arms again. "Both of you run. Whoever's in front, take it."

"Will, where's the spare drone?" Rav asked as he tossed a line to the dock.

"On its way," Will replied, "but the battery's almost dead."

A faint whirring passed overhead as the drone made for the boat. At least we'd have eyes on Jenn soon.

This was my fault. I'd insisted on taking the disc, a stupid, unnecessary risk. Why? Pride? Revenge? Ego?

And she was the one paying for it.

"We'll get her back safely," Rav said as he secured the boat.

"This is my fault," I muttered, barely keeping my voice steady. "If I—"

Dante burst through the door behind us. "Emmett! Did you find her?"

Exactly what I needed. A target. "What are you doing down here, De Rosa?"

"You left in such a hurry, I—" Dante started, his eyes wild with concern.

"Your father and his merry men took her," I spat, the words tasting bitter in my mouth.

Mr. Thatcher's warning from years ago echoed in my

mind. He'd told me I would hurt Jenn, and now it had come true in a way worse than either of us could have imagined.

Dante's hands balled into fists, and he pressed them against his forehead. "Tell me she's not working with them?"

His words ignited a fury deep inside me. I advanced on him. He'd pay. For bringing her here. For getting her involved.

"Working with them?" I threw my hands in the air, holding back the need to punch him or throw him into the water. "They kidnapped her!"

Dante's lip curled, and his fist flew—lights burst in my vision—straight into my cheekbone. The impact sent me reeling.

A bag flew over my head. Next came the fist to my ribs. The boot—

Snap out of it, Emmett!

You're not in New York. You're not in Venice. Get the fuck over it.

I shook off the memory, slamming my fist into Dante's face.

Rav's thick arm materialized between us, his muscular frame a barrier between me and Dante. I hadn't even seen him climb out of the boat, but here he was, restraining Dante.

"If you lay another hand on him, you're going into the water," Rav growled.

"The guards are dead!" Dante struggled against Rav's hold, but fortunately realized he was outmatched and gave up quickly. His eyes darted between Rav and me, anger and fear flickering across his face. "Did you kill them?"

A twinge of disgust bubbled inside me. "I expect it was your father, Enzo, or Noah." The memory of the blood in the security room raced through my mind, and I suppressed a shudder. "Probably Enzo."

The same man who'd beaten me in Venice now had Jenn...

Dante's indignant voice snapped me back to the present. "My father would never do something like that." But doubt filled his eyes, even as he spoke the words.

I ran a hand over my sore cheek. *You aren't asking the right question yet, Emmett.* "Why did he leave without you?"

Dante's jaw flexed, and I could almost see the gears turning in his head as he considered his response.

"Upstairs, you said your father had people spying on you to ensure you kept his secrets," I pressed, noting the flicker of uncertainty in Dante's eyes. "You're not in his trusted circle, are you?"

Dante shrugged out of Rav's grip, his shoulders sagging slightly. "He's a criminal."

"And you're not?" I shot back. "Jenn told me about the *Wheatfield* painting."

Dante thrust a hand toward the water, his frustration evident. "Why are we talking about this instead of taking your boat and rescuing her?"

Because I'm waiting for the disc, and I can't go anywhere until I have it. Instead of telling him, I said, "Because your father has her, and I don't trust you."

Will said over my earpiece, "Drone's almost caught up to them."

Either I was relieved at that news or terrified about what Will would report back. I wasn't sure.

"I genuinely believed my father each time he told me it was a mistake." Dante took a step further down the dock, his back to us. "He blamed the conservator just like he blamed his accountant for the errors in his books. Now this."

I checked my watch, anxiety building in my gut. How long would Drew and Jayce be? What was going on aboard that little tender? Its lights were still visible, and it hadn't arrived at the yacht yet.

The yacht. What would happen there?

You're stronger than your emotions. I normally had excellent control when I needed it, but Jenn... Jenn was throwing me off in ways I couldn't afford right now. I had to channel some of Scarlett's control. Although from her silence, it was obvious someone—probably Brie—had muted her.

"Neither my brother nor my sister speaks with Papa anymore." Dante turned to face me, his expression hard to read in the dim light, but the tone of his voice gave me more— he was confessing. "He didn't bother concealing the truth when I confronted him at the auction. I wish any of this surprised me."

Fuck, how did Dante and I have so much in common? Both of us were dealing with fathers who'd let us down, who'd chosen a life of crime over their families. Both of us were standing on a little stone dock below the Monaco Rocher, wanting to save Jenn.

"We should call the police," Dante said.

Rav shook his head. "Too risky and too slow."

"What do you call standing around watching her disappear?" Dante snapped, gesturing angrily toward the water again.

I took a deep breath, trying to steady myself. "They have a ransom demand that's on its way here. We move when it arrives."

Drew's breathless voice came through my earpiece. "I'm ten minutes out."

C'mon, Drew. Move faster.

"When I met her in Nice, I thought it was fate." Dante turned back to the water, his shoulders slumping as the small boat winked out of view. "My father needed a painting cleaned, and I'd just met a beautiful art restorer." He sighed, the sound barely audible over the lapping of waves against the dock.

"Before you get any ideas, Dante," I began, knowing I was about to make a huge mistake by saying this out loud while on comms, but Dante needed to hear it, "Jenn is my woman."

"What?" Scarlett's shocked voice pierced my eardrum—apparently, she wasn't on mute. "Emmett, I told you—"

I tuned her out, my attention fixed on Dante's reaction.

"I know." He gave a small laugh and turned to share a tight smile. "You did a terrible job of hiding it. She didn't see it at first, but I did."

Was that why he regularly puffed up his chest when I was around her? Gave her those stupid macarons? Kissed her in the hotel lobby? *It was on the cheek, Emmett.* He'd been trying to win her over before I did, hadn't he?

"I think she came into my life to help me accept who my father is," he continued. "When she's safe on land again, I'll call my brother with the Carabinieri." He nodded, not looking at me anymore. These were words for himself. "I have enough information to ensure the moment Papa sets foot on Italian soil, he'll never be able to do this again."

Well, shit. Dante wasn't the bad man I'd thought he was. Maybe I'd been too quick to judge him, consumed by jealousy and suspicion. But now? Some sort of strange admiration was poking its way through all the negativity.

"My team's almost here," I said, glancing at my watch. Drew would arrive any second with the disc.

Rav moved past me, climbing into the boat and releasing the rope with practiced ease.

I followed, then turned to Dante. "Tell the manager about the guards down here. There aren't any alarms, and no one else has come down this way, so I suspect they interrupted the security feed."

The fucking irony. My team had done exactly the same thing to steal the disc—which had wound us up here.

Dante approached the boat. "Let me help."

I put up a hand before he could jump in with us. "We've got this."

But Dante wasn't backing down. "I'm done making excuses for my father. Done being in his shadow and being defined by him. I don't care if you understand, but I *need* to do this. To be my own man."

His words hit me like a gut punch. I didn't want to be defined by what my father did, either. I'd kept Jenn in Monaco against everyone else's recommendations to prove I was better than my father and to prove I was over all the things Fenix had done to me. Where had that gotten us?

And where had my stubborn insistence that I didn't need anyone gotten *me*?

"All right, but you play by our rules." I turned to Rav and asked, "Got your gun?"

Rav nodded. "Of course."

I faced Dante again, a strategy taking shape in my mind. "Does your father love you?"

Dante looked apprehensive. "Yes."

"Good," I said. "Because I have a plan."

CHAPTER 45

JENN

I WRAPPED my arms around my curled-up legs, shivering at the back of the speedboat. My ridiculously expensive evening gown did nothing to fend off the cold.

The lights of Le Rocher faded into the distance, and I strained my eyes, desperately searching for any sign of Emmett.

But it was too dark.

We were moving too fast.

The boat that had met him on the dock wasn't moving. Were they even coming after me?

"You're cold," Noah's quiet voice startled me. He was suddenly close, too close.

I recoiled as he wrapped his tuxedo jacket around my shoulders. The warmth was a relief, but I couldn't bring myself to feel grateful. Not to him.

The engine was too loud for his voice to carry, but still, he leaned in. "I won't let him hurt you. I promise."

I wanted to laugh. Or cry. Or both. Instead, I summoned

what little courage I had left and tried to sound brave. "Then turn the boat around and let me go."

Noah's lips curved into what might have been a reassuring smile, but it didn't reach his eyes. "I know Emmett and Rav. They'll deliver the disc."

The disc. One of two things Emmett and his team had stolen. Stolen? He hadn't debated with Noah, so it must have been true. How much of the past week was a lie? And how had I fallen for all of it?

"Fucking Reynolds Recoveries," Enzo shouted into the night.

Noah stood, raising his voice as he walked to the front of the boat. "We've got far more dangerous opponents to worry about than Reynolds."

I pulled the jacket tighter around me, my thoughts a jumbled mess. Maybe Simon *was* the wise choice after all. At least he never had me help with art forgery or a casino heist.

God, what had I gotten myself into?

Enzo hollered over the engine noise. "I should have put Joseph Reynolds in the ground instead of in prison."

Joseph Reynolds? Scarlett's father? What did Enzo have to do with Mr. Reynolds' imprisonment?

"That was twenty years ago," Noah said, confusion evident in his tone.

"It was my first job for the boss." A sickening pride filled Enzo's voice. "I wanted to kill him, but the boss insisted you never kill a resource you may need later. Instead, all we got was a pain in the ass from his whelps."

"They're a distraction," Noah said, but something on his face made me wonder if he believed it.

"You're still soft for the skinny one. Can't blame you. The

tits on her! Honestly, her mother's more my type. I've always wanted to fuck an MI6 agent."

"That *wasn't* why I tried recruiting her." Noah's jaw tightened. "Scarlett would have been useful for our team."

Scarlett was going to join Fenix? Evelyn was MI6? Their father was framed? My throat closed up. Scarlett had lied to me about even more than I'd thought possible.

"Useful? You're smarter than she is. I tell you, we should have used those photos to expose her. Throw her in jail along with her old man." Enzo turned, and I saw his profile, the control lights casting wicked shadows across his scarred face. "What do they call it in English? Poetic justice?"

"You're a sadistic fuck." Noah shook his head.

They're distracted. Neither of them is looking at you.

The engine was loud enough they might not hear the splash if I jumped. We were still hundreds of feet from the yacht, so its lights wouldn't give me away. But what then? Would Enzo circle around and pluck me out of the water? Shoot me?

And even if he abandoned me, what would I do? I couldn't swim all the way back to shore, especially not in the dress. It would probably pull me down like an anchor.

Enzo said something to Noah, but it was too quiet. The two men argued, and Noah grew agitated, waving his hands and rolling his neck like he was scanning the heavens.

This might be your only chance to escape. You can do this.

Slowly, I shifted my weight, preparing to jump. I glanced at the two men, then at the dark water we sped through. I needed to be quiet, stealthy—they were only ten feet away. More importantly, I had to jump far enough and at the right angle to avoid the motor.

Taking a deep breath, I gripped the bench, my arms trembling. I pushed up to standing and—

I was hauled back down to the bench. Noah wrapped his jacket tightly around me, pinning me to the seat. His voice was almost apologetic as he said, "Don't make him more angry than he already is."

I swallowed a scream. No one would hear me, anyway. "Stop pretending to be my friend."

Noah's eyes met mine, a flicker of hurt crossing his face. "I'm not pretending."

I looked back toward the shore, searching for any sign of rescue. There was movement and lights at the port, but nothing below the museum. Emmett *was* coming for me, wasn't he?

What if he wasn't? What if that was one more thing I'd misjudged about him? "What happens if they don't bring you what you want?"

"They will," Noah replied with unwavering confidence.

If only I could have borrowed some of his certainty. Why was he so sure of Emmett when I wasn't? I was the one who'd slept in his arms, made love to him, told him how much I wanted him. I was the one who'd been in love with that liar since the tenth grade. "Why do you want it so badly, anyway?"

"He genuinely didn't explain things to you, did he?" Noah sighed as he sat next to me. "I work for a man with... vision." His gaze drifted to the stars, an unsettling smile playing on his lips. "The disc is part of a set of ancient artifacts that, when combined, will change the world."

"Into what? Billions of crazy kidnappers?"

Noah extended his arm along the back of the bench and

stretched out his legs, as if we were old friends catching up. "A cure to disease."

"Which disease?"

He swept a hand across the sky, his voice filled with awe. "All of them. Everything."

I followed his gaze upward, searching the constellations as if they held some answer. Was 'all of them' supposed to include a cure for whatever insanity had overtaken Noah?

"I tried telling Scarlett about this," Noah said, his voice softer now. "But my teammates didn't treat her well."

My stomach lurched at the implication. If they didn't treat his former fiancée well, what did that mean for me?

Noah rolled his head toward me and said, as if reading my thoughts, "No one hurt her."

My imagination churned with nightmares of Emmett, beaten after his kidnapping. How bad had it been that he still had nightmares? Still slept with a gun under his pillow?

Oh, god. If they didn't bring the disc, would Noah, Enzo, and whoever was aboard the yacht hurt me to get it? Spots crowded my vision. *Stop breathing so hard.*

"And no one's going to hurt you," Noah added quickly. "I'm sure Scarlett was coordinating the op from HQ."

"HQ?" I echoed, swallowing the bile from my throat.

"The office in Halifax. I'm certain she's not in Monaco. Which means she was on the line and no doubt told the team your safety comes first."

I blinked, trying to process everything. "She's in charge?"

"When do you remember her *not* being in charge?"

The question hung in the air, unanswered, as the boat slowed and Enzo's voice cut through the night. "Open the garage door."

Ahead of us, the back of the yacht lifted, creating a space large enough to swallow our small boat whole. Terror screamed through my limbs, leaving me paralyzed. Once we were inside, I'd be trapped in the middle of this shitty situation with no way out.

"How does this work?" I asked, my voice trembling despite my best efforts to keep it steady. "They sail up to the yacht, toss over the disc, and you... what? Throw me overboard?"

"We'll be more humane than that." Noah's lips quirked into a humorless smile. "The last thing we want is a firefight. We only want the disc."

"And what do you do when you get it?" I pressed, desperate for any information to help me understand—or escape—this nightmare.

"Sail away, like we'd planned to all along." Noah waved a hand dismissively. "All the Reynolds team accomplished was slowing us down by an hour."

I clenched my back teeth to stop them from chattering as our boat glided into its designated spot. My eyes darted around, taking in two armed men patrolling the upper deck with scary-looking rifles. This was real. This was happening.

"Where are you going?" I asked, hating how small my voice sounded.

Noah stood, tsking softly as the boat settled into place. He held out a hand to help me up, but I couldn't bring myself to move. "We're going to visit our boss. And as pleasant as it was to see you again after all this time, I'm not divulging where he is."

I remained frozen in place, my body refusing to cooperate.

Noah leaned closer, his voice dropping to a whisper that

shot ice through my veins. "Don't make me pick you up again."

Bile rose in my throat again, but I managed a weak nod and forced myself to stand on shaky legs. As Noah helped me from the small boat onto the platform, a familiar voice cut through the air.

"This has been a disaster," Massimo drawled, as though a *disaster* were no more than an inconvenience.

"Your son stopped the painting auction," Noah informed him, while not letting go of my arm.

Massimo muttered something in Italian, his face contorting into anger. His gaze locked onto me, and I felt myself shrink under its intensity. "That was your doing, was it not? You've poisoned my son."

"Um... he..." I was going to be hurt while I was here, wasn't I? He'd take something out on me.

There was a sharp crack.

Blinding pain.

Bright lights seared my eyeballs.

I clutched the spot where Enzo had backhanded me.

Noah jerked my arm, spinning me behind himself so he stood between me and Enzo. "Don't touch her!"

"What are you going to do?" Enzo raised his chin, advancing on Noah. "Find another fire extinguisher?"

"So you *did* know it was me," Noah said, his tone cocky despite the tension sucking the oxygen out of the air. "Well, let me be clear—you need to get some fucking control. Martine did us a favor by letting us in. How do you think she'll react to you killing her guards?"

Enzo leaned in, his gravelly voice full of menace. "I should have thrown you and the skinny one into the pit in Venice."

"Your impulsiveness is going to ruin everything." Noah didn't back down, countering Enzo's intensity with confidence. "How many pieces of the phoenix would you have without me? So unless you've got something more impressive than framing an innocent man twenty years ago, shut up and do your fucking job."

I cowered behind Noah. How was I relying on this man who, only a day ago, I thought was dead? Who'd thrown me over his shoulder and taken me—by force—out of the Casino Rocher?

Such shitty irony.

At least Simon never hit me. But he *had* lied to me.

Tears blurred my vision. Again!

Everyone lied to me. Was I that gullible? That stupid?

You should have listened to your father.

"Come with me," Noah said, guiding me from the garage onto the boat's back deck. He kept himself between Enzo and me, a human shield I never thought I'd be grateful for.

As we stepped out into the night air, I squinted—sending a fresh wave of pain across my cheek—into the darkness, my eyes drawn to the museum in the distance.

Please, Emmett, please.

But then...

Was that...

Movement? Lights? *Yes!* Lights flickered at the base of the Rocher, just below the museum.

Noah followed my gaze, a slow smile spreading across his face. "Ahh! They're on their way."

They *were* coming for me.

But what would Enzo—or the other men with the guns—do when they got here?

CHAPTER 46

EMMETT

I LEANED FORWARD on the speedboat, my knuckles white as I gripped the windshield frame. My gaze remained fixed on the yacht ahead.

Be all right, Jenn. Just be all right.

"Tell me the safety's on." Dante stood at the helm, his voice betraying a hint of nervousness. Who could blame him, given the gun aimed at his back?

Rav's response was flat and emotionless. "My finger's not on the trigger. That's as close as you'll get to a safety."

The plan was risky, but it was all we had. Dante would be our insurance policy, ensuring Massimo kept Enzo and the guards from opening fire once I handed over the disc.

Such a stupid decision, Emmett. You just had to tell Jayce to grab the disc, didn't you? If you hadn't been so hot-headed and just stuck to the job, you'd be back at the hotel with Jenn, safe and sound.

"It's a solid plan, Emmett," Rav said for the fifth time.

I muttered, "It's not enough of a plan. There's too much playing it by ear."

"Never thought I'd hear you say that," said Rav.

Surprisingly, Scarlett didn't chime in with a sarcastic comment. She was the one who refused jobs that were too risky or lacked sufficient planning time. Yet here I was, rushing headlong into what could very well be a trap.

"I can't talk my way out of things with Enzo there." *If I even could talk with him there.* He was the one who haunted my nightmares. And now that monster had Jenn.

"She's going to be all right, Emmett," Rav reassured me, but his words did little to ease the knot in my stomach.

"This is my fault."

Will's voice carried through my earpiece. "Noah's holding Jenn. Enzo, Massimo, and another guy are with them. I count four guns. She's wearing a black jacket. I'm guessing Noah's, since he's without one. She's... shit... she's holding her cheek. They were out of view for a few minutes while I surveilled the rest of the yacht. I think he—"

"Don't say it." I already knew—Enzo had happened. Rage surged through me, trying to push the nerves away.

Will continued his report, detailing the positions of the staff and potential threats. I barely registered his words, my mind consumed with images of Enzo's hands on Jenn.

"Slow down, Dante," Rav said.

"I know what I'm doing." Either Dante was as indignant as he sounded, or he was getting into character as we got closer to our target.

Across the distance, Massimo's face contorted with rage. He stepped ahead of the others, shouting something I couldn't make out over the boat's engine.

Good. The plan's already working.

Two armed men on the yacht—one on the top deck and a

bodyguard next to Massimo—trained their guns on me. Someone else guided a spotlight onto us.

I reached into my jacket pocket, fingers closing around the golden disc. I pulled it out, holding it high in the air so everyone could see. "We're only here for the trade, not to make trouble!"

"Then let my son go!" Massimo shouted back.

I shook my head slightly. "As soon as we get back to shore safely."

Dante skillfully maneuvered our boat alongside the deck at the yacht's stern and cut the engine. He handled the vessel with impressive skill. Of course he did, if he grew up around yachts like this. If my own father hadn't been in prison for most of my life, maybe he'd have taught me skills like this.

Focus, Em.

"I'm all right, Papa," Dante called out, raising his hands in a placating gesture. "We can speak of revenge when I'm safely back on shore."

Rav's voice came from behind Dante, who he was using as a human shield. "Noah, you can confirm I pose no danger, unless your team thinks of double-crossing us or opening fire."

Enzo's face twisted into a snarl. He'd been on the wrong end of Rav's fists after my kidnapping, and was likely stupid enough to want to try round two. Enzo grabbed Jenn by the hair, yanking her away from Noah. My stomach lurched as he pressed the muzzle of his gun to her head. "I don't trust you."

Jenn squeezed her eyes shut, trying to shrink away from the gun, and let out a tiny whimper. The sound tore at my heart, and I had to fight every instinct not to leap onto the yacht and tear Enzo apart with my bare hands. We had a plan. We had to stick to it.

Noah took a few steps toward our boat, his expression unreadable. "Rav's telling the truth. He's a man of honor."

"Honor." Enzo spat on the deck, his contempt evident.

Noah's eyes turned heavenward for a moment. Had Scarlett been right about the fracture in the Fenix team? Or was it only Noah and Enzo who appeared to hate each other?

"Guns down, everyone!" Noah commanded, his voice ringing with authority.

To my surprise, the armed men lowered their weapons, with the exception of Enzo. It might have been Massimo's yacht, but Noah held control here.

Noah extended his hand toward me. "Let me see it."

Will said over my earpiece, "The second drone's five minutes out."

You've got this, Em.

Cautiously, I stepped onto the yacht's deck and passed the disc to Noah. My gaze locked with Jenn's, all her fear and desperation on full display. Infusing my voice with every ounce of confidence I could muster, I said, "It's almost over, honey."

Noah walked toward a light, holding the disc up to examine it.

Enzo jostled Jenn, and she sobbed, a strangled noise that cut through me like a knife. "She makes the same noises when I hit her that you did. Crying like a little girl."

Fire built in my gut, threatening to consume me. *Keep control of yourself.* My hands clenched into fists at my sides. This was a job, but she was my woman. I couldn't risk her life by doing something foolish, like attacking him.

Not until the right moment.

Enzo stepped closer, dragging Jenn by her hair. "Maybe I should taste her before you go."

She sniffled, tears spilling down her cheeks.

Scarlett whispered in my ear, "Stay calm, Emmett."

I took a deep breath, forcing my voice to remain steady as I addressed the scarred asshole. "We agreed to a fair trade."

Enzo growled, swinging his gun to point at me instead of Jenn. "We win again, don't we?"

That's it, Enzo, stay with me. I took another step, this time sideways, further from Noah and closer to the water's edge. "I suppose you're just better than us."

Enzo took the bait, sidestepping to match my movement. "We always have been."

"Thirty seconds," Will's voice came through the earpiece.

I sidestepped again, and Enzo mirrored me, his attention on our dance rather than the world around us.

Massimo stormed over to Noah. "Why are you so quiet?"

Noah's response was measured. "I need to be sure."

"Four. Three," said Will. He paused and then, with a tinge of regret, added, "Goodbye, baby."

I shifted in the opposite direction I'd been moving, my eyes locked on Jenn.

"Drop!" I shouted.

A small explosion erupted from the yacht's starboard side.

Enzo's head snapped toward the noise, his gun pivoting away from me.

Jenn dropped to the ground.

I lunged forward, adrenaline spiking exactly when I needed it. I grabbed Enzo's gun arm, forcing it upward and away from Jenn. With my other hand, I drove a punch into his gut, his grunt of pain satisfying a need inside my soul.

Rav's calm voice came through the earpiece, "Guards have moved starboard."

A gun blast cracked across the water as Enzo staggered backward, his finger clenching the trigger. The wild shot triggered chaos on deck, and Rav provided an update I couldn't make out over the ringing in my ears.

I fought through the pain in my eardrums and grappled with Enzo. *Fuck, he's strong.* But I had surprise on my side, and more importantly, I had my woman to protect.

My. Woman.

I surged forward, colliding with Enzo to tip him off balance.

As he brought the gun back down, I kicked one of his legs out, and he toppled. His gun dropped. He flailed for my jacket, but I freed myself as he fell into the water.

I spun, searching for Jenn. She was still on the deck, dazed but unharmed. I hauled her to her feet, my grip probably too tight, but it wasn't the time to be gentle. We darted for our boat, and I kept myself between her and every Fenix player I could.

Checking over my shoulder, I spotted Noah at the light. He gave me an almost imperceptible nod, then stepped in front of Massimo, preventing him from coming after us. What did that mean? I filed the information away for later analysis—right now, getting Jenn to safety was all that mattered.

Rav's voice rang out from our boat, "If I hear any more gunshots, Dante's dead!"

"I'm going to kill you all!" Enzo bellowed from the water. No gunshots, though. He must not have found his gun.

I practically tossed Jenn into the boat, jumping in after

her. I tackled her to the ground, covering her body with mine, and shouted at Dante, "Go!"

The boat lurched forward as we sped away from the yacht. A minute—or five or ten—later, Dante said, "The yacht's engines are starting up. You can take the gun off me."

Rav's reply was terse. "Not until we're out of sight. You don't want them to suspect you were working with us."

Beneath me, Jenn began to struggle. "Get off me!"

I eased up, but only enough to grab her hands, preventing her from hitting me. "Not until you're safe."

Jenn continued to fight against my grip. "I'm cold, my face hurts, and the floor of this stupid boat hurts, especially with all your stupid weight on top of me!"

Fuck. I sat up quickly, pulling her with me into a sitting position. I took inventory—torn dress, messy hair, mascara-streaked cheeks, and a swollen eye. And Noah's jacket! I yanked it off her and threw it overboard. "He might have put a bug or a tracker in there."

Jenn wrapped her arms around her body, her teeth chattering. "Who are you people?"

Rav came closer, positioning himself beside us. He kept his gun trained on Dante, but his eyes on the men aboard the yacht.

I removed my jacket and wrapped it around Jenn's shoulders. Cupping her face gently, I tried to meet her eyes, but she swatted my hands away. "What do you mean?"

"I think we're clear," Rav announced.

"Noah told me everything," rasped Jenn. "I didn't believe him at first, but the disc, and the guns, and..."

How much had Noah revealed? How much damage control would we need to do?

"It's me and Rav," I said. "We're the same people you've known most of your life."

But Jenn wasn't buying it. "You're a heist crew. You stole the scarab, didn't you?"

She knew. There was no going back now. Everything I'd built with Jenn over the past week was crumbling in front of my eyes. The way she'd looked at me earlier? Gone. I'd known this moment would come, but I hadn't been prepared for it.

Jenn continued, her words coming faster now. "And the disc. And you're a con artist. Scarlett's your mastermind, like it's some freaking movie. Your mom's in MI6—"

Oh shit. I also wasn't ready for the team to hear that.

"And Enzo framed your dad for espionage. And Jayce—"

"Wait, what?" I grabbed her hands again, trying to slow her down. My father?

Jenn pulled her hands free to cover her face as she sobbed. "She's a thief!"

Every member of the team was chattering over my earpiece. Rav's confused "MI6?" Brie's shocked "Framed?" And Scarlett's disbelieving "Enzo?"

I gently dragged Jenn's hands away from her face, trying to focus on her despite the conversations in my ear. "Enzo framed my dad?"

Jenn's mouth gaped open in disbelief. "That's the only thing you can say? So all the rest of it's true?"

Scarlett's voice cut through all the others. "Tell her it's all a lie. She can't believe Noah."

I stared at Jenn, my mind a whirlwind of conflicting thoughts and emotions. "After everything Noah did to you, how can you—"

"Because I can see it in your face," Jenn interrupted, her

voice trembling. "Scarlett's listening in, isn't she? Noah said you have earpieces to communicate during a heist. If it's a lie, show me there's nothing in your ear. Or in Rav's."

"Shit," whispered Scarlett.

"I can explain," I began, but Jenn turned away from me.

"No, you can't." She hiccupped a sob and huddled at the boat's edge, staring out across the water. "Just take me back to the hotel."

As much as I wanted to, this wasn't the time to press her. I stood and joined Rav at the stern. We watched in silence as Massimo's yacht moved, leaving Monaco behind.

CHAPTER 47
JENN

THE NEXT MORNING, I lay in bed, staring out the open balcony door. The warm breeze wafted in, the calm view nothing but a reminder of my shitty reality. How had this dream trip turned out like this?

A knock at the door startled me.

"We have an hour and a half until the helicopter picks us up," Emmett called from the hallway. It should have been a statement, but it sounded more like a question—or as though "Are you coming with us?" was meant to follow.

You should get up. Shower. Pack. Do something.

I couldn't summon the energy. All I'd managed to do this morning was open the balcony door. Some part of my brain thought the sounds and smells would carry me back to my first night in Monaco. Back to when my world was semi-normal, and my biggest worry was Simon cheating on me.

The morning sun glinted off the stupid gold bracelet. Love. Screw that. For the fifth time, I tried wrestling it over my wrist, but it wouldn't budge. I should have searched for something to fill in for the screwdriver, so I could take the damn thing off.

Emmett knocked again. "Jenn?"

I closed my eyes, memories of last night flooding back. The tense, silent ride to the hotel. Requesting a separate room from the front desk, only to be told nothing was available at three in the morning. The way I'd followed Emmett upstairs without a word, locking myself in this room the moment we arrived.

Scarlett had called several times, but I'd let every call go to voicemail. I wasn't ready for either of them yet.

"I'll be back in fifteen," Emmett said.

I lay still, listening to the world outside my room. Cars honked on the street below. Tourists laughed as they passed by. Birds chirped in the palm trees, and gulls soared overhead.

A bitter laugh escaped my lips as I thought about Dante. The guy with the stolen painting was the only one who hadn't lied to me. My cheating ex, my lying lover next door, my best friend, all of my other supposed friends in town, Massimo, and even Noah—I was a pawn in everyone else's games.

"Recovery agents," I whispered to myself, rolling my eyes. "Right."

My father's warnings about the Reynolds family replayed in my mind. But if Joseph had been framed, were any of those warnings justified? Unless Enzo was lying about that part, too. But why would he? It's not like he had anything to gain by bringing it up.

Movement on the balcony caught my eye, and I startled, shooting up to sit. Emmett stood there, wearing worn jeans and a light gray golf shirt. His hands were up, as if trying to calm a spooked animal.

"I had a feeling you weren't coming out." He stopped just outside the open door. His whole body seemed tense, uncertainty written across his face. "So I climbed around the divider between our balconies."

On my first night in this suite, I'd walked out onto that balcony, wishing Emmett would follow me. Wishing he would have joined me to stare down at the city, wrapped his arms around me, and kissed me. The memory felt like it belonged to someone else now.

"Picking the lock might have been smarter," Emmett continued, attempting a weak smile, "but Jayce would be proud of me."

"I'm going to book my own flight home," I said, trying to keep my voice as neutral as possible so he wouldn't figure out how deep he'd gotten under my skin. I wouldn't give the con artist that satisfaction. "And I'll call a cab to take me to Nice."

"Can I come in?" Emmett asked, his voice soft and hesitant.

"No."

He shifted his weight, clearly uncomfortable. "Can I apologize?"

"No."

Emmett sighed, dragging a hand through his hair. "Explain?"

"Explain what?" My voice cracked, betraying the emotions I was trying so hard to hide. "About how my best friend is a complete stranger? Or how you're exactly the same as every other man I've ever fallen for?"

'You keep dating these bad boys, then you're surprised when they treat you... badly,' Scarlett had once said to me. That's why I didn't tell her about Simon. Because she was right.

I lay back down and rolled away from him, wincing as my bruised cheek touched the pillow.

Fucking Enzo.

"Or maybe," I continued, "you can explain how my father was right about you all along?"

There was a long pause. Long enough, I figured he'd given up and left.

But then his voice wrapped around me one more time. "That's what I thought for most of my life. It's why I stayed away from you."

"Stayed away?" I scoffed. "Until you conned me into sharing a room with you. You probably staged the break-in, didn't you?"

"Jenn, I wouldn't—"

"You and your little crew, pretending you were all protecting me."

"That was Enzo," Emmett said, desperation in his tone. "He thought you were an undercover agent using Dante to get to Massimo."

I shot up again, spinning to face him. "That's rich! Considering Dante and I are the only two honest people in this whole fucking country!"

Emmett raised his hand, placing a barrier between us. "Noah told me last night. And we found two bugs inside your room. That's why I brought you here. I was afraid they..." He trailed off, looking down at the balcony floor and clenching his fist.

Feeling exposed in my little sleep tank, I pulled the cover up.

"I was afraid Fenix was here, and they might come for you."

A weak laugh escaped me, tears pricking at my eyes. "And you were right, weren't you? Except you threw me right in their path."

"I've made a lot of stupid choices in my life, but trying to protect you was never one of them." Emmett gripped the doorframe and looked up at me again. His eyes glistened. Tears? Seriously? From the con artist? "That's where I failed last night. I chose the team over you, and I almost—"

His voice broke, and some gullible part of me considered forgiving him.

I really, really wanted to.

But how could I? After everything that happened, all the lies and deception, how could I *ever* trust him again?

"Despite everything, I almost lost you. When I realized they had you—"

A sudden clatter above us, like cutlery on porcelain, interrupted his words. Someone above him was having breakfast.

"Can I come in?" he asked again. "Please?"

I swiped the back of my hand across my eyes, clearing away the tears threatening to fall. "Fine."

In two long strides, he was at the side of my bed. He fell to his knees, leaning his elbows on the mattress. "I would have switched places with you in a second. Would have taken Enzo's bullet if it got you home safely last night."

The memory of Emmett fighting with Enzo on the yacht flashed through my mind. The terrified look in his eyes when he told me to drop, and the fierceness he went after Enzo with. The struggle for the gun. Enzo's curses from the water.

"Those wouldn't have been stupid choices, either," he said.

He'd crushed me to the floor of the speedboat, shielding

me with his body. His weight, the scent of his cologne mixed with sweat, and the rapid beating of his heart against me all came rushing back.

"Giving in to my feelings for you wasn't a stupid choice, Jenn. Making love to you wasn't, either."

I clutched the blanket tighter to my chest, as if it could protect me from the choices my heart wanted to make. "I don't even know who you are."

"You don't understand my *career*. That's all."

"You're a thief!" That was so much more than a career.

"A recovery agent. We use our skills to return stolen items." Emmett shook his head, leaning forward slightly. "You knew that already. Just not *how* we do it."

Was this another con? Another way of twisting words to manipulate me? But why? He'd already gotten me into bed. Already gotten away with the scarab he was after.

"I don't know how to explain it any better or how to apologize or how to make you change your mind." Emmett's words came out in a rush. He extended his hands across the bed toward me. "Let me try. Please, honey."

My heart clenched. God, I wanted to believe him. I'd been in love with him for so long, and I'd honestly thought this was my chance.

"I don't know if I deserve it or not. I've lived so much of my life thinking I was no better than my father, and now? Now, I'm just... I'm lost." Emmett's shoulders sagged. "Scarlett and I only learned about Mum's MI6 connection two months ago. We hadn't talked to her or the team about it yet."

"Really?" The word slipped out before I could stop it, but he kept talking through my surprise.

"And my dad?" This man, always confident and in

complete control, was slowly breaking down in front of me. "I had no idea, but did Mum? Why did he confess if he was innocent?" He let out a long sigh and closed his eyes, a tear rolling down his cheek. "I'm tired of secrets. After I came home in April, I couldn't even go out in public for weeks until everything healed. There would have been too many questions."

My hand twitched, wanting to reach out and comfort him. To tell him everything would be all right.

"But when I woke up next to you Thursday morning, I thought my life could go back to normal." Tears streamed down his cheeks, and he didn't try to hide them. "And then that night? I wanted to tell you everything. Let you into my crazy world and maybe earn a little of your love."

I shuddered.

Did he say love?

"I don't know if I've lost my chance or if you can find it in your heart to let me back in," Emmett whispered, "but I swear, I will do everything in my power to make it up to you."

Despite everything, despite the lies and danger, I reached out. My hand trembled as I took his. "Where would you start?"

Emmett's brows knit together as he twined his fingers with mine. "Wherever you want."

I stared at our hands, letting the warmth of his skin against mine melt away a little of the pain. "I want the truth. All of it. No more lies, no more half-truths or omissions. If you want me for more than this week, that's what I need."

He stood slowly, his rich brown eyes locked on mine until he slid under the covers beside me, wrapped me up in his arms, and kissed my unbruised cheek. "First, the bracelet is equipped with an advanced GPS tracker."

A what? I stiffened as a hint of anger seeped back through the sympathy.

"I won't apologize for that."

He was tracking me? Maybe the truth wouldn't fix everything.

"It's how we found you before they got away." He lifted my left hand to his lips. "I'll have Will remove the tracker, but I'd like you to keep the bracelet."

And the smidgen of my anger receded again. "Is this sort of thing normal in your world?"

"It's standard practice for all of us, but..." He chuckled, rubbing his thumb over the side of my hand. "Why don't I tell you about the time Jayce and I got stuck in a museum for four hours one night, and then we can discuss what *normal* means?"

CHAPTER 48
EMMETT

"I wish I'd been there to see that jerk go over the side!" Jayce swatted my knee as the driver opened the limo door for us. We'd made the short ride from Monaco to Nice via helicopter, then taken a transfer to the airport and our company jet.

I couldn't help but smile. In the moment, I hadn't been thinking. But now? "It was supremely satisfying."

Drew slid out first, and Jayce shimmied after him, practically bouncing out of the vehicle.

As Will exited, Rav's glower caught my attention. "I can't believe you and Scarlett hid the truth about Evelyn."

I'd wanted to share with the team when we found out two months ago, but Scarlett had insisted. "I'm sorry. We—"

"Told Drew, but not me?" Rav cut me off.

"We needed confirmation first." Such a hollow excuse. I stepped out of the limo. A figure appeared at the jet's door before I could turn to offer Jenn a hand. "Shit."

"What?" Jenn asked, climbing out to stand next to me.

Jayce called out, "Hey, boss lady! What brings you to Nice?"

"We have a lot to talk about," Scarlett called out before disappearing into the jet.

Jayce and Drew grabbed their bags, with Rav and Will following them. The group of four made their way to the jet while Jenn and I hung back.

I leaned closer to Jenn, trying not to focus on her bruised cheek and black eye, keeping my voice down. "You ready for this?"

"You think she knows?" Jenn asked, her eyes searching mine. "About us?"

This was my sister we were talking about. I retrieved our bags and took Jenn's hand as we headed for the jet. A few of my brain cells suggested getting back into the limo and leaving. "Of course she does."

Hell, I'd called Jenn *'my woman'* on open comms last night, and Scarlett had heard it.

The rest of the team climbed the stairs, and Jenn followed, her shoulders tense. Once she was inside the entry, Scarlett met her with arms wide. Jenn stepped into the embrace, both of the women stiff and awkward.

I positioned myself next to them, not prepared to leave Jenn's side. The space was cramped, although everyone else was taking their seats.

"There's a private cabin at the back," Scarlett whispered. "I was so worried about you, I—We need to talk, and I didn't want to wait until you got home."

Jenn pulled back from the hug but kept her hands on Scarlett's arms. "Emmett explained a lot already."

Scarlett's gaze drifted to me. "He did, did he?"

I wasn't interested in the argument, but said, "Jenn's a smart woman. After everything she witnessed last night, I wasn't about to tell her more lies. She's in the loop now, and you'll have to deal with it."

Scarlett's expression softened when she faced Jenn—a look my sister rarely revealed unless she was with her closest friends. "I was trying to protect you."

"I understand." Jenn's smile was tense. "After last night, I *really* understand."

The entry grew tighter as Malcolm wedged himself into our crowded space. "C'mon, sugar muffin. We need to brief the team. Jenn can wait in the VIP cabin until we're done."

"Yeah, about that…" I clasped the back of my neck. "I've explained a *lot* already."

Scarlett and Malcolm's gazes landed on me. Information about what our core team did was on a need-to-know basis. Even some of the Reynolds staff were in the dark.

"She's loyal," I said. "She won't share anything with people she shouldn't."

Scarlett's eyes narrowed dangerously. "You slept with her, didn't you?"

I opened my mouth to respond, but Scarlett smacked my chest.

"I told you hands off!" she hissed.

Jenn put up a hand. "I'm a grown woman."

"With a boyfriend!" Scarlett shot back.

"I broke up with Simon weeks ago," Jenn countered.

The anger drained from Scarlett's face, replaced by hurt. "You didn't tell me?"

"He cheated on me," Jenn admitted quietly.

"Why didn't you…?"

Jenn sighed, her whole body deflating for a moment. "You

knew he'd do something like that, and I didn't want to hear it."

"I wouldn't have said anything like that," Scarlett protested.

Few people stood up to Scarlett, but here was my woman, holding her ground. She was so strong—as if the events at the Casino and on the yacht hadn't already proven that.

"You've kept so many secrets from me, Scar, but you never hid how you felt about the men I've dated. Maybe I should have listened, but..." Jenn turned to me, a gentle smile on her lips. "Maybe I had to kiss a lot of frogs on my way."

Everything about Scarlett's posture told me a lecture was forming.

Instead of letting her start, words tumbled out of my mouth, "And I'm in love with her."

Stunned silence blanketed the jet.

Did I just say that?

"You're what?" Jenn asked, a mix of surprise and something else—hopefulness?—tinging her words.

Wait. That strange feeling in my chest for the last few days? It was love. Real, deep, terrifying love. How long had I felt this way?

"You're brilliant, talented, and caring," I said, voicing all the things I'd never dared to admit. "Beautiful. You've always stood up for what you believe in." I glanced at Scarlett before returning my focus to Jenn. "When we were kids, people teased us about our dad, but your friendship—your love— never wavered. How could anyone *not* love you?"

She raked her teeth across her bottom lip, conflict obvious in her eyes. She still had a long way to go in learning to trust me again, but I'd give her all the time she needed.

Scarlett's attitude shifted again. It was a rare sight—my sister letting her emotions show. Normally, she was guarded, clenching her toes inside her shoes to help hide every emotion. But today? Her eyes darted between Jenn and me. "If you hurt her—"

"I'll break his knees for you." Malcolm cleared his throat and took Scarlett's hand. "But we need to sit if we're ever going to leave."

Scarlett blinked, no more words coming, and let Malcolm tow her into the forward cabin.

"Did you mean all that?" Jenn whispered.

I took her hand, placing it over my heart. "I promised to be honest, right?"

She nodded. "I love—"

I pressed a finger against her lips. As wonderful as hearing the words back would have been, they didn't matter. "I don't need to hear it just because I said it."

She moved my finger away, her touch gentle but firm. "But I *do*."

For a moment, I considered whisking her into the VIP cabin. Having her all to myself behind a locked door was tempting. Instead, I leaned in and kissed her, soft and slow, savoring the moment. But more importantly, not hiding anything from Scarlett or the rest of my friends.

Jenn loved me.

And I loved her.

Malcolm's voice, louder than necessary, broke our bubble. "Remember how I said we need to sit if we're ever going to leave?"

I pulled back from Jenn, unable to keep the smile off my

face. This strange feeling in my chest, this love, was over-whelming in the best way possible.

And Jenn? She was radiant again.

I led her to the leather divan in the mid-cabin, across from the television. Rav, Will, Jayce, and Drew had taken seats in the aft cabin. Our flight attendant, Patricia, bustled through, checking on everyone before ducking into the cockpit.

Scarlett let out a long breath as she and Malcolm swiveled their chairs to face the rest of us. "All right, here's the latest I'm sure everyone's curious about. First, we're not heading to Cairo."

"What?" whined Jayce from the back.

"I'm dispatching a courier with the scarab when we land in London. So we're dropping Will off, then flying home. We've got more important things going on than a courtesy delivery, like a team that doesn't listen. I said to leave the disc alone, and next time, I expect you to make better choices."

"I was point on this job." I straightened in my seat as the plane taxied. "That means—"

"Honestly, Em, you can save the martyr shit. It was reckless. You, Jayce, *and* Drew could have stopped it before things spiraled out of control, but none of you did. The team's safety always comes first." Scarlett's eyebrow quirked in the way that meant I wasn't to cross her.

But I was an adult, not a child—not the spontaneous guy who got by on his charm and good looks. And not even the guy who froze when he heard Enzo's voice anymore. When I'd sped out onto the dock last night, seeing the boat leave, seeing Enzo, my knees had gone weak.

But when I'd seen Jenn on the yacht, everything changed.

You didn't even think about your poker chip. Just thought about getting her to safety.

"Scarlett," I drawled. "I'm not *trying* to be a martyr here. It was my op—my call—not yours. Jayce and Drew did exactly what I told them, so I'm the only one who failed last night. It was the wrong decision, and I'll admit it."

Jenn placed a hand on my thigh and squeezed.

Honesty. That's what Jenn had asked from me, and that's what I'd give her. "We can discuss it further at our debrief, but rehashing things right now won't accomplish anything."

Scarlett frowned at me, a cover for how much she was seething inside.

"It gained us an ally, though," said Rav, changing the subject before Scarlett or I could start an all-out fight. "I spoke with Dante at length last night, after everyone else left the waterfront. He's contacting his brother with the Carabinieri in preparation for the yacht's arrival in Naples. He'll hand over information about fraud, tax evasion, and several other crimes. If no one else, Massimo will go to prison."

I hummed aloud. "And Noah gets what he wants."

"Yet again," muttered Rav.

What Noah actually wanted was Scarlett. That, and to teach his team a lesson.

The bastard had played us one more time.

"And finally..." Scarlett took a long look at Malcolm, who smiled at her as though giving her the strength to continue. "Mum was monitoring the op from her office yesterday. After Jenn shared Enzo's bombshell, I went to talk to her. She was already gone."

I stretched an arm along the back of the divan. "And let me guess, you haven't been able to get in touch?"

Scarlett nodded, her expression grim. "I expected her to deny the MI6 part, but I wouldn't have accepted that, given the intel Drew has. And no, she hasn't answered my calls or texts. Brie checked Mum's place after I left, and she wasn't there, either. I don't know where that leaves us."

"Is Brie tracking her?" Rav asked.

Scarlett shook her head. "Evelyn's not a target. My guess is she's either regrouping, dealing with the emotional fallout of her secrets coming to light..." She paused, scanning the team. "Or she's planning."

The thought of our mother 'planning' in secret made me uneasy. It couldn't be good.

Jenn voiced the question I suspected everyone had. "What do you mean by planning?"

Scarlett's gaze shifted to Jenn, my sister's calm exterior masking the turmoil beneath. "Fenix has gotten the better of us several times this year. Nothing we couldn't recover from, but I suspect she's done turning the other cheek."

I was surprised it had taken this long. "And Dad...?"

How many questions could that lead to? Was our mother aware he'd been framed? Did she fight it? Had she covered it up? Had the Russians gone after her?

Hell, had the Canadian and British governments gone after her?

"I don't know if she knew or not." Scarlett's expression tightened. "Until we talk to her, I've asked Brie to—respectfully—not dig any further."

So where was our mother?

CHAPTER 49

WILL

I CLIMBED the narrow staircase up to Mum's maisonette apartment in Oxshott, England, the events in Monaco on an endless loop. The familiar creak of the steps under my feet was a stark contrast to the luxurious surroundings I'd left behind only hours earlier. As I reached the landing, I fumbled with my keys, exhaustion settling over me.

"I'm home," I called out as I pushed open the door.

"We're in here, George!" Mum's voice came from the kitchen.

I froze, my hand still on the doorknob. George. My father. Dead for over a year now. I closed my eyes, willing away the sudden tightness in my chest.

Not one of her better days, apparently.

The conversation with Emmett and Jenn about assisted living replayed in my mind, followed quickly by my sister's daily reminders while I was away.

She's not doing well, Will, Katie had said after day one. After three, it became, *How long are the waitlists?*

"And you'll never guess who's here!" Mum's voice, bright

and eager, carried a clarity that deepened the ache in my chest —it was only a fleeting echo of the woman she used to be.

Leaving my suitcase by the door, I went to the kitchen. As I rounded the corner, I stopped short.

Evelyn Reynolds sat at our worn kitchen table, a chipped teacup held between her fingers. My mother beamed at me, her eyes bright with an excitement that came and went with the weather.

"Evie came for a visit!" Mum exclaimed.

"This is a surprise," I said. Why was she *here* instead of at home?

"Good to see you again," Evelyn said smoothly, deftly avoiding using my name.

"Of course," I replied, my tone carefully neutral. My fingers itched to grab my phone and alert Emmett or Scarlett, but I resisted.

The sound of the front door opening again rescued me from having to say more.

Katie appeared in the kitchen doorway, carrying a grocery bag and a small, distinctive bag from Harrods. She pulled out a box of chocolates, handing them to Mum with a smile.

"Thanks for staying while I went out, Auntie Evie," said Katie.

"Katie," I said, keeping my voice steady, "I want to take Evie upstairs to show her the addition."

Mum looked up from inspecting the chocolates, her brow furrowed in confusion. "We only have one floor, George."

"I meant the attic space." My chest tightened again, but I forced a smile. We'd converted the attic almost a year ago when I moved home to care for my mother. I leaned down to kiss her cheek. Turning to Evelyn, I gestured toward the back of the kitchen. "The stairs are this way."

Evelyn squeezed Mum's hand before standing to join me.

The stairs groaned as we ascended to my workshop. Upstairs, Evelyn's attention roamed over the cluttered workbenches, the shelves lined with gadgets and prototypes. Her gaze lingered on a half-finished device near my main workstation, and a flicker of pride passed over me despite the circumstances.

I walked to the large worktable in the middle of the room, running my hand along its edge. How many scale models had I constructed here? "Scarlett's been looking for you."

She didn't respond immediately, instead touring the perimeter of the room. She inspected the 3D printers, slowing in front of my electronics table before moving to the upright cabinet where I kept most of my tools.

Was she looking for something? Or avoiding me?

"The relationship between mother and child is fascinating," Evelyn finally said, giving nothing away with her tone. "We spend much of our lives trying to ensure our children will be happy and successful. We educate them about the dangers of the world, while trying to shield them from those dangers."

Where was she going with this?

Evelyn paused in front of a 3D model of the Albrecht house. I'd built it for Emmett's rescue mission in April.

"You kept this one?" she asked, eyebrow raised. "That was a risk."

She was right. I shouldn't have kept it. If the authorities came here for some reason, it would be evidence tying me to that recovery. But I couldn't separate myself from that job. Until this week, it was the only job I'd physically been present for in ages. It was a reminder of the old times before I moved to Oxshott. Before my father died. Before I found out about my mother. Before I left my life behind.

"I'll get rid of it."

Evelyn nodded, then changed tack abruptly. "Brie says your mother needs additional care."

Like the London job, I didn't want to give up on her, either. "Katie and I haven't decided yet."

"I've spoken with some people at home and found somewhere that will take her." The same regret I'd seen in Katie's eyes after she came for her first visit flashed behind Evelyn's. "Somewhere I'd approve of."

"Really?" I'd been looking casually for a few months, and the waitlists were over a year long. How had Evelyn managed it so quickly?

Stupid question, Will. Because she's Evelyn Reynolds.

"First, they took Emmett." She nodded, lifting the roof off the house model and inspecting the garage. "Then they manipulated Scarlett. Tried to kill Declan and Rav. Tried to kill Jayce and Drew." She placed the roof back on. "But this time, they took Jenn. I'd planned on going slow. Watch them and find out what they were up to. I'd thought we had time to find the photos they took of Scarlett. But if they'd touch someone outside our team..."

Scarlett was right. Her mother *had* been planning.

"You and your mother are too exposed here," Evelyn continued. "When we make our move, I'll need you both at home, where I can protect you."

Protect us? Didn't Noah take Jenn because she was already at the Casino Rocher? Or was something else going on? What sort of *move* was she intending?

"Does this have to do with Joseph?" I asked, voicing the question that had been nagging at everyone on the jet. "And his apparent framing?"

Evelyn's eyes snapped to mine, sharp and assessing. "We need the team to regroup. But locally. Not remote anymore."

Was it finally time to go home again? Instead of settling Mum somewhere in England, I could take her back to Halifax. Back to the office where Brie and I worked side by side, our desks so close I could hear the quiet hum she made when deep in thought. Back to the space where my tinkering surrounded us, her suppressed laughter always within reach. And back to the team, of course. "When?"

"The room is opening up for her in two weeks, and I'll ensure it stays available. Plus, I'll cover the fees as part of the relocation expenses."

It was sudden. I'd discussed distant plans with Brie and Katie but hadn't thought it would happen so soon. "I'll have to get the house ready to sell..."

"You kept your condo, didn't you?"

My condo overlooking the waterfront.

Brie had been with me the last time I was there. She'd tried not to cry when I told her I didn't need a ride to the airport. But her boyfriend had been with her, and I wouldn't accept a ride from him. As far as I knew, they'd broken up before Christmas, and she was still single.

I pushed those thoughts aside, focusing on the matter at hand. "So we're going on the defensive?"

"Ahh, William..." Evelyn's voice trailed off, and I couldn't help but notice the hint of an RP accent that always came out when she was tired.

I used to think it was because Evelyn had spent so much

time with my mother back when we lived in Halifax, as if Mum's accent had rubbed off on her. But after what we learned about her past last night, things were so clear. I'd missed clues about her past, too.

Evelyn's lips curved into a wicked smile. "You know what they say about the best defense..."

EPILOGUE

EMMETT

Two months later...

I scanned the room, taking in Scarlett and Malcolm's house. The air was thick with the aroma of roasted meats, mulled cider, and so many sweets I couldn't distinguish one from another. All around us, the Reynolds crew mingled with their significant others, Scarlett's friends Heather and Kelley, and a handful of faces I didn't recognize. It was a potluck dinner in October, perfect for what Malcolm had planned.

He stood in the archway separating the dining and living rooms, his usual cool replaced by an uncharacteristic nervousness.

"You sure everything's a go?" I asked in a low voice, doing my best not to laugh at my best friend.

Malcolm swallowed hard. He wore his favorite cologne, had spent a half hour on his hair, and was wearing the cream half-zip sweater Scarlett loved him in best. "Tell me I'm not about to make a fool out of myself."

I clapped him on the shoulder. "You looked calmer when we were facing down the armed clowns in April."

"That was only our lives at risk," Malcolm muttered. "This is a lot scarier shit."

"Much scarier, but the payoff's far better." I nodded, feigning gravity. "Or significantly worse."

With a chuckle, I turned to see Jenn standing at the dining room table. She selected food, placing bite-sized pieces on a small paper plate.

The sight of her sent a rush of emotions through me—desire, love, and a fraction of the nerves Malcolm was experiencing. "Just give me enough time to maneuver Jenn into the room. She won't want to miss it."

Malcolm's face practically blanched. "You have ten minutes. Any more, and I'm ducking out like a coward."

I laughed before leaving his side for Jenn's. As I approached her, she smiled at me—a beaming smile that warmed me from the inside.

"What's with Mal?" she asked. "He doesn't seem like himself tonight."

I slid my hand down her left arm, over the Love bracelet she still wore—without the tracker—and over the custom-made bracelet that held the blue scarab from Naukratis. I pressed my lips to her cheek. "We got a text from Evelyn."

Jenn's brow furrowed. "Was she supposed to be here?"

I sighed inwardly, thinking about how my mother had become obsessed with mission planning since Enzo's revelation about framing my father. "We're flying out tomorrow for a short recon job. Shouldn't be more than two days."

Jenn put her plate down and placed her hands on my chest. "Shouldn't be?"

Over the past couple of months, I'd done a lot of local

work. The job we were preparing for would be the first long, high-risk trip I'd leave her for.

"I can't give you the specifics," I said, "but it got me thinking..."

Jenn tilted her head, curiosity replacing the worry in her expression. "Thinking what?"

I took a deep breath, steeling myself. Malcolm was waiting for us. I didn't have time to hem and haw over this. *Just say it, man.* "We've spent almost every free minute together since we returned from Monaco. I want to make it more permanent. More than one drawer and your own toothbrush."

Jenn's eyes went wide. "Two drawers?"

I couldn't help but brush my thumb over her cheek. "Let's stop pretending this might be temporary. When I get home, I want you to move in with me."

Jenn inhaled deeply, her gaze drifting back to the table behind her. The silence stretched between us, and a sinking fear settled in my gut. Was I rushing things? I glanced over at Malcolm, who gave me a *hurry-up* signal.

"Unless..." I started, but my throat was too thick to continue.

Jenn snapped her attention back to me. "No unless." She threw her arms around my neck, linking her wrists there. "I was thinking about my father. He's part of my life, too. You think you can handle that?"

I winked at her. "You may not remember me tossing Enzo off a yacht, but—"

"My dad's pretty scary. But in the end, he wants me happy." She lifted onto her tiptoes and gave me a peck on the lips. "And that's what you make me. So if you're willing to deal with him..."

That odd feeling in my chest started again. The one I was growing more familiar with by the day and had even started to crave. "That's a yes?"

Jenn tightened her grip around my neck. "That's a hell yeah."

I leaned in and kissed her deeply. My life was turning around. Everything had seemed near-perfect before the kidnapping in April, but now? I'd been missing so much, and I hadn't realized it.

Malcolm tapped my shoulder. "I'm doing this without you."

I separated from Jenn, trying to calm the ridiculous smile that was half love for Jenn and half laughter at Malcolm. "We should go to the living room."

Jenn looked to where Malcolm had gone and reached for her plate. "What's going on?"

I put her plate back on the table, then towed her behind me, between a few people, and around the corner into the living room.

Malcolm was already lowering to one knee in front of Scarlett, opening a jewelry box. "You're the most remarkable woman I've ever met, and no one—"

Jenn squeezed my arm, practically jumping in place. She whispered, "You knew?"

I mock frowned at her. "He asked my permission to ask Evelyn months ago." After working for Evelyn for six months, Malcolm had a well-placed fear of my mother. "He finally worked up the courage to talk to her last week."

Scarlett didn't take her eyes off Malcolm while he talked, and when he finally asked her to marry him, she nodded vigorously. Malcolm placed the engagement ring on Scarlett's finger and stood, wrapping her in his arms.

I took in Jenn's radiant face, and a crazy thought popped into my head. I was going to marry *her*. Not yet, but soon. As soon as I won over her father. "Go congratulate her."

"Oh, right!" She slipped out of my grasp and rushed over to hug her best friend.

I slid my left hand into my pocket, rubbing the poker chip. It didn't hold the same power it used to. Standing up to Enzo, seeing my therapist regularly, and having a wonderful woman in my life were all helping me heal. What happened to me in New York and Venice would always be a part of me, but I was getting closer to it being a single chapter in my history instead of the climax.

Jenn took Kelley's baby as Kelley hugged Scarlett. The image of marrying Jenn flashed to one of having children with her—of her holding our child, and not just Kelley's.

These were the defining moments. Not the games, not the danger, but the softness. The smiles. The moments that made me reflect on the good in my life. Because these were the moments that would pull me through the darkness.

Finally, I walked into the center of the celebration to hug Scarlett. "You really didn't see this coming?"

Scarlett cocked an eyebrow, her way of admitting Malcolm had pulled it off. "Jenn said you invited her to move in with you?"

I scratched my short beard, glancing over at Jenn, who was cooing at the baby. "I love her, Scar."

"Took you long enough." She nudged me and hugged me again before Rav stepped in.

I hugged Malcolm, said my congrats, and returned to Jenn's side. "I know it's early, but what do you say we take off?"

Jenn smiled at me, handed the baby to Kelley, and took me by the hand. "Let's swing by my place, grab some things, and head home?"

There was that light feeling in my chest again. "*Some* things? You want to move in sooner rather than later?"

Jenn's smile widened. "Abso-freaking-lutely."

I took her face in my hands and kissed her, despite all the people around us, and that the focus was supposed to be on Scarlett and Malcolm. Who cared? Because I had my woman, and nothing else mattered in the world.

THE END OF BOOK 4

BOOK 5: Will and Brie go undercover at the infamous data center, searching for intel on Fenix's operations and plans. Disguised as a newly hired married couple, they infiltrate the high-security facility hidden beneath Gideon Tremaine's exclusive resort in the Bahamas. A fake marriage, only one bed, and two best friends who crossed the line once and swore never to risk their friendship again. What could go wrong?

Discover Will and Brie's story at

https://janetoppedisano.com/the-honeymoon-hack

BONUS SCENE: Fifteen years ago, one kiss broke two young hearts. See the moment Jenn and Emmett gave in to their first sparks of teen attraction, then watch Mr. Thatcher ruin it all.

Join Janet's author newsletter and get this bonus scene plus
behind-the-scenes details at
https://bf.janetoppedisano.com/kpof37stin

AUTHOR'S NOTE

This book took on so many variations over its life. Originally, Emmett's post-traumatic stress was going to be far worse, Noah wasn't going to make it out alive, and Dante wasn't going to let go of Jenn quite so easily. And, I was going to skip the third act breakup! But, the characters tend to find their own stories and sometimes convince me to change my plans.

In large part, I think the changes arose from how difficult writing this book was. While I was finishing book 3 in the series, I started slipping into a low-level burnout. Many of my author friends were dealing with the same thing this year and 'mental health' inched its way into the foreground. So I slowed my book production while I dealt with those challenges, both craving writing and fearing it at the same time. It's a strange thing to feel when I've loved writing for as long as I can remember.

I think what my brain wanted was more of a warm hug rather than extreme angst. And so, the story changed, veering as close to a warm hug as a book with lies, secrets, and a kidnapping can be.

Happily, as I'm writing this note, I'm coming out of the burnout. I'm looking forward to next year, and all the plans churning in my brain. I've got Will and Brie's story to write, as well as Rav's (and his mystery woman), to close out this series. I'm also planning some other special books that will weave their way into my art crime universe.

I'd like to thank those who've been with me through it all. From my alpha readers and constant cheerleaders, Paula and Pat; to my editor and book coach Miranda; and everyone on my team, including my beta team, my ARC team, and my amazing cover designers at The Book Brander.

And as always, thanks to you, my dear reader. Without you, the books would just be words on a random piece of paper. But *with* you, they become stories of hope and resilience.

Here's to happily ever afters!

- Janet

ABOUT JANET

Janet Oppedisano delivers award-winning romantic suspense with smart, driven women and sexy, protective men that will keep you on the edge of your seat. Her heroines excel in their fields and aren't looking for love—until they meet the charismatic heroes who fall hard and fast for them. Throw in gripping mysteries, heart-pounding danger, and a touch of history or legend, and you've got stories that keep you hooked.

With a Mountie father and a Navy diver husband, Janet's life has been steeped in adventure, inspiring her high-stakes stories. She's lived all over Canada, from the Maritimes to the Prairies, and her books reflect the authenticity and depth of her journey.

When she's not plotting her next twist, Janet is baking, hiking, traveling, or cheering for her hockey goalie son.

And if you're wondering about her last name, it's pronounced oh-ped-ih-SAH-no—just like it looks. Honest!

**You can find Janet and all her social media profiles at
https://janetoppedisano.com**

www.ingramcontent.com/pod-product-compliance
Lightning Source LLC
Chambersburg PA
CBHW030940010826
48974CB00011B/444